Stepping Stones

Stepping Stones

ANDREA HERLONG

For information about this title or to order other books
and/or electronic media, contact the publisher:

Cover and interior design by The Book Cover Whisperer:
OpenBookDesign.biz

979-8-9905208-3-7 Paperback
979-8-9905208-4-4 eBook

Printed in the United States of America

FIRST EDITION

For everyone, that we may all know the love
of God and the love of others.

Enjoy your journey.

Let the music add to your experience as it guides the
story of Sergio and Celeste. Follow along at Spotify.com.

Playlist: Stepping Stones SC by Andrea Herlong
https://open.spotify.com/playlist/5wnrkWhlU4
GndnduqQSvqm?si=1f135011cff64053

Chapter 1

CHICAGO

The ring pinched her finger. It had been her mother's ring, a vintage cross of silver, wrapped in a velvet box and opened on her sixteenth birthday. Celeste wore it on her left ring finger, the one whose vein led directly to her heart. She was told it looked like a wedding ring, and she shrugged at the thought. The ring was her safety net, the shield that protected her heart. No one bothered her, men didn't approach her. Perfect. She couldn't do that again. She wasn't brave enough to take the ring off or let love in. She absently twirled it around her finger with her thumb as she considered her 30 years, and then she shook her head, hoping the hard memories would simply fade away.

She pulled the white duvet up to her chin and snuggled deeper into the covers. Her eyelids wavered and closed. She pushed aside all thoughts of the ring and focused instead on her recurring dream. It was a strange dream, and it made no sense to her. In the dream, she found herself standing in a small, empty room. The only thing visible was an ancient door. She had never walked towards it or even reached out to touch it. She opened her eyes and stared at the ceiling. *Is the door significant? Is there a deeper meaning?* She turned and burrowed into her pillow. Her eyelids drooped. She felt sleep coming swiftly. As her breathing slowed, she wondered what would happen if, this time, she approached the door and maybe even tried to open it. Could she be that brave? That night the dream returned.

She was back. Celeste stared at the door before her. It was always the same. Slivers of pale light shone through tiny cracks along the outer frame and poked through well-worn hinges. She turned around slowly, but once again, she found only a dark and windowless room. There was no beckoning light, no other visible exit.

She faced the door like an idle character in a video game, waiting for the player to direct her movements, waiting for someone else to decide for her. But there was no one else. She had to make the choice herself.

With determination, she slowly stepped forward, reached for the door handle, and pulled. It opened easily and gave her a small sense of assurance. But then a howling wind rushed into the room, and she pulled at the edges of her open coat. She shivered, took a deep breath, and stepped across the threshold. As her foot landed on the other side, she was propelled into the midst of a blizzard.

Icy pellets swirled around her in dizzying speeds without purpose or direction. She turned around, but nothing was visible. The door was gone. She took a tentative step. A rope tightened at her waist, a sudden lifeline in the storm. She grasped onto it and pushed forward. A tremor of fear coursed through her, but she wouldn't surrender to it. She could do this. After all, she had purposely walked through the door.

Then suddenly her grip slipped, and she plunged into the snow face first, the rope stretching tight around her. She rested her cheek on the frigid ground. She willed herself to move, dug her toes into the snow, and rose awkwardly onto her knees. She staggered. Out of nowhere, a hand appeared. It steadied her until she could stand, but when she grabbed onto the rope and stood straight, no one was there. Instead, a tiny snowflake glimmered in the distance. She shook her head in confusion, but strength rose within her, and she knew she would not give up. She would survive the storm.

The blinding snow transformed into a slow-moving wave resembling the curtains fluttering at her window. She became fully awake, pushed back the covers, and stepped cautiously out of bed. She closed the window, disrupting the gentle flow of the heavy cotton, and looked out at the clear night. Stars were visible, and the moon was bright. She breathed a sigh of relief. There was no snowstorm in sight. She reached for a pair of crumpled socks from the floor, pulled them on, and returned to bed. Her mind whirled with images of the blizzard, and she shivered, snuggling down further into the covers. *Is there a new storm looming in my life?* She plumped her pillow as thoughts raced through her head. *I was thrust into a storm, but I had help. There was a lifeline and a hand that lifted me up. So, there was hope within the storm. I need hope right now. I don't understand it, but I'm glad I opened the door and walked through it. But what happened next?*

She flopped over onto her side, clasped her hands together, and prayed. *Lord, is my life just a series of storms? I don't know your plan, but I trust you. If there are doors you want me to walk through, please give me strength. I choose to believe there are good things through those doors. Whatever is beyond the doors you place in front of me, I will trust you to lead me, to protect me, and to guide me. I am putting my trust in you. Amen.*

Chapter 2

CHICAGO

Celeste closed her laptop, slid it into her backpack, and glanced at her phone. She had spent an entire Saturday working on designs at the office to keep her mind off of last night's dream, but dramatic images of a blizzard and an old door ran before her eyes like a movie reel. Her head ached, and she rubbed her temples to ease the pain. Was a storm on its way? What door had she opened?

The autumn sun beckoned, and she left the building, walking to the Red Line lost in thought. Choosing a seat on the L at Jackson, she turned her face to the window. The swaying motion of the train was familiar and somewhat comforting, and she settled in for the ride. As the old brick buildings sped by, she wondered about her life and about the dream. Was there a correlation? Was she about to face a storm? She was restless, and in all honesty, she was lonely. *Am I destined to be alone? Was I lost in that storm?* She crinkled her eyebrows together. She'd been alone most of her adult life. *Would it always be this way? No. I believe love will come when the timing is right, but it never hurts to ask. Lord, please send me who and what I need. I trust in your plan for me, and I know you will hold me and shelter me in trouble and in storms.*

A movement from across the aisle pulled her back into focus. She glanced at the teen. His eyes were closed, his headphones covered his ears, and the air around him throbbed with the beat. Suddenly his eyes opened, his head swung her way, and he looked directly at her. He leaned forward, tilted his head, and asked her, "What is it you really want?"

Before Celeste could register the question, he closed his eyes and lost himself once again in the music. She turned to look around, but no one made eye contact. *Had anyone else heard the question?* She saw a woman playing *I Spy* with her children as they looked out the windows. She watched an older man working a crossword from a tattered puzzle book, but everyone else was either looking out the windows or looking at their phones. Then she noticed a man about her age. She thought he looked nice, if that even made sense, but she quickly looked away. Then she turned back to the teen. She could feel the beat of a drum solo in the air, and her heartbeat raced to match it.

The question unnerved her. *What do I really want?* She exhaled and then sat up a little straighter, as if the answer needed strength. *I want a man to spend my life with: a husband who will be my companion, my friend, and the love of my life. Someone who will grow with me, travel with me, and laugh with me. Someone I can trust. Someone who loves me just as I am. Someone who will walk through storms with me or even shelter me from the storms. My person.* She nodded her head as if a great decision had been made and glanced back across the aisle. The teen was lost in his music, his eyes still closed, but his face held a knowing grin.

The train slowed and Celeste adjusted her backpack. As she stood, she looked through the crowd but didn't see the teen again. His question was so simple, and yet, so profound. She whispered a prayer of peace and protection for him and then stepped off the train. A little smile graced her lips as she realized she knew exactly what she wanted. Was she ready? She shivered and fidgeted with her ring.

As she walked home, she wondered why the teen had asked her the question. *Why me? In last night's dream I walked through a door and into a storm, and just now a young man asked me a profound question that made me evaluate my life. Is God trying to get my attention? I do think God sends people to us as messengers throughout our lives. Maybe the teen was sent to ask me that question. I don't know… but I did ask God to send me what I needed.*

Thinking of storms brought up old feelings from her past. Her parents had died in a tragic accident when she was eighteen. She missed them every day. And then in college, her boyfriend had just walked away. He left her, left Northwestern, and was suddenly gone from her life. It was grief upon grief. *What now?*

Still reminiscing, she headed to her favorite section of Lincoln Park. It was quiet and peaceful, and she chose a bench near the fountain. Last night's dream rose to the surface of her thoughts again, and she hoped it was not a metaphor for her life or a vision of things to come. *But I was taken care of because I had a rope around me. I had a lifeline. Hmm… I've always had a lifeline, haven't I? God is always with me. I've never really been alone. I need to remember that.*

She exhaled and listened to the water, comforted by the peace it gave her. She knew they'd drain it soon for winter, but for now, it still beckoned. Benches were situated around the fountain as invitations to rest, and English Ivy softened the scene, encircling the entire area.

Closing her eyes, she thought of the teen's question again. She felt good about her answer on the train and told herself to be patient. *You walked through the door. Be patient. Trust.* She opened her eyes and brushed a few leaves off the bench. They floated to the ground and scattered along the brick walkway.

As she watched them, she saw a man appear from the opposite side of the enclosure. She looked more closely and realized he was the man from the train, the one she thought had looked nice. He was tall and moved comfortably, as if he knew who he was and what he wanted out of life. The color of his hair was a mixture of chocolate brown and copper, and his tanned skin gave a healthy glow. His jeans were faded and well-worn. Celeste couldn't help but smile. *I wonder what he does for a living. What's his passion?*

It was a game she liked to play. She had assigned occupations to people all over the city as she walked or rode the train. In her musings, there had been the undercover spy stocking shelves in the grocery store, the shy bookkeeper whose passion was racecar driving, the man in the five-thousand-dollar suit who dreamed of being a trapeze artist in a circus, and one of her favorites, the school crossing guard who moonlighted as a Scottish dancer. *Hmm… I'll have to think about this.*

Turning to a bench, Sergio paused as he saw a woman watching him. He noticed her pretty face and how her brown hair fell around her shoulders in soft waves. He couldn't tell what color her eyes were, but they looked kind. Her smile was sincere with a hint of amusement in it. As he took in her features, he realized she was the woman from the train. He had noticed her, but he couldn't walk up to someone on a train and begin a conversation. It just wasn't done, especially on the L in Chicago. He had been disappointed at the time, thinking he'd never see her again. *Wow, God. You do answer prayers.* He looked up to the heavens, opened his eyes wide, and nodded. *Thank you!* He wanted to meet her. What was stopping him now?

The reels began playing in his head as he wondered what to do, what to say, and how to act. *Should I walk over to her? Should I just smile and walk away? Maybe she doesn't want to meet me. Maybe she just wants to be alone.* He glanced at her again. She was looking at him as if waiting for his reels to finish playing, and that gave him courage. As he began making a mental list of pros and cons, he found that his feet had already begun moving in her direction.

Celeste watched him curiously as he approached. *Is he a lawyer?* she wondered. *No, he's much too relaxed to be a lawyer.* She liked the way he walked, it was a comfortable gait, not too hurried, but not lazy. *He may be a teacher or maybe a writer. Maybe he does something outdoors.* She didn't believe in love at first sight, but her heart picked up its pace, and she felt something new. Hope? She had seen him twice in an hour, and that never happened in Chicago. She took a deep breath as he neared.

"Hello. You're sitting in my favorite spot," he began with a grin.

"It is the perfect spot. I love it here!" She looked up at him and grinned back. *He looks even nicer up-close.*

"May I sit with you?" He held his breath as he waited for her response. She could easily say no, but she nodded, and he joined her. "My name is Sergio. Sergio Conti. I think I saw you on the train." He turned his body to face her and crossed one leg over the other, his hand resting on his thigh. He hoped he looked relaxed and calm on the outside. He was nervous on the inside, and he wondered about that as he looked at her. He usually wasn't nervous around women.

Sergio. His name filled her thoughts. It was a different kind of name, somewhat exotic and mysterious. As she looked at him, she realized he must be waiting on an answer. "I'm Celeste James, and I, uh, I saw you on the train as well." She was not in the habit of being so personal with strangers in the park, but somehow it felt right. She felt at ease and comfortable with him, and she wanted him to know her name. She wanted to hear him say it. She suddenly felt the need to be known.

"It's nice to meet you, Celeste. What brings you to the fountain?

What do you like about it?" His eyes scanned the fountain as he spoke.

Celeste thought about his question and liked that he was curious about her opinions. "I love the beauty of this place. It's serene and peaceful, and it takes me out of the rush of the city for a while. It's like entering another world, like a hidden sanctuary."

Sergio nodded. "I agree. We need that in the city, don't we? It's a touch of beauty in a world of concrete."

"Do you ever get out of the city to explore the non-concrete world?" She asked as she picked up a leaf and turned it in her fingers.

"Actually, yes. I work for OEC, the Outdoor Equipment Company. I head up the IT department, and I get to travel the world. I just got back from Alaska. It was gorgeous. Have you been there?"

"No, not yet." Celeste smiled and vaguely wondered what it would be like to travel with him. *Well, that's a bold thought. Travel with him?* "It's on my list. What do you do on your trips?"

"I set up cell service via satellite for out-of-the-way places and establish IT hub stations for small towns. Really, though, I get my work done as fast as possible so I can experience the place. I use the company gear and hike, run, and climb. I feel close to God outdoors. It's a cool experience to just be with him in nature." He wondered how she would react to his admission of experiencing God, but he had noticed the cross around her neck and took a chance that she would understand.

Celeste looked at him with her head tilted slightly to the right. "Hmmm, that's nice. There's no better place to pray and talk to God than in his own creation."

Sergio nodded, looked at her, and wondered. He loved his job and his travels, but it was a lonely life. He wanted someone to share it with. He wanted to travel and discover new places with someone. *Woah, I'm thinking about traveling with her. Stop it, man. Get a grip.*

He found himself answering her, "I agree. I definitely like mountain trips best, although too much snow makes me edgy. I love the majesty of the mountain, but I also like the thrill of the climb. I like to have a goal, then reach it, and then enjoy the view." He stood up, needing to move, and motioned to the fountain. "Would you like to walk?"

Celeste stood up, threw her bag onto her shoulder, and answered, "Sure." His job sounded amazing, much better than her desk job.

They walked around the fountain and then stopped at a strip of mosaic tiles embedded in the wall. He gestured to the tiles and continued, "I always like to make a wish here. I don't know why. I guess it's a silly habit. I have been throwing coins and making wishes in fountains for years. I like to consider what I most want, and then I wish for it. It's different, of course, from praying. There's just something childlike and hopeful about tossing a coin in a fountain." He pulled two coins from his pocket. As he handed one to her, his fingers brushed against hers and electricity sparked through his skin. He caught her eyes and held the gaze. *Had she felt it, too?*

His eyes reminded her of the sea: greenish blue, deep, and full of mystery. Current still tingled where his fingers had touched hers, and she tentatively took a breath. He blinked, and she looked away.

The question from the teen on the train took shape in her mind, and she knew exactly what to wish for. As she tossed the coin, she made her wish and heard the plop of his in the water as well. Celeste closed her eyes and whispered a quick prayer of thanks.

He turned to her, noticed her eyes were closed, and closed his own. He thought about his practice of tossing coins and how the wishes in fountains represented a tangible hope. As he thought about hope, he realized he should probably pray more as well. They opened their eyes and smiled at each other, each wondering what the other had wished for.

Sergio cleared his throat. "Would you like to go for a cup of coffee? There's a great little diner nearby." He gestured to the path leading away from the fountain.

Celeste detected a bit of hope in his question as he looked at her. Should she agree to have coffee with a stranger she had just seen on a train and then met in the park? Was there risk, excitement, love, and adventure possible with her answer? *Wait… love? Why am I thinking about love?*

"I'd like that." She took the first step. He fell in beside her, and they walked out of the park together. She felt completely relaxed and not at all surprised that she had agreed to accompany him. Celeste stole a glance and regarded his handsome features. Her mind wandered to the ancient door in her dream. She had stepped through it for a reason. Was he the reason?

She looked forward again as Sergio turned his head to her. His mouth curved into a smile, and then he looked skyward and nodded. *Thank you, Lord. Thank you.*

Chapter 3

CHICAGO

Celeste was good at her job, and the clients were impressed by her personal touch, but she wasn't passionate about it. She had loved the idea of helping small companies promote their products through marketing, but after eight years, it just wasn't what she wanted anymore. She was getting that itch, and it was time for a change. *There's a reason I majored in marketing, but for the life of me, I can't remember why. Maybe it had something to do with wanting to make things better, brighter, and shinier, and in the process, make people happier. But I just don't think this is my life's work.*

The late afternoon sun caught her attention, and she glanced at her phone to confirm the time. She logged out of her devices, gathered her things, and left the building.

She walked slowly, looking at store window displays and thinking of Sergio. A longing gripped her heart. She hadn't known him long, but there was something about him that was magnetic. Her eyes grew wide as she pictured his face. Then she glanced at her ring and twirled it with her thumb. Could her heart handle these emotions?

A car honked its horn at oncoming traffic, and she looked up as a bus sped by, its side brandishing an advertisement for OEC. She grinned, hoping he would call or text soon.

She ducked into a clothing shop to escape the street noise, picked up some dark jeans and a cream-colored sweater, and headed to the fitting room. Twenty minutes later, she left the store with both items, including a bracelet and a new pair of earrings. As she stepped outside, her phone dinged, and her face broke into a smile as she glanced at the screen.

"I apologize for the last-minute text. I'm at the 4th Street Pub on Alexander. I'd really like to see you. Are you free?"

She considered her response and texted, "I'd love to. I'm not too far away. See you in a few."

It took ten minutes to walk to the pub, her mind a blur and her heart thumping fast. Taking a deep breath, she eagerly opened the door, the irony not lost on her. This was definitely a door she wanted to open and walk through. Noise welcomed her: laughter from the bar, heated discussions about a game on the television, and the clinking of glass, while aromas from the kitchen hung in the air.

Sergio saw her walk in. He watched as she spoke with the hostess, noticing how her whole face lit up as she laughed. When the woman turned to point in his direction, his eyes met Celeste's, and she smiled again. She walked towards him, and all he could think about was how beautiful she was. He stood up as she approached. He wanted to say something perfect, something that conveyed all the feelings he'd stored up since they'd met, but he simply asked, "How was your day?"

Celeste sat down across from him, placing her shopping bag beside her on the bench seat. "I've been doing a bit of retail therapy. How was yours?"

As Sergio talked, she watched him. She wrapped her fingers around her water glass and ran them along the condensation to give them something to do. He was a handsome man. His gorgeous sea-green eyes were kind and deep but also full of fun. She loved the way his lips rose slightly higher on the right side, giving him a constant grin. There was just something about him that she couldn't yet explain, but she felt at ease and comfortable simply being herself. She took a sip of water and relaxed.

Sergio watched her. She was a bit shy and careful, as if she'd experienced grief or some traumatic event first hand. Maybe her heart had been broken, but she wore a ring on her left ring finger. He glanced at it and wondered. He looked up as her laughter enveloped him, and when she replied with a funny story or reaction, he liked her even more.

"What are you thinking about right now?" Sergio asked. "You have a far-away look."

She smiled, loving that he had noticed. "Music, actually. I like that song playing through the speakers. When I run, I listen to music and it, um, it speaks to me. It flows into my ears and through my body, and my feet move in time to the beat. The tune keeps me running and the words guide my thoughts. It's like the music becomes the soundtrack of my life at that moment. I feel the longing, the excitement, the love, or whatever emotion is brought to me through the song. I run a lot. It helps me when I'm sad or angry or in a mood. I think it helps me deal with life." She looked at him with strength in her eyes and wondered how he'd respond.

A flirty grin appeared on his face as he met her gaze. "I don't run as much as you do, but I get it. It's your outlet. I really like how the music affects you as you run and how it becomes the soundtrack of your life at that moment." He winked at her and cleared his throat. "So, if you're thinking about me when you run, what song would be playing?"

"Ha! Well, it depends on my mood." She twirled a napkin on the table and looked up at him. "I could laugh this off and tell you it would have to be a polka or some cartoon classical piece, but no, that won't do." She took a breath and decided to be brave. "Because I've been thinking of you each time I run lately, there are many songs that fit."

Sergio nodded and met her gaze. Her eyes were bright and intelligent, and he stared into them until he had to take a breath and look away. He sipped his water and then cleared his throat. "Well then, I have an idea, because I love music and lyrics too. When we're thinking of each other and a song comes to mind, let's text the title of the song and the singer. No other comments. It will convey what we're thinking at that exact moment. What do you think? Are you game?"

"I love it! It's like flirting with music!" She reached out her hand, and they shook on it across the table. Sergio held on for an extra moment and would have been happy to never let go, but another song began to blast through the speakers and Celeste laughed.

As he recognized the song, he laughed as well. "Please don't ever text me this song!"

Celeste dried her eyes with her napkin. "Same goes for you!" As the Chicken Dance continued, people jumped up and acted out the movements. Sergio stood and reached for Celeste.

"Let's Chicken Dance!" She joined him, and as she laughed and clapped and kept up with the motions, she watched the man across from her moving to the music. *Life is fun with him. I think I could get used to this.*

Too soon the night was over, and Celeste was wonderfully tired. As Sergio paid the bill, he turned to her. "I drove here tonight. May I give you a ride home?"

"Yes," she answered with relief. "That would be great. Thank you." Sergio picked up her shopping bag and led her down the street.

As he started the car, he glanced at her beside him. She sat with her left leg crossed under the other, looking comfortable and relaxed. He looked at her knee, which was close enough to touch. The desire to reach out was strong. *What would it feel like to place my hand there? Comforting? Friendly? Something else entirely?* Their eyes met, countless thoughts passing between them. He cleared his throat and turned back to the road, his emotions pinging off the interior walls of the car.

Celeste navigated and thought about the exchange that had just taken place. The electric currents filled the air and left her breathless.

He pulled up in front of her apartment but was tempted to keep going. He wanted to drive with her beside him, listen to her voice, and hear what she had to say. He wanted to see her again.

He reached for her hand as they climbed the stairs. The simple act joined them in a way Sergio couldn't put to words. It just felt right. At the door, he turned to her, his fingers clasping hers. "Would you have dinner with me next week? No Chicken Dance required." He grinned, his mouth forming the smile she couldn't resist.

Celeste looked at him, his face visible from the glow of the nearby porch light. Waiting for a response, his eyes searched hers. He looked hopeful. Her hand was still in his, and she loved the connection. She whispered, "Yes, I'd love to."

They moved towards one another, and she wrapped both arms around his neck, her head landing on his shoulder. His arms found their way around her, holding her tight. She felt warm and perfect in his arms, but the embrace also felt safe, good, and electric all at the same time. It was an abundance of emotions and feelings. He felt alive.

She didn't want the hug to end. Her emotions were bursting like fireworks on the Fourth of July, but she needed to think about the intense feelings. She stepped back, pulled her arms to her side, and smiled up at him. "Thank you again for a great night. I had a lot of fun." It wasn't even close to what she really wanted to say. She couldn't allow herself to feel something this strong. Could she?

He took a breath and answered, "I had a great time too! I'll see you again soon." She nodded, opened the door, and slipped inside. Sergio made his way back to the car, feeling suddenly very alone. He sat in the quiet and looked at the empty passenger seat. How could he feel this much for her after so short a time? How could his heart already miss her? He shook his head, his pulse racing as he anticipated seeing her again. His phone dinged as a text came through, and he grinned at the song title. As he drove away, he knew she was an answer to his prayers.

Song: *More Than a Feeling* by Boston

Chapter 4

CHICAGO

The steady pace of her feet on the path immediately calmed her, and the beat from the music energized her. It was the perfect combination. As she ran and listened to the music, her mind began to wander to Sergio.

As she approached a small bridge, she stopped to look at the creek below. The water rushed and bounced against rocks as it coursed to its destination. Celeste considered it and compared her life to the water. Lately, she seemed to rush along her path, causing her to hurry towards an unseen future. It reminded her of the busyness of the city and how she felt about her job. *Do I just stay because it's all I know? Should I change course?* She frowned. *Hmmm, my life might need a slowdown. I want to be able to know where I'm going, but I also trust God with my life. He leads me where I'm supposed to go. I guess I just need to listen to him, be attentive, and watch out for the rocks. I also wonder how Sergio plays a part in God's plan for my life.*

As if on cue, the music paused as her phone rang. She smiled and answered. "Hello, I was just thinking about you."

"I like that. Where are you and what are you doing?" Sergio asked. Celeste could hear the smile in his voice.

"I'm running in the park." She told him about the comparison of her life to the running water. He listened and agreed with her.

"I actually understand the comparison. It makes sense. Sometimes we get going so fast that we forget to slow down and take in the sights. If we don't look up, we may turn the corner and head straight for the waterfall. Speaking of dangers, are you safe there by yourself?"

Celeste reassured him she was. "I run this path quite often, and there are others nearby. I'll just finish a quick run and then head back home. I feel safe, but thank you for caring." She leaned against the bridge railing, the sturdiness grounding her.

"Please be careful. If you get lost, stranded, or taken captive, I'm your guy. I'm here for you."

Celeste laughed. "Thank you. If I ever need help in any of those situations, I'll call. I'd better get to it, though, or it will be dark. Thanks again. Talk to you soon."

As her playlist resumed, a text came through with a song title, and she grinned at the screen. Her heart skipped a beat. She was falling fast for this man. She finished her run faster than usual as thoughts of Sergio filled her mind and warmed her heart.

Song: *I Only Want to be with You* by the Bay City Rollers

Chapter 5

Celeste sat in her cubicle, switched the background color on a template, and clicked save. She sighed, closed her eyes, and imagined the creek. The water coursed swiftly towards some unknown destination. The water itself didn't even know. She smiled with understanding. *Ah… it goes where it's supposed to go. It has a certain course and is led where it is meant to be. Hmm… Where am I supposed to be? I think I need to discover what God intends for me. But I think I might be open to changing the direction of my life.* Her skin tingled with that realization, and she shivered.

A new chat dinged on her laptop and brought her back to the present. She looked at it quickly, although distractedly, and her eyes widened.

"Ms. James, we would like you to represent the company at the product convention next week. I've emailed you the details. Please let me know if you are able to go."

Celeste checked the email and scanned the itinerary. The Inn at Shepherd Falls in the North Carolina mountains was expecting her, and she would be there for a week. She quickly messaged back with a resounding, "Yes, I will happily represent the company. Thank you!"

"Woo hoo!" she exclaimed. She saw heads turn and smiles light up tired faces. Someone gave her a thumbs up from across the row of cubicles, and she wondered if anyone in this place found joy in their job. She hurriedly finished her work, and then she closed her eyes for a moment. *Thank you, Lord. I'm ready to go where you lead me.*

As she rode the train, she made a list of items to pack. She thought of texting Sergio, but then decided she would send pictures instead and have him guess where she was. He often spoke of loving the mountains of North Carolina. Maybe he would guess correctly. She knew he was out of town for a couple of weeks, and he would be surprised and intrigued that she was traveling as well. It sounded like fun to her, and she chuckled at the thought.

The flight from Chicago to Asheville took nearly five hours, with one stop in Atlanta. Once she was off the plane, she followed the signs and made her way to passenger pick-up. She walked towards an SUV whose side door was emblazoned with the Inn's name. Below it, a picture of two mountain peaks and a scattering of pine trees completed the picture. She noticed that the driver was on his phone, his back to her as he leaned against the driver's side door. He was wearing a dark blue jacket and a black baseball cap, and she couldn't see his face. She opened the back door to put her bags in, and then plopped down in the front seat as a gust of chilly air slammed the door behind her. She shivered and then turned to greet the driver as he opened his door and sat down. She gasped. Her mouth dropped open, and she swallowed hard.

"Sergio?"

Sergio's expression was a combination of surprise and disbelief. "Celeste? What are you doing here?"

Celeste stared in wonder but then gulped as a wave of unease arose. Had he lied to her about being out of town? She had assumed his travels had been for work. "Why are you here? Are you representing OEC's products?" She buckled her seatbelt and waited for his answer.

Sergio stared at her incredulously. "Actually, my brother Luca owns the Inn and asked me to help out this week for the convention. He tossed me the keys this morning so I could pick up guests from the airport. I had no idea you were going to be here. When did you plan this trip?" Sergio maneuvered through traffic as he headed out of town, and Celeste breathed a sigh of relief.

"I was just recently asked to attend the convention. I was going to send you pictures and have you guess where I was, but I like having you here in person much better!" She turned to the window, the scenery taking her breath away: rolling hills thick with trees that arched into mountains, the sparkle of a river below, winking every so often in the sunlight, and a peacefulness that made her sigh. "It's all so beautiful."

"Yes, it is," he said as he gazed at her.

She turned to him, her green eyes sparkling with excitement. A song began playing on the radio, and she reached over to turn up the volume. Grinning, she held her phone to her mouth like a microphone and sang with gusto. Sergio laughed out loud and joined her, thinking that life had just gotten infinitely better. He shot a thank you to the heavens and sang even louder.

Song: *Happy* by Pharrell Williams

Chapter 6

NORTH CAROLINA

Celeste awakened to a gray, chilly day, the mountains hidden by fog and rain. She soon ventured downstairs to the coffee bar, her jeans, boots, and thick sweater keeping the chill away.

The convention was over, people had started leaving yesterday afternoon, and there weren't many guests around at this early hour. The work had been fine, but the time she had spent with Sergio had been wonderful. When they weren't working, they had roasted marshmallows over a campfire, watched the sun rise and set from the upper deck, walked in the woods, and spent time in lighthearted, flirty conversation. The more time she spent with him, the more she liked him. He was fun to be around, but he was also kind and caring. Her heart danced with a lightness she couldn't remember ever having before. She grinned, and as she ordered her coffee, she looked forward to what the new day would bring. Turning around, she saw him walking towards her. He wore faded jeans and a black crewneck sweater that defined his muscles well. Her heart raced. *Wow! The scenery here is very nice.* He took her breath away.

"Good morning. You look lovely," he said as he leaned in to give her a hug. *I could get used to this,* he thought. The hug ended, but his gaze lingered on her mouth. He longed to kiss her, but a first kiss had to be special. He needed to wait.

"Good morning," she was able to whisper breathily. "Would you like to join me? I've already ordered." Celeste's hand motioned to the coffee bar.

His eyes followed the motion, and he replied, "Yea, I'd love to." He ordered his coffee and a plate of scones, handed the mocha to her, and then motioned to a big leather couch near the fireplace. They walked over and settled onto it comfortably, sitting side by side. He loved sitting so close to her, the nearness producing a mixture of comfort, contentment, and electricity within him.

"I don't want to leave tomorrow," Celeste said. "I love it here."

"You can visit anytime. My brother would love to have you." Sergio took the coffee and scones from the server and nodded thanks. "There's a trail out back that leads to a beautiful garden. Would you be up for a little hike this morning? It looks like the rain is about to stop."

Celeste watched him as he talked. The light from the fire touched his hair, accenting the bronze wisps, his eyes grew large as he talked about something he cared about, and his voice was honey smooth.

She cleared her throat. "I'd love to go for a hike this morning. I'm not leaving until tomorrow afternoon. How often do you get to visit the Inn?"

Sergio took a sip of his coffee. "I try to come as often as I can. I like to help my brother, and I love being on the mountain. It's a very special place. I feel close to God here."

"Do you go to church in Chicago?" she asked as she held the hot mug. She tugged a throw off the back of a nearby chair and pulled her legs up under her. Faith in God was very important to her, and she wanted to know what he believed. She thought the time was right to have a deeper conversation.

"I do. I've been attending a small chapel near Northwestern. It's an older congregation, but I like it there. The pastor is a friend of mine, and I help him with IT issues in the building whenever I can. The thing is, though, I haven't been going as much as I should. Sometimes I don't think I need God, and so I sleep in or go hiking instead. It's kinda hard to admit that, but I want to be honest with you about something so important."

"Thank you. Can you tell me your God story? You know, how you came to know and love God?" She took a sip and waited.

He stared into the fire for a moment, wondering exactly how much to share, and then turned to her. "I was hiking the Appalachian Trail one autumn about ten years ago. It was my first solo trip, and I was young and a little too sure of myself." Celeste listened as the fire crackled nearby. "A few days in, I had made it to a high outcropping and camped for the night. I remember sitting on the ledge watching the sun set and suddenly feeling God all around me. I had gone to church when I was young, and deep down I loved God, but I hadn't truly given my life to him yet. You know?" Celeste nodded.

"I started praying out loud, and then I was on my knees. I began crying and thanking God for all he had given me, for all the blessings, for life, and love, and family. I was so grateful that he loved me. Then suddenly I stopped crying, and I stood up. I raised my arms over my head and shouted, 'I love you!' over and over again into the mountain and the valley below. The echo was incredible! It was a symphony of 'I love yous' all around me. It was my love to Jesus and his love back to me. Then I felt a joy so intense that it lit me up from the inside. I fell to my knees again. I asked forgiveness for my sins, and I asked him to always be with me. At some point later, I have no idea how long, I crawled into my tent and slept like a baby." He shrugged and continued.

"I've always wondered if anyone else heard the echoes that day. That would've been something!" He shrugged. "The next morning,

I began my day with prayer, realizing how his love had changed me. Now, I talk to God as if he's my best friend. I guess, he really is. I gave my heart to God that night, and my life was transformed." He blew out a breath. "I knew I belonged to him in a way I had never imagined possible." He took a sip of coffee and looked into Celeste's eyes. "It's good to remember that experience. I'm glad you asked."

Celeste nodded. "I love the image of you yelling 'I love you!' from the cliff and how it echoed all around you."

"Yeah. I think being alone helped me understand that I am never really alone. God is always with me." He took a gulp of his coffee and reached for a scone. "The thing is, though," he looked at Celeste sadly, "it's not as vibrant as it was then. I mean, I love God, but I don't put enough into my end of the relationship. I need to do better. A relationship takes two, after all." He knew he had left out important details, but he wasn't yet ready to reveal his whole story. His gut clenched at the omission. He nodded and then asked, "What about you? Do you have a church family?"

Celeste told him about her church in Atlanta and how the pastor's family had taken care of her when her parents died. "I was almost out of high school, so it wasn't long-term. They were great, and the church was mobilized to help with whatever I needed. My grief was intense. My pastor's wife suggested a weekend retreat for kids who had experienced a death in the family, and she signed me up. It happened to be the weekend that changed my life." She shifted her position and patted the throw around her. Sergio watched her and waited.

"I had always loved God. He was a huge part of my life, and I first told him how much I loved him when I was ten years old. But I didn't really understand the depths of that love until I went on that retreat." She fiddled with her coffee mug and then looked at him and continued. "That weekend was full of stories about how much God loves us. There were also stories from each other about the deaths in our families and the grief we were processing. But then, one pastor got up in front of the group and told us that Jesus had died for each of us. He went around the circle and looked deep into our eyes. He looked at each of us individually and said the same thing: 'Jesus died for your sins. He loves you that much. He died for you.' It wasn't accusatory or guilt-ridden, it was beautiful. Looking back, I guess it was strange to hear about Jesus dying for us at a grief retreat, but maybe that made it even better. I don't know. I had always heard that Jesus had died for us, but at that moment, it hit me all at once, and I got it. I finally understood Jesus' love for me. He died for me and for my sins so that I could be forgiven and have eternal life. Me. I was bowled over by this information. I cried, and then I rejoiced! I felt an overwhelming joy and lightness. I asked forgiveness for my sins and asked Jesus to come into my heart and never leave. That experience changed my life. I love Jesus, I read my Bible, and I try to be a light to others, especially to those who are grief-stricken." She took a sip of coffee and watched Sergio's reaction over the rim of her cup. It was always a leap of faith to share your most personal story.

Sergio reached over, pulled her close, and whispered, "Sometimes we can hear the truth all our lives, and then one day it just hits us right in the heart. Thank you for telling me your story." Celeste rested her head on his shoulder, closed her eyes, and silently thanked God for this moment.

A server wandered over to check on them. "How are you two this morning? Looks like you're having fun."

Celeste sat up and answered her, "Yes, we are, thanks. How are you today?"

"I'm doing okay. It's a cold, bleak day," she sighed. "I like to see two people so happy together. It's good you have each other." She walked away, but her words lingered.

Celeste and Sergio looked at each other, both wide-eyed, each knowing the truth of that statement. It was indeed very good that they had each other.

"Well, how about that hike?" Sergio asked as he stood up.

Celeste's heart was full. The server's words had somehow closed a circle. She felt connected to Sergio in a solid way. It was secure, right, comfortable. She looked up at him with a contented smile. "Yes. What do I need?"

Dressed for the weather, they met in the lobby fifteen minutes later. Sergio led her down a set of stairs along the back of the building and down a narrow tunnel. "The staff uses this area to come and go. It'll lead us right to the path." She followed him down the passageway and around the corner. It was getting colder, but she was interested in what he wanted to show her. Suddenly a burst of icy air hit them head-on, and they stopped short.

Sergio turned to Celeste. "Are you okay? That was intense! It's strangely cold for this time of year. Are you sure you still want to do this?"

Celeste nodded and pulled her parka closer to her body. "That felt like the Chicago wind right off the water!" Her recurring dream came to mind as she pictured a blast of icy air sweeping through an open door.

Sergio stood in front of her, blocking the wind, and tucked a bit of escaped hair behind her ear. The need to kiss her was suddenly all he could think of. His hand played with the bit of hair destined to escape, giving him the excuse to touch her. He brushed his fingers along her jaw and looked into her eyes. Butterflies took flight in Celeste's stomach. But as the frigid wind picked up, she shivered, and her excitement turned to determination. Pulling her hat over her ears, she looked up at him. "Let's go. You lead. I'll follow."

He captured her hand, led her out of the tunnel, through the staff parking lot, and into the woods. The path was covered in pine needles, and it acted as a cushion under her heavy boots. She liked holding his hand and being linked to him that way. It was a comforting and safe connection.

"Up ahead," he began, "is a little garden that's hidden if you don't know it's there. Not much farther now."

She nodded, and they walked in silence. The wind whipped around them, dry leaves scooting across their feet. No birds or animals were seen. Sergio slowed and turned.

"Here we are." He dropped her hand and motioned for her to follow him. There were no special markings, but the pine-needle path turned to stepping stones. The path grew smaller, almost as if to prevent visitors. Sergio held back a branch for her. As she moved past him, the scent of sandalwood and pine filled her senses, and she looked up at him. His face beamed with anticipation, as if he couldn't wait to share this secret with her.

She turned back to see where she was going and froze. Before her was not just a lovely garden, but a garden so perfect, it looked as if it had been taken out of a fairytale. The path opened up into a hidden cove. At the far end was a simple waterfall flowing down the rocks and into a pond. Brown moss covered the edges of the pond, as well as the stones reaching up the back of the waterfall. She imagined that in spring and summer, the moss would be a luscious green color giving off an emerald tint to the falling water. Pine needles scattered into the water from the trail, and two wooden benches sat at the edge as if to welcome visitors to this hidden treasure. Twinkle lights had been strung around the trees to add to the enchantment. She took it all in and sighed.

Her gaze followed the path, and she wondered about the stepping stones. *Why would someone place them here? Stepping stones are invitations to follow where they lead. If this place is special to him, wouldn't he want to keep it private?* Sergio watched her face as thoughts ran through her mind. Her face was so readable, he could almost see the thought process, and it intrigued him.

"Sergio, the pine needle path was soft and quiet. Why are the stones here?"

He led her deeper into the garden. "I like stepping stones. I put them in places that are important to me. Each stone leads to another, and eventually we arrive at someplace extraordinary. I like the imagery of small steps leading to something great. It's the beginning of a journey with a wonderful surprise at the end." Celeste nodded with understanding.

With the tumble of the waterfall as background music, she felt his hand slide into hers. He turned to her. His other hand touched her cheek and then traced her lips with his finger. Celeste's heart beat strong and steady, her lips tingling in response to his touch. He looked deep into her eyes and then lowered his gaze. He moved closer and pressed his lips to hers. He then breathlessly whispered her name, and then he kissed her again.

Celeste had been kissed before, but this, this was different. The intensity was incredible, a combination of shooting stars, bright sunlight, and joy all bursting forth together. She reached her arms around his neck and fused her mouth to his. The world seemed to pause, nothing else mattered, and Celeste felt completely at peace and on fire all at once. The embrace was a bridge between darkness and light, between being alone and being known, between being unloved and being loved.

As if awakening from a dream, she was startled when something cold touched her cheek. She reluctantly broke the seal their lips had formed and looked at the sky. Sergio opened his eyes and followed her gaze upward. He held her close while the snow descended gently in whispers around them. Celeste rested her head on his shoulder and sighed. Everything was suddenly right in the world. The question from the train floated into her thoughts: *What is it you really want?* She knew the answer immediately: *This. This is who and what I want. Thank you, Lord.*

Song: *Yours* by Russell Dickerson

Chapter 7

NORTH CAROLINA

Celeste burrowed under thick blankets, watching the snow fall outside her window. As she thought of Sergio and the secret waterfall garden, she wondered how she could ever return to the city. She pushed back the covers and walked to the window. The view through the glass was beautiful. Everything was white. The snow sparkled as if the sun had sprinkled glitter from above. It was different from the snow of the city. This snow was clean and begged for walks, snowmen, and sledding. She grinned in anticipation of the day ahead.

She pulled her hair into a messy bun, applied a bit of lipstick, and headed downstairs. Coffee first, and then she could think about her plans to leave. She noticed a group of people hovered around the front desk, and she vaguely wondered about them as she veered towards the barista.

"Celeste." She heard him say her name. She turned to find Sergio standing nearby, watching her.

He walked towards her, his eyes locked on hers, his heart pounding. "Good morning." He looked at her as if she were the only one in the room. He liked how her hair was haphazardly thrown up in a bun. Some of it hung down in waves framing her face. Her green eyes sparkled, and her creamy skin glowed. She was beautiful. Sergio also loved her excitement and her anticipation of upcoming adventures. He grinned as he imagined how fun life could be with her.

"Good morning!" She greeted him and then breathlessly ordered her mocha.

"The roads are all closed, and there's no way down the mountain." He gestured towards the windows. "We've never had such a snowstorm this early in the season. We're stuck here until the plows can clear the way."

Celeste beamed. All she wanted to do was stay there with him. The rest of the world just faded away. Her phone played a text tone he had not heard before, and he glanced at it quizzically. It sounded like a cat meowing. Celeste held it up to him with a grin. "It's my friend Olivia. She loves cats!"

"Nice! Why does she call you G squared?" he asked as he nodded at the screen.

She picked up her coffee, reached for his hand, and pulled him over to the fireplace. He smiled, and they sat comfortably as she answered.

"Once we were in San Francisco on a girls' trip. We visited Ghirardelli Square, and I had a fit over the chocolate. It's kind of a passion."

"Oh, really? I now understand your love for mocha in coffee!" He teased her but held onto her hand. He was enjoying this.

"It's not just the mocha in my coffee, it's a mocha/coffee love affair!" She laughed out loud and looked longingly at her cup. "Anyway, on that trip I discovered dark chocolate caramel bars. I liked them because they were hard on the outside and soft on the inside. Those two sides made it complete, whole, perfect. So, Olivia started calling me G squared or G^2. It's short for Ghirardelli Square and for the chocolate with the soft center."

"Just because you liked the chocolate?" he asked.

"Well, no, not exactly." She took a sip of her chocolatey brew and considered her explanation. "Olivia knows what I've been through. Most of the time I keep up a hard exterior to block pain. It's like a protective coating to a soft, mushy inside. The chocolate reminded us both of how I sometimes project a hard exterior while really, I'm a mushy mess inside. I think I have to be so strong, but I'm really just vulnerable and alone."

Sergio squeezed her hand still in his and interjected, "You do know that you're never alone, right?"

"Oh, I know that God is always with me, but sometimes I stay inside my protective coating to keep from getting hurt. Hence, G^2."

Sergio rubbed his thumb over her hand as he slowly sipped his coffee. "I think we're both trying to figure out who we really are and what God's purpose is for us. I like your soft vulnerability, but I also like your strength. You're an amazing woman, and I'd like to think I'll be around to stand beside you and protect you if you ever need it." He reached over and enveloped her into a hug that melted her heart and any of the hard shell that may have still been holding on.

Celeste breathed in his scent and felt his arms close around her. Home. His embrace felt like home.

Song: *You Take my Breath* Away by Rex Smith

Chapter 8

Luca tossed a log to his brother and smirked. "So, what's up with you and Celeste? You like her?"

"Yeah. I like her a lot. She's the most incredible woman I've ever met. We're so much alike, and she has a very strong faith. That's important to me." As they moved firewood from the outside rack to the inside totes, Sergio reached up for the log that was hurtling towards him. He caught it easily and admitted, "I'm messed up."

Luca began, "Messed up, huh? How so? She's beautiful, too." Sergio looked at him knowingly. "It's easy to see," said Luca with a pained expression. Don't give me that look."

Sergio took the logs from the stacking rack and met Luca's gaze. "She's beautiful inside and out. I'm really falling for her. I can't stop thinking about her. It's unsettling, but in a good way. I don't know, just messed up. She's in my head and in my heart, and I can't think of anything else. Messed up."

"Huh. How'd you meet her?"

"We met at the park, but I saw her first on the train. She had this thoughtful expression on her face, and I wanted to know what she was thinking about. I was intrigued, and I thought she was very pretty. Then I lost her in the crowd. I actually prayed I'd see her again, and then I saw her in the park. Our eyes met, and I walked over to her. We struck up a conversation, and here we are." Sergio thought back to that day and shook his head in wonder.

"Things like that don't just happen," Luca protested.

"I like to think they do," replied Sergio. "It's holding onto hope that God will send you exactly who you need. It's dreaming of the one you want to meet, and it's an answer to prayer. Things like this really can happen." Sergio side-eyed his brother and wondered if he should say more. He sighed and continued. "Look, good things can happen. It's all about hope, trust, acceptance, and forgiveness."

Luca looked up at him and shook his head in disagreement, but he didn't answer. They finished the chore and carried the totes inside to the fireplace. Both men were thinking of Celeste, but they kept their thoughts to themselves.

Snow and ice covered the roads and made driving impossible. Those still at the Inn were hunkered down and carried blankets with them wherever they went. Most people preferred to stay downstairs where the fire in the huge stone fireplace roared happily. Boardgames littered the tables along with decks of cards, snacks, and bottles of water. The mood wasn't somber at all. It was almost like camp, just a bit cold if you got too close to the windows or doors.

Celeste had brought her blankets to the lobby. She was wearing thick socks inside her boots and held a mug of steaming hot chocolate that kept her hands warm. She sat cozily in front of the fire talking with Sergio. The fire crackled and popped whenever bits of snow fell through the chimney, and Sergio stretched out his long legs towards the heat. He chuckled and looked at her.

"Can I share a secret with you?" He covered his eyes with his hand and grimaced. "I've never told anyone what I'm about to tell you." He removed his hand and looked at her, his eyes sparkling with intrigue.

"Oh, yes. Share!" She turned towards him and waited, and then pressed, "Come on! I have to know what this is all about!"

"Okay, but don't laugh." He looked at her sideways and then continued. "I have a nickname for this fireplace." He released his breath and shook his head.

Celeste turned towards the brick structure and then back to him. "I need the back story on this. Why did you name this fireplace, and what's the name?" She tried not to laugh, but a giggle escaped. "I'm sorry, it's just that I love this side of you. Please tell!" When he wasn't immediately forthcoming, she playfully nudged him in the ribs.

"Okay, okay! I'll tell the story and then make you guess." He paused and then looked as though he might reconsider. She started to nudge him but instead took a sip of hot chocolate and waited. He focused on the fire and spoke quietly. "One rainy day, I was hanging out on this couch reading the Bible story of Moses and the burning bush. I looked up at the fire, and I was suddenly very grateful for it. It just made me feel comfortable. I've always loved this fireplace. It has been my refuge, a place where I could be safe and sheltered from any storm. So, one day," he looked up to observe Celeste's face. She wasn't laughing. He could tell she was intrigued. He continued. "So, one day, because I saw it as a refuge, I decided to name it. I was thinking about the fire of the burning bush. You know, how it didn't burn out. It just kept burning, but the bush wasn't consumed. I liked that. It just felt safe, like as long as the fire didn't go out, all was going to be okay. I like to think of it as a place to hear from God. Moses stood with God in front of his burning bush, and he heard God's plan. I think this is a good place to be with God and to listen for his guidance. You can sit in front of this fire and just think about your life and pray for God's presence and direction. That's why we have it going continuously. It's always here for those who need refuge." His eyes met hers.

"Wow. I love that description." Celeste looked at the fire and then reached for his hand. "Thank you for sharing your secret with me." She looked at him and then nudged him again. "But what's the nickname?"

"Can you guess?" Sergio squeezed her hand. Celeste looked at the fireplace, watched the flames licking at the wood, and knew exactly what it was. She turned back to him.

"You named it Moses." She watched for his reaction.

"Yep! That's it! I named this fireplace Moses." He looked pleased with her guess. "But, no one else knows I named it. Don't go around mentioning Moses. Let's keep it between us. Okay?"

"It's just between us. And Moses. I love that we share this secret. Thank you!" She tucked her arm through his and rested her head on his shoulder. They sat in front of the fire watching the flames, lost in thought.

Celeste rubbed her hand along Sergio's arm and asked, "You once said snow made you edgy. Are you feeling okay with this snowfall?"

"This is fine. It's the blinding snow, constant wind, and no visibility that makes me tense. And I'm here with you in front of Moses. All is good!"

"I'm glad to be here with y…," she began to reply.

"Celeste, I really like you a lot." She paused, curious to hear more. Sergio sat up and held her eyes. "Let me explain. There's love and there's like. Some people just fall in love and that's that. They may never really like each other, and then they're in a relationship with not enough substance to make it work. But I think it's important for you to know that I really like you. I like your heart, I like your mind, I like the person you are, and it feels really good to be here with you right now." He reached for her hand.

Celeste enjoyed the warmth of his hand on hers. It grounded her body while her heart sped to the stars. Once she found her voice, she answered. "I don't know how this happened so fast. It's like we're best friends or an old married couple that has had a lifetime of happiness." She paused. "Thank you for seeing me, for listening to me, and for liking who I am. I really like you a lot, too." He linked his fingers with hers and gazed at their hands.

"Well, objects of worth and beauty incite love and awe. The more I get to know your mind and heart, the more worth and beauty I find." He took a breath and cleared his throat. "Celeste, there's something sweet but also exciting about holding your hand. When we're separated from each other, just reach out and imagine me holding it. It will seem like we're never apart." He brushed his thumb against hers and searched her eyes.

For a split second, an expression of pain crossed his face. *Did I just imagine that?* Celeste managed a smile as she wondered. "I'll remember that, but I'm hoping we won't have to be very far apart." She looked at him, noticing the shape of his face, the color of his hair, and the upturn of his smile. She whispered, "It is truly a gift to like each other for who we really are. It's the best way to start."

He nodded and squeezed her hand again. "It certainly is." Their lips met and sealed the moment with a kiss.

Song: *You and Me* **by Lifehouse**

Chapter 9

Celeste woke early and stood at the window. The old feelings of insecurity and doubt crept into her thoughts again. *Why can't I just believe he is good? He mentioned being separated. What does that mean? He told me how much he likes me. Why am I doubting?* She pressed her forehead to the glass. *God, please take away my doubts. You know I have issues with people I care about leaving me. If I get too deeply involved with Sergio, will he leave? Will I be able to live without him? Will the grief tear my heart apart? I trust you, Lord. I need your guidance. Help me believe that he is genuine, and that he won't leave. Thank you. Amen.*

Celeste and Sergio met in the lobby for a sunrise walk. The storm was over, and it was bitter cold, but they wanted to get outside, breathe the fresh, cold air, and walk together. When they headed out the front door, Sergio grasped her hand.

"I want to show you something. Let's go!" Celeste laughed out loud as they took off. They ran around the corner of the building, the snow crunching beneath their feet, and then they slowed to a walk.

Celeste navigated the snow and asked, "Where does this path go?"

"You'll see." He squeezed her gloved hand as they rounded a corner and headed into the woods. When they came to a fork, he led her to the left and then around the bend. Directly in front of them was a small gazebo overlooking the valley. It was made of wood that had weathered to a fine gray, but it was sturdy and had stood the test of time on the windy overlook.

Celeste gazed at the expanse before her and murmured, "This is beautiful!" They stood at the snowy railing, still holding gloved hands, and fell silent. She pulled out her phone and asked, "Quick selfie with the sunrise?"

Sergio posed as she took the picture, and then they watched the sun make its slow ascent to begin a new day. He wrapped his arm around her, and when the sun had risen, he turned and gathered her in his arms, holding her tight. Celeste enjoyed the embrace for a few moments, but then she pulled back and looked at him seriously.

"Sergio," she began, as she cleared her throat. "You know my parents died my senior year of high school." He looked into her eyes and nodded, watching her face as she chose her next words. "Well, in college, I dated a guy who said all the right things. He spent time with me, cared for me, and I thought I loved him. I found out, though, that he wasn't ready for love, or for me, and he left Northwestern at the end of the year. He never returned, and I never heard from him again. He was just gone. It was too soon to go through that loss after my parents, and I didn't date anyone else the rest of the time I was in school. It made me distrustful of people, and I held onto my heart tightly so that it wouldn't get hurt again. I even wear my mom's ring as a safeguard and for a sense of security. I've been through a lot with my heart, and I, uh, I just wanted you to know." She looked up at him and shrugged while he pulled her into his arms again.

He whispered in her ear as he held her close, "I know that grief that comes from losing parents, and I know how fragile we are afterwards. I'm so sorry you were hurt by that guy in college. I'm really glad you're here with me now."

She lay her head on his chest, allowing herself to feel safe. She was in the arms of the man she had prayed for, and as she held on, she dared to dream of a future together. She snuggled in and wrapped her arms tightly around him.

Sergio was holding the woman of his dreams, and he didn't want to let go. He closed his eyes and silently thanked God for her, while also asking for help with what he knew he had to tell her. He sighed, brushed his cheek against her hair, and whispered in her ear, "I can feel your heart beating."

She smiled into his sweater and sighed. She had found her person, and she was beginning to trust that she could fully give her heart to him.

Song: *Something Just Like This* by The Chainsmokers and Coldplay

Chapter 10

Celeste's phone chimed from the table beside her bed, startling her awake. She turned and reached for it sleepily, wondering who was texting her before the sun rose. She focused her eyes on the phone as Sergio's message appeared.

"Good morning! Want to go to an early service at Shepherd Falls Chapel? The roads have been cleared, and I'd love to begin the day with you. Meet downstairs in 20?"

She glanced at the time display and then responded, "Yeah, sounds great! See you in 20!" She yawned and stretched and grinned at the anticipation of seeing him, and then jumped out of bed to get ready. The outdoor temperature was 19 degrees, and she shivered as she headed to the closet. She'd be downstairs in 15 just to grab a coffee before they headed out.

She made her way into the silent lobby and saw him waiting for her with coffee in hand. He turned as she approached and walked to her. Their gazes locked, and her heart fluttered. She stopped on the second step so that her face was level with his, so that she could look directly into his eyes. He leaned forward and whispered a quiet good morning as his lips found hers. She wasn't sleepy anymore as she placed her hands on his cheeks and returned the kiss. She then whispered a good morning to him when he reluctantly pulled away.

"Well, that's a great way to start the day!" He handed the coffee to her, and as she took it, he kissed her again.

"Thank you for the coffee and the kiss," she answered. He grinned and grabbed her hand as they headed outside to his truck.

Shepherd Falls Chapel was a small church that had been built in the early 1940s as a place of worship and refuge. It had been used as a hospital during the war, and had held weddings, funerals, baptisms, and services in the restored brick building. The sunrise service wasn't very well attended, especially with the snowy weather, but Sergio liked it. It was quiet and peaceful, and it suited him. He knew Celeste would be leaving soon since the roads were open, and he wanted to share this experience with her. He pulled into the parking lot and maneuvered around snow drifts.

As Celeste turned to open the door, Sergio placed his hand on her arm. "Wait, please." She glanced at him and recognized the look in his eyes. He reached over to her, brushed her cheek with his hand, lifted her chin, and pressed his lips to hers. The moment was breathless, warm, and exhilarating.

Sergio tore himself away and looked into her eyes. He relished this moment with her in the quiet of the truck. Was he wrong to bring her to church when he had so much more to tell her about his journey. He dismissed the thought and asked huskily, "Shall we go on in?" Celeste nodded. They entered the chapel together and sat down in a back pew. They joined in the singing, their voices mingling in tune, and then they listened to the message. Celeste watched as the stained-glass windows began to glow from the lower sections. As the sun rose, the pictures shone in an upward pattern, telling a story with the sunrise.

As the service ended, Celeste leaned closer to Sergio and whispered, "We began our worship in the dark, and now the church is bathed in light. That's significant. And did you notice the light shining in the windows? I'm glad we came."

Sergio nodded and squeezed her hand. "I'm glad you were here with me today. Worshipping with you was really special." They walked outside hand in hand, dodging snowdrifts in the parking lot. A sense of peacefulness surrounded them.

Sergio opened the truck door for Celeste, and she turned to step inside.

"Hey," Sergio said as Celeste looked up at him expectantly. "I, uh, I didn't want that to end. It was so peaceful to worship and to sing with you, to hold your hand, to be with you. I need, I really want to hold you right now." Celeste nodded in understanding and wrapped her arms around his waist, resting her head on his shoulder. He pulled her close and held her gently. He knew he would never forget this warmth, this feeling of security, safety, and closeness. She felt like home.

Celeste reluctantly headed back to Chicago while Sergio stayed at the Inn. She flew back home with such joy in her heart she could barely sit still. Her hopes, dreams, and thoughts swirled around Sergio and her possible future with him. Love. She felt so much love for him but knew it wasn't the right time to say anything. But still, her heart was bursting with joy. Life seemed brighter, happier, and more intense. When tiny doubts tried to edge into her thoughts, she pushed them away with a wave of her hand. *Not everyone who cares for me leaves me. I have to believe this!*

She fell into bed and clasped her hands together in prayer. *Thank you, God, for Sergio. I know he's the one I've been praying for. Thank you.* And as she fell asleep, her hands unclenched, and her ring slid off her finger.

Celeste stared past her coffee cup at her left hand. She had woken up with an empty finger, the ring glinting in the sunbeam from the bedroom floor. She rubbed the skin where her ring should be. *It fell off last night. I should put it back on.* She considered her finger and wondered. *Am I brave enough to be without my shield? Olivia told me to take it off years ago, saying it sent a message to men to stay away. Do I still want and need this defense? Lord, help me.*

Life in Chicago was busy, but thoughts of Sergio kept a spring in her step and a smile on her face. As Celeste unloaded groceries in her small kitchen, her phone rang, and she answered, trying not to sound overly excited.

"Hello!"

"Hey, how are you doing?" Sergio asked. She answered him and put the phone on speaker as she rambled on about missing the Inn. She noticed he wasn't responding and instantly wondered what was wrong.

"Hey, what's up? Is everything okay?"

He sighed. "Actually no, it's not. I have some news to share with you. This is horrible timing." He took a breath before he continued. "Unfortunately, I have to go away on an extended work trip. OEC is sending me to Iceland tomorrow to set up a new IT hub in a small village. I'm leaving straight from the Inn. I'll still be able to text, but I'm not sure how often I'll be able to talk. The work is complex and time consuming, and the time zones are so different. I'll be thinking of you every single day, but I won't be able to talk much. I'm so sorry."

Celeste stood still, her heart beating crazily out of control. *Was he blowing her off? Had he meant anything he had said?* She took a deep breath and remembered who he was. *Maybe, just maybe, he was the real thing: honest and true. But, what if he's not?*

"I can't even explain how much I'll miss you." She needed to keep herself together to keep her heart from shattering. She took a deep breath. "I'll look forward to your texts and pictures. I'll send song titles, too. I will pray for you every day. How long will you be gone?"

He didn't want her to feel abandoned, and his gut clenched at the thought. "It looks like this trip will be at least three months." Celeste couldn't speak. "Are you still there?" he asked.

"Yes, I'm just sad. I'm really going to miss you," she whispered as her heart raced and her stomach churned. She stopped what she was doing as a disturbing thought surfaced. She had to ask. "How long have you known about this trip?"

Sergio grimaced, hoping she'd understand. "I've known for a while that it was a possibility, but I didn't want to say anything. I guess I was hoping it wouldn't happen or that someone else would get the assignment. I just didn't want you to feel abandoned."

Celeste's vulnerability turned into anger. "You thought springing it on me at the last minute was okay? Really? This is worse!" Celeste dropped the phone onto the counter and pushed it away from her. It was still on speaker, but she didn't want the device close to her at the moment.

"Celeste, please hear me. I didn't want to hurt you. I wanted to have time with you without the dread of an extended trip hanging over us. I will miss you too. So much. Celeste, I am with you, and you are very much worth whatever it takes. I am willing to wait and be patient and trust God one day, week, and month at a time solely for the privilege of being with you. I'm going to enjoy this journey with you."

She nodded as tears ran from her eyes. She pulled the phone back to her. "I want to believe you, so I will trust that this is just part of our journey; it's a stepping stone. We will be stronger because of it."

Sergio took a painful breath. "Yes, it is. We will be okay." He paused and then asked, "Hey, would you pray with me, right now over the phone?"

"Yes. Will you start?" she asked.

"Yeah." He closed his eyes and quieted his mind. As he spoke, he thanked God for Celeste and for their relationship, for watching over them, and for keeping them both safe and free from danger. He asked for protection, for guidance, for wisdom with decision-making, and for God to guide and direct their steps.

Sergio paused and Celeste began. She thanked God for their relationship and for the journey they were on. She prayed for Sergio as he traveled, that he would be a light to others, using the wisdom and leadership skills God had given him. She prayed that he would always know God, no matter the situation or how far he was away from home, and she prayed he would come back safely.

They ended with, "Amen." Afterwards, they were both silent as they thought about the experience they had just shared. It had been intimate and holy, and as they took their worries, their fears, and their gratefulness to God, they both felt his peace.

Sergio cleared his throat and said, "I have to go now, but I'll be in touch as often as I can. Hey, can you text me that picture of us at the gazebo? I really like it." She could hear the uplift of his voice and could imagine he was trying to smile.

"Of course." She clicked on the photo app. "I just sent it to you."

"Ah. Thank you. You're so beautiful. I really have to go now. Goodbye, Celeste. I'll be in touch soon. And," he paused, "thank you for the prayer."

She held the phone and managed to whisper something that sounded like, "Goodbye." She ended the call, rested her head against the kitchen cabinet, and cried.

Sergio silently hoped all would be well. He should have said more. He should have told her everything, but he couldn't bring himself to. What if she never wanted to see him again? He couldn't risk it. His heart already ached for hurting her. He texted her the only song title he could think of and pressed send.

Song: *Tragedy* by the Bee Gees

Chapter 11

CHICAGO AND ICELAND

Sergio texted pictures of the Arctic landscape: beautiful snowy drifts, sparkling snow, and frozen waterfalls that looked as though they stopped in mid-tumble to the rivers below. Every beautiful site reminded him of her. He loved telling Celeste how much he thought of her, how beautiful she was, how much he missed her, and how he longed to see her. He knew texting could only say so much, but it could be enough in the moment.

Celeste filled him in on her days as well, and they fell into a rhythm of pictures, jokes, questions, feelings, song titles, and virtual togetherness. They didn't hold back, and their texts became more and more important to them.

Sergio got into bed and opened his phone. He looked up at the ceiling, took a breath, and then texted, "Hey. You know how much I like you. I want to be able to talk to you about everything, and there are some things I've never told you. Maybe this time apart is a good time to share the good and the bad."

Celeste heard the text come through as she stood in her Chicago kitchen. She opened it with excitement and anticipation, and then read his words while sliding into a kitchen chair. "I like you too. I'm always here for you. This is sounding kinda serious. You can tell me anything." She paused, thumbs at the ready, but then closed her eyes to think. *What does he want to tell me? I want to tell him exactly how I feel right now. Isn't it good to be honest with your feelings?* She grimaced. *I'm just going to say what I feel.* "No matter what you need to tell me, please know that I really miss you. I can't wait until I can see you in person, feel your arms around me, and kiss your lips."

Sergio read her text and dropped the phone. He missed her so much it hurt. He could push the serious conversation to another time. Grabbing the phone, he paused, and then texted, "I miss you like breath." He sent it and waited.

Celeste stared at the phone and willed her heart to continue beating as she read his words. She took a deep breath and read them again. *He misses me like breath. Woah.* She rested her head in her hands and closed her eyes. *I've never had someone miss me so much they couldn't breathe.* She suddenly realized he must be waiting for a response and sat up and stared at her phone. *But how do I respond to that?*

She stared at his words and then texted, "That's the most beautiful thing anyone has ever said to me. I miss you with each breath I take. I pray we will see each other soon."

He responded, "I'm praying too." He then texted a song title and closed his eyes. He pictured her face and sighed. He was counting the days until he could hold her again. He prayed that would be soon, and he prayed all would be well.

Song: *Real Good Thing* by Marc Broussard

Chapter 12

ICELAND

The Christmas celebration was magical. Sergio walked through the small Icelandic village like a little kid, excited and full of wonder. He preferred this out-of-the-way hamlet over the city of Reykjavik. Thinking of Celeste, he took in the sights and sounds of the festival. The snow sparkled, the wind whipped around him, but he didn't feel cold. Children ran through the crowd, couples held hands while walking, and somewhere music was playing. He walked through the booths selling jewelry, hand-made scarves and toys, and thought of her again. At a jewelry booth, he spotted a beautiful snowflake pendant on a silver chain. Each point of the snowflake held a tiny diamond that sparkled in the moonlight. He picked it up and thought of her. *She's my snowflake, my one-of-a-kind Celeste. There's no one else like her in the world.* It brought back a memory, and he smiled a quiet smile. He bought it and placed the wrapped package in his jeans pocket. *This is perfect. It's amazing how I feel more alive and joyful and full of life because of her.* Suddenly, the music grew louder, and he heard his name being called.

"Sergio! Come on up here!" He moved quickly, recognizing the voice of one of his work buddies. "Get up here with me. It's that song you like!"

"No way!" Sergio yelled over the music as his friends laughed.

Clapping began as the crowd recognized the song. Sergio was so happy with the celebration, with the necklace in his pocket, and with the feelings in his heart, that he headed to the stage. The crowd parted, and he grabbed two friends to join him. They started dancing and lip synching as the crowd roared in appreciation, and they put on a show that brought everyone to their feet. As Sergio sang, he thought of Celeste, and he grinned even more. He couldn't wait to tell her about it.

As he walked home later that night, Sergio wondered what Celeste was doing at that very moment and guessed she might be on a run in the park. He closed his eyes and imagined taking hold of her hand, weaving their fingers together, and then pulling her into his arms. He imagined looking into her eyes and then kissing her tenderly.

He shook his head to clear his thoughts and then prayed, "Lord, thank you for Celeste in my life. I love her heart and her mind. I love being with her, listening to her, and imagining a life with her. I love that she loves you so much, and I really believe she helps strengthen my commitment to you. Thank you for bringing us together." He texted the title of the song he had sung on stage and wondered what she would think of it. He chuckled and hummed the tune as he headed home.

Song: *Rubberband Man* by The Spinners

Chapter 13

CHICAGO AND ICELAND

The day was cold but sunny in Chicago, and Celeste took advantage of the light as she sat on the little deck outside her kitchen. Her chimes blew gently in the wind as she sipped coffee and thought of Sergio. Her phone rang, and she absently picked it up.

"Hello?"

"Where are you and what are you doing?" She nearly dropped her coffee in surprise. She placed her mug on the table and pulled her sweater up around her as she settled in for a much-needed conversation.

Sergio described the beauty of Iceland and how he longed to share it with her. "The people here love a good party. They celebrate outside even when it's cold and dark. I went to an outdoor winter festival recently, and it was such a great time!" Sergio paused and asked, "What's that noise? Is it a wind chime?"

"Yes, I'm on the deck, and the wind is blowing. I like the sound," she answered as she glanced upwards.

"I like the sound too. It's nice. It must not be very cold if you're on your deck."

"It's one of those bright chilly days, and I'm taking advantage of the sunlight." He imagined her sitting with her legs pulled up, sipping coffee, and a beautiful smile beaming from her face. How he wished he were there beside her. He listened to her voice, loving the way she sounded. It was soft and graceful with a mixture of Chicago strength and southern drawl. His office door opened, and he pulled himself back into focus as his team entered the room.

"Speak to me for a minute. I just want to listen to your voice," he whispered, as his team tried to give him some privacy. Celeste understood, and she described what she saw before her: the bare trees, the dogwalkers and their dogs exploring the street down below, and the sound of the train in the distance. She knew it didn't matter. He just wanted to hear her voice and see what she was seeing.

"Thank you. I love hearing your voice. It makes me feel like I'm home. It soothes me. Celeste, I…" he turned to look at his colleagues in the room and made his way to the far corner to continue. "I dream of your voice. I hear it in my head, and it just makes everything seem better. I know that must sound odd, but it means a lot to me. I imagine the way your eyes light up and how your cheeks grow big when you smile. Sorry, I know this is a lot, but I think we should be honest." He paused as he was called from across the room. "I'm so sorry. I really have to go, but hopefully we can talk again soon." He quickly said goodbye without giving her a chance to respond, and the call ended.

Celeste stared at the phone and then set it down slowly. She placed her fingers on her lips and spoke his name, feeling her breath tickle her fingers. *He dreams of my voice.* She looked out at the world she had just described to him, but it was suddenly different. She smiled at the view and then up at the chimes. She knew that every time she heard the soothing melody, she would think of him. Her heart was joyful, and a feeling of peace washed over her. She texted a song title and prayed he would come home soon.

Song: *Everywhere* by Fleetwood Mac

Chapter 14

Work kept Celeste busy, and as she had not heard from Sergio in four long days, she was grateful for the distraction. *Where is he? What is he doing? Is something wrong?* She wondered about him constantly. She worked, she exercised, she cleaned her apartment, she checked her phone, and then she checked her phone again. There were moments when her lashes were suddenly damp, and she had to remind herself to be strong. *He's just on a work trip. It's okay. I don't know what's going on, and I'm afraid something has happened to him, but, ugh, I just miss him. I miss him like breath.*

She bought a journal to record her thoughts, feelings, and desires, and she began writing a list of random questions to ask him to get to know him even better. She giggled at some of them as she wrote, and it helped her relax.

Ding! A text came through, and she automatically reached for the phone. Her heart raced as she saw Sergio's name appear on the screen. *Oh, thank you, Lord.*

"Hey! So sorry I haven't been in touch. We've had technical glitches here. Winter in this small town has caused some problems with our communication. Where are you and what are you doing?

I miss you!" He stood in his room lifting weights with one hand while texting with the other.

Giddily, she reread each word, and then responded, "Hey! I've missed you! I have a new journal, and I'm writing down questions to ask you!"

"Fire away!" He switched the weight to his right hand.

"Have you ever done anything embarrassing in public?"

"Yes!" he answered. He put down the weight and texted about his karaoke performance at the winter festival. She laughed out loud and imagined the crowd going wild as he told the story. It was then that she understood the reason for his most recent song title. They texted back and forth, playfully enjoying the exchange. He walked away from the weights and stared out the window. *I miss her so much.* "What is something funny I don't know about you?"

"Hmmm…" Celeste crinkled her nose and looked up to the left as she pondered his question. "Well," she texted, "there's a lot you don't know yet, but I must confess, I'm a messy tooth brusher."

"I didn't expect that!" he texted as he chuckled. "Hold on, now, explain please. I need an image!"

She giggled as she replied. "I don't know what it is. I'm such a neat, orderly person, but I'm all over the place with a toothbrush in my hand. It's quite messy, really."

Sergio laughed so hard his phone fell to the floor. "Oh, this is great! Thanks for sharing." He took a moment for a deep breath and chuckled again.

"I have a very serious question to ask you now, Miss messy tooth brusher." She waited for the words to reveal themselves on her screen. "Did you ever watch Star Trek?"

"Yeah, I actually liked it. Why?" She waited for his response.

"They had these machines that transported people to different places. I need a transporter."

"Oh, yeah. I remember those. Why do you need a transporter?" she responded.

"To get you." Sergio shook his head and took off for the gym. A hard workout seemed to be the only option at the moment. He missed her so much. He couldn't wait to get back home to her.

Celeste stared at the phone and didn't know what to say. But she prayed he would suddenly be transported to her and whisk her away. She texted a song title and then headed to the bathroom to brush her teeth.

Song: *Help is on Its Way* **by Little River Band**

Chapter 15

CHICAGO AND ICELAND

Celeste stretched out on her couch. She yawned, pulled the blanket, and closed her eyes. Another dream came swiftly.

The Inn is quiet and dark. She walks in, looking around for someone. Anyone. She's alone. The glow of a computer screen gives her just enough light to see. She walks to the fireplace, lights a match, and holds it to newspaper stuck between the logs. It catches and begins to spread quickly. She rubs her arms for warmth and looks around. She isn't scared. She senses that everything is going to be okay. She sits down on the couch and waits.

Someone's coming. She hears footsteps on the fallen snow. She turns to the door. Sergio walks in balancing wrapped packages in his arms. Then he notices the fire crackling in the fireplace and looks at the couch. Their eyes meet, and he walks to her.

"Celeste," he whispers. "Celeste."

He joins her and pulls her into an embrace. He wraps her in his arms, and she melts into his. She feels safe. She lays her head on his chest, and he pulls her in tighter. Peace. Sanctuary. Refuge. Celeste sighed in her sleep.

It begins to rain, and Celeste has a desire to run out into it. It's a crazy, joyful feeling, and she suddenly jumps up.

"Let's go!" She pulls on her boots and runs outside. He stands

in the doorway watching her run through the rain with her arms outstretched to the sky. He is captivated by her joy. Then the rain stops, and Celeste stands still. She looks up at the stars but knows he is near. The pine trees stand tall around her and whisper with the wind. He stands beside her, places his hand on her shoulder. She turns in to him, and his hand caresses her cheek. She looks up into his eyes and sees love looking back at her. He leans down gently and brushes her lips with his. Little drops of rain drip off her hair and moisten his cheek. He pulls back, looks into her eyes, and smiles. Then he gently lifts her face to his and kisses her again.

Celeste woke slowly, not wanting the dream to end, and stretched languidly. *I love his kisses.* She tried to remember each aspect of the dream, to feel his lips, to feel the rain and the wind on her face. But there was something more. *Why was he carrying packages? Is that significant?* She opened her eyes wide to consider. *Packages can be gifts. They contain something special inside. They were all wrapped up, so they were probably gifts. Is Sergio the gift himself, or is this relationship the gift. Hmmm, but wait, I didn't open them.* She was analyzing this dream too much. She just needed to sleep. She headed to her room, fell into bed, and whispered Sergio's name.

Sergio looked at his watch and frowned. It was 2:00 a.m. in Chicago. He wanted to text her, to begin his day with her, but he also didn't want to disturb her sleep. *Maybe she has her volume muted.* He grabbed his phone and texted, "Hey, just thinking about you. Kinda hard not to." He added a heart emoji, tossed the phone onto his bed, and headed for the shower.

Celeste was instantly alert as she heard the incoming ding of a message. She reached for her phone, her eyes coming into focus as she read his text. Grinning sleepily, she responded, "Hey. I was just dreaming about you, but this is better." *Adding a heart emoji and a sleep emoji now.*

Sergio's phone sounded and he immediately turned around. *Could it be her? Did I wake her up?* He returned to his phone and picked it up. "What are you doing awake? Are you missing me?" He laughed as his thumbs flew across the keypad.

"You woke me up. I'm not complaining, though. You can wake me anytime!" She held her phone with anticipation.

Warmth spread through Sergio as he read her words. He responded, "Go back to sleep now and keep dreaming of me!" *Winky emoji added.* He stared at his phone thinking of her, imagining what she must look like at that very moment: hair mussed, sleepy eyes, beautiful face. *I wish I could start each day with her.* He shook his head and froze. *But what if she walks away after hearing about my past?* He headed back to the shower, his mind focused on hope and forgiveness and the story he knew he needed to tell.

Celeste willed her phone to light up again, but eventually, she texted a song title, thanked God for Sergio, and drifted off to sleep.

Song: *Adventure of a Lifetime* by Coldplay

Chapter 16

CHICAGO

Staring at her phone, she wondered if she should do what she longed to do. The days had turned into weeks, and she couldn't wait. She picked up her phone, but her hands were sweaty, and it dropped. She picked it up again and stared at it. *I love him, and I just want him to know. He did say we should be honest with each other.*

She closed her eyes and took a deep breath. Then she sat down and talked it out. *Here's the thing. I feel so much love for this man, but it doesn't just stop there. This love I feel for him is affecting everything else in my life. I feel God's love in a shiny, new way. I see friendships, colleagues, and even strangers with new eyes. I see God working in the world through love, and I want to share in it, be a part of it, and help it grow. I have to tell him. I love him.*

She touched his name on her texting app. *But what will he say? How will he react?*

What if he doesn't love me? Will it change things? Will it be awkward?

She began to text and then erased it. She took a deep breath and prayed, *Lord, I love this man. I pray that my words to him today bring him joy instead of worry. I pray they bring him excitement and hope for the future. Thank you, Lord, for Sergio and for our relationship.*

Thank you for this journey we are on; I know you are here with us. I'm going for it.

She looked down at her phone again and texted, "I just want you to know that I miss you, and I love you." She pressed send. With her heart beating wildly, she grabbed her ear buds and dashed out the door for a long run. There was nothing else she could do. She had thrown the proverbial ball, and it was now in his court.

Chapter 17

ICELAND

Sergio heard the ding of an incoming message. Work was all consuming and there seemed to be too many problems. An hour later, he pulled the sleek black phone from the front pocket of his jeans. He saw her name on his screen, took a breath, and let it out slowly. She was what he needed right now. A sweet message from Celeste would make his day, no matter what it said. *Well, it does matter what it says. I hope it's something that makes me smile or laugh. God, I miss her.* He opened her text and read the words she had sent. *Woah. She loves me. Couldn't she have waited to tell me face to face? She just couldn't wait. How do I respond? What's my heart telling me?*

He immediately stood up, jogged into the hallway, and headed to the lounge where he could sit down comfortably in one of the oversized chairs. He needed to relax and think before he responded.

Love. I want it to be real and lasting. To tell someone you love them takes guts and faith. Those are big words with huge meaning. All walls come down when you utter those words to the one who holds your heart. But I know what I want to say. God, will you bless these words I'm about to text to Celeste? Please let it be the right thing to do and the right timing. Here goes.

"Celeste, I miss you too. Very much! I can't wait to see you, but until I can see your face and tell you in person, here's my response: I love you too. I like who you are, and I love you. Just the thought of you makes me happy, and knowing you are in my life and that you love me, well, it's just so good and real. I'm thankful. I love being on this journey with you. On another note, it's possible they're going to send my team north into Greenland. Send warm socks! Ha-ha! It makes me really happy to say this, so I'll say it again: I. Love. You."

Song: *Love is Alive* **by Gary Wright**

Chapter 18

CHICAGO

Celeste poured a glass of water and stared at her phone. *Did he answer?* Her heart practiced flipping within her chest. Then she sat down feeling strangely calm. *I don't know what he's going to say, but I know I love him, and I'm glad I told him. Sure, a text wasn't the best way to say it the first time, but I just couldn't wait. When you know, you know.*

Her phone dinged, but she couldn't look. She walked around the room, she took off her shoes, she drank more water, and then she slowly picked up her phone and glanced at the message with one eye closed. *He loves me too.* She curled up on the couch with her favorite blanket, and then she jumped up and danced around her apartment. She was so happy and so thankful she had found him that she just couldn't contain her emotions. Then she stopped and closed her eyes.

"Lord," she whispered. "Thank you for sending Sergio to me. Thank you for blessing us with each other. Keep him safe, Lord, and bring him home in your good timing. I love you, and I trust you. Amen." As she hugged her blanket, she wondered how she could mail warm woolen socks to him in Greenland. Instead, she let the music and lyrics of a song convey her feelings.

Song: *Walking on Sunshine* by Katrina and the Waves

Chapter 19

CHICAGO

Celeste needed to run. She needed to think, listen to music, and pound all her emotions into the pavement. Soon her body fell into the familiar rhythm. She was oblivious to other runners on the path. She ran, listened, and thought of Sergio. Her music paused to allow a call to ring through, and she answered it excitedly.

"Sergio?"

"Hey, Celeste, I miss you!"

"Hi! I miss you too! I'm so excited to hear from you!"

"I had a bit of a break and wanted to call you. I've been thinking about you all day. It's been difficult to stay focused."

Celeste couldn't speak. She was overcome with happiness. She sat down on a park bench smiling from ear to ear.

"Celeste? Are you still there?"

"Yes, I'm here. I'm just excited to hear from you and so happy that you're thinking about me. Talk to me and tell me everything."

"I'm working and staying busy. It's cold here, but the work is interesting. But what I really want to tell you is that you are in my thoughts during the day and in my dreams at night. I can't wait to come home to you."

Celeste started to respond, but she heard voices in the background, so she waited.

"Celeste, I have to go, but before I do, I want to say something. I miss you. I know I've said this before, but I have to say it again. I'm with you, and you are worth whatever it takes. I will wait and trust God for the privilege of being with you. The waiting is hard, but you are worth the wait. This is just part of our journey. I'll talk to you soon. I love you."

"I love you. I will wait for you." His words completely filled her heart, and she knew there would never be anyone else. She was his, and her heart belonged to him. She texted a song title, and she prayed.

Song: *I Will Wait* by Mumford and Sons

Chapter 20

ICELAND

"Serg, can we talk?" Sergio looked up from his laptop and nodded at Liam. He knew what was coming. He took another quick look at the code he was working on and then pushed his chair back and stood up.

"Let's take a walk." Liam, the site supervisor, strode ahead, bouncing on his toes. The toe-walking made him look lively wherever he went, but knowing what was coming, Sergio shook his head, thinking it looked comical instead. He led Sergio to the break room and poured coffee for them both without saying a word. As they walked towards a square, gray table in the corner, Sergio frowned.

"So, Liam. When?" He reached the table, pulled out a chair, and sat down. Liam straddled one across the table from him, his movements sloshing his coffee beyond the rim of his cup.

"Two days. Look, we know it's not ideal, but someone needs to go up there." He paused to take a sip and then continued. "We need to see if anything is salvageable. You are the right guy to lead the team. Here's the plan: you'll leave on Thursday. We'll fly you and four of the guys to Tasiilaq: specifically, Henry Gonzalez, Trevor Lewis, Colin Perry, and Joe Campbell. Then they'll transport you an hour inland by helicopter. Once there, you'll walk to the site. It's about two miles from the drop-off, but we can't risk getting any closer. It is, after all, the Arctic. There's a generator in the cabin, and there are bins stocked with freeze-dried food and coffee from before. We just need your team to be secluded in the wilderness, use the company products, take lots of pictures, and come back with the gear that was left up there five years ago, including the tech." Liam took a swig of coffee that made a sickening noise in his throat. Sergio looked at him in disgust and wondered if he could just resign. Liam's explanation was callous. He didn't care about anyone or anything except himself and the job.

"I don't want to do this now." Sergio folded his arms and set his face. "I don't think it's safe. Greenland in February? Really? Didn't the last team have to be evacuated due to severe frostbite and near starvation? Let's just take a loss. It's not worth it."

"Yeah, well, we think it is worth it. You and your team will be highly compensated, and we'll have incredible pictures to promote the products. Plus, we really need the tech and gear left there. There's no one better than you to lead this team. Will you do it?" Sergio stared into his coffee and didn't answer. "Well?"

Sergio stared at Liam with contempt. He'd finish this job, deposit the money, and resign. It wasn't what he wanted anymore. *One more job. Then I'm done.* "I want contracts written for my team and for me. I want the compensation stated, and if something happens, the money goes to our designated person. We get all the gear we request, and if there's an emergency, the chopper comes to get us immediately. I want it all written, signed, and notarized." His eyes held Liam's.

"Done. I'll set up a meeting for the entire team, and we'll have the contracts ready. You'll be back here in five days. Think how amazing the pictures will be! We'll put you guys in next month's online spread." He pushed his chair to the table and hurried to the office.

Sergio let out a breath. He didn't want to go, and he knew his team felt the same way. He wondered if the money would be enough of an incentive. He shook his head knowing he had to share the news.

"What do they think we can do?" A brawny man named Henry carelessly threw socks and hats into his bag as he complained. "They tried setting up a data hub there years ago, but it failed. It's the middle of Greenland! Do they know it's an ice sheet? Now they want us to try again? And they also want us to use the gear and take pictures in it? Are you serious? We'll just be up there with the muskoxen, and we'll be freezing. Greenland in February?" Mutterings and under-breath grumblings faded away as Sergio thought about their situation and wondered what muskoxen looked like.

The men weren't happy, but Sergio knew the sooner they went, the sooner they could come back. He packed his warmest company gear and zipped his bag. Looking around the room, he noticed the package containing the snowflake necklace he had bought for Celeste at the winter festival. He carefully took it out of the bag, wrapped it in tissue, and placed it in an envelope. Then he sat down and wrote a quick note:

"My sweet Celeste, you are one of a kind, like this beautiful snowflake. Wear it near your heart and think of me. I love you. Yours, Sergio."

He addressed the package to her and placed it on his desk. *I'll give it to her myself when I see her. It'll be safe here.* He turned around to look at the room and picked up his bag. Then he sat down and pulled out his phone. He had to text her one more time.

"Hey, beautiful! I'm heading to Greenland. It's doubtful I'll be able to text for a while. Don't forget about me! There's so much more I want to share with you, but we'll have all the time in the world when I return. I love you! See you soon!"

He closed his eyes and whispered a prayer of protection, texted a song title, and walked out of the room.

Song: *Hold Her* by For King and Country

Chapter 21

The two-mile trek to the hub was painful. Due to the abysmal weather conditions, it took longer than anyone had expected. The biting wind whipped around them, making their progress agonizingly slow. With each step, Sergio tried to stay positive. His thoughts focused on Celeste as he plodded on. Images of her sweet face warmed him, and knowing she loved him gave him strength. He could think of her, and suddenly everything seemed better and brighter. He loved the effect she had on him. He thought of her again as he placed his foot into the deep snow to lead those behind him. *When I return, I don't want to waste a single day. I love her. How did this happen so fast? It's as though we're connected… like I don't know where she ends and I begin.* He stomped his foot into the snow with renewed energy. He had to get back to Celeste, and he prayed it would be soon.

Heads down, they walked in a straight line using each other's footholds to move forward. When the hub came into sight, their spirits soared, and the men found the energy needed to keep going. Visibility was low and light was dim, but the hub stuck out like a beacon. Sergio whooped and the men answered with cheers as they trudged on in the deep snow.

When they arrived, they found the door unlocked. Sergio worried what they would find inside, but he bolstered the men with high fives as they entered one by one. The team soon discovered that nothing was left. There was no food or gear. *Where was it?* Sergio's thoughts sprang into action as he mentally calculated their supplies. They had several days' worth of food they had brought with them, but that was all. They would melt snow for water.

"It's going to be okay, guys. We will rest for a day, take some pictures in the gear we brought, and then we'll leave. We can do this!" Sergio tried to sound confident and strong, but he was angry. This was a bad situation, and he wanted to leave as soon as possible. They settled in and then took stock of the small building.

Sergio worked on placing the food in a secure place and getting the generator started. His main goals were to stay safe, to keep his team alive, and to get home soon. He thought of Celeste and wondered what she was doing. He clutched a shelving unit with both hands, pressed his forehead against the metal, and closed his eyes. He saw her face, and it gave him strength to stay strong. He didn't just love the way she looked. Yes, he admitted he was attracted to her physically, but it was her heart that made her so beautiful. More than anything, he loved that she was good and kind, and the more he got to know her, the more deeply he fell in love. As he pictured her in their waterfall garden, he could almost feel her arms around him, pulling him close. His thoughts turned to love. *I know she loves me too, and I love feeling lovable. Does that even make sense? She has brought so much joy to my life. I thought I understood love, but I never truly knew what love was until I fell in love with her. God, thank you for Celeste, and thank you also for being here with me. I know that when I am afraid, I need to put my trust in you. Together, we can do this. Together, we can make it home.* He opened his eyes and released his grip on the shelving unit. He pulled out his phone and texted a song title. He knew it wouldn't deliver, but it made him feel better. He left his phone on the shelf and got to work.

Song: *Here Without You* by 3 Doors Down

Chapter 22

CHICAGO

Days crept into weeks. News reports explained that a team of five men had been lost in the Arctic wilderness.

The dramatic tone of the reporter caught her attention. "We know they made it to the facility. Early reports showed they were making good progress and spirits were high. But the latest reports and drone footage show a cave-in of the building. We will keep you updated." The grim look on the reporter's face was too much. Celeste jumped up, not knowing what to do. She wanted to call someone at the hub in Iceland, but who? No one there knew her, and she had no idea how to get through. She called Sergio's brother, Luca, but he had not heard anything either. They promised to keep in touch. She fell onto the couch and cried.

Celeste walked through each day in a daze. She played the last song he had texted her on replay and cried at the words he had written. She imagined him shivering and calling her name. She brushed away tears with the back of her hand and looked out the window at the winter sky. She saw a flock of birds flying freely, dipping and soaring on the wind. She wondered if she could ever feel that free again. Would she ever be happy? She brought her gaze down to her phone and texted a song title. She cried and she prayed. There was no word.

Song: *O* by Coldplay

Chapter 23

CHICAGO

Celeste and Luca tried to keep in touch, tried to reach out, call, or text, but it was difficult. It had been two months without a word from OEC or the media. Her heart ached, and her breath sounded jagged and harsh on the phone with him, almost as if her lungs had forgotten how to breathe. To say she missed Sergio like breath was a true statement if there ever was one. *Does he still miss me?* She held onto hope and tried to breathe deeply for him, not even letting herself consider that he might not be breathing at all. She withdrew from her normal, everyday life. She worked and she came home. She watched the news whenever she could, often waking up in the middle of the night to watch the international reports.

Trudging home from work, she noticed that people seemed happy, going on with their everyday lives, and she couldn't imagine why. Didn't they know she was missing the love of her life? She didn't want to go grab a pizza with friends after work. She wanted Sergio.

She stopped in her lobby to get the mail, turned the lock, and opened the small, metal door. There was more there than usual, and she carefully pulled out the contents. She piled it all in her purse and turned the lock, nodding at others who were there.

Once inside her apartment, Celeste turned on the TV, muted the volume, and fell onto the couch. She wiped sudden tears as she scanned the headlines and rested her head on the pillow. There was still no word. She thought about her parents. They would have loved Sergio. But now… now… were they all gone now? She took a breath and gritted her teeth. The forceful action somehow gave her strength and determination.

She thought back to the day her parents died. She remembered standing on the back deck of their house at eighteen, staring up at the sky and wondering if she would ever feel safe again. She was alone. Scared. Empty. She remembered how the clouds had darkened, how lightning had streaked the sky with jagged light, and how the thunder had rumbled. The tension and drama of the night sky had matched her emotions, and as the clouds released their torrent, she imagined they had been crying with her. She remembered walking out into the rain, feeling angry, wanting to yell and scream, but instead she had prayed. She had fallen to her knees in the muddy yard, looked up at the sky through the downpour, and prayed with all her might. She needed God, and even in her heartache, she had known she was not alone. She knew God had never left her. She knew he would not leave her now.

She sighed, wiped her tears on the pillow, and noticed an envelope sticking up out of her purse. *What is that?* She grasped the purse strap, pulled it closer, and reached inside. Her fingers brushed over a small, padded envelope, and she picked it up. She gasped. "It's from Iceland!" She sat up straight and took a deep breath, and then jumped up to get scissors from a drawer in the kitchen. She opened the envelope carefully so as not to break or cut anything inside and pulled out a note.

"Hello, Celeste. I'm from the OEC job site in Iceland, and I found this envelope in Sergio's room. It was already sealed and addressed to you. I thought you'd like to have it." Sincerely, Oliver Adams

She reached in and pulled out another envelope. It was smaller and was addressed to her. She held it carefully, knowing Sergio had wrapped it himself. *He left me a package?* She stopped in mid-thought. *Wait, didn't I dream about Sergio walking in with an armload of packages? Could this be what my dream foretold?* She pulled gently on a piece of tape, and a small pad of tissue fell out into her lap. She opened it carefully and brushed away a tear with her sleeve. The snowflake hung from a beautiful silver chain, its tiny diamonds shining and sparkling in the light from the TV.

"It's so beautiful," she whispered to the room, as if the necklace itself needed to know how very special it was. She read the note, held them both to her heart and vowed. "I will never take it off. Thank you! I love you, my Sergio. I love you."

Song: *Talking to the Moon* **by Bruno Mars**

Chapter 24

GREENLAND

Cloudy dizziness engulfed him. His mind could not grasp anything real, and he hurt all over. One word floated into his mind, and he whispered it as if it were a prayer. "Celeste."

Chapter 25

"It's an open invitation. Please come anytime you'd like to get away." Celeste heard Luca speaking to her, but his words hardly registered.

"I can't come to the Inn, Luca. It would be too hard. I just can't."

"I understand, but if you change your mind, please don't hesitate.

Celeste hung up the phone and stared at the wall. It had been three months without a word from Sergio or the company, and the news reports were rare these days. Maybe she should go to the Inn, spend time there, and talk to Luca. Spending time with Sergio's brother might even be a good idea. She also really wanted to go to their garden, to walk the trails, and to spend time in the places that were special to him. She had a vacation coming up. *Why not?* She called Luca back, made the arrangements, and planned her trip.

A week later, Celeste walked through the airport feeling uneasy. She looked around expectantly, as if Sergio might be right around the corner coming to greet her. An SUV waited in the exact spot as before, causing her heart to pause momentarily. She walked towards it slowly, trying to figure out how to deal with her emotions. *I know Sergio won't be here, but what if he is? What if the accident in the Arctic never happened? What if he just left me?* She opened the back door, placed her bag on the seat, and glanced at the driver.

"Hi, Luca."

"Celeste. Welcome back. Will you sit up front?"

She climbed in and closed the door. Her stomach started to clench, and she just wanted to stop along the side of the road and throw up. Why was she here again? She couldn't remember.

"Maybe this is a mistake," she whispered. "I don't know if I should be here."

"I'm really glad you are." He turned the car into traffic and set off. Luca was quiet on the drive and kept his eyes on the road. Celeste stole a glance at him and compared him to Sergio. They resembled one another, that was true, but Luca had dark brown hair and looked more European than Sergio. She sighed and closed her eyes, not sure at all what she was doing.

By the time they arrived, Celeste truly felt ill. Everything looked the same, smelled the same, and brought back too many memories. Once inside, she dashed to her room. It was too much. She took a long shower and then crawled into bed. Sleep soon overtook her, and the anxiety of the day faded.

She spent her days walking through the woods, sitting in the secret garden, watching the sunrise at their gazebo, and writing in her journal. She was crying less these days, but the heaviness in her chest was a constant reminder. One verse that repeatedly came to mind was Psalm 28:7 – *The Lord is my strength and my shield; my heart trusts in him, and he helps me. My heart leaps for joy, and with my song I praise Him.* It gave her peace and reminded her that she was never alone, and she repeated it often to herself.

Luca was attentive, making sure she was included in outings, festivities, dinners, and games. The distractions helped, and she even laughed out loud once. It surprised her, and Luca smiled. They were becoming friends, and Celeste was grateful for him.

One evening by the fire, Luca told stories of their brotherly childhood antics. They both laughed when Luca told of Sergio building a boat out of cardboard and trying to sail it down the river. Then they stared silently at the fire, lost in their own thoughts of the man they both missed and loved. Celeste stood up to leave, and Luca reached for her hand.

"Do you have to go?" The touch on her hand surprised her, and she pulled back.

"What? Yes, I'm tired. I'm headed to bed. Good night." She walked away with a strange feeling in her stomach. He looked so much like Sergio, but he wasn't Sergio. He was Luca, and he had wanted her to stay. She turned back to look at him, and then she walked away whispering Sergio's name.

Song: *Whenever I Say Your Name* by Sting

Chapter 26

GREENLAND

Figures moved before him, sometimes stopping nearby. He felt hands on his arm and on his head. Then he felt nothing. The cloudiness reappeared, and he drifted through snowy mounds searching for something. Something. What was he searching for? He could almost see it. It was so close, but his mind couldn't quite reach it. Suddenly everything turned black, and the iciness returned. Then the heat. He was on fire and thrashed around trying to put it out. He yelled to get someone's attention, but the figures did not return. He whimpered and succumbed to the void.

Chapter 27

CHICAGO

Celeste returned to Chicago. Loneliness settled into her and grew deeper and more intense. She looked at the city and saw only despair. She needed the mountains and the clean air. She needed Sergio. She wrote letters to him describing her days, her activities, and her deepest longings, but they were a poor substitute for the real thing. She kept the letters in an empty box made to look like a rare book. She knew it was a bit old fashioned, but she found the actual writing with pen on paper to be therapeutic and comforting. She stored the book on her bookshelf, the visual reminder giving her a sense of peace and purpose and hope. It helped her remember everything. It wasn't just a dream. Their relationship was real and good. He would come back one day. He had to. He just had to.

Daily life settled in, and she found solace in church. The people there were a kind and prayerful group, and she needed them in her life. They were her community. She was able to pray, to spend time studying her Bible, and to listen for God's voice. She realized her pain was a lot like the grief she felt when her parents had died. *Where there was great love, there is great grief.* She had heard that quote somewhere and realized how accurate it was.

She was sleeping better at night, but she still dreamed of Arctic winds, blinding snow, and strange animals wearing woolen socks.

Awake or asleep, her fingers found their way to the snowflake necklace she wore around her neck. The action was now involuntary, and it helped her feel closer to the man she loved.

Luca called, and they fell into a rhythm of talking once or twice a week. It was nice talking with someone who knew Sergio so well. *I think Sergio would like that I'm becoming friends with Luca.* She pulled out paper and a pen and began to write:

> "Dear Sergio, I miss you. But I am so grateful to have had a connection… to have expressed love for you, to know you and to be loved by you. I will hold you in my heart forever, and I pray I will see you again. Keep trusting in God. Don't give up hope. We both love you.
>
> With all my love, Celeste.
>
> P.S. Here's a song title for you: *Always in My Head* by Coldplay."

Chapter 28

CHICAGO

"Can you help me for the holiday weekend? Free room and board!" Luca's voice sang over the phone. "Come on, say yes!"

She had a few days off and thought she could handle helping out. "It could be fun," she said as she thought about it.

"I'm booking your flight and will have a car waiting for you at the airport. Thanks for your help, Celeste. I can't wait to see you!"

Celeste hung up the phone. She was happy that she was going to be helping Luca, but her hand automatically reached for her necklace, and she closed her eyes. She thought of Sergio. *Can I be there again at the Inn where I fell in love with him? Can I really be there without him?* She walked out on her deck and sat in the sunshine. Pulling her knees up, she hugged them while thinking of the man she loved. *I miss you, Sergio.* The wind began to blow softly around her, and she smiled though her tears as the chimes began moving with the wind, serenading her.

Song: *Til Kingdom Come* by Coldplay

Chapter 29

GREENLAND

His brain was fuzzy and disjointed, as if the pieces didn't know how to sort themselves. He couldn't move, but he could hear, and he strained to hear something familiar. *Are those dogs barking in the distance?* Something soft moved against him, but he wasn't able to turn his head to see what it was. Everything was dark. He felt a cool hand on his forehead. It felt good, and a whispered moan passed through his lips.

The soft thing brushed against him again and a kind voice said, "Eat." He attempted to open his mouth, but the pain was excruciating. He took a breath through his nose and tried once more, and then he knew nothing.

A noise woke him from a dream that did not make sense: a montage of snowflakes and wind chimes dancing under pine trees, but the images drifted away as he sensed someone near him.

"Eat." He tried to open his mouth at her gentle word, and was able to part his lips slightly. He felt a spoon touch his bottom lip and then the tiniest drop of broth made its way down his throat.

He closed his eyes and tried to make sense of things. He wondered where he was and why he couldn't see. He heard other sounds as well. He listened carefully and thought he heard whispers not too far away, but he couldn't make out any real words. Something soft brushed against him again and a hand touched his forehead. *Ahhh, he thought. I like that cool hand on my forehead.* He felt the spoon on his lips and was able to take four or five drops of warm broth before he had to stop. The pain was unbearable. Everything hurt. It was hard to breathe. Sleep was the only relief, and he surrendered to it.

In his dream, he saw a beautiful woman walking along a path, smiling at him. She turned away and started down another path, pushing away overgrown branches. She looked back and motioned for him to follow. She vanished into a dense fog that turned into a waterfall, and as he followed her, an unfamiliar song led the way.

Song: *O-o-h Child* by The Five Stairsteps

Chapter 30

Celeste walked through the airport towards a small alcove of lockers near baggage claim. "Locker number 15, where are you?" she muttered as she searched. Upon finding it, she punched in the combination Luca had texted her. It opened easily, and she reached in for the small, black leather pouch inside.

A handwritten note from Luca read: "Welcome back! See you soon!" She took the car keys from the pouch and walked to the parking lot, rolling her suitcase beside her.

The drive was easy, and she arrived right on time, but she sat in the car for a moment and calmed her thoughts. *I'm here to work. It's going to be okay. Guide my steps, Lord. Please guide my steps.* A quick nod of her head finished her prayer, and then she pulled her suitcase from the back and walked to the entrance. A soft breeze picked up her hair, causing it to swirl around her face. She brushed it out of her eyes and then heard wind chimes faintly in the distance. The sound brought Sergio to mind, and her heart ached. She paused as she wondered if she could handle being here again.

"Celeste, thank you so much for coming!" Luca walked quickly towards her as he continued, "This convention is a huge one, and my assistant manager is out with the flu. I really need your help. The guests begin arriving this afternoon at 4:00." He took her suitcase from her and ushered her into the main lobby. "Here's your key. If you can take your bag to your room, change clothes, and be back down in twenty minutes, we can go over the logistics."

Celeste nodded. *I think this will be fine. It's all about business, and Sergio used to help his brother. I can do this. I'm here to help his family.* She stepped into the elevator, pulled out her phone, and texted a song title. Even though her texts and songs weren't delivered anymore, she continued the game. It helped her feel closer to Sergio as she chose the right songs for her moods. She added each song to her running playlist. They were her accompaniment along the journey, giving her words to express her feelings when she couldn't express them on her own.

Song: *Baby Hold On* by Eddie Money

Chapter 31

GREENLAND

He lay perfectly still as if being motionless would help his thoughts fall into place. It was no use. He remembered nothing. Nothing but the cool hand that touched his forehead and fed him broth. He heard the faint sound of dogs again and realized he knew what they were. *Good. Maybe there's hope for me yet.*

He turned his head but couldn't see a thing. There was something covering his eyes, something that blocked out all light. As he lay still, a sound reached his ears, and he froze. *I know that… I think I know that, but what, what is it?* The noise came closer, and his toes began to move to the beat. *It's a song. I recognize the song!* It got louder and louder and then went away, softer and softer until it was gone. But he had heard it, and he knew it from somewhere. He tried to remember the lyrics as they faded, but instead, he fell asleep, exhausted from the exertion.

Nearby, Margret watched him and noticed his toes had moved to the beat of the music. "We need more music for this one," she said as she watched him with interest.

Song: *Gotta Be Somebody* by Nickelback

Chapter 32

NORTH CAROLINA

Celeste dropped into bed, tired but happy. The stars peeked into her window, and she stared at them as she fell asleep. Her thoughts of the day mingled with images of Sergio, and she dreamed.

She stands on a beach, the sun warm on her skin. "Remember the Sea," a voice whispers in the wind. "Work towards the sea." She moves closer to the water. She feels the force and power of the tide and swims out into its midst. Suddenly she is unsure and afraid. Her mind whirls with thoughts of love, and it overwhelms her. She turns back and swims swiftly towards the shore. Once there, with her feet on the sand, she faces the water. She's afraid, but she can't keep away. Love calls to her. Again, she walks into the sea. She can do it, even if she's afraid. She must follow her heart. She must work towards the sea.

Remember the sea? Work towards the sea? She groaned and looked at the clock. The numbers 4:15 glowed from the rectangular shape on the bedside table. She reached for her journal and pen to record the dream. As she wrote, the words took shape in her mind and formed a poem:

You, my love, are the sea:
Deep, beautiful, mysterious.
I wade in cautiously
not quite understanding the risks of love.
I then turn back towards the shore, but
You serenade me and pull me back
to you with laughter, warmth, and songs
and I feel at home.
But again, I start back to shore,
Doubting and unsure.
Then with determination,
I turn around to face you.
You are real.
I move towards you confidently
I can't keep away…
Love encircles me; Joy consumes my soul.
I am yours.

She closed her journal, turned off the light, and sighed, knowing her heart would always belong to Sergio. *He's the love of my life. I love him, and love is always worth the effort.* She closed her eyes and imagined being on a great journey working towards the sea.

Song: *Dream Weaver* by Gary Wright

Chapter 33

NORTH CAROLINA

Traffic was bumper to bumper. Celeste fiddled with the radio and checked her phone, but there was no information. They were simply not moving.

"I'm so sorry," she said to the guests she had just picked up. "Hopefully, we'll be on our way soon."

She stared out the window at the mountains in the distance and tried to relax. She took a deep breath, ran her hand through her hair, and breathed again. *Where are you?* she wondered as she choked back a sob. She coughed a couple of times to hide the sound of the cry, and then took a sip of water. The ladies in the backseat were happily chatting and did not seem to notice her burst of grief.

Resting her head on the headrest, she looked at the truck in front of her. It was a work truck with heavy materials in the back, and she tried to figure out what they might be. Then she looked down at the license plate and gasped as she read the word SERGIO. She sat up straight and stared.

"What?" she asked out loud. "What on earth?" But the guests in the back were laughing at something on a phone and did not hear her. She tried to make sense of it, shaking her head, and then the traffic started moving. The truck turned right and was soon out of sight. Celeste drove in the direction of the Inn, her thoughts clanging against one another. It was a sign; she just knew it. *And we didn't start to move until I had seen it. It was there for me to see.* The sign renewed her hope that all would be well. *Thank you, Lord, for this sign. Thank you.* A song came on the radio, and she smiled, making a mental note to text it to him later.

Song: *Am I Wrong* by Nico and Vinz

Chapter 34

NORTH CAROLINA

The conference kept Celeste busy. She welcomed the attendees, directed them to registration, gave tours, put out fires, drove to and from the airport, ran errands, and fell into bed exhausted at night. As she drifted off to sleep, she thought of the license plate with the word SERGIO on it. *Whose truck, was it? How many Sergios were there in this town?* She whispered a thank you to God and was instantly asleep.

The next morning, Luca talked with two conference attendees as Celeste made her way to the barista in search of her beloved morning mocha. She was dressed in her uniform shirt with the pine trees stitched neatly on the left pocket, her favorite pair of jeans, and tennis shoes. Luca watched her as he continued talking with his guests but quickly found his way to her side.

"Celeste, thank you so much for everything you are doing. You're amazing, and I appreciate you so much," Luca reached for her coffee and handed it to her. Celeste took the drink and held it to her lips.

"I'm happy to be here, and I really enjoy the work. I love hospitality and helping others." She sipped the coffee and sighed. "So good," she said, and then took another sip.

"Would you run an errand for me this morning? I need something picked up in Shepherd Falls. Actually, why don't you take several hours and just enjoy the time there. It's a great little town about twenty minutes away." Luca smiled at her as he spoke, but Celeste didn't notice. She simply heard the words *several hours and enjoy yourself,* and she was ready to go. She had been to the Shepherd Falls Chapel with Sergio, but they had never gone into town. She was soon out the door with coffee in hand. She welcomed the opportunity to explore and to wander by herself for a few hours, and she was grateful for the time.

The drive was beautiful. The road curved and wandered through the mountains, tiny waterfalls tumbled from high bluffs, the sun shone brightly, and every now and then she saw deer munching on grass. She took a deep breath of the early spring air and relaxed.

The town looked as if it had been plucked from a painting and placed down gently in a lush valley. She drove slowly into it and parked along the street in front of The General Store. She turned off the ignition and looked around. *I think Norman Rockwell may have painted this, and then it just came to life.* There were cheerful flowers in window boxes, children riding bicycles, people taking the time to stop and talk, and the cutest store fronts she had ever seen.

She stepped out of the truck, locked it, and walked in. The General Store was jam-packed with goods, and she had to be careful not to step on anything. She stopped and stared at the array of items everywhere: on shelves, on chests, on the floor, on ladders, inside cabinets, and strung on lines hung from wall to wall. It would take weeks to see it all, so she got started. Along the wall, there were bowls of silver jewelry with stones of every color, as well as necklaces and bracelets. She wandered closer, her eyes catching a sparkle in the sunlight. She stopped and stared. It was a snowflake bracelet very similar to the necklace Sergio had given her.

"It's so beautiful," she whispered as she picked it up.

"Here, let me," she heard a warm, soothing voice insist. She looked up to see an elderly man. His white hair was cut close to his head, and he was tall and dark-skinned. His kind face held a permanent smile. He nimbly picked up the bracelet and clasped it to her wrist. "It suits you. The name's Bert. Welcome to my store." Then he turned and walked to the back, calling for someone named Daisy.

Celeste looked down at her wrist and then reached for the snowflake necklace at her throat. Taking a deep breath, she wondered at the coincidence. She continued wandering around the store, picked up an item or two, and then headed to the register to pay. She saw Bert and asked for the item Luca had requested. A spry older woman walked up and smiled hugely at Celeste. Her dark, creamy skin was smooth and her eyes lit up her face.

"And hello to you, my dear. Who are you?"

Celeste couldn't help but smile back at her. "My name is Celeste James. I'm helping out at the Inn for a few days. I'm a friend of Luca's. I'm dating his…" but she couldn't continue. Her eyes suddenly became watery, and she wiped at them and then latched onto her necklace for strength.

"Oh, dear. Now, Celeste, you come right over here and tell Daisy all about it," the old woman said, as she led Celeste to a chair.

Bert pulled up a stool and handed her a bottle of water, looking like he was ready to listen to a good story. For some reason, Celeste felt compelled to tell the entire tale of her relationship with Sergio to these two complete strangers. As she spoke, she held onto her necklace, while Daisy and Bert looked on with interest.

"Mercy," Bert exclaimed as he took a deep breath. "Well, what do you know? Daisy, S and C!"

Daisy turned to him, wide-eyed, "Gracious, that's right. S and C."

"Now, Celeste, I have a story for you." Celeste took a sip from the bottle and turned to Bert. "Two nights ago, I couldn't sleep. I kept tossing and turning, so I got up and went to my workshop. I like to build things, you see, so I picked up some wood, but nothing came to mind. I sat down in my recliner out there in the workshop and fell asleep. Now, this is the good part. I dreamed of letters, specifically, the letters S and C. Now, why on earth would I be dreaming about letters? Strange, right?" Celeste sat on the edge of her seat, waiting for more.

"In this dream, I made a wooden bowl with a silver band about one inch tall going all around the upper rim. At the base of the bowl, I carved the initials S and C in an intricate design. I'd never seen anything like it before. So, when I woke up, I knew I had to recreate that bowl. I've been working on it for two days, and I just finished it this morning. Would you like to see it?"

Celeste just nodded. She couldn't speak. The letters S and C ran circles in her mind until they formed the words Sergio and Celeste. She shook her head in wonder. Daisy patted her back, gave her more water, and told her everything was going to be just fine. Bert stood up and looked at Celeste and then left to retrieve the bowl.

Daisy filled the time by telling Celeste all about her new oatmeal raisin cookie recipe while Celeste listened distractedly. When Daisy got up to retrieve a plate of cookies for her, Bert returned. He sat down beside Celeste and paused.

"I don't know why I dreamed of this, why I made it, or why you walked in here today, but I know for certain that I am giving this bowl to you." Bert gingerly placed the gift in Celeste's hands.

She felt the warm wood, traced the intricate carving, and ran her fingers over the silver band.

"Oh, it's lovely." She stared at the letters and felt warm, salty tears fly out of her eyes. "Sorry, I seem to be doing a lot of that," she explained as she hurriedly wiped them with the back of her hand.

Bert patted her on the shoulder. "Now, young lady," he began, "you are taking this bowl. It was certainly made for you. If I have more dreams about letters, I may begin a brand-new business and just wait to see who walks into my store!"

Celeste couldn't help but laugh. Daisy took the bowl, wrapped it carefully in soft tissue, and then placed it in a bag. Celeste thanked them both, gathered the packages, and headed for the truck, feeling a bit like dancing.

Song: *You Should be Dancing* by The Bee Gees

Chapter 35

GREENLAND

He was frustrated. Whatever was wrong with him, he wanted to know what it was, and he wanted to fix it. The soft thing rubbed against his hand, and he was able to reach out and grab it. It stopped. His fingers reached out to explore it. Was it a fur coat? His mind couldn't quite figure it out. He sighed and let his hand drop.

A gentle voice whispered next to his ear, "Eat." He felt the soup in his mouth before he realized he had opened his lips. "Music," he heard the voice say. "You like music." Another spoonful of warm broth trickled down his throat.

Music, he wondered, but before he could muster a real thought, he heard it. Someone had come near with music. He did not know the tune, but it was sad, and he didn't like it. He turned his head away from it and tried to drown it out. The music stopped immediately.

The young nurse typed on his chart while observing him, her fingers clicking over the keys. She wrote, "Does not like sad song #1." Her soft jacket brushed against his arm as she recorded her observations, and he turned towards it. *I'll try another,* she thought and carefully looked at the playlist. *Here's one.* She pressed play, and he smiled slightly. She watched him as he listened to the music, and she wondered who he was.

Song: *Running on Empty* by Jackson Browne

Chapter 36

NORTH CAROLINA

Celeste strolled through the town of Shepherd Falls in a happy daze. She dropped off her packages in the truck and set out to explore. Stopping at an outdoor café, she enjoyed a quick lunch and then wandered into a nearby bookstore. After buying a travel guide, chocolate bars, and a scarf the color of cinnamon, she slowly made her way to the truck. She needed to get back, but the time away had been good, and she felt refreshed. Her bracelet caught the light and sparkled as she walked. She hopped up into the truck and sighed. *I wish Sergio were here right now. I'd love to wander through this town with him.* She put the key into the ignition and looked at the car in front of her. It was parked too close to hers, and she couldn't get out. Instead of making a fuss to find the driver, she grabbed a chocolate bar and a bottle of water and turned on the radio. Within minutes, two women walked into view and towards the car. Celeste recognized one as a guest at the Inn. She turned the radio off and rolled down her window to speak to them, but they were deep in conversation.

"We love the Inn," she was saying, "you have to come visit. The owner is a dream, and we really like his girlfriend, too." They got into the car, pulled away, and left plenty of room for Celeste to leave, but she sat, stunned.

"Girlfriend?" she muttered. "Surely not! They think I'm his girlfriend? They must mean someone else." She pulled away from the curb with a sick feeling in her stomach and took her time getting back to the Inn.

Luca glanced up at the front windows as Celeste pulled into the parking lot. He smiled and then stopped himself. *Stop it, man. Stop it. She's in love with your brother!*

Celeste walked in holding her packages and was approached by a group of guests. Luca watched her deal with their problems in such a kind way that they relaxed and left feeling satisfied.

He made his way to her. "How was Shepherd Falls? Any problems?" he asked.

"No problems. It's a picture postcard town, and Bert and Daisy were so sweet." She handed his bag to him and continued. "I'll put my things in my room and then get to work." She walked to the elevator. The conversation she had overheard was still ringing in her ears, and she wasn't sure how to act around Luca. She needed to think.

"Hey, Celeste, hold on a minute," Luca called after her. "Can we meet in my office in a little while? I need to talk to you about something."

"Of course," she answered. "I'll be down in a few minutes." Celeste placed her things in her room and tucked the bag containing the bowl into a corner of her closet. She sat down on the bed and thought about recent events:

1. *I saw a license plate on the back of the truck that said, "SERGIO." Traffic was held up, but as soon as I saw the plate, we began to move. It was as if I was meant to see it and to keep hope alive.*

2. *I found a snowflake bracelet almost identical to the*

necklace Sergio gave me. Then the owner of the store placed it on my wrist as a gift.

3. *The storeowner had a dream about the letters S and C on a bowl. He replicated the bowl and then gave it to me once he heard my story. That's actually incredible.*

I think these are signs telling me that Sergio is okay, that he's coming back, and that I should confidently continue to wait. I love him. After all, I opened the door. I walked into this relationship willingly.

She touched up her hair, grabbed her phone, and headed downstairs to meet with Luca.

Song: *Got to Be Real* by Cheryl Lynn

Chapter 37

Luca stood at his office window. He stared out at the pine trees swaying in the wind, their needles dancing to and fro in graceful bends and turns. The mountain laurels waved as if wanting to show off their spring blooms. He missed his brother. *Where is he?* He dropped his head and wished he could do more. He had been in touch with Sergio's company, but they had no news. They would call him when they had more information or when they found him. He had received a check for $25,000 as Sergio's next of kin, but he had deposited it into Sergio's account. It wasn't his to spend. It also made everything seem so final. What he couldn't do was have feelings for Celeste. It was the last thing he should be feeling, but he enjoyed her company so much and… *No. I will not even think about it. But I wonder if Sergio told her everything. If not, I could fill her in…*

He turned around as he heard a knock at his door. "Come in." His voice sounded stronger than he felt.

Celeste walked in looking relaxed and beautiful. Her hair was pulled up with little wisps hanging down at the sides. He gulped and made himself focus on the work at hand.

"Hi. Thanks again for running into town for me. I really appreciate everything you're doing here and how hard you're working. Let's sit down," he said as he gestured to the pair of leather chairs by the window.

Celeste sat down. "I loved the sweet little town. In fact, I love this whole area. It's so beautiful. I feel better in the mountains." Her voice was whispery soft. She cleared her throat, looked at him and said with more strength, "What can I do for you?"

Luca looked at her and wondered if the time was right. She was perfect. "Celeste, I have a proposition for you."

Celeste jumped up from her chair in surprise. "What?"

Luca quickly realized how his statement had sounded. "Oh, no, no, no. Celeste, I have a business proposition for you. Please, will you listen?" He handed her a bottle of water from the mini fridge as she sat back down and took a deep breath.

"I own this Inn, and Sergio helps me, err, helped me out as much as he could. But his dream, well, our dream, was to run it together. He was considering resigning from OEC and coming here this spring. It was our plan. Now, I have so much to do on my own, and I need help. You are doing an amazing job, and you fit in perfectly. This is my proposition. Will you consider coming here to live and work full time to help me run the Inn? You would have your own suite, free food, medical plan, and all that. I just, you're just so good at your job, and people here love you."

Celeste sat quietly listening to him. First of all, she was glad his interests in her were completely work-related, and second, she was flattered.

He leaned closer to her from his chair. "Here is the offer. Please take this, read it, think about it, and let me know. I would want you to begin as soon as possible." He looked at her hopefully.

Celeste took the papers he handed her, thanked him, and told him she would be back in an hour. He watched her as she walked away but could not read her expression. The door closed with a thump, and he sat down to stare out the window again.

She knew exactly where she was headed as her feet took the pine needle path they knew so well. She could not get there fast enough. She needed to think, but then she stopped suddenly. Why was she in a hurry? She closed her eyes and stood still, enjoying the warm air and the smell of pines. Opening her eyes, she walked down the path to the waterfall. Once there, she brushed stray pine needles off the bench and sat down. "Let's do pros and cons," she said out loud.

"Pros:

    1. I'll be closer to Sergio when he returns.

    2. I love the Inn and the work.

    3. I can visit Shepherd Falls.

    4. Free room and board.

Cons:

    1. Giving up my apartment in Chicago.

    2. Missing my friends.

    3. Not being near the places I went with Sergio in the city.

    4. Luca without Sergio.

There's no question. I want to be here." Celeste opened the packet and looked at the details of the job. The pay was comparable to her job in the city, and with no room or board to pay for, she could start saving money.

She stared at the waterfall and spoke out loud, "Sergio, I'm going to take this job at the Inn. When you come back, I'll be here for you. I don't know where you are, but I know you're alive and that you'll be here one day. I just know it. I love you." She sat a little while longer staring at the water, then stood up, stretched, and walked back to tell Luca the good news.

Song: *Learning to Fly* by Tom Petty and the Heartbreakers

Chapter 38

*C*eleste walks into the massive conference center holding Sergio's hand. He looks at her as they head to the registration desk, his mouth expanding into a smile. Celeste wanders off while Sergio signs in. He collects the conference materials and then turns to look for her. She's gone. He turns around, walks in the direction he last saw her, and then is intercepted by colleagues. He resumes his search, calls to her, and panics. He throws the folders and lanyards into his messenger bag and goes in search of her. Loud music blares from hidden speakers and his heart starts pounding in tune with the beat. He turns a corner and is suddenly on the edge of a garden conservatory within the conference center. Its beauty is stunning. Lovely trees and flowers of every kind and color fill the space. Paths beckon to be explored, little bridges curve over flowing streams, lampposts light the way, and twinkle lights shimmer everywhere. It's magical. Sergio stops, stunned at the sight, but then enters the gardens to find her.

Celeste suddenly finds herself in the garden, unsure how to locate the exit. The garden paths are beautiful but never-ending. She follows routes around waterfalls, clusters of trees, flowering shrubs, and flowers. They all start to look the same.

Sergio begins to think he's entered some type of maze that has no ending, and his heart begins to race. "I've gone left, right, down that *path, over that bridge, past those flowers, and through that tunnel of vines. What now?" He stops and tries to figure it out. "Am I still in the conference center? What is this place? Where am I?"*

Time doesn't exist. Has it been minutes, hours, or days? The only thing that keeps them going is the thought of finding each other. Finally, exhausted, scared, and frustrated, Celeste reaches the exit, finding it suddenly there! She runs down the path and falls onto a bench at the edge of the garden, crying from sheer exhaustion.

Sergio continues to search but somehow, he's forgotten what he's searching for. He wanders more deeply into the tangle and disappears from sight.

Celeste woke up and stared at the ceiling. "Good grief," she muttered, "what a dream! Did he ever find me?" She leaned over, grabbed her journal, and wrote it down before she forgot the details. The dream consumed her thoughts all day long, and something in the back of her mind made her wonder if there was more to it than she realized.

Later that evening Celeste sat in front of the window in her suite and pulled her journal closer to her, images from the dream filling her head. She clicked her pen and stared outside at the mountains. *What did it mean?* She opened her journal to make a list. She understood things better when she could see them on paper.

1. There was a maze in the garden, conference center, conservatory. A maze is hard to navigate. There are false starts, endings, turns, twists, dangers, surprises, and finally the exit.

2. A conservatory is full of beauty. Plants, flowers, trees, streams, arched bridges, twinkle lights… it was lovely,

but there were dangers unseen, weren't there? Or were the dangers just in my imagination?

3. Sergio and I were both lost within it. We were close to one another, but we were separated. Did we eventually find one another?

4. How was I able to see it from my point of view and Sergio's? How did I feel his anxiety and know his thoughts? Is it strange to dream both sides?

Celeste closed her journal. She needed sleep. As she closed her eyes, a song title drifted into her mind and she fell asleep dreaming of the lyrics.

Song: ***Ordinary World*** **by Duran Duran**

Chapter 39

GREENLAND

Margret sat watching her mystery patient, taking his vitals, and wondering about him. Today she would remove the head wrappings to look at the wounds and evaluate the healing process.

"He's a good-sized man, about six feet tall, possibly 180 pounds, although he has lost weight, with good muscle tone and good reflexes," she typed on the chart. "No name or ID on him, possible amnesia, but likes music," she continued. Out of all the patients, she liked taking care of him the best. There was something about him that intrigued her, like the way he looked hopeful while trying to remember something important. She hoped he would get well soon, and she wanted to be the one to help him.

She spoke quietly near his ear, "I am going to take the wrappings off your head. We will remove the eye patches gradually so that your eyes aren't damaged by the light. I will be very careful. Do you understand?" He moved his head in her direction and nodded. He felt the soft material brush his arm, and he relaxed. It took a long time to remove the wrappings, and he heard the voices of others who came to help with the process.

When the last strip was taken off, she whispered, "There now, let's have a look." He heard the clicking of keys on a keyboard and some muted voices, but then she spoke. "This looks better. I'm going to place dark glasses on your face to keep the light out of your eyes." He felt glasses take the place of cloth. He tried to open his lids, but the pain was too intense.

"It will take time," she said. "Be patient." She started to leave but then turned back. "Sir, do you know your name?" He did not know his name. He knew he had one, but for the life of him, he couldn't recall what it was. He slowly shook his head. "It's okay. I'll help you figure it out. Now, try to rest. I'll be back soon."

Margret came back multiple times each day to visit, asking him questions and trying to help him remember. He was able to speak now without his throat burning, and he thought he might know his name.

He reached up to touch her soft jacket and uttered six short, detached words, "I. Think. My. Name. Is. Joe."

"Well, that's wonderful! It's nice to meet you, Joe. You're getting better every day!" She patted his hand and marveled at the strength of it. Even in his condition, his hands were large and lively, and she liked the feeling of them in hers.

Song: *Here Comes the Sun* **by The Beatles**

Chapter 40

GREENLAND

Joe was able to sit up. He wore the sunglasses he had been given even though the lights in his room were turned off. They helped ease the headaches and the pain behind his eyes, and they allowed him to see. His whole body ached, and he still didn't know where he was or what had happened to him. He knew there was something he was supposed to remember, but it drifted in and out like the wind, and he couldn't grab hold of it.

"Good morning, Joe." We're going to try more questions today." He nodded to the nurse but then grimaced from the pain.

"Okay," he said.

Her beautiful blonde hair was worn in two long braids, she had a pretty smile, and he liked the way she bit her bottom lip as she considered the day's plan.

"Today we are going to look at pictures. If you know what they are, tell me. If you don't, that's okay. Don't worry if you don't have an answer."

He looked at the pictures. Some he knew, like a dog, a car, a tree, and a house, but there were some he didn't know that were specific to places in the world. It was frustrating, and it was exhausting.

Someone brought him a cup of hot coffee, and he sighed with relief. "Thank you. I miss this. My friend likes a good mocha." He stopped and stared at the nurse. "I remember. I remember I have a friend who likes coffee! Is that a breakthrough?" He looked anxiously and excitedly at her for a response.

"That's wonderful! Yes, it's a breakthrough. Let's stop for the day. Enjoy your coffee and relax. I'll come back later."

Joe eased back in his bed, pulled a thick woolen blanket around him, sipped his coffee, and wondered exactly who it was that liked a mocha. Pieces of a song floated in from distant memories, and he had the faintest desire to text it to someone.

Song: *I'd Really Love to See You Tonight* by England Dan and John Ford Coley

Chapter 41

NORTH CAROLINA

The transition had been seamless. Living and working at the Inn was life changing for Celeste. She didn't miss corporate life or the city at all, and she even enjoyed working with Luca. The air was clean, she was surrounded by natural beauty, she enjoyed helping people, and she felt close to Sergio. It was where she needed to be.

Today was the last day of a 300-person conference, and although it had gone well, she had to admit, she was ready for them to leave. Only the party remained, and she had everything arranged to run smoothly. After seeing to the last details with catering, servers, and the florist, she snuck away to rest and change clothes. She made it to her room without being bombarded with questions and sank into her cozy chair with a cup of tea. She glanced towards the closet door, which was slightly ajar, and her eyes locked onto a bag in the corner. Remembering the wonderful day in Shepherd Falls when Bert had given her the bowl, she retrieved it and looked at it closely, rubbing her fingers along the carved letters.

"Sergio, I miss you so much. Where are you? I believe you are still out there somewhere. Do you know how much I love you? Do you know that I see your face when I close my eyes?" she whispered as she held onto the bowl. A moment later her phone dinged and her heart leapt with anticipation. She sighed as she quickly glanced at her phone, and then she carefully placed the bowl back into its bag. She wasn't yet ready to display it.

Luca had nothing pressing to do. He sat in his office looking out over the mountains and thinking about Celeste. He was glad to have her on staff. He had no idea how talented she really was until she took over and turned the place around. She was remarkable, but he couldn't sit still and just think about her. He kicked at a rough place on the carpet and watched the dust float upward in a beam of fading light. He thought of Celeste again and smiled. Then he shook his head, jumped up, and took the stairs to his room on the 5th floor to release some energy.

Celeste walked into the great room and saw that all was going well. The music was lively, the food was delicious, and the guests were happy. As she walked through the crowd, people stopped to thank her and to compliment her on the party. She was glad it was such a success.

Luca entered the room after he had run the stairs several times and then taken a shower. He watched her as she made her way through the crowd. She was beautiful and so at ease with the guests. He walked towards her slowly, knowing he shouldn't. "Celeste, you look beautiful. Would you like to dance?"

While telling herself it was only a dance, Celeste took his offered hand and followed him to the dance floor. As he smiled at her and began to move to the music, she relaxed and enjoyed herself. It had been a while since she'd danced or even had fun, but she felt guilty, as if having fun wasn't quite fair. They danced for two upbeat songs, and then the strains of a slow song began. Celeste moved to the edge of the dance floor, but Luca slid his hand into hers and pulled her back to him.

"May I have another dance?" he asked while staring into her eyes. Celeste hesitated. Luca pulled her into his arms and pressed his body to hers. He whispered into her ear, "Thank you." Celeste danced, but her mind was elsewhere. All she could think about was Sergio and how she wished she were dancing with him. *Does Luca have feelings for me?* she wondered. *No, of course not.* But in the back of her mind, she wasn't quite so sure.

When she noticed several people smiling at them, she had had enough. "Thank you for the dance, but I need to check on something in the kitchen," she muttered to Luca as she let go. Once in the kitchen, she took a look around and then headed straight to her room. She was done for the night. She changed into sweats, lay down across the end of her bed, and stared out the window at the mountains. A tear slowly made its way down her cheek as she searched the stars for answers.

Song: *Your Song* by Elton John

Chapter 42

GREENLAND

Joe needed answers. The four walls seemed smaller every day, and he craved more than they offered. As soon as his nurse came in, he would start asking. He was able to remove his dark glasses for a few hours each day but kept the lights off in his room to help handle the pain. His head ached nonstop. Even though it was getting better, he still felt dizzy and disoriented when he stood up for too long. He sipped coffee and tried to think.

"Why can't I remember anything?" he said out loud.

"Are you doing okay, Joe?" a sweet voice asked from the door. "Is now a good time to do some work?" Margret walked in, took his vitals, and watched him closely, sensing his discomfort. *We may make some progress today.*

"I just need answers. Why can't I remember?" he said a little more loudly than he had intended.

"That's good. Let's work together," she said as she sat down next to him. She pulled up a small table so that it fit between them and lay her tablet on it.

Joe watched her. She was so precise. He liked the way her braids stayed perfectly in place, and how her soft nurse's jacket fit snugly around her hips. She had a calming effect on him, and he relaxed.

"What is your name?" she asked.

"Joe. All I can remember is Joe."

"That's all right, Joe. Where do you live?" She glanced up at him as she asked.

"I don't know where I live," he answered. "I don't know who I am or where I live or if I have a family. I don't know what I do for a job. I don't know!" he shouted. He hung his head. "I'm sorry. I'm just frustrated."

"I understand. No apology necessary." She tried a new tactic. "I'm going to play some music for you because I think you have definite likes and dislikes when it comes to songs. She pulled out her phone and searched a playlist. "Here's one I like." A song belted from the speaker, and his fingers tapped out the beat.

"Good," she said as she added a note. Next was an instrumental song that was more classical in nature. Joe shook his head. She then played a love song that had a nice beat, and he liked it. She made a note. They continued listening for an hour as she recorded his preferences. He watched her and wondered about her. She was beautiful, with her long blonde hair and bright smile.

"What's your name?" he asked suddenly. "You've never told me your name, and I think I should know who you are."

She placed the tablet back on the table. "It's good that you're questioning. It's a sign of improvement. My name is Margret, and I'm a nurse here at the hospital," she said.

"Margret," he responded tentatively as if testing the new name with his lips. "Thank you for helping me. Where are we and why do you wear a fur coat?"

"Well, first of all, a fur coat is important where we are. Lots of us wear them when it's practical to do so. We are in a remote region of Eastern Greenland. Do you remember Greenland?" she asked.

Joe looked at her and wondered, but he had no recollection of his life before, so he wasn't surprised. "I don't remember Greenland at all. Can you show me a map of the world?" Margret left to find a paper map while he waited.

A knock sounded at his door. "Hello, Joe, how are you today?" the man asked as he placed the lunch tray on the table.

"Hello. I'm trying to get better every day. Thanks for lunch." The soup felt good on his throat as he sipped it. *Greenland. Do I live in Greenland?*

Margret walked back in with a map of the world she had found in the lounge. She helped him into the chair near his bed, and they spent most of the afternoon searching the paper world, pointing out countries, oceans, deserts, mountain ranges, and major cities, but nothing seemed familiar. She watched as he looked earnestly at the map before him. *Who was he? Where was he from?* She noticed that the scars on his face were healing. She made a mental note to request a shower and a shave, and then she placed her hand on his.

"I will leave this map with you. I'll see you later."

Joe liked the feeling of her hand on his. It made him feel less alone. "See you later, Margret," he said as she walked out of the room. She turned around as the door closed and smiled at him.

Song: *Hold the Line* by Toto

Chapter 43

GREENLAND

J oe was drawn to the map. He spent hours looking at it, learning from it, and trying to figure out where he might have lived or visited before his accident. It was like looking at the world for the first time and discovering how big and interesting it was. He loved the mountain ranges best and marveled at how they reached and stretched over large parts of the world. He began memorizing their names and where they were. Then there were the continents, the oceans, and the deserts. He was fascinated and couldn't put it down, but the hours strained his eyes, and he closed them. The map slipped to the floor as he fell asleep.

Joe dove into the vast blue ocean and swam in long strides. Turning around, he saw someone on the beach. It was a woman, and he called out to her. She walked towards him, smiling and waving, and then dove in. Suddenly she stopped, turned around, and swam back to shore. He treaded water and called out to her again. She turned, put her feet back in the water, and looked at him as if waiting for some kind of sign. Finally, she nodded, and then with a look of determination, she dove in. She swam closer and closer and then propelled herself into his arms. "I am yours," she said. "I am yours."

Joe woke slowly and felt a bit out of sorts from sleeping in the chair. The early morning nurse came in to check his vitals and directed him back to bed. She checked the scars on his face and determined he was ready for a shower and a shave as Margret had suggested. The hot water pummeled his skin and massaged his muscles. He emerged feeling a bit more human but was weak from the effort. She shaved his thick beard and then helped him to the bed where he immediately fell asleep. He dreamed again of waves in an ocean and of someone swimming out to him.

Margret walked into his room and was taken aback. She drew nearer while he slept and marveled at his face. He looked so different without the beard. *He's even more handsome than I thought.* She noticed the map on the floor and picked it up. *He's working so hard to remember.* She watched him sleep, checked his pulse, and turned to leave. Then she stopped, selected a playlist from her phone, set it on the table, and left the room.

Song: *Listen to the Music* by The Doobie Brothers

Chapter 44

NORTH CAROLINA

Celeste woke up early, dressed in jeans and a t-shirt, laced up her hiking boots and grabbed a light hoodie. She needed a hike. The only bad thing about working and living at the Inn was that she was always there. She loved her work, but every now and then she needed to get away. Today was one of those days. She walked into the lobby, ordered a coffee, and waited for it at the bar.

"Good morning." She could hear the smile in his voice as he came near.

"Good morning, Luca. I'm waiting on coffee, and then I think I'll go for a little hike before the day starts."

"Would you mind some company?" he asked. "Sometimes I just need a break, but I don't want to intrude on your time." Celeste wanted to sigh loudly, but she refrained. She understood. She wanted time alone. Time to think, to hike, to wonder, and maybe to scream a little to relieve some frustration, but the look on his face said he needed a bit of that as well.

"Of course. 15 minutes?" she asked softly.

"Great! Yeah, I can be ready in 15," he replied as he jumped up to give directions to an assistant.

Celeste picked up her coffee, thanked the barista, and sipped it while staring out the window. She then turned to the large fireplace.

Hey, Moses. No matter the season, the fire always burned. She loved it and the guests did as well. It was comforting, and it offered refuge from whatever storm one was facing.

She noticed a young woman sitting near it now. Celeste walked over to her to see if she needed anything. "Good morning. Can I get you a coffee?"

The woman looked up at Celeste and shook her head. "No thank you. I'm not much of a coffee drinker." She turned back to the fire and sighed. Celeste sat down in a nearby chair.

"Are you okay?" She recognized the look on her face. She knew it well.

"Can I ask you a question?" she looked to Celeste with teary eyes.

"Of course," Celeste answered.

"Do you think absence really does make the heart grow fonder?" She looked young, earnest, and in anguish.

"Ah, what a great question." Celeste looked into the fire as thoughts of Sergio swirled in her mind. "I think it depends."

The young woman turned abruptly to Celeste. "Really? How so?"

"Well," Celeste began, "if two people are in love and they are apart, several things can happen. One, they miss each other but then life gets in the way and fills their time, and they begin to miss each other less and less. Pretty soon, the relationship is over, and they've both moved on. In that scenario, they just weren't meant to be. Two, one person loves more than the other and it becomes one-sided. It won't work, and the relationship fizzles out. That scenario is really hard on the one who is still holding on. Three, both people love and miss one another. They write love letters to one another, even if they can't send them, they think of one another non-stop, and they dream of the day they can be together. In this instance, absence does make the heart grow fonder because they realize they don't want to be without the other. This is love. This is patience. This is part of God's plan for them both. They are each other's person and it's part of their journey." Celeste stared into the fire, forgetting where she was.

"Huh. I didn't know there was that much to consider. My scenario may be the second. I think about him all the time, but he doesn't seem to miss me as much. I thought his heart would grow fonder, but I guess our absence shows us that it really is not meant to be." She wiped a tear and looked at Celeste. "That was brutally honest, but it helped. Thank you." She stood up, nodded to Celeste, and walked away.

Celeste watched her and worried that her explanation may have been a bit harsh, but on the other hand, maybe it had helped. She looked at the fire again. *Sergio and I have the third scenario, right? I will believe that we are part of each other's plan. It's all part of our journey.*

She finished her mocha and waited for Luca to return. Five minutes later they were headed out the door, walking briskly to the woods, Luca leading her to a trail she had not been on before. The air was crisp, the sky was brilliantly blue, and the world seemed to welcome her with a strength she needed.

Luca pointed out new growth, taught her the names of plants, and stopped when he noticed some small animal near them. When he called a chipmunk a hedgehog by mistake, she laughed out loud. Luca laughed too and walked closer to her. They sat down on a large rock together and caught their breath, Luca moving so that his thigh touched hers. Celeste continued to laugh and ask where the hedgehogs were as Luca pulled snacks from his backpack. They sat on the rock, talking and eating granola bars, and Celeste felt better than she had in a long time. Luca was enjoying himself too. He wondered how long he had to wait before he could hold her hand or kiss her lips. He knew the feelings were wrong, but he couldn't help himself. He was falling in love with her, and he didn't know when or if his brother would ever come home.

Song: *Can't Stop the Feeling* by Justin Timberlake

Chapter 45

Celeste's mood matched the cool, gray day. Staying focused on her work was impossible. She looked to the window, noticed the slowing rain, and left the office. Taking the service elevator, she made it to her room without being seen, grabbed her raincoat and boots, and was outside within minutes. She knew exactly where she needed to go. She took the tunnel at the back of the building and headed to the waterfall garden. She felt better as her feet stepped upon the wet pine needles. Her breathing slowed, her fists unclenched, and she began to relax. She pushed past the hanging limb and stepped deliberately on each stepping stone as she entered the garden. The twinkle lights were off, and the rain hushed all sounds. Celeste made her way to the bench and sat down on it, not caring in the least that it was wet. She stared at the waterfall as the rain poured upon her.

"Where are you?" she whispered. "What are you doing? Are you okay?" She stared at the falls and then stood up. She felt empowered and said aloud, "Where are you and what are you doing?" Then she yelled at the waterfall, "Sergio, where are you and what are you doing?" The rain fell in torrents, the sky crackled with electricity, and thunder boomed nearby. Celeste stood waiting for an answer. The answer did not come. She sat back down on the bench and thought she would cry, but instead, she felt peaceful. Deep in her heart she believed Sergio was out there somewhere. She knew one day he would gather her into his strong arms and kiss her once again. She began to hum a song, and then realizing that most of the lyrics fit her mood, she pulled out her phone and texted it to him.

Song: *You are the Reason* by Calum Scott

Chapter 46

GREENLAND

Joe woke up in a good mood with renewed energy. A glance at the clock told him it was noon and the rumble in his stomach confirmed it. He pushed a button on the hospital bed to move it to the upright position, pulled the covers up around him, and reached for the map. He was looking forward to learning more about the world he'd forgotten.

The door opened and Margret walked in. "Oh, good, you're awake. I thought we'd try a walk today. Are you up for it?" she asked.

"Well, I think so, but I'm really hungry. Any chance I could eat first?"

Margret glanced at his chart and scrunched up her face. Joe knew she made this facial expression when she was thinking about something. He thought it was cute.

"Well, the food is brought in at certain times, but I think I can find something for you in the nurse's lounge. Let's try it."

Margret helped him out of bed, made sure he was wearing thick hospital socks, and led him out of the room. She held onto his arm and named things as they walked by them, hoping to refresh his memory, but he wasn't much interested in doors, floor tiles, or rolling carts.

Twenty feet later, Joe sat down on a mustard-colored vinyl bench to rest, and Margret asked a passing nurse to sit with him while she slipped into the nurse's lounge. The walk had sapped his energy. He felt weak and disoriented and didn't feel like answering questions from someone new. After a few minutes, Margret returned with a tray on wheels that pulled right up to him as he sat. The hot soup helped him feel better right away, and in addition to the soup, he ate two sandwiches, pudding, and a cookie, and he washed it down with hot coffee. He paused as a noise caught his attention.

"Why are there dogs at the hospital? You know, I think I remember hearing dogs when I first woke up." He looked at Margret for the answer.

"Joe, let me show you something. Can you walk to the window?"

"I'll try," he answered as he held onto a second cookie. Margret led him around a corner to the window to look outside. She wanted him to know where they were and what the weather was like. Surely every bit of information would help him remember. But she had to be careful.

Joe walked to the window and stared. It was beautiful but stark. The huge expanse of snow was solid white and held a dull tone in the dim light. He pushed his glasses up the bridge of his nose and saw dogs pulling a man on a sled as they shot past the window. They were quickly out of sight.

"Something tells me I'm far from home," he said sadly as he turned to Margret. "I'm ready to go lie down."

Her hand reached for him, and he felt the soft jacket she wore. He liked the way it felt on his arm, and he let her lead him back to the room. He was suddenly exhausted, and now that his stomach was full, he drifted off. As he hovered over the bridge between wakefulness and sleep, he heard a woman's voice yelling and asking him where he was and what he was doing.

Song: *Love is the Answer* by England Dan and John Ford Coley

Chapter 47

GREENLAND

A snowstorm took over the tiny slice of the world he knew. Lights flickered, unnecessary machines were unplugged, and the hospital was quieter than usual. There was no light coming through the windows, and the darkness gave an eerie feeling to the place. Joe sat in his chair wrapped in several blankets, two pairs of socks, and a wool hat. Margret sat across from him. He watched her, liking the way she studied his chart. He noticed she held her mouth in a side pucker as she concentrated. He suddenly wondered how it would feel to have her arms wrapped around him. Would it feel safe? Warm? Secure? Or maybe something else entirely? He shook his head and quickly asked a question to divert his thoughts.

"What happened to me?"

Margret looked at him with concern and paused. She began carefully, "I can tell you what I know but only a little at a time. I don't want to worry you unnecessarily."

Joe looked at her and shifted in his chair. "Okay, tell me what you can."

She shivered, pulled her coat closer, and began, "There was an accident in a building you were working in. I don't know all the details, though. Do you remember anything at all about an accident?"

Joe sat very still and looked off into the distance. "No."

Margret continued, "A dog sled brought you here because the weather was too bad for trucks to traverse the ice. Due to the harsh conditions, no one can get back in to investigate, and it will be months before the weather breaks."

He turned his face back to Margret. "Why don't I have a wallet or ID or anything personal?"

Margret looked at him with concern and pulled her coat closer. "You were found outside the building. All of your personal items were probably inside. You were hit hard on the head, and that has caused your memory loss. Joe, you're lucky to be alive. You were placed in a medically induced coma for months so that you could rest and heal." Margret reached out to him and placed her hands around his. "I know this is difficult, but I'm here for you. I'll help you regain your strength and your memory for as long as it takes."

Joe looked at his hands in hers and then into her eyes. "Thank you."

Margret watched him intently. "We're going to get there, Joe. You'll remember little bits at a time, and hopefully, your memory will return completely."

A loud popping noise suddenly surprised them, and the electricity went out. The hospital was covered in darkness. "I need to go check in," Margret exclaimed as she jumped up. "Stay here and try to keep warm."

Joe got into bed, pulled every blanket over him and closed his eyes. All he could do was wait for someone to come back. He soon drifted off to sleep.

The violent snow blew all around him, but he kept going. He held onto a rope, knowing that if he let go, he would be lost. The rope was his lifeline, and he trudged on. Suddenly a sound like thunder roared nearby and then there was nothing.

Joe woke with a start. The hospital was still covered in darkness. His hands and feet were numb, and he knew he had to move his body to get his blood flowing. Wrapping the blankets around his shoulders, he stepped into the hallway. Everything was dark, quiet, and still. There were no lights, no beeping of machines, and no voices. The darkness mingled with his fear, but he shook his head and continued. *I'm not afraid because I'm not alone. I can do this.*

Chapter 48

Luca ordered two coffees and headed to Celeste's office. As he approached, two employees walked out laughing and waving goodbye. Everyone loved Celeste. As Luca entered, they smiled at him and continued happily on their way.

"Knock, knock," he said as he walked in.

"Well, hello there. Ah, coffee. Thank you," she replied.

Luca handed her the steaming mocha and sat down. As she took a cautious sip, he looked around. She had transformed the office. Everything was serene and comfortable and cozy all at the same time. Small plants and candles had been placed on shelves and tables, white and cream-colored pillows sat invitingly on the chairs, and a long, white wooden sign had been hung on the wall behind her desk: *Be still, and know that I am God. Ps 46:10.*

"Celeste, I need to talk to you about something," he began as he focused on the sign.

She put the coffee down and folded her hands. "Gotcha, what's up?"

"I have an investment opportunity I'd like to look into. It involves a resort in Colorado. I'm thinking of buying it." He tilted his head towards her but kept his eyes on the sign.

"Oh, wow. I didn't expect that. I had no idea you were interested in another resort."

His eyes met hers. "Well, I wasn't, but they contacted me out of the blue. It seems one of our recent guests is a relative of the owner of this other resort and made the recommendation. I'm surprised as well," Luca stated. "I want to talk about a plan. I'm going to go see it in two days. I'd like to look around, work the numbers, and decide if I want to purchase it. Will you be okay running the place without me?"

"Yes, of course. Our guest list is light this week. Thanks for trusting me with it." She picked up her coffee for another sip. "Are you excited about it? Do you want to run two resorts?"

Luca answered, "I'm actually really excited about it. Here, let me show you." He pulled his chair closer to hers and entered the website information on her laptop. They looked at it together, and she jotted down notes as they scanned the property. She asked questions about employees, number of guest rooms, restaurants, and square footage. He was impressed. He loved how precise she was and how she seemed to think of everything. He was certain she would have more questions for him later, and he looked forward to it. *I don't want this time with her to end.*

"Will you have dinner with me tonight to talk more about this new venture?" he asked suddenly.

"Um, sure, I can do that." Distractedly, she picked up her phone and added a calendar reminder.

Luca stood up to leave and then motioned to the sign behind her desk. "What exactly do those words mean?" He glanced at it again. It didn't make sense to him.

"It's one of my favorite Bible verses. It comes from Psalm 46. 'Be still and know that I am God' means that whatever you are going through, if you believe in him and know him, you can rest and be still and know that God is in control. It gives me hope. When everything is chaotic, I just breathe and remember to be still and let God handle it. The 'I am God' part is so personal and beautiful to me. Look at the word 'am.'" She turned and pointed to it and then continued. "It is present tense. God is here, he is with us. Yes, he's in the past and in the future, but I love that he is also present. I can rest because he is God. There is no other. It's faith, hope, and trust in God. It grounds me."

"I had no idea. Huh. That makes sense. Does it really take the pressure off?"

"It does if you believe it," she answered, looking at him hopefully. "Do you want

to talk about God?"

"Sure, but later. I'll see you soon." Walking out of her office, he looked at his watch to see just how long he had to wait until he could see her again. He didn't care what they talked about, he just wanted to be with her.

Song: *Every Breath you Take* by The Police

Chapter 49

Celeste loved running the Inn. Luca had been gone for four days, and all had gone well. A reunion group was arriving at 10:00 a.m., and she looked forward to having them. They were ready. She sat at the coffee bar eating a quick breakfast and admiring the beauty through the panoramic windows as the sun rose over the mountain. When a movement caught her eye, she turned her head and spotted an old truck pulling into the parking lot.

"Oh, it's Bert," she exclaimed as she hopped down to greet him. She hurried to open the front door and welcomed him in with a hug. "Bert, it's wonderful to see you. How are you? Come in," she said to the older man.

Bert grinned from ear to ear and returned the hug. "Oh, I'm fine, just fine. But I need to talk to you." His face shone with excitement. Celeste invited him to the chairs by the fire and ordered coffee and breakfast for him as she wondered about his visit.

"Please sit down. It's so good to see you. How's Daisy?"

Bert sat down in the comfortable leather chair and accepted coffee from the barista. "Thank you," he said and then took a sip. "That's good." He took another sip, put his mug on the table, and then looked at Celeste. "Now, my dear, I need to tell you about my dream. I woke up early and headed this way before Daisy even got out of bed. She said to tell you hello, by the way."

Celeste was intrigued, and Bert continued, "Last night I went to bed, and it was a fitful sleep. I tossed and turned, but then I began to dream. First, there was a snowstorm and a blizzard, and everything was bright white. Someone was walking in the snow holding onto a rope, you know, the kind that keeps you from getting lost. Anyway, then it was dark, and the snow was gone. Suddenly I saw a waterfall in the mist. Now, this is the part I want you to hear. You and your young man walked out of the waterfall holding hands while green leaves fell from the sky and floated on a warm breeze." He picked up his mug and looked at her for a reaction, his eyebrows rising as he smiled.

Celeste gazed at the fire for a long moment and then turned back to Bert. "Thank you, Bert, but, uh, what does it mean? He left for Iceland over seven months ago, and there's been no word. Is he okay? What about the waterfall? And what do green leaves mean?" She blinked to hold off tears and glanced back at the fire.

"Celeste, dear, I'm sorry. I just thought you might want to hear my dream. I don't know what happened to him, but I know you cannot give up hope. I also don't know the significance of the waterfall, but I do know that green leaves symbolize new growth and new life. I believe my dream is a dream of hope. You must believe," he soothed, as he looked at her with kindness. She returned the look, but now she needed to think.

Bert finished his breakfast and told her stories while they sat together. She then showed him around and invited him to bring Daisy for dinner one night soon.

"Give her a hug for me," Celeste called as she waved goodbye.

"Thank you so much for coming to see me." Bert blew a kiss and waved from the truck as Celeste walked back inside. She felt restless and on edge. She didn't want to be there. She wanted to go in search of Sergio.

Images of a dream suddenly came to mind, and she paused. *Someone was holding onto a rope and walking in the snow.* A shiver of fear gripped her for a moment, but then she pushed down the dread as she remembered something else. *I dreamed about that. I remember a hand emerged from the snowstorm, saving the person.* She recalled a verse: Isaiah 41:10 – "Do not fear, for I am with you; do not be dismayed, for I am your God. I will strengthen you and help you; I will uphold you with my righteous right hand." *God was there in my dream. He was the lifeline. Oh, it was God's hand that saved me! Hmmm….* She made her way quickly to the privacy of her office. As she thought about her dream, the images intertwined with those from Bert's dream, and she curled up in her chair to think about them. She closed her eyes and tried to recall more, but she knew she had remembered the most important part. Whoever was lost in the storm had God's steady hand nearby to save him from danger. *Thank you, Lord. Thank you.*

Song: *Rescue* by Lauren Daigle

Chapter 50

GREENLAND

Hearing hushed conversations, Joe made his way cautiously down the dark hallway to investigate. His hospital socks made no sound on the polished floor, and the frigid air kept him moving forward. As he walked, he wondered why the electricity had been off so long in a hospital. *Don't they have a generator?* He continued slowly, but nearing a corner, he came to a stop.

He heard a male voice say, "What should we do? We can't move the patients to a new facility, but we have no electricity. The generator doesn't work, and it's freezing."

A female voice answered, "Let's go down to the basement, collect all the blankets, and take them to the patients."

Their rhythmic footsteps hurried across the floor, and then a door closed. Joe stood motionless in the dark and frigid silence and then continued. It was too quiet, and he wondered where all the people were. Turning a corner, he saw the dim outline of a counter and walked forward with his arms outstretched. Once he reached it, he kept one hand on the edge as he walked. Suddenly he stopped. Something in his mind nudged him to remember. *I was walking and holding onto something. It was cold. I could barely see.* He shivered but tried to remember more. *There was snow everywhere. Think, man. Get it together!* But then he realized where he was, and he felt weak again. He needed to sit down, and he needed food. He made his way around the desk, found a chair, and collapsed. He rested his head on the desk for a moment, feeling some type of paper spread over it. He sat up and searched as his hands moved over the pages. The feel of it reminded him of something he had completely forgotten. *It's a newspaper.* He gathered it together and shoved it down his shirt. Next, he opened desk drawers and found what he was looking for. He picked up three candy bars and a soda can. Then he stood up and maneuvered his way around the desk, the counter, and down the hallway to his room. Once again, he wondered where everyone was. *How many patients are here with me?* He opened his door and walked to the bed. It was pitch black, but he knew the room well enough to find his way. He climbed in bed, pulled the blankets around him, and dug into a candy bar. He placed the other ones in his bedside table for later. He had a feeling he would need to ration what he had. After taking a sip of the soda, which turned out to be ginger ale, he pulled the newspaper out of his shirt and placed it in the drawer. He couldn't see it now, but he knew, at some point, he would want to read it.

Hours passed and no one came. *What happened to the two people who went for blankets? What's going on? Where's Margret?* Joe lay in bed, wrapped in his blankets, and worried. Finally, exhausted, his eyes closed, and pieces of a song guided his dreams.

Song: *What is Life* by George Harrison

Chapter 51

NORTH CAROLINA

"Oh, you startled me," Celeste exclaimed as she swung away from the window. Luca sauntered in and apologized as he settled into a chair. "I'm sorry, Celeste. I didn't mean for my knock to frighten you. Will you sit with me for a few minutes? I want to talk to you about my trip."

Celeste sank into the chair opposite him. Her thoughts had been consumed with Bert's dream, and she had to refocus. She curled her legs under her as she waited for him to speak.

Luca loved how comfortable she could be in his presence. She looked beautiful with her hair down and her eyes wide open. "Colorado was wonderful," he began, "and the place is incredible. I want to make an offer, and I'd like to discuss it with you."

Luca talked on and on about the new resort, and Celeste could tell he was excited about it. She tried to pay attention, but her mind kept wandering. "And so, this is what I'd like to offer you," she heard Luca saying.

She sat up straight. "Wait, what? I'm sorry. I lost track of the conversation for a moment."

"That's okay, I understand. It's a lot to take in. Here's the thing, though. I'd like to purchase the Colorado resort and leave you here in charge of this one. I'd fly back and forth every few months, but I would legally put you in charge of The Inn at Shepherd Falls. What do you think?" Luca slipped out of his chair and knelt down in front of Celeste. "I trust you completely, and I can't imagine leaving this Inn to anyone but you." Luca took her hands in his. "Say yes, Celeste."

At that very moment, a housekeeper walked by. She heard the last part of Luca's declaration, saw him on his knees, and recognized the look in his eyes. She beamed and quickly walked away.

His question stunned Celeste. "You want to move to Colorado and leave me here to run the Inn? I'm overwhelmed." She took a deep breath and asked, "You trust me to run your family business by myself?"

His hands were still holding hers as he answered. "Yes, that's it. You are family now, and I want this to work." As he spoke, he moved back to his chair and looked out the window. "This was our dream. Sergio and I wanted to make this Inn the best in the southeast and then purchase another one. We had a great plan." He looked at Celeste. "Will you please help me with this dream?"

Celeste reached over and squeezed his hand. "Yes, I would love to! Thank you for trusting me with it."

Luca stood and reached for her hands, pulling her up to face him. Then he wrapped his arms around her and swung her around and around. They both laughed, giddy with the new adventure ahead.

"Congratulations, you two!" came the voices of several employees. "Let's celebrate!" A bottle of champagne appeared, the cork popped, and the bubbly flowed. "To Luca and Celeste! Hear, hear!" several voices chanted.

Celeste wondered vaguely how the staff knew of the deal that had just been made but accepted hugs from the staff and smiles from all. She wasn't a fan of champagne but grabbed a ginger ale from the fridge and poured it into her champagne flute. Then she toasted with the group. For a moment, she was happy with the present, not thinking of the past, or of the future. Luca had said she was family now, and her heart warmed with the thought. She was part of a family again. She looked at each of the people celebrating with her, and she raised her glass to them all.

Song: *We are Family* **by Sister Sledge**

Chapter 52

Celeste and Luca spent every waking hour together. He taught her each aspect of running the Inn, from hiring employees to keeping the books.

"You already know how to work with people. Everyone here loves you, and anyway, that's not something to be learned. Someone either has it or they don't. You've got that down pat." He stole a look at her and continued. "The accounting can be tricky, but we can work on that over the phone." He turned the page in his manual. "You're going to be great. Thank you." He rested his hand on hers and smiled at the picture their hands made.

She was excited about the new opportunity, but losing Sergio's brother was tugging at her heart. *Another piece of him is leaving. I'll be totally alone.* She pulled her hand away and stood up. "Luca, I need a little break. Can we meet in a couple of hours?"

"Yeah, I guess we've been working non-stop. Take a break, and I'll see you at 5:00." He turned back to the manual and made a notation.

The question from the teen on the train suddenly sprang to her thoughts, and she paused. "Luca," she faced him with a questioning look. "What is it you really want?"

He glanced at her blankly. The ringing of his phone interrupted the silence, and he picked it up. Answering the call instead of Celeste told her what she needed to know. His focus was on work. She watched him as he took the call. *Am I just a placeholder for what he thinks he wants? Who am I to him?*

Celeste shook her head, left the office, and made her way to her room. She changed clothes, grabbed her ear buds and phone, and set out for her favorite running path. She started off easy, then worked her way up to a full-on sprint when the path allowed. She felt the worry slipping away as the run energized her, and then she eased back into a moderate pace. As she approached a sharp curve near an ancient white oak, she slowed to a walk. She climbed the trail as it wound up and around a cluster of pine trees and into a small clearing, and then she sat down on a moss-covered rock to catch her breath.

As she looked out at the beauty surrounding her, she noticed a partially hidden stepping stone. It was definitely man-made, as it was perfectly round. Curious, she walked over to it and squatted down to get a closer look. Then she noticed another one a foot away covered mostly in dirt and brambles. She moved closer and carefully smoothed the dirt aside. It was round, as well, and in good condition. She looked for another near a cluster of ferns. She brushed back the spindly leaves and found it, but this one was a bit crumbly. *What on earth?* She looked for more. She moved deeper into the thicket and found another, then another, and then one more. There were six in all. She swept the leaves and twigs away from the last one and noticed a strange etching on it. It looked like the letter O. She suddenly sat up straight, her heart lurching wildly, as if it already knew what she was about to discover.

Calming her heart, she made her way cautiously back to the first stone and looked at it carefully, clearing the leaves away. There it was: the letter S. She could hardly breathe as she looked at the next one. Sure enough, she found the letter E. Then she crawled to the next stone and found an R, then a G, then an I, and finally she was back to the last stone with an O carved into it. She sat down next to it and thought about the man she loved. *Sergio, when did you put these here? Why did you put these here? Aren't stepping stones supposed to lead you to something? They are a path to a destination, but what does this lead to? What was it you said about stepping stones?* She crinkled her brow as she tried to remember. *You said you put them in places that are important to you. Each stone leads to another and eventually you arrive at something extraordinary. It's a journey with a surprise at the end!* She brushed the dirt, twigs, and leaves away from the last stone as if touching it would give her answers. As she moved a twig along the edge, it crumbled a bit more, and she quickly stopped so that it wouldn't completely fall apart. She ran her fingers along the far edge and felt a slight depression in the dirt. She sat up on her knees, used the twig to remove some of the dirt, and then tried to pick it up. She carefully rocked it back and forth little by little so it wouldn't crumble. Gradually, it began to give. After a few minutes of careful movement, she was able to pull the stone up from the ground and gently set it aside. She looked down at the dirt and into the hidden hole below. Without hesitation, she reached in and pulled out a small metal box. She sat down slowly and placed it before her. She wiped her forehead with her sleeve and swallowed hard. *This must be his. Should I open it? Would he want me to open it?* Her pulse quickened, and she suddenly felt weak. She took a fortifying breath and let it out slowly. Curiosity was too strong. Lifting the latch, she opened the lid and discovered several items. She picked them up carefully, one by one. The first was a toy pine tree. It was about an inch tall and was something you might place on a cake as a decoration.

"Hmm," she said out loud, and continued looking. Next, she pulled out a piece of wire that had been formed into a snowflake. It was silver and about two inches in width. She automatically reached for the snowflake necklace around her neck and closed her eyes. Taking a breath and letting it out slowly, she put it down carefully and then picked up the next item. It was a silver dollar with the date showing two years ago.

"Okay, this gives me a timeline. It hasn't been here more than two years," she said as she gained strength from her own voice. She put it down and pulled out a piece of paper folded up in a plastic baggie. "I don't know if I can read this." She looked out at the forest before her as if a sign telling her what to do might appear, but nothing was revealed. She had come this far, and she would continue. Opening the baggie, she pulled out the paper and read,

> "One day I will fall in love, and I will love her forever. She will be one-of-a-kind, like a snowflake, and our love will remind me of a beautiful evergreen. It will weather the storms and stay strong. When she is away from me, I will miss her like breath, and I will count the moments until I see her again. These stepping stones represent our relationship because each of our encounters will be a step on the pathway of our journey together. One day, my love, one day."
>
> All my love, S E R G I O

She held onto the note and took deep, rasping breaths. "Come back to me, my love. Come back." She didn't know it was possible to love him more, but her heart ached with longing and love and grief all rolled together. How could her heart still be beating under all that weight? Her eyes were dry for once, and she sighed as she looked at his treasures and remembered him.

As the light faded, she laid the items carefully on a rock and took a picture of each with her phone. She replaced the items and then held the box to her heart. She wasn't sure what to do.

"Do I bury it again or keep it?" Eventually she decided it wasn't hers to move. One day, she prayed, they would dig it up together.

Song: *I Will Walk with You* by Bruce Hornsby and the Range

Chapter 53

Joe opened his eyes and felt surprisingly warm in his bed. As he woke fully, he realized something was breathing down his neck, and he jumped. "What?" he started. "Who are you?"

"It's me, Joe. You're very cold; I'm just trying to warm you up." Margret had gotten in bed with him. She thought their two bodies together had to be warmer than one, and so she had snuggled under the covers with him while he slept. Her fur coat tickled his skin. "The electricity is still out. Are you okay?" Margret asked as she rubbed her hand along his arm.

"I'm okay, I think," he answered. "What's going on?" He did feel warmer with her in bed beside him. He pulled the blankets closer as he turned towards her.

Margret continued to rub his arm. "There's a bad storm out there, the piteraq is dreadful, and there's no one coming to help. We've brought up all the reserved canned food, but we'll have to ration it. Of course, we opened the emergency supplies and gathered survival blankets for everyone. They will help immensely. There are only a few patients here, so that helps."

"What about the machines the patients are on? Don't they need them?" Joe was worried about patients dying without life support. "What's a piteraq?"

"It's a very dangerous wind," she explained as she shuddered. "In the Inuit language, it means 'that which attacks you.' As for the patients, this is a rehabilitation hospital. They are all recovering from orthopedic injuries or surgeries. No one here is on life support. That's a blessing. You were brought here because it was the closest medical center to the accident, and the dog sled team could get here easily."

"Then why aren't the others from the accident here?" he asked.

"I'm not really sure. The storms have been brutal since then, and they are still raging." She stopped rubbing his arm and shivered.

Joe had a feeling she wasn't telling him everything she knew, but he pulled his arm out of the covers and reached for a candy bar. "Would you like half of this?" he asked as he picked it up.

"I sure would," she said, as she reached for her half. "Where did you get this?"

Joe looked guilty as he answered. "I went for a walk and found some candy bars and a soda in a desk drawer. I guess I was too hungry to think that they might belong to someone. I'm sorry."

She lay on her back, enjoyed the chewy chocolate, and sighed. "It's okay. We keep extras up at the front. I'll check later to see if there are any more. We do need to ration what we have, though." Worry showed on her face, but as she relaxed, her eyes closed and she fell asleep.

Joe felt awkward with her asleep in his bed, but he had to admit, the warmth was nice. He turned his back to her and thought about his situation. He pulled one of his socks off each foot and placed them on his hands as gloves. Then he pulled the covers up closer and tried to remember his life, making a mental list:

1. My name is Joe.

2. I was working in a building in the middle of Greenland.

3. I had an accident that took away my memory.

4. A dog sled team brought me to a rehabilitation hospital.

5. I like maps.

6. I like ginger ale and chocolate.

7. Margret takes good care of me.

8. Is anyone missing me?

9. Do I have a family?

10. Where do I live?

He looked at the window but saw nothing but blinding snow. It looked like it might be late afternoon, but it could be morning for all he knew. He glanced at Margret, but she was fast asleep. Restless and needing to move, he decided to take a walk down the hall. He eased out of bed and made his way to the door, feeling the cold floor through his single layer of socks. He glanced at his chair and saw the bright red emergency bag waiting for him. He opened it and pulled out a shiny blanket that would radiate his body heat back to him and keep him warm. He thanked God for the blanket and wrapped it around himself. Feeling immediately better, he turned left out of his room and wandered down the hallway. He had never been this way before, and he wondered what he might find. The hall was eerily empty, and he heard nothing but his own breathing as he walked silently on the cold linoleum. Ahead of him was an open door. He walked up to it cautiously, expecting to see a patient, but the room was empty. Once inside, he opened the drawers beside the bed and found two pairs of hospital socks in plastic wrap. He placed two on each foot and was instantly warmer. As he was coming out of the room, Margret ran into him.

"Oh, there you are," she said, sounding flustered. "I've been looking for you." She wrapped her arms around him and hugged him tightly. "I was really worried."

Joe pulled his blanket around her to offer warmth and comfort. She placed her head on his chest and snuggled closer.

"We're going to be okay. I've been praying, and I know God is with us," Joe whispered. Margret squirmed within his blanket to get warm. Talk of God made her uncomfortable.

She mumbled from within the folds of the blanket. "Joe, how is it you have no memory, yet you remember God. How does that work?"

"Huh. I guess my faith in God is something so deep within me, that it can never be forgotten. I know he's with me, I know he's in control, and I know we'll be okay. I trust him with everything that I am." He pulled the blanket tightly around them and wondered about it himself. *I'm basically in the dark, literally and physically, yet I have the light of Christ within me. That light will never go out, no matter what.*

"I don't know much about God," Margret admitted. "Would you tell me about him some time?"

Joe smiled in the dark. "Yes, Margret. I will be happy to tell you about God."

Song: *Burn the Ships* by For King and Country

Chapter 54

Celeste thought about Sergio's secret as she walked back home. *I wonder why he placed six stepping stones in a hidden place in the woods. And why did he bury mementos and a note under one of them? Should I tell anyone about it?*

She showered, changed clothes, and made it to the office a few minutes late, but Luca wasn't there. She pulled a water bottle from the mini fridge and stood at the window facing the mountains. *He loves it here*, she thought. *He'll come back here one day.*

Luca stood in the doorway watching her. "That's a beautiful view," he said as he walked up beside her. "I'll miss it." He put his arm around her and stood quietly with her as the light dimmed and the mountains began to darken. "I have an idea," he said. "Let's go into town for dinner. Would you do me the honor?"

Celeste did not want to go anywhere at that moment except to her room to think about the day, but she didn't want to be rude.

"Sure, that sounds nice."

They met in the lobby ten minutes later and headed to the truck. The evening air was cool, and Celeste pulled her light jacket closer to her. Her jeans and boots had that comfortable lived-in feeling, and she relaxed as she stepped up into the truck and buckled herself in.

Luca talked about the new resort as he drove to town, and then he pulled up to an Italian restaurant Celeste had never noticed. The hostess led them to a table in the corner near a small bubbling fountain. It was peaceful and pleasant, and she was glad she had come.

She studied her menu, chose a pasta dish that sounded delicious, and picked up a breadstick. She nibbled it while Luca spoke of the adventures he and Sergio had when they were younger.

"We've always loved this town and this mountain," he shared. "I have so many good memories here."

Celeste looked at him. "Luca, thank you for trusting me to manage the Inn. I will do my absolute best to run it the way you and Sergio would."

"I know you will. I have no doubt. Celeste, I, um, I'm not usually at a loss for words, but uh, there's something I need to say to you tonight," he stammered.

Celeste felt uneasy, and her stomach suddenly tightened. She looked at him as calmly as she could manage as she wrung her hands beneath the table.

Luca would have held her hands, but he noticed they were nowhere to be seen.

"Celeste, you know I trust you completely with the Inn because I consider you family. I know you were in love with Sergio, but we don't know if he'll ever be back. I know this is harsh, but I just have to say it. You are incredibly important to me, and I…"

"Luca," Celeste interrupted him, "you are about to move to Colorado. It's across the country, and you will be running a new resort. I will be here running this one. Whatever you think you need to say must wait. You can't say something important and then just leave. You can wait until the time is right." She pulled her hand from her lap and placed it on his. He nodded.

"You're right, and you make good sense." The waitress brought their food and then the check, and before long, they headed home. Celeste was exhausted and had a splitting headache. She said goodnight to Luca, but he lingered and watched her as she walked away.

Celeste got ready for bed, slipped between the sheets, and fell asleep instantly. She dreamed she was in a forest full of ferns and was looking under each one for a stepping stone.

Song: *Follow You Follow Me* **by Genesis**

Chapter 55

GREENLAND

Joe held Margret in his arms with the blanket wrapped around them both. He still had no idea who he was or what had happened, but he was beginning to feel more energetic. He needed to do something. Anything.

"Margret, can we walk? Maybe there's something we can do to help." Margret nodded but didn't want to leave the warmth. She dug in deeper to Joe's shoulder and then reluctantly pulled away.

"We can walk this way," she said as she pointed down the hall. "This building is laid out in a U shape. We are on the first floor right now. There's no one on the second floor, and there's a basement for the laundry and extra supplies."

"How many patients are there?" he asked. "It's too quiet." They walked slowly down the hall as Margret spoke about the hospital and its staff.

"There are four nurses and one doctor employed full time, but right now, there are only three of us here. Five patients are recovering from orthopedic surgeries, so that makes six patients total including you. We're a small out-of-the-way facility. We don't get many patients."

"I'd like to meet the other patients. Would it be possible to move them all to the rooms closest to the lobby? If we're all close together, I think it would be easier for everyone," Joe explained.

"Yes, we can do that. It's a good idea," Margret answered as she glanced up at him. "I can tell you are used to being in charge and making decisions."

Joe shrugged. "Well, maybe so." They spent the rest of the afternoon meeting patients and moving them to their new rooms. All the beds were on wheels, so it was easy to do. Joe sat and talked with each patient while Margret and one other nurse collected supplies from the empty rooms. Each patient was given extra blankets and socks, and the general mood of everyone increased. Soup was found in a pantry, and the nurses poured it into dishes and heated it with candles placed underneath. Joe sipped the hot soup, and felt good about what they had done. The room was freezing but he had a hot meal and extra blankets, and he had met new people.

Margret hurried in with a flourish and made her way to the chair. She sipped her soup from a cup and shivered. Joe threw a blanket to her. She grabbed it with one hand and snuggled into it, patting it down around her.

"It was a good day, Margret. It felt really nice to help the others." He took a sip and looked at her. She tipped the cup all the way up to get the last drop. He chuckled, and Margret grinned.

She placed her cup on the table and turned to him with a questioning look. "Why aren't you mad at God?" she asked, looking serious again.

"What do you mean? Why would I be mad at God?" He shivered, rubbed his arms for warmth, and gathered his emergency blanket close.

"Well, you still love him after what he did to you. I don't get it."

"Margret, God didn't do this to me. He's helping me through it. I know God loves me and will be with me every step of the way." Joe pulled the blankets up around him. "Can I tell you a story?"

"Sure. I'm up for a good story." She hugged her knees and arranged the blanket around her while Joe thought the position looked somehow familiar. He shook his head and concentrated.

"In the beginning, God created the world. He formed everything, including the sun and the stars, plants, and living creatures. Then he created man and woman. Adam and Eve were the first people, and they were given a beautiful garden. God told them not to eat the fruit of one particular tree in this garden, although they could eat anything else. Then a serpent came along and tricked Eve into eating some of the forbidden fruit. Eve believed the serpent instead of God and ate it. She gave some to Adam, and he ate it too. Their disobedience caused them to hide from God, and it created a distance between them. They had sinned, and they were ashamed. They were banished from the garden, but not banished from God's love. God still loved them so.

Many years passed by. They had children and their children had children, and so on. There were prophets throughout the years who told of the son of God coming one day to save all the people from their sins. People looked forward to this man, this messiah, who would save them all. They waited and they waited." Joe took a breath and watched Margret. She sat still and hung onto every word.

"One day an angel of the Lord came to a teenage girl in Nazareth and told her she was going to have a baby through the Holy Spirit. She was to name him Jesus. He was the Son of God. At this time, Mary was engaged to a man named Joseph. She trusted God, and so she said yes. Then Joseph had a dream of an angel visiting him and telling him what was going on. Joseph decided to believe the angel in his dream. He also said yes to God. Mary and Joseph married, and Jesus was born in a town called Bethlehem. Now, I'm skipping a lot, but there's a great book that can fill in all the details."

"Okay. Keep going, I'm intrigued." Margret pulled a knitted hat from her pocket, put it on, and waited for more.

"Jesus grew up, and when he was an adult, he began preaching and healing. He gathered twelve disciples to teach them about the Kingdom of God. They traveled with Jesus from town to town, listening and learning from him. So many miracles happened. People were healed. Many people followed them and wanted to learn more from Jesus' teachings. Then, after about three years of ministry, Jesus was condemned to die on a cross."

"Wait. What? This good man, God's son, who healed people and loved people was going to be killed?"

He pulled the blanket closer as the room suddenly felt colder. "Those in authority didn't like what Jesus was doing and saying. He healed people on the Sabbath and said things they didn't believe or understand. So, they condemned him to death. Margret, they nailed him to a cross and he died."

Margret jumped up in outrage. "I think I've heard parts of this story, but is it really true? How could he just die? Wasn't he God's son?" Feeling defeated, she sank down into the chair and pulled the blanket around her again. "What happened next?"

"This is the most amazing part! He was put in a tomb with a large rock rolled in front of the door so that no one would try to steal his body. On the third day, a couple of his women friends went to the tomb and saw that the rock had been moved. They went into the tomb but didn't see the body. Instead, they saw an angel. The angel reminded them that Jesus had said he would rise again on the third day. They remembered how Jesus had told them what would happen, and they left to go tell the disciples. Margret, Jesus, the son of God, was crucified on a cross, laid in a tomb, and rose from the dead in three days. It was all part of the plan." He took a breath and then continued.

"After this had happened, Jesus appeared to the disciples and opened their minds to understand the scriptures. He sent them to preach love, forgiveness, and repentance, to baptize and to make disciples. These disciples spread the good news of Jesus to the ends of the earth. They went to many countries preaching the words they had learned from him, and people believed. And it continues. Here I am telling you the story, praying you'll believe it. And one day, hopefully, you'll be a believer and you'll tell the story. We are all disciples on the journey of our lives, telling the most important story in the world. The Bible is true, Margret, and it is the most important book ever written." Joe sat back and looked at Margret expectantly.

"I have a lot of questions. Like, why would God send his son just to die? That doesn't make sense." She looked thoughtful. "I had a Bible once. A friend gave me one from a yard sale, but I held it in my lap and just stared at it. I had no idea where to begin. It seemed like a monumental task just to open it. I don't know where it is now."

"We can get you a new one. God sent Jesus to save us all from our sins. He loved us so much that he sent his one and only son, so that whoever believes in him will not die, but will have eternal life with God. That's your first Bible verse. It's in the Gospel of John, chapter 3, verse 16. You see, God wanted to save the people of the world because he loves us so much. Jesus' death on the cross means that our sins can be forgiven and that if we believe in Jesus as the son of God, then we will have eternal life with him. I know it's a lot to take in, and I'll always answer your questions. But Margret, I hope you know that you are loved by the one who created the world and who created you. He died for you." Joe looked at Margret with compassion and saw that she was silently crying. He got out of bed and walked the few steps to her, pulled her up out of her chair, and wrapped his arms around her.

Margret returned the hug and let the tears fall into the blankets that surrounded them. She whispered, "I don't know how you remembered all of this, but I'm grateful. Thank you." *Life isn't meaningless,* she thought. *There is hope, and his name is Jesus.*

Song: *Don't Look Back* by Boston

Chapter 56

Managing the Inn gave Celeste a sense of purpose. She was making decisions that mattered, and it felt good. Bert's hand-carved bowl came to mind, and she retrieved it from her closet. The intricate designs and details revealed his care for his craft. *Isn't that what life is supposed to be about; to actually care about the work and craft of our life?* She ran her fingers over the S and C carvings and thought of Sergio. *I love him.* It was a simple statement, but it held promise and hope. It was time to display the bowl properly. She headed to her office to give it a new home.

"Sergio, where are you and what are you doing?" She walked over to the windows and stared out at the mountains as if they would reveal the answers she needed. She closed her eyes. "I trust you, Lord. You know my path, and you know what I need. I trust you even when I have doubts about Sergio. Is he ever coming home?" She opened her eyes as a song title drifted into her thoughts. She pulled out her phone and texted it to him in faith that he would one day receive it.

Song: *Photograph* by Ed Sheeran

Chapter 57

Joe lay in bed listening for the noise that had woken him. He wondered if he should get out of bed to check, except that it was too cold to leave the warmth of the covers. His eyes closed momentarily, but the noise forced them open once again. It sounded like voices a long way away. He grunted and swung his legs over the side of the bed while gasping at the onslaught of frigid air. He pulled two blankets and wrapped them around his shoulders, wondering again what he had heard. The halls were dark and icy cold. Every now and then he paused to listen, but he thought he was going the right way. He made it the length of the hallway and stopped, pulling the covers closer, and looked around the corner. He knew he couldn't be seen by anyone because of the dark, but he sensed he needed to be quiet to learn what was going on. He heard two people arguing, and he could tell one of them was Margret.

"You can't keep it from him forever. You have to tell him. You have made a commitment to help, and that's not what you're doing." The male voice was impatient.

"I will tell him when he's ready, and he's not ready," Margret answered.

"We don't know how long we're going to be here. It might help with his amnesia," the male voice countered.

                    Andrea Herlong

"I'm going to go check on the patients. Just… just let me do this in my own time," Margret said emphatically.

Joe quickly turned around and headed back to his room. He was under the covers and had them pulled up when his door opened. Margret walked in, but he pretended to be asleep. She stood over him and watched him for a moment. He didn't know how long he could keep up the ruse. He wondered why she was just standing there watching him. It was a unnerving. Margret placed her fingers on his wrist and checked his pulse.

"Hmmm… his pulse is higher than normal. I'd better check his blood pressure," she whispered.

"I'm fine, Margret. I was just up walking around to get warm. I'm sure that's why it's faster than normal." Joe tugged on the blankets as he explained.

"Oh, I thought you were asleep," she started. "Now my heart is racing."

"Sorry. I didn't mean to scare you." He wondered if he should tell her what he had heard but decided against it. Margret walked over to the chair and sat down. She covered herself with a blanket and closed her eyes.

"I hope you don't mind," she said sleepily. "I just need to rest for a little while."

Joe watched as she closed her eyes and fell asleep. He was glad she had chosen the chair and not his bed. As he looked at her, he wondered what secrets she wasn't yet ready to reveal, but then he focused his thoughts elsewhere. The woman in the sea came to mind. *Why the sea? Who is this woman? Why am I in the water, and why is she swimming out to me? Nothing makes sense, but I hope someone is missing me. Do I miss her?*

Song: *All I Can Think About is You* **by Coldplay**

Chapter 58

"Special News Report: The storms in Eastern Greenland are unprecedented. Everything is shut down. Buildings, schools, hospitals, and homes have no electricity. The situation is bleak, and help is needed. Food boxes, as well as matches and firewood, are being dropped in remote locations. Blankets, sweaters, wool socks, and gloves are essential. If you can help, please visit the website to donate."

Celeste knew the reports were grim, but something about them also gave her hope that Sergio was out there somewhere and still alive. She continued to watch, she sent in a monetary donation, and she prayed.

As she headed out for an early morning run, she asked herself questions that had been creeping into her thoughts on a daily basis: *Why do I love Sergio so much? I mean, I miss him even after all this time. What is it about him that won't let my heart let go?* Her feet pounded out a steady beat while she reflected and answered herself. *Well, first of all, I trust him. I felt as though I could tell him anything on our first date in that pub. That's surprising, especially for me. Second, he gets me, and he likes me. Third, I can talk to him as though he's my best friend. He listens to me, and he doesn't judge me. Our conversations are real and good, and they make me feel seen and heard.*

She swerved around an inconsiderate squirrel in her path and continued. *Fourth, he brings out the best in me. He makes me want to be a better person. Fifth, he's adventurous. Sixth, he's thoughtful and kind. Seventh, he makes my heart flutter. Eighth, there's no one else I want to be with. Ninth, when I told him I loved him, I meant it with all my heart; and tenth, I love that he loves Jesus. His faith is strong, and I'm sure we're both relying on him right now. I will keep praying. God will send us what we need.* As she continued her run, she remembered there had been several times Sergio had tried to tell her something about his past. *I wonder what that was all about?*

She slowed down, came to a stop, and wiped her face on her shirt. Turning into the wind, she whispered, "All I can do is continue to wait, to pray, and to work hard here at the Inn. We'll talk about everything when he gets back." She kicked a rock on the path, accidentally jiggling her phone loose from her pocket. It fell with a thud and bounced once into a pile of leaves. She sat down on the ground, retrieved it from the leaves, and scrolled through her recent pictures. She stopped on the pictures of the stepping stones and looked at each one. Her eyes widened in surprise as she looked more carefully at the closing of the written note:

All my love, S E R G I̲ O

Even though she had looked at the pictures many times, she had never noticed that the letter *I* was underlined. *Was it a smudge or was it a clue? What did it mean?* She stared at the letters until her eyes hurt, and then she laughed at herself. *Look at me, just staring at a smudge on a note until my eyes are crossed.* She shook her head, pocketed her phone, and made her way down the mountain.

For the rest of the day, she managed problems that arose, greeted guests, and interviewed several candidates for job openings. All in all, it was a good day, and as she lay down to sleep that night, she closed her eyes and imagined Sergio touching her cheek, staring into her eyes, and moving towards her with a kiss. She fell asleep as the lyrics of a song guided her dreams.

Song: *Once in a Lifetime* by One Direction

Chapter 59

Joe slept later than usual, yet when he opened his eyes, the room was eerily dark. The storm raged, and there was still no electricity. His tongue ran over his teeth, and he cringed. He reluctantly headed to the bathroom to brush them in the icy water. It was a jarring experience, but he was thankful for the water and the toothbrush. As he placed the brush in its holder, a faint memory flashed through his mind, and he wiped up the sink so as not to leave a mess.

He quickly got back under the covers and reached for a candy bar. As he chewed, he remembered the newspaper he had hidden in his bedside table drawer. He leaned over in anticipation, opened the drawer, and held it in such a way as to make out the words in the dim light. He quickly discovered, though, that the words didn't make any sense. The paper wasn't written in English, and he couldn't decipher it. He focused on the pictures and slowly turned each page. As he came to the last page, he folded the newspaper in half to make it easier to hold and squinted at it. In the top right-hand corner, he noticed a small article with a blurry picture. The article was written in a language Joe didn't know, but underneath, the article was repeated in English. It told of a building that had collapsed due to heavy snow and how the authorities were not able to get into the building to save the people inside. Dog sleds were sent to help, but they were only able to transport one man. It went on to say that this man was believed to be named Joe (no last name known) from the U.S.

Joe read it again and then looked at the blurry picture. He could see the dog sled team, but he couldn't make out the picture of the man being transported. *Were those people still inside the building? Was I the only one to survive?* He threw the paper down on the floor and jumped out of bed. He looked around for something to hit, thinking that the pain in his hand would ease the pain in his heart. But instead, he knelt by this bed, buried his face in his hands, and prayed.

Margret walked in, saw the paper on the floor, and knew it was time for the truth to be told, at least as much as she could.

"Hey, maybe we need to talk."

Joe sat down on the bed, shivering. "I need to hear everything."

Margret sat down on the edge of the chair, drummed her fingers on her leg, and took a deep breath. "Okay. You were in a remote building doing some kind of technical work. For some reason you were outside when the collapse… when the building collapsed. There was a rope tied from the door to the generator at the back of the building. You must have been using it as a guide in the blizzard. An alarm rang at the fire station, and the dog sled team was called in, as the conditions were too hazardous for trucks. They, uh, they couldn't get into the building, but as they searched, they found your rope, and they found you hanging onto it. Well, they saw your legs. The rest of your body was under part of the roof that had fallen off. They dug you out of the snow, wrapped you up, and brought you here. We didn't know if you were going to make it, but you were a fighter. You pulled through, and now you're up and moving. We're so proud of you. Please don't be mad at me for not telling you everything sooner. I just didn't know if it would hurt your recovery. I'm sorry." She watched him intently for his reaction.

Joe stared at her as she spoke, and he had to control his emotions as he asked, "Am I the only survivor?" He clenched his fists and took a deep breath. He didn't remember the other men, their faces or their names, but it hurt anyway. He had to know.

Margret looked at him sadly. "We believe you are the only survivor, but they can't access the building because of the storm."

"So, they could still be alive in there?"

Margret looked grim. "It's been months, and there's nothing to be done until the conditions improve." She reached out to him but Joe needed to move. He shook his head, grabbed his blanket, and walked out the door. He needed to think. He needed to just do something. He climbed the stairs to the second floor where he could walk the halls alone.

Celeste couldn't sleep. She tossed and turned and then finally reached for the remote and turned on the TV. She flipped through the channels and settled on the international news. As she listened, she tensed, sat up in bed, and concentrated on the words that were now echoing in her head.

"And so," the reporter announced, "the sole survivor of the accident is a man named Joe from the U.S. We're assuming it is Joe Campbell, a member of the OEC tech team, but the storm is preventing an investigation to take place. Once the team can access the building, they…" Celeste felt her body grow cold.

"One survivor. A man named Joe. One survivor," she mumbled. She picked up her phone and called Luca.

"Celeste, are you okay?" she heard him ask. "Celeste, what's wrong?" His words were more urgent now, edging towards panic. Celeste's ragged breathing turned to sobs. Luca jumped up and paced the floor.

"International news. Turn it on," she sputtered.

Luca turned on his TV and found the channel. There was nothing that would've upset Celeste until he heard, "and just a recap on the incident in Greenland…" He stared at the screen as the meaning became clear. After what seemed a long time, Luca heard his own voice. "I'll get on the first flight tomorrow. Will you be okay tonight?" He was numb. Could this really be happening?

"No, I won't ever be okay," Celeste whimpered. "Will you talk to me until I fall asleep?"

Luca assured her he would. He rattled on about Colorado, not knowing what else to talk about. When she didn't answer anymore, he ended the call and made a reservation to return to North Carolina. Then he headed for his car, wanting to drive fast around dangerous curves and steep drop-offs. He needed to feel alive, but as he drove, great hiccupping cries burst from him, and as they waned, he drove safely back to the resort. He thought about the plans he needed to make and the stupidity of his frantic driving. He shook his head and berated himself. He would calm down, he would pack, and he would return home to Celeste.

Chapter 60

GREENLAND

Joe's emotions ranged from frustration to anger to grief and back again. There was nothing he could do to help the situation, and he couldn't stand knowing he was the only one who had been rescued. *Were they okay?* he wondered. *How many were with me? Were they still alive? How could they be?*

Margret walked cautiously into his room with a pack of peanut butter crackers. "Hi, I hope you're not mad at me." She handed him the treat.

Joe took the crackers and sat down in his chair with a determined grunt. "Thanks. I'm not mad at you. I'm just frustrated that there's nothing I can do."

"Joe, the most important thing you can do right now is remember who you are," Margret said matter-of-factly. "Regaining your memory will help you and possibly the others."

He looked at her and knew she was right. "But what else can I do?"

Margret walked over to him and pulled him up so that he was standing in front of her. She looked him in the eyes. "You will get there. You need to rest. Being stressed and anxious will not help you get better. I know we're stuck in this hospital with no electricity, and things seem bleak right now, but look at all you have: you are here, you have socks and blankets, and you have food. These are things to be thankful for." She reached her arms around him and gave him a big hug. "And you have me here to help you," she whispered into his ear.

Joe returned the hug and then stepped back. "You're right. Those are all things to be thankful for." Pulling blankets from the bed, he wrapped them around himself. "What can I do, though?" he asked. "I can't just sit here."

Margret smiled. "I have an idea. I'll be right back." Joe opened the pack of crackers, threw two into his mouth, and sat back down.

She was back within minutes. "Here are some books and magazines. It's possible that reading may help you remember. You just never know what will open the door to a memory." Looking pleased, she placed a stack of English-language magazines and a couple of books on the table beside his chair. "Now, read up. I have to go check on the other patients, but I'll be back."

Joe looked at the stack and picked up the magazine on top. It was a fishing and hunting magazine with pictures of rivers, lakes, and snowy fields. He looked at the images, but they weren't helpful. He placed the magazine underneath the others and decided to go for a walk. Patients called out to him from their rooms, and he spent time with each one, talking and listening. It made him feel good to visit with them. Margret had told him that children in Greenland learned Greenlandic, Danish, and English in school, and he was grateful he could communicate with them in English. They were all local, but they didn't know anything about the building he had been working in. They were good men, and Joe enjoyed getting to know them. They in turn, liked him, and they saw him as a leader, even though he had no idea who he was.

Chapter 61

Celeste didn't get out of bed. She texted her assistant manager, took a sick day, and ordered two mochas from the coffee bar. He brought them up himself and left them at her door along with some bakery items. She pulled herself out of bed and cracked the door to make sure no one was there, and then she pulled the tray inside. She lay sprawled on top of the covers thinking about the news report. She began to sob again.

"He can't be," she cried. "He just can't. I don't feel like he's gone. I think if he were really gone, I'd know it." She wiped her eyes, blew her nose, and drank her coffee. She lay in bed staring at the wall and thinking of the man she loved. Old feelings from the past rose up in her: the grief that had engulfed her at eighteen when her parents died, and the abandonment of the guy she thought she had loved in college. She remembered how her faith had sustained her then. She knew it would also sustain her now.

"I will focus on the good things. I will remember our happy times. I will remember that he loved me," she whispered to herself over and over. Making positive statements out loud was a technique her grief counselor had taught her, and she found that it did help to focus on the good. But even as she made her positive statements, tears slid from her eyes in defiance. A verse from Romans 8:26 made its way through the thickness of her thoughts: "…the Spirit helps us in our weakness. We do not know what we ought to pray for, but the Spirit himself intercedes for us through wordless groans." She groaned and allowed the Spirit to pray for her. She could find no more words to say.

Several hours later she wandered over to the breakfast tray and picked up two of the scones and the second mocha. It was cold by now, but she didn't care. Soup was delivered, but she never opened the door to get it. She finally got up the nerve to turn on the news, but there was no update. She turned it off, pulled the covers over her head, and cried.

Luca rented a car at the airport and drove the familiar road. He hadn't slept at all on the flight and was exhausted. He just couldn't believe Sergio was truly gone. He slammed his hands into the steering wheel and yelled at no one in particular. Wiping his tears, he tried to get a grip on his emotions, unsure of what awaited him.

Celeste heard a soft knock on her door. At first, she ignored it, but then her phone dinged, and she saw it was Luca asking if he could come in. She looked at herself in the mirror and quickly pulled on sweatpants and a sweatshirt over her pajamas. Then she grabbed an elastic band for her hair.

"Luca," she mumbled as she opened her door. "I'm glad you're here."

"Celeste, are you okay?" Luca asked as he walked into her suite. He saw her face and the tears brimming in her eyes, and his chin trembled. He reached over and pulled her into a tight hug. They cried together in each other's arms until the tears stopped. Then they just held onto each other, remembering the man they missed and loved.

Finally, Celeste pulled away. "Thank you for coming. I was a mess last night. Not that I'm any better now, but I'm just kind of numb, and I think that helps."

Luca nodded, understanding what she meant. "Would you like to go for a walk? The weather is nice, and it's still light."

"No, I don't think I'm up for a walk, thank you. I think I just want to go back to sleep."

"Okay. Get some rest. I'll head to my room and get some sleep as well. See you in the morning." Luca walked out and closed her door. He stood with his back against it as he wrestled with his need for Celeste. Her tear-stained face and swollen eyes tugged at his heart. He needed to hold her again. He turned around and started to knock but stopped himself. He knew he shouldn't return to her. It wasn't the right time. He shook his head and quickly walked away.

Celeste made tea and picked up a croissant. She turned off all the lights and opened her curtains. "These are the mountains Sergio loves. He has to come home." She watched the sun set and the shadows darken. When all was dark, she sighed and reached for her phone, texting Sergio a song title that promised she would see him again.

Song: *See You Again* by Carrie Underwood

Chapter 62

Why had she not thought of it before? She quickly pulled on the sweats she had thrown onto the chair and picked up her master key. Earlier, Luca had mentioned going to his room, and the idea had crept into her mind until it woke her with its urgency. She made her way silently down the hall in her sock feet, accessed the service elevator, and pushed the round, glowing number 5. She had been so intent on her new job and all of its responsibilities that she had never even thought about Sergio's room. Because he was part owner, he kept a private suite on the 5th floor. She had never seen it, but her heart now raced at the thought.

She peeked into the 5th floor hallway to make sure Luca wasn't around, and then she headed towards room 511. She paused at the door. *Should I go in? But why shouldn't I? It will be fine, but can I handle it?* Taking a deep breath, she opened the door and hurried in. She turned on the light and stood with her back against the door, taking in her surroundings. IT journals and books littered the desk, a notepad and several pens rested on the table, and the digital clock glowed 3:00 a.m. She glanced at the books and then made her way to the small table near his bed. She saw her name written on a notepad, and a smile touched her face, followed by a gulping sob. She glanced at the other items on the table and picked them up one by one: a brush, a pen, some loose change, and a worn baseball cap. She placed the cap on her head, and took it off again. Then she turned around and headed for his closet. Sergio's scent permeated her senses as she opened the doors. She recognized the clothes and reached out to touch them. Her breath caught. She pulled a navy-blue t-shirt and a gray sweatshirt from the hangers and held them to her face. They still smelled like him, and she pulled them in tighter. Holding them close, she sat down on the bed. A feeling of peace washed over her, and a sense of calm infused her thoughts.

"I will not believe he's gone. I have faith that he will come back," she said to herself out loud. She looked at the notepad on his table, leaned for a pen, and wrote, "I believe you are alive. I love you." Returning the pen to its place on the table, she made a plan. *I will come back often and write to him as much as I can. He'll see the notes when he returns.*

She brushed his shirt against her face and breathed its scent. She stood up with determination, left his room, and took the elevator down to the 2nd floor. She changed back into her pajamas and pulled his sweatshirt on over them. Then she slipped into bed, clutched his t-shirt tightly to her, and fell sound asleep.

Song: *Fire and Rain* by James Taylor

Chapter 63

GREENLAND

Margret walked into the room smiling, and Joe wondered why she looked happy in a freezing, dark hospital with limited food and no way out. She was carrying a box and two cups, and he could see something else sticking out of her pocket.

"I have a surprise for you!" With a twinkle in her eyes, she walked straight over to him and handed him a cup of coffee. She pulled the little table between them and placed the box on it. Next, she surprised him with a roll of Ritz crackers. "Look what I found!" she exclaimed. "Let's dig in!"

Joe sipped the hot coffee appreciatively and nodded. "Thank you. How did you make coffee?" He held onto it like a life raft in the ocean and sighed as it warmed his hands and throat.

Margret grinned. "I found instant coffee packets in a cupboard. I heated water in a pan using candles, and then poured the hot water over the instant coffee. It's not great, but it's hot!"

"You're amazing!" he said and then looked at the box on the table. "What's that?"

"I found a puzzle in the basement. Who knows how long it's been there, but I thought it would be fun, and it will be good exercise for your brain."

Joe was intrigued. He looked at the picture on the top of the box and saw that it was a beautiful mountain landscape. "500 pieces, huh? Well, let's get started before it gets even darker in here." He took the lid off the box, and they began by looking for the border pieces. Joe searched for colors, edges, lines, and sizes to fit and realized it really was good exercise for his brain. Every now and then he stopped to sip his coffee and eat a Ritz. He spent a lot of time looking at Margret, as well. He noticed her hair was braided a different way, one big braid down her back instead of two, and she smelled nice. It was a sweet kind of smell, possibly vanilla and mint. He liked it. He realized he needed to take a shower but shrugged and pulled his blanket in a little closer.

"Do you need a break?" Margret asked. She looked up at him and noticed he was watching her. She put her puzzle piece down, rubbed her hands together for warmth, and waited.

"Margret, you've been with me from day one, haven't you? I remember your soft jacket brushing my arm. I remember how nice it felt on my skin."

"Yes, I have. You've come a long way since that day," she answered. "I was so worried about you, but look at you now!"

"Was there something I did or said to give an indication that I was getting better?" he asked.

"Well, yes, there was," she began. "Your fever broke, you began eating the broth, and then there was the music. I noticed early on that your toes moved to the music when you heard a song you liked. It gave me hope that you would recover. I do think it helped," she said.

"I wonder why music is so important to me. But thank you for recognizing it and playing the songs. I'm sure it helped."

"You're very welcome. Now, let's work on this puzzle." He grinned, picked up a piece, and concentrated on the picture before him.

Joe woke up the next morning and knew something was different. It was quieter than usual, and it was bright. He shielded his eyes and searched for his dark glasses. He found them in his bedside table drawer and walked to the window. The snowy landscape was beautiful, although that was all he could see. He looked away reluctantly and closed the curtains to dim the light. Deciding to start this new day with a cold shower and a shave, he headed for the bathroom.

When he emerged from the icy torrent, he dressed quickly in clean scrubs and old socks, while also praying for heat to be miraculously restored. He glanced at his closet and wondered what it held. Wrapping his blanket around his shoulders, he walked over and opened the small door. Two plastic hooks were stuck to the back of the wall, and he started to turn away, but then he glanced down at the floor and smiled. His boots lay forgotten where someone had left them long ago. *How long had it been?* He sat down on his bed to put them on. They were stiff, and with two pairs of thick socks, they were a bit tight, but they felt wonderfully warm. He stood up to test them and wondered if Margret was making coffee.

As if on cue, Margret walked through the door carrying a steaming cup. She handed it to him and greeted him with a cheery, "Good morning!" She sat in his chair as he climbed back into bed, boots and all, and she continued, "Well, the storm has passed, but the electricity is still out. Hopefully, a sled team can bring in some supplies, and maybe a generator. We can't leave, but it's possible they can come to us." She picked up a puzzle piece, found its place, and then picked up another. "Would you like to help me with this puzzle?"

Joe got out of bed to join her as she stood up from his chair.

Glancing at his feet, she nodded. "I forgot about your boots. I'm glad you found them. They must be much warmer." She looked up at his face and noticed his hair. Shaking her head, she declared, "And put your hat on! You have wet hair!"

Joe gave her a nudge with it before covering his head. Then he gathered his blanket around him and sat down to work on the puzzle.

She settled into the chair opposite him, and they worked for a while in comfortable silence, each engrossed in their own thoughts. Joe thought the puzzle was difficult but liked the challenging task.

The door opened, the doctor walked in, and he greeted Joe warmly, "Good morning. It looks like you are hard at work. How are you feeling?"

Joe looked up. "Actually, I'm really hungry right now. I think it's a good time to take a break."

The doctor glanced at the puzzle. "Ah, beautiful, green mountains. I like this one." He picked up a piece and fit it perfectly into place. "There you go," he chuckled, "only about 475 more pieces to go."

He took Joe's vitals and looked into his eyes with a light as Margret quickly left to find something for breakfast. He spoke about the storm passing and his hopes that help would come soon. Then he sat down opposite Joe, pulled his clipboard close, and stated, "Now, I'm going to ask you some questions. Just say whatever comes to mind first." Joe nodded and sat up a little straighter.

"What is your name," he asked.

"Joe."

"Where do you live?"

"I don't know."

"What is your occupation?"

"I don't know, but I like music."

"Are you married?"

"No. At least, I'm not wearing a ring."

"Where did you go to school?"

"I don't remember."

"Do you like sports?"

"I think so, but I don't remember any particular teams."

"What's your favorite book?"

"I have no idea."

"What kind of car do you drive?"

"I drive a truck."

The doctor stopped his questioning and looked at him curiously. "You remember you drive a truck? Tell me about it."

Joe looked at the doctor and smiled. "I remembered something!"

"Yes, you did. It's a good start. What color is it?" the doctor asked.

"It's black, and it has a picture on the door."

"That's very good," the doctor said. "Can you remember anything else about it?"

Joe tried to remember, but he couldn't recall anything else. "No, I'm sorry."

"Let's take a break for now, and then we'll try again later," the doctor said as he stood to leave. "Keep working on the puzzle."

Joe stared at the puzzle and tried to remember more about his life. At least he remembered he had a black truck with a picture on the door. *That's something.*

Margret walked in with more coffee, a bowl of soup she had heated by candlelight, and a pack of crackers. "I've brought you a feast," she said as she walked carefully to him. "I heard you remembered something." She set the food before him and sat down to listen.

"I remembered that I drive a black truck, and the truck has a picture on the door," he said proudly.

"That's great progress. I think working on this puzzle is helping.

I'll come back in a little while and finish this bottom corner. Maybe you'll remember something more." She brushed his hand with hers and then walked out of the room. Joe watched her go and noticed her blonde hair hung down her back in two braids today.

He ate his soup quickly before it got cold, sipped his coffee, and ate every one of the crackers. He was starving but knew it would be a while before getting more. He moved the empty soup bowl to the sink and sat back down to work. The puzzle was coming together, but he wanted to see more of it. He picked up the box and studied the picture carefully. There were three mountain peaks with pine trees covering them and a beautiful sky the colors of blue and pink and yellow, as if the sun were setting, or maybe rising. Deer and other animals could be seen grazing, and colorful flowers dotted the landscape. A sparkling river ran through a valley and trees lined each side. He paused to study the river and looked at it closely.

"Home," he said out loud. "It looks like home."

"Hi, Joe. Did you say something?" Margret walked in with his chart.

"I was thinking about this river." He glanced at her, shrugged, and pointed to the puzzle.

"Oh. I think rivers are wild, scary, and full of things that can hurt you. I'm not really a fan." Margret shuddered.

He looked at her and then back to the box. "Huh. Well, for some reason when I think of a river, I immediately think of a woman." Margaret's head jerked back to him as he picked up the box top and considered it again. "A river is beautiful, deep, strong, mysterious, and intentional, but also unpredictable. Can't that also describe a woman? I don't know who I'm describing, though. Those words seem to be meaningful in some way." He placed the puzzle box on the table and glanced at her.

Margret was still. She wondered who he was thinking of and wished it was her. She shook her head and gathered herself. "Those are great descriptive words, Joe. I think you are definitely getting better." She took his pulse just to be able to touch him and then made her way to the door. "I'll be back later."

Joe closed his eyes. He could see a glistening river journeying through a lush valley. The smell of pine tickled his nose and the gurgle of water splashed in his ears. A song made its way into his thoughts, and he began humming a tune he couldn't name.

Song: *Carolina in My Mind* by James Taylor

Chapter 64

NORTH CAROLINA

Celeste woke up before the sun. She lay in bed thinking about her discovery the night before and held Sergio's t-shirt a little tighter. Then she reluctantly got out of bed, splashed water on her face, brushed her teeth, and pulled on sweatpants. She was still wearing Sergio's sweatshirt, and just having it on made her feel closer to him. She laced up her sneakers, grabbed her journal, and headed downstairs. Making her own coffee, she added extra chocolate and then slipped out the front door. She knew exactly where she wanted to go to watch the sunrise. The air was chilly and fresh, and she filled her lungs with it. The mountain air invigorated her, and she wondered how she had ever lived in the city. She made her way down the stone path and towards the gazebo. She noticed the dew on the grass, the birds beginning their morning songs, a chipmunk darting across the path, and a squirrel or two looking for breakfast. She sighed and slowed her pace.

The gazebo sat on the ridge waiting for her. She walked to it, stood at the railing, and watched the sun put on a dazzling show to begin the day. Feeling inspired, she sat down with her back against the railing, opened her notebook, and wrote a letter to the man she missed and loved.

Luca slept in and ordered room service. He had not slept well, and he wasn't sure what the day would bring. He didn't want to disturb Celeste too early, so he worked from his room and watched the news. *What am I going to do? Will she be okay when I have to return to Colorado? Do I even want to go back? Maybe I need to be here.* He worriedly paced the floor of his suite.

Celeste walked back to the Inn and chatted with a few of her employees who were concerned about her.

"I'm feeling better," she assured them. "I'll be down in an hour." She went back up to her room, showered, and changed clothes. She remembered what the news had reported, but she didn't believe it. She couldn't. She placed the letter to Sergio in the secret book and noticed how full it had become. She would continue writing, no matter how long he was away. She brushed her hair, dabbed on some lipstick, and headed downstairs.

Luca decided he couldn't wait any longer. He needed to see Celeste. He knocked softly on her door, but there was no answer. *She must still be asleep.* He looked at his watch. *Last night was so hard for her.* He walked downstairs and headed to her office. *Maybe there's something I can do for her down here.* As he walked in, he was surprised to find Celeste sitting behind her desk looking just fine. He thought she would be a red, puffy-eyed mess today, but instead, she looked beautiful and calm.

"Celeste, good morning," he said, a bit confused. "I thought you'd still be in your room."

Celeste looked up and gave him a quick smile. "Good morning, Luca. No, I got up early, went for a walk, and then decided the best thing to do was to get to work." She picked up her coffee and gestured to the chairs by the window. "Would you like to sit with me?"

Luca made his way to the opposite chair. Trying to gauge her emotions, he watched her and finally asked, "Celeste, how are you?"

Celeste looked out the window and ran her fingers over her necklace as she spoke. "I'm better than I was last night. I had a good cry, but then I realized that my heart doesn't think he's truly gone. I have to keep believing he's out there somewhere, he loves me, and he'll be home one day. I will not give up hope." She turned and looked at him and was surprised at the look on his face.

Luca stared at her in disbelief. "But the news report said the only survivor was a man named Joe. Joe Campbell was the only man named Joe on the team. Celeste, I think we need to face the fact that he's gone."

"Think what you want, Luca. But I know he's coming home." Celeste stood up and walked out of the office and straight into the ladies' room where she immediately burst into fresh tears. She allowed herself to cry until she was spent, then she splashed cold water on her face, and gathered the courage to face him.

Luca was waiting for her. As soon as she saw him, she broke into tears again, and he pulled her into his arms.

"It's okay," he soothed. "It's okay."

She rested her head on his shoulder and sobbed. After a few minutes, she lifted her head and wiped her tears.

"Thanks," she said. "I'm sorry I spoke to you that way. I know you miss him too."

He reached up and brushed a strand of hair off her wet cheek. "I have an idea. Let's go to town and keep busy today. I think it may help."

Celeste nodded in agreement. She made a few appointment changes and then went upstairs to change. Her mind was a whirl of memories and thoughts, and she wondered if spending the day with Luca was really the right thing to do. She looked down at the yellow sundress she had chosen and pressed it with her palm. The lemony yellow was a joyful color, and it reminded her to smile. She could do this. She would be strong; she would hold on. She closed her eyes and took a deep breath, and then she headed for the lobby. Luca was waiting for her, and they walked outside, hoping the excursion would give them both a tiny bit of relief from the pain they felt in their hearts.

Song: *Hold On* by Michael Bublé

Chapter 65

GREENLAND AND NORTH CAROLINA

Joe picked up his notepad and pen and wrote down the things he remembered:

1. My name is Joe.

2. I have a black truck with a picture on the door.

3. I live somewhere in the U.S. with mountains, a river, and pine trees.

He stood up, walked to the window, and hoped to remember something more, but nothing came to him. He was suddenly tired, and his head began to hurt. He wandered back to the bed and pulled up all of the blankets over his emergency one. The covers did a fine job of fighting off the chill, and he was soon asleep.

Fog covered the mountain as he made his way along the curved path. He saw her walking in front of him, just out of reach. He moved faster but couldn't catch up. The sun was rising; streaks of red, yellow, and orange splashed across the sky. He looked back for her, but she was gone. Six stepping stones shimmered on the ground in her place. He sat down on a bench and felt the heat of the sun on his hand.

Margret walked into the room to find him sleeping. One of the blankets had fallen off the bed, and she picked it up and tucked it in around him. She checked his pulse and then placed her hand on his, hoping he would be well soon.

Celeste wasn't sure she wanted Luca to leave. She felt angry as she tried to figure out her fluctuating emotions and exactly why she felt the way she did. She read the same paragraph on an accounting report for the fourth time and gave up. *I just can't think today.* She closed her laptop and stood up to stretch. *I need to run.* They had few guests at the moment, so she didn't think she'd be missed. She passed by the lobby on her way upstairs and saw Luca drinking coffee. He was sitting in the big leather chair that Sergio used to sit in, and he looked lost in thought. He sipped and stared out the window as if he were trying to make a decision. It made Celeste nervous, and she made her way upstairs without being seen.

Fifteen minutes later she was on the trail with her music blasting through her ear buds. She decided on a well-traveled path for the run. She relaxed as her breathing evened out and her music sang to her. The songs on her playlist led her through emotions of happiness, longing, sadness, and joy. Music always spoke to her, and she relied on it to help her, to calm her, and to change her perspective.

Two miles in, she slowed to a walk, turned the volume down, and tried to think. She had been glad when Luca arrived because she could cry on his shoulder. He understood the pain of losing Sergio as no one else could. He could tell stories about Sergio growing up, and he could make her laugh, but he was getting too close. Celeste wondered if Luca wanted to take Sergio's place and stay at the Inn with her. She stopped walking and sat down on a nearby bench. Wiping her face on her sleeve, she took a deep breath. *He doesn't understand that I love Sergio with all my heart. I will not just lose hope and take up with his brother. I guess I need to stop avoiding him and have a good talk.* She stood up and saw him walking up the path towards her. With dread, she figured that now was as good a time as any.

"Hello, Celeste," Luca said as he approached her. "How was your run?" His face was a mixture of sadness and delight as he looked at her. She was glistening with sweat, her face pink from exertion, and he thought she looked beautiful.

"Well, hey, Luca. What are you doing up here?" She sat back down on the bench, wishing she had brought a bottle of water.

Luca sat down beside her and picked up her hand. "Celeste, I think we need to talk." Celeste wanted to jump up and walk away, but she knew this was important.

"Yes, we probably do," she whispered.

Luca let go of her hand and turned to face her. "Celeste, I'm going to go back to Colorado tomorrow. There are two reasons. One, I need to be there for a large group that's arriving on Tuesday, and two, because I'm in love with you." Celeste started to argue the point, but he placed his finger on her lips and continued. "Shhh, don't say anything yet. Let me explain." He stood up and faced her as she stared up at him.

"I know you love my brother. I know you miss him and long for him. I understand that you will love him forever, but I also know he's not coming back. I want you to know that I love you. I can make you happy." Luca sat down beside her and ran his fingers along her cheek. "I'm going to go away, but I'll be back in three months. During our time apart, I'd like you to think about the possibility of us being together. Maybe you'll miss me while I'm gone. Maybe you'll want to call me for no reason at all. Maybe you'll want to hear my voice before you fall asleep or, maybe not. Anyway, I had to tell you how

I feel, and that I need to go away. Maybe when I return, you'll have decided." He smiled at her and leaned in.

Celeste was caught up in his eyes and sat transfixed. Luca used the moment for what he wanted and pressed his lips to hers. They tasted like Sergio's, they felt like Sergio's, and she relaxed. She let herself believe she was kissing Sergio, and she returned the kiss. Luca reacted and wrapped his arms around her, holding her close, unable to believe his good fortune.

Celeste suddenly realized what was happening and pulled away, wiping her mouth with her hand. She was disgusted with herself for the moment of weakness. She had imagined herself kissing Sergio, but it wasn't right. It also wasn't fair to Luca. She suddenly felt cold. Standing up, she walked a few feet away and then turned around to face him.

"Luca, thank you for telling me how you feel. I love you too, but I love you like a brother. I'm in love with Sergio and only Sergio. I'm sorry to hurt your feelings, but I have to be honest."

Luca stood up and joined her. He picked up her hands to hold them again. "I understand, Celeste, but that kiss said more to me than any words you will ever say. Call me whenever you feel like it. I'll always be here for you." He pulled her in for a hug that lasted too long, kissed her forehead, and then walked back down the path.

Celeste immediately put her ear buds in again, pushed play on her phone, and took off running. She knew the music would allow her to think, and she hoped it would give her the answers she needed.

Song: *I'll Be Around* **by The Spinners**

Chapter 66

GREENLAND

Joe was working on the puzzle before the sun rose, hoping the exercise would help his memory return. He had attached his list of things remembered to the wall, and he desperately wanted to add to it. The electricity was still out, and he was still freezing, but the blankets, extra socks, and boots helped. He placed a piece into the puzzle and felt a sense of accomplishment. It was coming along.

Margret knocked on the door and walked into Joe's room. "Looks like breakfast is coffee and beef jerky today, but I can bring you some soup once it's heated. How are you feeling?"

"I'm feeling okay this morning. I have a bit of a headache, but I'll work through it. Thanks for breakfast."

Margret sat down to work on the puzzle and told stories of her childhood in the Arctic and how she had always wanted to be a nurse.

She held a piece up in the air for a moment and then placed it perfectly in its spot. "I knew I wanted to help people, and I thought nursing would be the perfect profession for me. I wanted to be with people at their most vulnerable times as well as their most joyful times. I was right. I really love it."

"Tell me about your family," he said as he sipped his coffee and looked at her.

She glanced at the puzzle pieces, searching through them as she began. "I have a mom, a dad, and four brothers. They all live in a village not too far from here." She grinned, picked up a piece, and continued, "We got a dog when I was 15, and he's still with us. His name is Eeriuffi. It means warrior wolf. He's a mix of breeds, but I think he mostly looks like a husky. It's nice to have a good dog when you grow up with four brothers." She looked pensive and then inserted the piece into the puzzle. She glanced up at him, hoping that some bit of information might trigger his memory.

The doctor strode into the room. "Margret, we need you next door. "Joe, have you remembered anything more?"

Margret patted Joe's shoulder as she left the room. It felt good to Joe, comforting and warm. He told the doctor about his headache. It was still pounding, but he was starting to wonder if it was due to hunger. His stomach growled in protest.

The doctor glanced from his notes. "We need to get you a proper meal. I think that will help a lot. Continue working on the puzzle and try keeping some type of journal. It might help you remember more if you write something every day."

After the doctor left with the hopeful promise to find food, Joe stood up, stretched, and walked to the window. He put his glasses on, although the light was dim, and opened the curtains. He saw two nurses talking to a man on a snowmobile. He watched as the man unfastened several large coolers and brought them to the steps of the hospital. The nurses looked overjoyed and one of them reached up to hug the man. He returned the hug and then drove away. Joe prayed he had brought food.

A few minutes later Margret walked into his room with a tray laden with fish, potatoes, vegetables, fruit, bread, and steaming coffee. "Look what I have for you! It was brought up from the village. They know we're up here without electricity, and they've promised to send food every single day now that they can get through!"

She placed the tray on the table, chatting happily about the generosity of the townspeople. "You'll love the bread! It's my favorite. Auntie Imi makes it, and it's known far and wide." Joe sat down, barely able to contain himself, but he closed his eyes for a moment to give thanks. He then took a bite of the broiled fish and groaned at the deliciousness. Margret promised to come back soon, but she turned to watch him, and then smiled and walked away.

Joe didn't notice anything but the food he was devouring. His stomach had shrunk considerably, so it was soon full. He sighed contentedly, picked up a piece of Auntie Imi's bread, and walked to the window. All he saw was snow. He tried to remember more about his life and didn't hear Margret approach. She walked up behind him, slid her arm through his, and stood beside him.

"You'll remember," she said as she rested her head on his shoulder. "You'll remember."

Chapter 67

Luca had been gone a month and Celeste hadn't called him once. She didn't want to. When there was a problem, she figured it out. When she was lonely, she had a good cry, and when she was confused, she went for a long run. She started attending Sunday services at Shepherd Falls Chapel, and it brought community and a sense of peace to her life. She remembered the morning she and Sergio had attended the sunrise service, how he had held her hand, their fingers intertwined, and how their voices had mingled in song. The message that morning had been about God's provision, his presence in their lives, and his guidance. The words from that morning's message floated into her mind: "Trust God, walk with him, and lean on him in your times of trial." She closed her eyes and repeated them to herself, needing their strength and their assurance now.

She was falling into a routine, and work was going well. Staying busy helped numb the pain. She welcomed guests, trained new employees, and kept the Inn running like a well-oiled machine. The staff noticed she wasn't quite herself, but they thought she simply missed Luca. Celeste hadn't talked to any of her friends about the situation, and it kept a safe wall around her heart. She knew if she talked about how much she missed Sergio, she would fall apart.

She couldn't even think about what Luca might say to her in

two months when he returned. She shuddered at the memory of the passionate kiss they had shared. If she refused him, as she knew she would, would she still work at the Inn? She loved her life in North Carolina and couldn't imagine leaving, but could she work at the Inn Luca owned? She stood up, headed for the coffee bar, and chatted with the barista as the mocha was prepared. Celeste took a sip and immediately felt better. She walked to Sergio's favorite chair and sat down with a sigh, pulling her legs up under her and sipping her coffee while staring at the fire.

I'm the one he loves. I'm the one longing for him, loving him, and praying for his safe return. If he were not alive, I think I would feel the emptiness deep in my heart. I miss him, and I am grieving his absence, but I believe he will come back. I will not give up, and I will not just settle for Luca because he's alive and well. Sergio will return to me, and I'll be waiting for him. She stood up with renewed energy and headed back to the office.

When she got there, though, she sat at her desk and stared at her phone, willing it to light up with a text or message. As she scrolled, she opened her picture app and looked at the photos she had taken in the woods. She read and reread the note and then focused on the closing:

"One day I will fall in love, and I will love her forever. She will be one-of-a-kind, like a snowflake, and our love will remind me of a beautiful evergreen. It will weather the storms and stay strong. When she is away from me, I will miss her like breath, and I will count the moments until I see her again. These stepping stones represent our relationship because each of our encounters will be a step on the pathway of our journey together. One day, my love, one day."

All my love, S E R G I̲ O

Why is the I underlined? She stared at it and concentrated on the spaces between the letters. *Why are the letters separated?* The first pains of a headache began forming above her eyes, and she closed her phone. She grabbed a water bottle from the mini fridge, threw two Advil into her mouth, and promptly forgot about the underlined letter.

Celeste wandered into the lobby feeling out of sorts and irritable. Her headache lingered, and she needed a distraction. She noticed a woman at the reception desk who looked familiar, and when she turned around, Celeste grinned and hurried to greet her.

"Olivia! What are you doing here?" Celeste pulled her friend into a tight embrace, and Olivia knew she had made the right decision.

"Celeste, it's so good to see you! We need to talk!"

"Absolutely. Let me show you to your room, and you can tell me why you're here without letting me know ahead of time. I'm so glad to see you!" She walked with her friend to the elevators and listened while Olivia chatted about her trip.

As the door closed to her room, Olivia sat down in a chair and motioned for Celeste to join her. "Celeste, I'm here for a reason. I'm here to check on you and to see if you're okay. What's going on?"

"What makes you think I'm not okay?" Celeste asked as she fidgeted with her necklace.

"Ha! You've stopped texting me and the girls in Chicago. You've stopped posting on social media, and you've stopped being you. Talk to me." Olivia looked at her sympathetically, and Celeste sighed. She summed up her worries about Sergio and Luca, and then looked to Olivia for support.

"It's just a lot, and I am doing the best I can," she whimpered.

"Nope. This isn't the Celeste, the G², I know and love. Go change clothes and meet me downstairs in five minutes. We're going for a run." Olivia stood up and opened the door for her friend.

Celeste walked out of the room obligingly and then hurried to her room to get ready.

Olivia rummaged through her suitcase, changed into running clothes, and was stretching outside within minutes as Celeste joined her.

"Take me on your favorite run, as long as it's level," Oliva stressed as she looked at the mountains around the Inn.

Celeste nodded as she recalled their old Chicago runs and how it had taken her some time to manage the hills here. "Let's go this way, I think you'll like this one." Celeste led her down the mountain towards the river, and they fell into step together. When they neared the river, she led her friend to a grassy area, and then sat down on a rock to catch her breath. Olivia followed suit and sat on an opposite rock to face her friend.

"It's beautiful here. I can see why you love it so much. It's definitely different from the city." Olivia regarded Celeste and shook her head. "I'm worried about you."

"Thanks, but I'm going to be okay," Celeste responded as she picked a dandelion and played with it while glancing cautiously at her friend.

Olivia cleared her throat and faced her. "You are an amazing person because of who you are. You are not amazing because of a man. You are smart, kind, thoughtful, funny, and beautiful, and you are all that because of you."

"But I…" Celeste tried to interrupt.

Olivia continued. "Celeste, I know you love this man, but this relationship should not define you. You've lost yourself. Where is that strong woman on the train who knew what she wanted? Where is the woman who believes in herself and who believes strongly in God? You have to be the woman God created you to be. Yes, you can miss him and love him, but listen to me: don't forget who you are! Stop being all whiney and sad. God has given you an amazing life, and you are not making the most of each day. This is your wake-up call." She reached over and hugged her friend.

"I love him," Celeste whimpered as she held on.

"I know you love him, girl, but this relationship can't be everything you are. It's like you're caught up in a maze with no way out!"

Celeste sat up abruptly. "A maze with no way out?" Olivia nodded with an all-knowing look. "Wait," Celeste exclaimed. Olivia's eyes opened wide as Celeste continued.

"I dreamed once that Sergio and I were lost in a maze. It was beautiful, but we couldn't find one another. We searched and we searched, but I eventually found the exit. I don't remember if Sergio got out, but I think I woke up feeling safe. Exhausted and emotional, but safe." She looked at Olivia expectantly.

"Huh. Okay. So, you were both lost in a beautiful maze, wanting to find each other, but you couldn't. There were obstacles in your way. You finally found the exit, and you felt exhausted and emotional, but safe. Could this maze dream have a deeper meaning?" Olivia swatted at a bug and regarded her friend.

Celeste looked off into the distance and started to speak and then stopped. She needed to sit with her thoughts. She had gotten out, but what about Sergio? *I woke up feeling safe, so he must have found the exit too, right? But maybe he's lost somewhere and trying to find the way home!*

She spoke slowly as her thoughts became clear. "I haven't lost myself. In fact, I've found myself, and I know I will find Sergio again.

If he's lost, I'll keep searching. I'll keep praying. I'm not giving up hope. It's just that, he is so important to me. He showed me what true love really is." She paused and then continued, "I am still the strong woman you know. I trust God with all my heart, and I speak with him daily. You know my grief was so hard when my parents died, and then my epic college breakup really did a number on me. Well, this grief is like that all over again, except in this case, there's a possibility he'll come back. I'm holding out hope that he does. If not, though, I'll be okay. I have wonderful friends like you, and I have this place, and I have God to help me through." She looked to the mountains. "I'm going to be okay."

Olivia reached out and hugged her again. "It's good to hear you sounding confident and strong. I'm sorry I came on so harshly, it's just that I've been worried about you. Make sure you share your concerns with friends who love you. Don't keep it all inside."

Celeste smiled and motioned to the road. "Race you to the Inn! I want to take you to the cutest little town you've ever seen!" She took off running and Olivia laughed out loud as she raced to keep up with her friend.

Song: *The Power of Love* by Huey Lewis and the News

Chapter 68

GREENLAND

Joe was tired of looking at snow. He was tired of everything, and his boredom made him irritable. Rubbing the back of his neck with one hand, he stood at the window and complained, "I wish this headache would go away." He suddenly turned around and headed for the door. He didn't know where he was going, but he knew he needed to move. He needed something different, something more. He walked down the hall, pulling his shiny blanket close, and saw Margret coming towards him.

"Hey, are you okay?"

"No, I'm bored, I'm tired of not remembering who I am, and I have a headache."

Margret guided him into a small room off the hallway and offered him a chair. The light was dim, but he could see where she directed him. He sat down, shivered, and waited for her to speak. He knew her well enough now to expect it.

"Now, listen here, Joe. I know you are bored, tired, cold, and hungry. I know you are having chronic headaches, but you have been through a traumatic event. You have to be patient and allow your body to heal. It's only then that your memory will return. Now, what do you have to say about that?" Margret looked at him expectantly.

Joe's mouth turned up at the edges. "You're right, of course. I'm just tired of the monotony. Do you think I could walk out and touch the snow? I can't remember what it feels like."

Margret looked at him and considered his request. She'd have to have help and make sure he didn't slip on the ice, but maybe it could work. "I'll see what I can do. Actually, dinner will be delivered in an hour. It's possible we can take you outside when the others will be there to help. Maybe the snow will trigger a memory." He looked hopeful. She grabbed his hands, pulled him to a standing position, and led him back to his room.

An hour later, Margret and Joe walked to the front entrance. He was excited to feel the wind in his hair and on his face, to touch the snow, and to experience something different. The doctor opened the door and a nurse reached for Joe's hand. Margret grasped his other one, and together they walked outside. Immediately the frigid air hit him head on, and he gasped. Tears ran from his eyes as the wind whipped around him, but he wasn't able to brush them away. He had worn his boots, but his thin scrubs, robe, and blanket were not enough protection from the cold. Joe knew immediately that this had not been a good idea. Margret looked at him and knew he would not last long. She let go of his hand, motioned to the other nurse to hold on tight, and ran out to the snowbank to scoop snow into a cup. The doctor took up Margret's spot and led Joe back through the door. It was cold inside, but it was nothing like what he had just experienced. The doctor led him to a wheelchair and wheeled him back to his room where he was put to bed, given hot tea, and covered in woolen blankets. Margret watched him and worried. *It was too much.*

Joe shivered under the covers and held the hot mug between his hands, taking small sips. He didn't focus on anything or anyone.

"Joe, I'm going to bring you a hot meal. I think you'll like tonight's supper. I saw some of those rolls you like. I'll sneak an extra one for you." Margret looked at him hopefully. He just stared at the wall and sipped his tea.

As she turned to leave, he whispered, "Where's the snow?"

Margret breathed a sigh of relief and answered, "I have it right here. Would you like to touch it?" She waited for his answer, and he turned to her and nodded. She brought the cup of snow to his bedside and held it out to him as she took his tea. He took the cup of snow and touched it, feeling the hard iciness. It had molded to the cup and felt like stone. He rubbed his fingers over it and grimaced.

"It looks better than it feels. I think I'll take that hot meal now."

Margret patted his hand and traded his mug for the snow. "I'll be right back."

The snow hadn't jogged any memories, yet there was something about it. The rigidity of the snow in the cup didn't make sense to him. Maybe it was snowflakes he wanted to know more about.

Margret opened the door and pushed in a rolling cart holding two meals. "Mind if I join you for dinner?" She placed his meal in front of him and helped him sit up in the bed.

He picked up a roll and answered, "Please. That would be nice. Tell me about snow. I think there's something I need to know about it."

Margret sat down in the chair, sipped her coffee, and nibbled a roll. "Well, each snowflake is different. There are no two snowflakes alike."

He listened to her monologue on snow as he ate and hoped something would nudge his brain into remembering, but he soon felt the weight of sleep come over him. His head drooped, and she jumped up to take his tray.

"Goodnight. We'll talk more tomorrow." She pulled the blankets

   Andrea Herlong

around him and held his hand in hers. She watched him fall asleep and then silently left the room.

The forest beckoned, and the winding path led deeper and deeper into the trees. He saw what he was searching for: stepping stones. He stepped on the first one, and then turned to the left and stepped on the second. Then he walked around a tree and found the third just where he knew it would be. Then the fourth one was found under a fern, the fifth beside the fallen log, and then finally he stepped on the sixth one. He looked at it and smiled, tracing the letter O on top of it. A single glistening snowflake fell from the sky. He placed his hand out flat, and the snowflake rested on it, shining like a star.

Song: *Doctor My Eyes* by Jackson Browne

Chapter 69

GREENLAND

Joe lay very still with his eyes closed as he tried to remember the dream: a path in the woods, trees with green leaves, stepping stones, a snowflake. His brain felt fuzzy, but a door was trying hard to open to reveal a memory. It was like a scab that had grown over a wound that, as soon as he picked it off, would allow the blood to flow freely. He just needed to scratch the itch to open the floodgates. He opened his eyes and reached over to the bedside table for his notepad. He wanted to write down every detail he could remember. Was there something written on one of the stones? He thumped his head with the pad as if the gesture would dislodge the memory, but it was no use. The dream was gone. Instead, he reached for his world map and sat up in bed to study it.

"I'm American, so let's concentrate on that country," he said out loud. He circled the United States with his pen. "I dream of mountains, so let's cross off any desert or ocean areas. Wait, I've dreamed of oceans, too." He put the pen down and sighed.

The doctor and Margret walked into the room together, the doctor with his chart, and Margret with his breakfast.

"Good morning. You had a rough day yesterday." He checked the chart and asked hopefully, "How are you feeling today?"

"Hey, doc, I'm all right. Just frustrated I still can't remember more."

"Joe, it takes time. I know it must be discouraging not to remember yet, but it will come. Did you have any memories after seeing and touching the snow?"

"Not really. I dreamed of a snowflake, but that's all," he responded as he took the offered coffee from Margret. "Thank you. Oh, I also dreamed of stepping stones," he added as he sipped the hot liquid.

"That's very interesting. Possibly the stepping stones represent a journey or steps you must take before getting where you need to be," the doctor suggested as he made a note on the chart. "The mind is incredible, and dreams can give us clues to our lives. Make sure you write down any little thing you remember, no matter how insignificant it may seem." Margret slid his tray onto the table. "After you eat, I'd like Margret to run through some questions with you. We're going to try everything we can to help." He made another note on the chart and left the room.

Margret settled into the chair and pulled a blanket over her legs. "Do you mind if I start the questions now?" She shivered and adjusted her hat as she watched him.

Joe's stomach grumbled as the smell of food wafted towards him, and he eagerly picked up the crisp bacon. "No, I don't mind," he answered, "as long as I can keep eating." Margret began with the usual questions and answers, but then she placed the clipboard on the table.

"I think I want to ask different kinds of questions and be less formal about it." She glanced at Joe as he devoured his breakfast, paying particular attention to him as he licked his lips. "I'm glad you like the food."

He sipped his coffee and picked up another piece of bread. "It's really good."

"Joe," she began, "I'm going to ask you more personal questions as if I'm really trying to get to know you. Are you comfortable with that?"

"Sure. I don't think I'll remember anything, but let's try it."

"What's your favorite childhood memory?" He looked at her but had no answer.

"What school did you go to?" Joe crammed more bacon into his mouth and shook his head.

"What do you do for work?" He paused and looked pensive.

"Maybe something where I need a truck. Maybe something outside?"

Margret nodded thoughtfully. "What's your wife's name?" Joe stopped chewing and looked at her.

"My wife's name? I'm not married, Margret."

"How do you know for sure?" she leaned forward in her chair as she asked.

"I guess I don't really know for sure, but I'm not wearing a wedding ring. I also think that if I had a wife, I would remember her." He held his coffee cup in midair as he thought about it. Margret watched him as he wondered about her question, and then she grew excited as she spoke.

"Joe, I have a surprise for you! We're going to be moving all the patients out of this freezing cold hospital to the village. There's an empty hotel there with a working kitchen and rooms for all of us. And best of all, it has electricity. We'll be warm. I think seeing new things and having new experiences will help you regain your memory. What do you think?"

"That's incredible news! How will we get there? Will the other patients be okay traveling? When are we going?" He looked up at her with hopeful eyes. Margret loved that he was concerned for the other patients. It showed what a kind heart he had. She sat back and responded in her methodical way.

"We're going to begin the move today. They brought in some warm clothes with the breakfast run to help keep you all warm. Most everyone will ride on snowmobiles, but dogsleds will be used for the patients who can't sit up for that length of time. It'll be slow going, but by tonight, you'll be in a warm bed, and you'll have more good food. Also, there's a great fireplace in the lobby that always has a roaring fire."

Joe's head jerked up. "Oh, Moses. I love that fireplace. There's also a leather chair. I like to drink my coffee there."

Margret stared at him. "Do you realize what you just said? I think you remembered something." She watched him closely as he searched his memories.

"I can see it." He closed his eyes and concentrated. "It's a big, comfortable oversized leather chair in front of the fireplace. The fire crackles and smells good. It's one of my favorite places. But I don't know where it is." He opened sad eyes.

Margret stood up, walked over to him, and placed her hand on his. "It's a great start. I think you're really starting to remember." She took his empty tray and walked to the door. "Keep thinking about that fireplace and how it made you feel, what the fire sounded like, and what it smelled like. I'm proud of you. I'll be back in a little bit. I have lots to do to get ready for this move today."

He watched her leave and sat up in his bed, pulling the covers in tightly around him. He reached for his notepad and began trying to describe the fireplace and leather chair that were stuck in his memories.

After an hour of thinking and trying to remember details, his head ached, and his eyelids were heavy. He put the notepad and pen on his table and closed his eyes.

"Hey, Joe, it's time to go," Margret shook him awake. He frowned and groaned sleepily.

"I guess I fell asleep. What's going on?" he asked.

"You're up next for the snowmobile ride. I have some warm clothes here for you. There's a pair of ski pants, jeans, thermal under-wear, an anorak, a scarf, gloves, a wool sweater, and a ski mask. Can you handle this yourself?"

Joe nodded. As soon as the door closed behind Margret, he picked up the pile and began to dress. Once outfitted for the trip, he looked in the mirror. He turned slowly around, barely recognizing himself. The blue scrubs had been his uniform for the length of his stay, but he was glad to see them go. He felt warm and ready. He looked around the room and grabbed his hat, his notepad, pen, sunglasses, and map of the world, leaving the puzzle for someone else.

Margret walked in, gulped, and asked shakily, "Are you ready?" *Wow, he looked good.*

He nodded, looked around the room again, took the list of things remembered from the wall, and followed her out. The rooms leading off the cold hallway were empty and littered with discarded blankets and scrubs.

"How long will it take to get there?" he asked as the lobby came into view.

"It's about a two-hour trip. They'll be taking it slower than normal out of precaution for the patients. It'll be cold, but just keep thinking how much warmer the hotel will be, and you'll be fine. You'll have a helmet, of course, and you'll be on the third snowmobile, right behind the other two. Do you have your gloves?" Margret spoke quickly as she went through the procedures and instructions until he stopped her.

"Margret, are you worried?" He regarded her anxious eyes.

She stopped walking and took a breath. "I'm sorry; I guess I am a bit nervous. It's treacherous out there, and I want to make sure you get there safely." She looked up at him, her eyes radiating fear. She was scared.

Joe reached out to her and rubbed his hands along her arms. "Hey, I'm going to be just fine. I'll see you tonight at the hotel, and I'll meet you in front of the fire." He locked onto her eyes. "Thank you for taking such good care of me."

Margret looked up at him. She moved towards him slowly, slid her arms around his waist and lay her head on his chest. "Be safe out there and hold on tight. I'll see you tonight." She wanted to stay with him in that hallway that didn't seem cold anymore. She pulled away and reluctantly led him to the front of the building. It was time.

Joe held on tight to the driver. The wind was brutal, but the scenery was stunning. Snow sparkled as far as he could see, and he was grateful for the goggles he wore. There were no trees, and the mountains in the distance stood against a gray sky. The snowmobile maneuvered over mounds of snow, around frozen ponds, and through rock formations. Joe was impressed with the driver's skills; nevertheless, he was careful not to let go. Every so often the driver pointed to polar bears and caribou, and Joe spent the time looking for more. He spied several muskoxen along the way, and he marveled that he knew what they were.

They made it to the hotel with no problems. The nurses who had been transported earlier helped him off the snowmobile and led him carefully inside. He was stiff from the ride and was glad for their help. They directed him into the building and to his room where he took off his coat, ski pants, and boots. A nurse brought him hot tea, and he sipped it while resting in an old, but comfortable, rocking chair.

"It feels so good and warm in here. Thank you for the tea." He took another sip and held the mug appreciatively.

"You're welcome. Take it easy for a while. We'll let you know when dinner is ready."

He sighed with pleasure and looked around the room. A desk, two chairs, a dresser, and a large mirror filled the space, and the bed invited a nap, but he was most interested in the bathroom. The prospect of a hot shower was thrilling. How long had it been since he'd had a hot shower? He couldn't remember. He finished his tea, took off his heavy clothes, and made his way to the bathroom. He remained motionless as the hot water pounded his back. It was instant therapy, and as he stood under the water, he closed his eyes and thanked God for safe passage, warmth, and shelter. He fist-bumped the air and looked heavenward. *Thank you, Lord. Thank you!*

Margret sat waiting in front of the fire. Awkward feelings arose as she thought of him, and she reminded herself that she was his nurse. She cared for him and wanted him to regain his memory. Didn't she? She knew he would eventually, but right now, she was the most important person to him, and she liked that. If he remembered his life, would he leave?

Joe walked into the lobby and saw Margret sitting in front of the fire. She had an intense look on her face. He wasn't sure if he should intrude, and he paused. As he watched her, something wiggled around in his brain, something important that was almost there, but he just couldn't bring it to the surface. He shook his head and continued towards her.

"Hi, Margret, may I sit down?"

Margret looked up at him and took in a deep breath. He had showered and shaved, and he looked like a model for an outdoor magazine. Copper highlights gleamed in his clean hair, and he seemed different, rather confident and sure. *But how could that be? He doesn't even know who he is. With his hair down to his shoulders, no one would even recognize him at home, but he sure seems different, almost self-assured. Will he still need me?* She stopped her daydreaming and answered him. "Yes, please join me." She stared at him, noticing how good he looked in the new jeans and sweater. She had to look away.

Joe sat down in the chair beside her. "Now, this is nice: a warm building and a fire. I'm so grateful we were able to make the trip. Thank you."

"I'm very glad, myself. It's nice to be warm. Maybe this will help your memory. We'll still have to work on it, you know." Margret squeezed his hand.

He held onto her hand and looked at her intently. "Thank you for taking such good care of me. You've been away from your family, and you've worked hard to help us all. I won't forget it." He laughed as he realized what he had said, and she began to laugh as well.

"I hope you won't forget it!" Margret replied. "It has been my pleasure to take care of you." She squeezed his hand and then covered it with hers.

Song: *Think* by Aretha Franklin

Chapter 70

GREENLAND

Joe lay in the comfortable new bed, grateful for the warmth. As he relaxed, he retraced the day in his mind. He had traveled hours across the snowy plains on a snowmobile and had seen Greenland's natural beauty and incredible wildlife. He had showered in hot water, and he had enjoyed the warmth of a fire with Margret. He was grateful, but he knew his life lay beyond this frozen land. Would he ever find his way there? His eyes were suddenly leaden, and he couldn't hold them open any longer. Sleep came swiftly.

He sits on a couch next to a woman with the most intense green eyes. He reaches over and holds her hand, intertwining his fingers with hers. Rain patters gently outside the cabin, enveloping their world. He looks at her with love, and she returns the look with a sly smile. He watches in surprise as she pulls on boots, throws the door open, and runs outside. The rain stops, and she stands still among the pine trees. She looks up at the stars, and he walks slowly to her. He touches her shoulder, she turns to him, and his hand caresses her cheek. She looks up into his eyes and smiles. It's inviting, welcoming. The attraction is mutual. He leans down and gently brushes her lips with his. He pulls back to gaze at her with wonder and then kisses her again.

Joe woke up and tried to recall every moment of the dream. The woman seemed familiar somehow. Was she important to him? He had kissed her, after all. He pushed back the covers and walked to the window. The snow-covered landscape seemed even colder and more desolate than ever. He wanted pine trees, warm weather, and a woman with the most enchanting eyes. He wanted to sit with her in front of a fire and feel at home in her arms. *Does she miss me too? Where is this mystery woman? Have I dreamed of her before?* He lay back down and sought her face again as he closed his eyes.

Song: *Will you Still Love Me?* by Chicago

Chapter 71

Celeste was anxious about Luca's return. After seeing Olivia to the airport, Bert and Daisy came to mind, and she decided a quick trip would help calm her nerves.

Twenty minutes later she pulled up in front of Bert and Daisy's store. She rolled up the windows, straightened her hair in the rear-view mirror, and hopped out of the truck. Unsure of why she was really there, she stopped and considered. Maybe she was hoping for some good advice. A smile and a hug would be great as well.

The bell chimed as she opened the door, and she heard a voice from the back say, "Come on in!" Celeste entered, happy to be back in this welcoming place. She loved the chaotic décor as well as the feeling of comfort. As she wandered through the store, she relaxed. She picked up an item here and there, smelled a few candles, and made her way slowly to the rear of the store. Daisy saw her and called her name.

"Celeste! Bert, look, it's Celeste. Well, honey, come on over here. How are you? Bert, bring her some water, dear." Celeste embraced the older woman. She smelled like cinnamon and vanilla, and she wondered if cookies were baking somewhere.

"Daisy, how are you? It's so nice to see you! Hello, Bert!" Celeste accepted the glass.

"We were hoping you'd come today, honey," Daisy said as she smiled broadly and smoothed her apron.

"You were?" Celeste looked at them both quizzically. "I had the strangest feeling all morning that I needed to be here today. What's going on?"

Daisy nodded and reached for her hand. "Walk with me. I think my cookies are about ready to come out of the oven."

Celeste was led to the kitchen at the back of the store. She marveled at the coziness of the space: a mixture of warmth, light, and peace. A sudden realization made her pause. *This place reminds me of being home with my parents in Atlanta. I think the feeling is contentment.* She missed her parents desperately, but she now looked at Daisy and wondered if God had placed these wonderful people in her life for a reason. If so, she was incredibly grateful. She sat at the table and took a bite of the warm cookie Daisy placed before her. She closed her eyes over the deliciousness of it.

"Daisy, this is the best cookie I've ever had."

Daisy added another one to her plate as she refilled her glass. "Go ahead, now. Tell me what's bothering you." The older woman stood in front of her with her sweet face and kind eyes. Celeste was startled. She had felt such peace, but now she was hurled back into the unknown. Her feelings ricocheted through her heart, and then escaped through her eyes. Daisy held her gently until she had cried herself out. "Now, tell me all about it."

Celeste dabbed at her tears with a pretty floral napkin. She told Daisy about Luca's declaration of love and about the arctic news update. She expressed her feelings, her fears, her trepidations about Luca, and her love for Sergio. She talked until she was spent. "This may sound strange, but it's like there's a scar on my heart. I want it to heal, but I also don't want to forget that it's there." She exhaled. "I don't know. I think that's all for now."

Daisy stood in front of her and nodded. "You're having to run that place, lead the people, be professional, and then deal with the brother who wants to be your sweetheart, all while missing the love of your life who's lost in the Arctic." Daisy sat down beside Celeste and took her hands. "That's a lot for you to be carrying. No wonder you needed to come here today. You needed to unload in a safe place. Now, it seems to me that no one should be asking you to make any kind of a decision about your life while you're mourning your man. If he asks you any questions along those lines tomorrow, you just tell him you don't have an answer and you just might never have an answer. In fact, he may need to stay in Colorado and give you space. Honey, the storms up there in the Arctic have been the worst they've ever seen. They started early in winter, and they're still raging. There is no connectivity, the news is spotty, and many places have no electricity. You cannot depend on the news right now when it comes to this. There are too many unanswered questions. You have the right to your own timing when making decisions of this magnitude." Daisy looked at Celeste and then pulled her into a bear hug.

Celeste hugged her back, and then she began to laugh. "I feel like the weight of the world has been lifted from my shoulders. Thank you, Daisy." Bert walked in and reached for a cookie. Daisy saw him and tried to swat his hand away.

"Only one, Bert, we can't be eating all the cookies. We're sending them home with this dear girl." Bert grinned, took one cookie, and headed back out to the store.

"Now," she said, her face pensive, "I want you to have something."

Daisy led Celeste towards the front of the store and stopped at a shelf with painted wooden signs of all sizes and colors. Each had a Bible verse written on it. Daisy looked at them thoughtfully and then chose a small black one with white calligraphy that said,

"Trust in the Lord with all your heart and
lean not on your own understanding."
— Proverbs 3:5.

She handed it to Celeste and pressed it into her hands. "Trust in the Lord, sweet girl. When you are anxious, give him your burdens and trust in him." Celeste thanked Daisy and hugged her again as they heard Bert calling.

"Daisy, honey, a bus just pulled up."

"Could you use some help on the floor?" Celeste asked.

"Well, what a wonderful idea. Yes, that would be great. You can just wander around straightening stuff, and if someone has a question, you just answer it or send them my way." Daisy hurried to the front as Celeste slipped the wooden sign in her pocket.

Working in the store turned out to be a terrific idea. Celeste had never taken the time to look at the entire inventory. Now she worked her way from the back to the front. She looked at Bert's woodworking designs, candles, jewelry, scarves, notepads, books, purses, prayer stones, picture frames, paintings, little pine trees, stuffed bears, even statues of waterfalls with running water. She answered a few questions here and there, but mostly she lost herself in the sea of merchandise. It was good medicine for her, but she also began formulating an idea. When the bus pulled away, Celeste headed to the register with a sweater, two scarves, and a candle.

"I loved being here with you both. Thank you. This place is a treasure."

"Thank you for helping us. It's a big store, and we don't always see every person who happens to be wandering around. You can come by anytime." Daisy winked at her and placed her items, as well as a tin of cookies, in a blue cloth bag. She looked deep into Celeste's eyes. "You are strong, and you are going to be okay. All shall be well."

Celeste nodded. "Thank you for everything. I will come back soon, and I'll keep in touch."

She felt lighter and happier, and as she hopped up into the truck, she called Luca. When he didn't answer, she took a deep breath and left a message, "Luca, I don't think you need to come tomorrow. I will not answer any major questions right now, and I think I can run the Inn well by myself. If you still feel the need to travel, I am happy to talk about business, but that's all. I cannot talk about anything personal right now. Please give me time to process everything that's going on. Thank you." She hung up feeling proud of herself. She was more courageous than she had been earlier, and she knew Daisy had inspired her. She turned up the music, rolled down the windows, and sang loudly as she drove home.

Song: *Best of My Love* by The Emotions

Chapter 72

Celeste sat at her desk running numbers and researching plans. She had an idea, and she wanted to create a written proposal before presenting it to Luca. Maybe the word proposal was the wrong word. The plan was exciting, and it gave her a small reprieve from her grief. She wandered into the Inn's lobby to observe the guests. Some were drinking coffee, others were relaxing near the fireplace, and some were looking at the trail map. We need something more, and I think this idea will be perfect. She walked eagerly back to her office to call Bert and Daisy.

Celeste presented the idea to the two storeowners, and they loved it at once. Daisy was so excited, she bubbled with multiple ideas, and Celeste jotted them down as she spoke. As soon as the call ended, she dove into the vast online inventory, amazed at the quality and the quantity of the items.

The next morning, Bert and Daisy arrived at the Inn, their joy for the project lighting their eyes and widening their grins. Celeste welcomed them with hugs and then showed them to a table. The barista took their coffee orders, and Celeste recapped her idea.

"After being in your wonderful store and working with the tourists, I wondered if we could have a smaller General Store here at the Inn. It would be your inventory, but we could help sell it. I think the guests would love to have a place to shop, to buy souvenirs, to pick up a sweater or scarf if they're cold, or just to wander around in their spare time. We would hire staff to work the register and to restock, but the entire inventory would come from your shop." Bert and Daisy sipped their coffees and sampled the snacks before them as they listened intently to Celeste.

"I just need to create a pitch for Luca, but I wanted to have all my facts straight and of course ask the two of you before I present it to him. What do you think?"

Bert and Daisy reached for each other's hands. "We love the idea," Daisy exclaimed, "and we can't wait to begin. We can just take half our current inventory and clean out the store a bit. We might not even be able to tell!" Daisy laughed and Bert joined her.

"That's the truth," Bert said as he picked up another brownie. He held onto it and continued, "She loves to buy all the pretty things, and we just keep filling up the place." He turned to Daisy with smiling eyes. "Remember those little rocks you bought with Scripture on them? You loved them so much that you bought the entire lot. We had rocks everywhere! We eventually made a rock garden there were so many!" He popped the brownie into his mouth as Daisy laughed.

"I still love those rocks, and we've almost sold out!" She giggled and squeezed his hand. Celeste watched them happily, their joy tugging at her heart. She wanted a lifelong loving relationship like the one they shared.

"I'd like to show you where I think it could go," Celeste said as she stood up. "Would you like to see the space?" She led them to the far side of the lobby and explained how she would have a storefront built into the archway of the wall. "It will look like it has always been here. It will have a General Store sign just like yours in town with all the charm of the original, maybe with little trees full of lights placed in front. I'm imagining candles to make it smell good, soft music playing, and of course your wonderful items to sell. There's even an outside door in the back that will help with deliveries. I wish it was already here!"

Daisy's eyes sparkled. "It's a wonderful idea. Let's do it! What do you say, Bert?"

"I'm in!" He replied with a grin. They talked about specifics, and when they left an hour later, they were excited to begin. Celeste walked back to her office to add the handwritten notes to her presentation. She knew Luca would call on Tuesday for the weekly report, and she wanted to present it to him then. She hadn't heard from him since she had left the message. The thought of his reaction concerned her a bit, but she was too excited to think about it now. She shut her laptop, locked her office, and hurried to her room to change clothes for a run.

Luca's plane landed, and he called for a car through an app. He knew Celeste didn't want him there, but he needed to see her. The three-hour flight didn't give him enough time to decide what to say, but honestly, he was just hoping the words would present themselves. He rode along the familiar route and thought of her. He loved her, but maybe the best approach was one in which he agreed with her. He shifted in his seat as he considered the plan. He wouldn't say anything about his feelings; instead, he would work with her, talk about the Inn, and enjoy just being with her. Maybe she would find his indifference appealing.

Celeste finished her run and watched the sun set from the gazebo. She wondered if Sergio ever watched the sun set and decided she'd ask him in tonight's letter. She closed her eyes and remembered being in his strong arms in this very spot. *When he held me, the world fell away: the grief, the loneliness, and the fear that had been bottled up inside me for so long. His kiss was electric, and when his lips met mine, nothing else mattered.* She sighed and took her time walking the grounds. The air was crisp and cool, the sky was colorful, and the pine trees whispered to her in the wind. *Sergio, if you were here, I know you'd hold my hand and walk with me. I trust you will be one day.* She looked up at the sky and whispered a prayer to the one who made all things possible.

Making her way to the Inn, she walked through the tunnel and towards the back door. Her peaceful feeling suddenly turned to unease as she caught a glimpse of Luca. He stood in the kitchen laughing with the cooks.

What? Didn't he get my message? Slipping by unseen, she made it to her room without having to talk to anyone. She collapsed on the couch, sighed, and whispered, "Sergio, I need you to be here right now. I can talk to you more easily than I can to anyone. I love you, and I miss you desperately. Your brother is here, and he thinks he loves me. I don't really think he does; I just think he misses you, and he finds solace in me. It's time to come home now. Please, Sergio, please." She reached her hand out and imagined him reaching out to hold hers.

Song: *Everyday* **by Phil Collins**

Chapter 73

GREENLAND

Joe spent the day working through cognitive tests. The doctor gave him simple recall exercises to assess his thinking, his memory, and his judgment.

As the doctor checked off boxes on the chart, he explained, "You're doing very well. Everything seems fine, except your long-term memory. You are healthy, and I do think your memory will return."

Joe looked at him expectantly. "Thanks. How much longer will it take?"

The doctor placed his pen in his coat pocket. "We just don't know. Each case of amnesia is different. It might help to try to remember the day of your accident, what you were doing outside, who you were with, and so on. I know those memories might be painful, but I think it could help bring back all of your memories. I'll be back to see you tomorrow."

Joe waited until the door closed and then punched his fist into the pillow and shouted, "I try to remember that day all the time! I try, and I try, and I try! I just can't remember!" He crumpled onto the bed and rested his head in his hands. "I'm trying."

Margret rushed into Joe's room after hearing him shout. She knelt down beside him and asked, "Are you okay?"

"I just want to remember." He punched his pillow again, but this time with less force. She wrapped her arms around him. He grabbed on tight as if the action would save his life.

"It's okay. Just breathe," she whispered in his ear.

He exhaled. "Thanks. I just lost it, didn't I?" He felt Margret's hands rubbing his back to soothe him, and he relaxed. "I'll just keep breathing, like you said. One breath after another." He closed his eyes but then pulled away.

Margret missed his warmth. Her arms had felt so good around him, but now the emptiness felt cold and lonely. She clasped her hands together and cleared her throat. "I'm glad I was here for you. Would you like to go downstairs? We're going to play some music and games." She looked at him hopefully.

Joe nodded, and she left the room, closing the door quietly behind her. His emotions were raw. He needed something to divert his attention. Maybe the music and games were a good idea. He couldn't go anywhere else until he knew where to go, and besides, all the roads were closed. He couldn't call anyone until he knew who to call. But why, he wondered, was no one looking for him?

He stood up, threw the pillow back onto the bed, and walked into the bathroom to take another shower. He didn't need it, but he knew the hot water would massage his body and reduce stress. The pounding water did relax him, and as he stood there, he marveled at how the little things could make such a big difference in his life. He closed his eyes and took another long breath. As he exhaled, he thought about breath and its life-giving properties. A sudden memory shone through his foggy brain. He remembered talking to a woman on the phone. He had told her he missed her like breath. He opened his eyes, and his mouth turned into a sideways grin. *Do I love someone? Someone I miss so much that I compare the loss to breathlessness?* He shook his head, turned off the water, and emerged from the shower. *If I love someone and someone loves me, then no matter what we're going through, there is hope.* He smiled into the mirror, closed his eyes, and thanked God. He soon headed down to the lobby in a much better mood, ready to hang out with his friends. Someone loved him.

Margret sat near the fireplace with the patients and some of the nurses. She had brought snacks and sodas from the kitchen, and she had found a game of Pictionary. Joe joined the group, and Margret watched him carefully. He nodded to her, and she smiled at him. Margret's glances landed and lingered on Joe throughout the evening, and she told herself it was solely for professional reasons.

Joe soon discovered he was not an artist. His team had no idea what any of his squiggles were supposed to be, and the laughter was good medicine for all. The fun helped them forget about their troubles, if only for a little while.

As the game was nearing the end, Margret took the snack bowl into the kitchen for a refill, but when she returned, everyone was heading upstairs for bed.

"Goodnight, Margret. Thank you for the great evening!" The patients called out to her and waved as their chatter continued up the stairs.

Joe sat near the fire, and she turned to him. "Did you enjoy the evening?" She placed the bowl of pretzels on the table and sat down beside him.

He shrugged his shoulders. "It was a great night. There's so much to worry and wonder about, but tonight, I laughed. I think it was just what I needed."

Margret patted his hand. "I'm glad it made you happy. I think I'll put on some music." She walked over to an old record player, looked through the albums, and chose one she liked.

He rested his head on the back of the couch and stretched his legs. "I think music is important to me. It's as if the songs are messages of some sort. I wish I could figure it out."

"I'm sure you will. We just need to give it time." Margret reclaimed her spot on the couch and rested her hand upon his. She hoped her hand would send the message she wanted to convey.

Song: *Give a Little Bit* by Supertramp

Chapter 74

NORTH CAROLINA

Celeste made it through an early morning run, breakfast, and a few hours at her desk before she saw Luca. She wondered where he was and why he hadn't checked in with her. If she hadn't seen him yesterday in the kitchen, she wouldn't have known he was even there. She was reviewing a spreadsheet when he knocked on her door.

"Hello, Celeste, may I come in?" He leaned against the door watching her.

"Hi, Luca, yes, of course." He sat down in one of the chairs near the window and chatted happily about the weather while motioning for her to join him. She was curious and a bit anxious about what he was going to say and watched him closely. At his gesture towards the chair, she swallowed a sigh and sat down opposite him.

"So, tell me what's been happening. Any new updates?" Luca looked genuinely interested. His friendliness and businesslike demeanor confused Celeste, but she realized this was a good opportunity to tell him about The General Store. She retrieved the plans from her desk and explained her idea to bring Bert and Daisy's merchandise to the Inn. Luca held back a smile as he listened to her excitement. He liked the idea well enough, but he loved her enthusiasm. He looked at the plans, asked questions, and made comments, but mostly he listened.

"I know it's your place, not mine, but I really hope you like this idea. What do you think?" Celeste asked breathlessly.

Luca leaned forward. "I love it. Let's make it happen."

"Thank you! I'm so excited about this new addition! I won't let you down. Would you like to see where I think it should go?"

Luca stood up and looked at her. He loved seeing the joy in her eyes. "I haven't seen you this happy in a long time, Celeste. Sure, show me the spot." Luca struggled to contain his emotions. All he wanted to do was gather her up in his arms and hold her, and his lips ached to touch hers, but he had to be smart. He had to wait until she was ready. He grabbed a cold bottle of water from the mini fridge and followed her into the lobby.

Celeste invited Daisy to spend a day with her at the Inn. She planned to show her the building, the grounds, and the gardens, but she really just wanted to spend time with her friend. She needed the wisdom, the strength, and the fun that Daisy brought to her life. Celeste thought about Daisy as she worked at her desk. *She's like a mother figure to me. I really look up to her.* She thanked God for the friends he had sent into her life. *I am so grateful. Thank you!*

Daisy arrived the next morning with her signature homemade cookies. She hopped out of her car with a newfound energy, feeling almost young again. The excitement of the second store was giving her purpose. She looked to the sky as she walked to the front door, thanking God for Celeste.

Celeste greeted her with a hug and happily accepted the

cookies. She turned to the coffee bar, but Daisy paused. "Everything okay, Daisy?"

"Let's go for a walk," Daisy insisted. "I have so much energy, and I'd like to see the grounds."

"Great idea. Let's go." Celeste handed the cookie tin to the barista and grabbed her phone.

They walked outside through the back door and into the gardens. The paths were bordered by flowering splashes of color and with stone benches for sitting. Small gurgling fountains had been creatively positioned for quiet reflection. It was a lovely place for rest, for contemplation, or for prayer.

"My goodness, this is beautiful. If I lived here, I'd walk these paths every day. Could we sit on that bench over there? I want to look at all this beauty." Daisy led Celeste to the bench, and they sat down. "Now, this is nice." She watched a couple walk by. They were looking up at the tress, observing the birds and trying to name them.

"Do you ever see couples holding hands anymore?" Daisy asked without giving Celeste time to answer. "When people hold hands, there's complete trust, there's connection, and there's mutual affection. You see, I love Bert, but I also like him. I enjoy being with him, and handholding keeps us connected. We hold onto each other, we hold each other up, we stay beside each other. When you hold hands, neither one of you is in front of or behind the other. You walk side by side, walking through life together."

Celeste sighed. "Sergio and I used to hold hands. It felt so safe and comfortable to hold onto each other, and when our fingers linked together, it felt perfect." Daisy nodded and Celeste continued. "When Sergio was going away, he told me that whenever I needed him, I should place my hand out and imagine him holding it. I hope he does the same wherever he is now."

The older woman cleared her throat. She took Celeste's hand in hers as she began to speak. "When love is deep and true, we grieve when it's gone. You're grieving the absence of this love that filled you with so much joy. I think you should continue to place your hand out and imagine Sergio holding it, and maybe one day, you'll hold hands again." She closed her eyes and took a breath as she remembered what Celeste had told her about her past. She opened her eyes, squeezed Celeste's hand, and continued with quiet strength.

"I understand this is extra hard because of your past, and I know you feel alone. You haven't been abandoned by this man, and most importantly, you will never be forsaken or abandoned by God." She looked knowingly at Celeste. Then she tilted her head and asked, "Do you remember the wood block I gave you with the Bible verse on it?" She paused as Celeste nodded and then continued. "It said, 'Trust in the Lord with all your heart and lean not on your own understanding.' You know that's Proverbs 3:5, but do you remember what comes next in verse 6?"

Celeste knew it immediately, as it was one of her favorites. "Yes. It says, 'In all your ways submit to him, and he will make your paths straight.'"

Daisy patted Celeste's hand and looked at her with a matter-of-fact expression. "That's right, dear one. Trust God with all you are, don't get caught up in your understanding, acknowledge God in every aspect of your life, and God will make your paths straight."

Celeste nodded at her friend. They sat in silence and looked at the beauty all around them. Celeste glanced at Daisy and noticed her eyes were closed. Maybe she was praying. Maybe she was giving thanks for Bert, the beauty of the earth, or possibly for the new store.

She closed her eyes as well. *Thank you, Lord. I am grateful for all you've given me. I will trust in you. I pray you will lay the paths straight before me so that I can follow them.*

Out of the blue, a song title rushed into her thoughts. She pulled out her phone, texted it to Sergio, and then glanced at Daisy. Her eyes were still closed, but she had a knowing look on her face, as if God were whispering secrets to her.

"Well, dear one," Daisy began, as she shifted on the bench and opened her eyes. "Let's go have some cookies and some of your good coffee. Shall we go back inside?" She latched onto Celeste, and together, they made their way back to the Inn.

Song: *Missing you* **by Dan Fogelberg**

Chapter 75

GREENLAND

Joe looked down at his hand and saw Margret holding it. It didn't feel right, and he pulled it away to cover a yawn. "I think I'm a bit tired and need to get to sleep. Thank you for a fun evening."

Margret stopped him. "Hey, I'm sorry for trying to hold your hand. I just feel very close to you after all this time, and I'd like to get to know you better."

He turned to her. "Margret, I appreciate everything you've done for me, but I don't even know who I am yet. Is my name even Joe? I really don't know. I don't think it's a good idea to get involved." But even as he spoke, he looked at her and noticed how pretty her eyes were. There was a sparkle in them that intrigued him. Margret noticed him looking and placed her hand over his again. This time, he left it there.

"I don't want to rush you, but maybe I can help you remember who you are." She looked into his eyes and moved closer, and then she abruptly kissed him. They were both startled. Margret bubbled with nervous laughter, and Joe winced.

"I'm so sorry, Joe," she giggled, "I just couldn't help myself."

Joe stood up but wasn't quite sure what to say. He wasn't even sure how he felt, but maybe her presence really could help him. He took a breath, slid his hand through his long hair, and tried to think.

Margret apologized again. She joined him, placed her arms around his waist, and rested her head on his chest.

"I'll be here to help you remember," she whispered. He stood still, not knowing what to do, but then she felt his arms moving up to embrace her and she snuggled in closer. She felt comfortable in his arms, but she wanted more of him. She slowly pulled away, looked up into his eyes, and then gently touched his lips with hers. Joe didn't respond, but Margret took a chance and continued her pursuit. This time she kissed him fully, gaining courage, and liking the way his lips felt on hers. Joe remembered these feelings from somewhere in his past, and he relaxed as his body answered hers. Passion flared between them, and they responded to one other as if their embrace would take them far away from the ice, the cold, and the memory loss.

Margret pulled away first and then rested her head on his chest again. His heartbeat matched hers in pounding rhythm, and she sighed. Was she in love with him, or did she just need to feel held? She didn't know, but she didn't want the feeling to end.

Joe held on tight, his arms encircling her. The warmth and intimacy of the moment unlocked a door that led straight to his heart. He didn't understand it yet, but he knew he wanted to walk through it. He nuzzled her hair and then whispered in her ear, "Celeste… I've missed you so much."

Song: *Let My Love Open the Door* by Pete Townsend

Chapter 76

Margret froze as his words registered. She wondered if he realized what he had just said. Those were not the words she had hoped to hear after such a passionate embrace. She had wanted him to whisper her name. Instead, the passion seemed to spark the memory of a woman named Celeste. Maybe it was someone from his very distant past, someone from his younger years. She could hope, anyway.

He pulled away and smiled at her. He kissed her lightly on the lips and touched her cheek. "I think I'll go to sleep now. I'll see you in the morning." He turned and headed for the stairs. She waited for him to turn around, realizing what he'd said, but he didn't. Margret sat down slowly on the couch with a sad sigh. She knew what she would have to do in the morning. She would have to ask about Celeste. But tonight, she just wanted to remember being held in his arms and the feeling of his lips on hers.

Celeste said goodbye to Daisy in the parking lot and then turned around to see Luca watching her.

"Hi, Luca, I had a great meeting with Daisy. She's excited about the plan."

Luca looked interested. "I have some business to talk to you about, and I thought a walk would be nice. Are you game?" Celeste glanced at her phone to look at the time, nodded, and they headed for the trails. He walked a bit in front of her as the trail narrowed, but he continued to talk in a business-like manner, turning his head so that she could hear him. "I like seeing you so happy about the General Store plans. I'm curious to see how business goes, and if it is a success, it may be something to think about for our Colorado resort. There's space there, and I think it might be a good idea. We could also incorporate some local Colorado products for that venue." Celeste listened excitedly and was sure Daisy and Bert would be over the moon about extending it to Colorado.

"It's imperative that this launch goes well in order for the next one to succeed too. I have a feeling that with you in charge, it will go very well indeed," Luca stopped abruptly and turned to her. "You're doing a fantastic job."

Celeste halted to keep from running into him and then glowed with the compliment. "Thank you, Luca. I have to ask, though, if you were upset by the voicemail I left on your phone."

Luca shook his head. "Celeste, I understand how much you miss Sergio, and I'm here for you. This is a business deal, and we're in business together. I can't imagine a more capable person to run the Inn. I will enjoy your company while I'm here and that's all. Now, tell me more about the store." Luca looked at her sincerely, and Celeste trusted that he meant what he said. For a second, she tried to imagine what it would be like to hold hands with him as they walked, but she shook her head and knew she could never feel that way about him. She was connected to him in business and in friendship, and she knew she did not want to be together with him in any other way.

Luca turned and pointed to the hill. "Are you up for a climb?"

Celeste shrugged. "Sure." She wondered what he really wanted, but she knew she was definitely not up for climbing into any kind of relationship with him.

As they walked, Luca wished he could simply reach out and hold her hand, but the time wasn't right. He had to play it cool. He had to wait.

Song: *All I Want is You* **by U2**

Chapter 77

GREENLAND

Joe lay in bed thinking about the events of the evening. It had been fun, but then it had turned into something passionate and breathless. He wasn't sure how he felt about kissing Margret. Something in his brain told him there was more to it, but he couldn't get there. He had a feeling that when he did remember his life and who he was, it would all come back like a floodgate bursting free. Kissing her had been exciting, but something was missing. Even though the warmth, the passion, and the closeness had felt very good, he didn't think hers were the lips he needed. *I miss lips I can't even remember.* He tossed and turned, worrying about what he had done while also remembering how good it had felt. He imagined his arms around hers and his lips… *Stop it, man,* he said to himself as he bunched up his pillow and put a fist into it.

His thoughts and emotions kept him wide awake, and he realized staying in bed was useless. He made his way quietly downstairs to the kitchen. He knew just where the tea and snacks were, and they sounded like the best option at the moment. He turned on a small light, put water on to boil, and grabbed a bag of cookies from behind the soup cans. Then he picked up a magazine from the table and leafed through it as he waited on the water. It was a travel magazine, one that presented hotel and resort options from around the world.

It also held product advertisements, recipes, travel quizzes, and pictures of luxurious places to stay, from Las Vegas to the Maldives. He studied each picture, wondering if he'd ever been to one of these places, but nothing was familiar.

The teapot began whistling, and he jumped up to take it off the burner. This simple snack of tea and cookies would have been a luxury last week, and he was grateful for it now. As he sampled the cookies and sipped the tea, he turned the pages of the magazine and stopped at a picture of a stunning inn nestled in the mountains of North Carolina. He loved the way the building was situated so that every side had a beautiful view of the surrounding mountains. *It's everything this place isn't.* He turned the page to look at the next picture, but it was a resort in Las Vegas that was too showy for his liking. As he turned the pages, he learned about resorts, spas, and hotels from all over the world, and he was glad he'd had a chance to see what different areas really looked like.

I don't think I'm from Las Vegas or the desert because those places don't appeal to me. I don't think I'm from an area with a beach either. He finished his snack and yawned hugely. He wasn't sure he wanted to go upstairs yet, but he cleaned his dishes and turned off the light. He left the magazine where he had found it and returned to his room. Falling asleep almost instantly, he dreamed again of the woman in the rain. This time when he kissed her, he looked into her eyes and whispered the name, *Margret.*

Chapter 78

NORTH CAROLINA AND GREENLAND

Emma, the head barista, watched the comings and goings of the Inn. She could listen to a conversation, collect facts, and make observations from afar. She was proud of her investigative abilities. If anyone wanted to know anything about anyone, she was the one to ask. After all, the coffee bar was very popular, and it was set up in the perfect location to listen and to observe. She believed that by knowing the ins and outs and the drama of day-to-day happenings, she had gained great insight into people's lives. Knowing all the details, she could be helpful and supportive to anyone who needed it.

She loved her job, and she worked as much as possible. She thought Celeste was a terrific manager, but Celeste didn't share much of her private life. Of course, the staff all knew that Luca had proposed, and that she had accepted, but she wondered why they were hiding it and why Celeste didn't wear a ring. She'd never forget the day the housekeeper had told her of Luca and Celeste's celebration in the office. Someone had brought champagne, and they had all toasted. But something wasn't quite right. Celeste didn't look happy around him, and he spent much of his time in Colorado. She would try to ask some probing questions the next time Celeste came for a mocha.

After serving lattes to a group of women who were headed to

town, she saw Luca and Celeste come in from a hike. They were laughing, and they were headed her way.

Celeste couldn't help but smile as she thought about The General Store launch. She greeted the barista happily as she approached. "Hi, Emma, how are you today?"

"I'm well, thank you. How are you two doing?" she asked, hoping for a bit of news.

"Fantastic! We're excited about the future!" Luca exclaimed as he reached for two cold waters. They walked away and Celeste gave her a quick wave. Emma watched them, knowing she finally had information to share with the staff. Doing a little celebratory dance, she grabbed a towel and buffed the bar.

Margret stayed busy with her nursing duties. She had patients to see, even though no one needed much these days. They were all just waiting until the weather got better and for the electricity to be restored at the hospital. She stayed away from Joe as long as she could and asked another nurse to check in on him. She dreaded having to tell him what he had said the night before. She wondered if he remembered. She should never have kissed him, but she just couldn't help it. Not only was he handsome, but it also felt right being in his arms and being held. Plus, he was genuine, even though he didn't know who he was yet. His character shone through anyway. She wandered down to the lobby to check the weather and ran into him on the stairs.

"Hi, Joe. How are you feeling today?" She found the courage to smile and noticed that he smiled back.

"I'm doing okay today. Would you like to sit by the fire?" He turned back around and walked down the stairs with her. "Did you hear it snowed another foot last night? This weather is something else. Is it normal for this time of year?"

Margret sat down and chatted about the average yearly snowfall and the possibilities of the next weather front. It was a safe and mundane conversation. She could talk about it for hours, and it sometimes helped her avoid unpleasant topics.

Joe enjoyed their conversation, but something seemed lacking. He admitted to himself that everything seemed superficial with Margret. He didn't know much about her life besides her family and her dog. He wondered what her dreams were and what made her happy. What was her passion? Maybe she was afraid to open up to him. He decided to try.

At a lull in the conversation, he asked, "Margret, what's your favorite thing to do in the world?"

Margret looked at him blankly. "What?" she asked.

"What makes you happy? If you could do anything in the world, what would it be?"

She looked at him, wondering what he meant. "I guess taking care of people makes me happy. I always wanted to be a nurse." She looked a bit uneasy but continued. "I like it here, this place is my home, and these people are my people. I have no desire to go anywhere else."

He nodded and understood. "I think we must all have our place to be, a place where we call home, where we have people that we love and families that support us. I can't remember mine, but I'm sure I have one."

Margret knew he would never stay in the snowy Arctic. It wasn't his home. She took a deep breath, knowing it was time to tell him. Then she shook her head. But she had to do this, no matter how difficult it was for her.

"Joe," she began, "I want to talk to you about last night. You said something to me, and I need to ask you about it." He turned to her and leaned in a little closer.

"Of course. What is it?" He picked up her hand and waited.

Margret looked at her hand in his. She wanted him to like her and to kiss her again, but she also knew she had to be honest with him.

"Last night was very special, and I loved our time together. I loved kissing you, and right now, it feels really good the way you're holding my hand, but there's something I need to tell you." She squeezed his hand and continued. "Last night when you hugged me goodnight, you called me by another name. You said you missed someone named Celeste." She gulped and watched for his reaction.

Joe continued to hold her hand, but he looked confused. "I called you Celeste? I'm so sorry. I can't imagine how that must have made you feel. Margret, I enjoyed being here with you last night. I don't remember anyone named Celeste." He reached over and pulled her into his arms. He felt bad for having made a nice moment awkward for her. He whispered into her ear, "I'm glad you're here, Margret." She turned in to him, and throwing caution to the wind, lightly brushed her lips against his.

Joe felt her lips on his, but he didn't engage. Instead, he wondered about a woman named Celeste. Could she be the one I love?

Song: *Someday We'll Be Together* by Diana Ross and The Supremes

Chapter 79

"Come to Colorado with me." Celeste choked on her coffee, coughed, and then took a deep breath to calm her nerves. This was unexpected.

"Excuse me?" she replied warily.

"Celeste, if we're going to open a General Store at the Colorado resort, I'd like to get your expertise on-site. How about if we leave tomorrow afternoon? You can stay for a couple of days, get the lay of the land, meet the staff, and then head home. I'd really love to have you see it firsthand."

Celeste was wary about his intentions, but she'd never been to Colorado. Maybe seeing the resort in person was a good idea. She agreed to go, and he quickly made the reservations.

The flight was uneventful. Celeste lost herself in a new book and was oblivious to anything else. Meanwhile, Luca tried to focus on financial spreadsheets but glanced at Celeste as much as possible. Numbers on a spreadsheet couldn't compare to the loveliness of his Celeste. *His Celeste?* He shook his head and berated himself. He shouldn't have those thoughts. He pulled out his phone and played Sudoku to keep his mind occupied.

Once in the Denver airport, they made their way to valet parking where Luca's car was waiting for them. It had been detailed and washed, and it smelled richly of fine leather. Celeste sank down into the luxurious passenger seat and breathed it in.

He tipped the valet, sat down, and turned to her. "I'm glad you like it." He pressed the ignition, and the car roared to life. He felt as though he was coming alive as well, with Celeste by his side. He looked at her again and attempted a normal voice. "Here we go. The resort is located in the mountains an hour away. The drive is beautiful." He kept his eyes on the road while Celeste kept her eyes on the Rocky Mountains.

"The mountains are incredible! There's still so much snow!" Luca looked over at her again. He loved her enthusiasm and joy, and he knew this trip was going to be just what they needed. He tapped cruise control, adjusted his position, and moved his hands lower on the steering wheel. They talked about the mountains, the resort, and all the available outdoor activities, and he made sure not to mention their relationship, or Sergio, or anything that might take away her joy and her excitement.

When they turned off the main road, Luca anticipated her response. He knew she would fall in love with the resort and the grounds the moment she saw them. He also wondered if she would want to move to Colorado with him eventually.

Celeste looked out the window and commented on each new scene. She loved the creek that gurgled alongside the road, the tall wind-swept trees that lined the drive, and the signs urging caution for moose or bears that might be crossing.

Luca pulled into the parking lot and watched her face. Celeste's eyes opened wide. For a moment, she couldn't speak. She had seen the website, but the online pictures paled in comparison. The resort was made of wood, glass, and stone, which gave it a comfortable, but luxurious feel. It had been built to look like part of the mountain itself, the large glass windows reflecting the incredible views. Tall pine trees bordered it, as if they were sentries, displaying an air of importance and strength. The creek wound its way in front, giving the builder reason to construct an arched bridge to the front door. Celeste sat silently taking it all in.

Luca placed his hand on hers. "Would you like to go inside our Colorado resort?" Celeste did not pick up on the insinuation but nodded at the invitation. Luca grabbed the bags from the trunk and opened the car door for her. They walked over the bridge and paused as the front door opened automatically for them.

"It's part of the charm," Luca explained. "There's a sensor under the bridge, and the door opens when it detects weight. Guests love it!" As she continued towards the door, Celeste wondered how they kept the moose and the bears off the bridge.

Luca led Celeste into the lobby and was pleased again at her reaction. She took in the polished mahogany wood, gleaming floor-to-ceiling windows, and leather chairs grouped at small tables for cozy seating. She noticed the thick, textured rugs, and the two-sided gas fireplaces arranged throughout the lobby. It was an immediate effect of warmth, light, and luxury. She was enthralled.

"Celeste, I'd like for you to meet the staff," she heard him saying, and then noticed a group of people standing nearby. She turned her attention to them and shook their hands as she introduced herself. As she chatted with the staff, she noticed how much they all seemed to like and respect Luca.

"I heard you like coffee," said the barista as she approached. "I've made a hot mocha for you and placed a dark chocolate coffee bean on top. It's a little something extra. I hope you enjoy it." Celeste popped the chocolate bean into her mouth.

"Thank you! What a nice welcome. It's delicious!" She vaguely wondered how the barista knew she liked a mocha but forgot all about it as she took a sip.

Celeste put her things away in her room before the grand tour and was thankful for a moment to herself. She thought of Sergio and wished he were there to explore with her. She stood at the window and imagined the two of them holding hands, walking along the creek, hiking the mountain, and kissing behind a tree as the sun set.

Someone knocked at her door, but Celeste didn't respond. She looked out the window and imagined Sergio standing beside her. *I miss you, Sergio. I miss you like breath.*

Luca knocked again, ready to show off the new acquisition he was so proud of. He guided her through the restaurants, the kitchen, and the library. The library was a beautiful, comfortable room lined with books and oversized easy chairs. Celeste wanted to sink into one of them and relax with her book, but Luca pulled her away towards the spa.

The spa was opulent. It boasted a menu of incredible relaxing and rejuvenating options, and Celeste made a mental note to revisit it the next day. Luca laughed at her reaction and led her into his office. Unfortunately, the office was more business-like than cozy, and Celeste didn't think it fit with the rest of the building. It was more contemporary chic, but then again, maybe it was more Luca's style. Celeste sat down in a black chair that wasn't very comfortable but was probably purchased to complement the office décor.

"I can see why you bought this place. It's spectacular!" She looked around the office and noticed how sparse it was. There was nothing personal on his desk or on the credenza. His pencil holder held four pens, his laptop sat at a perfect 90° angle, and there were no papers or folders sitting out. *Strange,* she thought. *Does he have no personal style at all?*

"Yes, it is! Thanks. I've made some changes and added a bit of luxury, and the cooks I hired are really taking it up a notch. The guests seem to love it, and the staff has accepted the changes very well. Wait until you taste the food tonight!" Luca rambled on, but Celeste wondered if he was making too many changes. *After all, it's a mountain resort. Should there be so much luxury? It is nice, though, and really, what do I know about luxurious mountain resorts?* She looked up at him and nodded. Maybe this was the real Luca. Maybe she was getting a glimpse of his own style and vision.

Luca escorted her to dinner, and she complimented the chef on the delicious meal. Afterwards, she excused herself and booked a spa treatment for the next day and then headed outside to explore the grounds. She followed the creek, throwing stones every now and then, and was pleased when one of them skipped along the water. She hiked a trail to an outlook and sat on a bench that had been perfectly placed to simply stare at the view. Pine trees swayed in the breeze, and the lake below shone like glass. Her loneliness seemed deeper here, as it was far away from the places Sergio knew and loved. She stared at the view, blurring it with tears that landed on her lower lashes. She sighed and blotted them with her fingers. *When you love someone, you want to share your experiences. When I see this beautiful view, I immediately want to turn to the one I love and talk to him about it. I want to experience this beauty, this place, and this time with him. I miss my person, my friend, the love of my life.*

"Come back, Sergio. I love you, and I need you beside me." Celeste spoke into the wind, and her words were lifted up and delivered as a whisper to the mountains.

Song: *Dreams* by The Cranberries

Chapter 80

GREENLAND

Joe lay in bed trying to figure out his feelings and emotions. He felt as though he was supposed to know something or remember someone, but the feelings drifted away as soon as they appeared. He heard voices somewhere down the hall, but that seemed normal. He heard drips from the eaves outside, and he wondered if the snow was melting. He then thought about the magazine in the kitchen. He suddenly sat up. *The resort magazine!* He showered, changed clothes, and quickly made his way to the kitchen.

"G' morning, Joe." The cook smiled grandly at him and offered him a muffin.

Joe chose one as he greeted her. "Good morning! Do you still have the resort magazine that was here the other night?" He held his breath while the cook thought.

"Well, I don't know, but you can look in that recycle bin over there." She poured a cup of coffee for him and placed it on the table.

Joe rummaged through the bin and found the magazine. He turned the pages quickly until he found what he was looking for. "This is it!" He grinned at the cook, took a bite of the muffin, and called, "Thank you!" as he ran out of the kitchen. The cook laughed and picked up the coffee he had forgotten.

Margret walked into the lobby and watched as Joe intently studied a magazine. He sat by the fire, looking at the page as if it were about to come to life.

"Hi, Joe. Everything okay?" She sat down next to him, a bit apprehensive.

"Hey, Margret." He responded without looking at her. "The other night I looked through this magazine, and something has been nudging me to look at it again. Almost as if it held answers I needed to find. There's something about this page, this particular place, that seems familiar. I don't know, but I may have been there at some point. I think, maybe, I'm starting to remember." He continued to look at the pages as if they held secrets he couldn't quite grasp. He wanted to step into the glossy page and be transported immediately to this place.

He turned to her and asked, "When can I leave, Margret? What does the doctor say?" He immediately regretted his words as the hurt look on her face spoke volumes. "I'm sorry. It's just that I think this place is important to me. I think I'll find some answers there." He paused and took a deep breath. "I'm sorry."

"It's okay. I understand. You have found something that has sparked a memory, and it's exciting. The roads aren't open yet, and we have no internet, but I'll talk to the doctor. He'll be pleased to know how well you're doing." She smiled at him, but her eyes looked sad. She knew it was only a matter of time before he left her forever.

Chapter 81

COLORADO

Celeste emerged from the spa feeling relaxed and sleepy, and she had just enough energy to make it to her room. As she pushed the button to close the elevator, the doors reopened, and Luca stepped in.

"Hi, Celeste, may I see you for dinner in an hour? I'd like to treat you to a delicious meal and discuss some business." Celeste managed to nod once before he stepped out and the doors closed. Luca winced, knowing he had messed up.

She sighed. *All I wanted was a nap, and now I need to get dressed for dinner.* She rubbed her neck to keep the tension from forming.

The elevator made several stops before it opened on her floor. At one stop, a woman's purse fell, its contents spilling all over the hallway and the elevator floor. Celeste stopped the elevator and helped gather the items. As they collected the contents, Celeste grabbed a lipstick tube before it rolled into the shaft. They giggled over the situation and then activated the elevator once again. As Celeste finally walked to her room, a text dinged from deep within her pocket.

"Let's plan a late dinner instead. Enjoy the treats and get some rest." She turned around and saw a steward rolling a cart towards her. She held the door open, thanked him, and gazed upon an assortment of fruit and chocolates. There was also a hot mocha in a covered resort mug ready to be enjoyed. She chuckled and sat down to enjoy the treat. Turning her chair to the window, she looked out over the mountains and picked up a strawberry. She texted Luca: "Thank you! This is quite the luxury treatment!"

"You're very welcome. Will an 8:30 dinner work for you?"

"8:30 is fine. See you then."

"Wear jeans. You deserve a casual night after a spa day."

"Perfect!" She grinned at her phone, put it down, and slipped into bed. She was asleep within seconds.

Luca slid his phone back into his pocket and thought of Celeste, hoping she would never want to leave. He made his way to the kitchen to discuss dinner with the chef. He wanted the date to be unforgettable.

Celeste opened her eyes and wondered what time it was. *Is it morning? Middle of the night?* She suddenly sat up, remembering her dinner plans. *Oh, no! Did I sleep through it?* She touched her phone, saw that it was 8:00, and relaxed. She threw back the covers and made her way to the shower. *I can do this.* She walked out of her room twenty-eight minutes later wearing her favorite jeans and a cream-colored sweater that brought out the green of her eyes. She had even thrown on some earrings and a bracelet to tie the look together. She felt calm and comfortable but then was caught off guard with a memory. She had bought the sweater and jewelry the day Sergio had asked her out. It had been their first real date. It was the night the songs had begun. She considered changing, but then realized the memories could give her strength. They could even give her joy if she let them. She walked towards the lobby thinking of Sergio and was smiling when she arrived.

Luca watched her approach, his eyes taking her in. "Good evening. You look well rested." He wanted to pull her into his arms and hold her tight. She looked beautiful. Instead, he took her arm and led her to a back door. "Let's go this way."

Celeste decided the best thing to do was to keep talking. If she talked, her thoughts of Sergio would be kept at bay until she could gather them up once again. She chatted about the spa and the luxuriousness of the resort, paying no attention at all to where they were going. Luca guided her and listened to her chattering while smiling to himself. He could get used to this. He slowed his pace and led her down a slight slope. She met his pace and then looked up to see where they were. As they turned to the right of the path, she saw lights in the distance and looked up at Luca.

"What are those lights?"

"Come on. I want to show you." He held onto her arm and led her closer to the dinner he had arranged. As they approached, Celeste took in her breath and stopped short.

"What is this?" She gulped at his grand gesture.

Luca moved his hand down her arm so that he could grasp her hand. "It's a special dinner just for you." He wrapped his fingers through hers and led her to a gazebo in the middle of the woods. Twinkle lights were strewn all along the top and the sides, small portable heaters were placed on the floor, and a table was set for two. Luca led her up the steps to a chair. "Would you like to sit here?" He looked into her eyes as he asked and had to refrain from looking at her lips.

Celeste realized her hand was linked in his and saw the look in his eyes. She looked at the table and answered, "Yes, of course." She let go of his fingers and sat in the chair he held out for her. She was feeling a bit disoriented and fuzzy from her day at the spa and her nap, but she also realized this was an incredible gesture from Luca. It was also very romantic. *How do I feel about that?*

Luca took the covers off the food, and Celeste laughed with appreciation. Cheeseburgers, French fries, and potato salad filled her plate, and her glass held Ginger Ale with a cherry bobbing within the bubbles.

"This is perfect!" She gazed over everything again.

Luca grinned at her. "Well, you've been working very hard, and today was a total relaxation day that has probably left you a bit tired. What better way to end the day than with comfort food?" He picked up his glass of Ginger Ale and held it up to her. "Cheers!" She clinked glasses with him and then took a healthy bite of her cheeseburger.

They ate and talked and laughed until Celeste could barely keep her eyes open. Luca stood up and motioned for her to follow him. "I think we should go, but first, I want to show you one more thing." He led her down the steps and around to the far side of the gazebo. There was a golf cart waiting for them, and Celeste shook her head.

"You think of everything, don't you?"

Creases appeared around his eyes as he joked, "Well, I am the owner. It's my job." He chuckled as he sat down in the driver's seat and motioned to her. "Hop in!" Celeste followed his instructions and held onto the hand grip in front of her. She didn't ask where they were going. She wanted to be surprised again. Luca drove down a path just big enough for the cart. It led them deeper and deeper into the woods until Celeste could barely see the twinkle lights of the gazebo when she turned around. She glanced at Luca, but he was intent on the path before them.

"Now, just up here, you're going to feel as though you can touch the stars." Celeste looked around but still only saw trees. Then, unexpectedly, they were out of the woods and onto an overlook. The sky before them sparkled with a million stars shining and twinkling directly above them.

She looked at Luca and then back at the sky. "This is amazing."

Luca pulled a blanket from the back of the cart and lay it down on the ground. "I've discovered that if you lie down right here and look up, it's as if you are actually among the stars. Would you like to try it?"

Celeste nodded, sat down on the blanket, and then lay flat, looking straight up. She was immediately immersed in the night sky. The stars seemed only a touch away. She looked for constellations and shooting stars, but mostly she enjoyed the experience. After a while she realized Luca must be somewhere nearby, and she turned her head to look for him. He was sitting on the ground looking up as well.

"Luca, come lie here and look up. It's so beautiful. I feel like I can reach out and touch them." Luca wanted to lie next to her and look at the stars, but he didn't trust himself. He could barely look at her. She was beautiful, and the way she was looking at the night sky was intoxicating. Before he could answer, she asked again. "You have to see it this way. Won't you look with me?"

Luca walked over to the blanket and lay down. The experience of viewing the night sky with Celeste right next to him was overwhelming. He was in love with her, and he didn't know what to do about it. Savoring every moment, he lay beside her without saying a word.

Celeste pointed out one or two constellations she knew, but soon she was silent too. Luca quietly turned to her and realized she had fallen asleep.

She's had quite a day. He moved closer and brushed his lips against her cheek. Her hair smelled like coconut, and he breathed it in while enjoying the nearness of her. He watched her sleep, and then he kissed his finger and touched her lips. She moved and twitched her nose, and Luca nudged her gently.

"Celeste, it's time to go." She woke up and nodded. He held onto her arm, grabbed the blanket, and then helped her to the golf cart. "Hold onto this grip while I drive. I don't want you falling out."

Celeste laughed softly and agreed. "No worries. I don't want to fall out either."

They drove through the woods and up a new path that led directly to the back of the property. They arrived in a matter of minutes, and Celeste was very glad there was no more hiking involved. He used his key to open the door and parked the cart inside, and then they walked in through an employee entrance. Celeste glanced at her phone. It was after one in the morning. The lobby was empty; no employees were around.

"I can make a fire if you're cold," Luca suggested.

"Thanks, Luca, but I think I just need to go to sleep. This whole day has been wonderful, and you planned the perfect evening. Thank you so much!" She smiled sleepily at him and started to walk away.

"Celeste?" She turned back to face him.

"Yes?"

"I'm glad you had a great day. I'd like to give you lots of perfect days." He stepped closer and reached out to touch her cheek. "Celeste, you are beautiful." She looked up at him and couldn't move. She was mesmerized by his words and by the look on his face. It was so similar to the one she held in her heart, and she longed for Sergio to look at her like that once again.

Abruptly, Luca's phone rang, and the spell was broken. He answered the call and Celeste waved good night to him. She took the elevator to her floor, and as she breathed a sigh of relief, she thought about breath. *Sergio left me breathless. He took my breath away. He said he missed me like breath. Luca does not have that effect on me at all. There is no magic, there is no breathless feeling. With him, I just breathe a sigh of relief when he's gone.* She made it to her room, got into bed, and dreamed of the one who missed her like breath.

Song: *It Only Hurts When I'm Breathing* by Shania Twain

Chapter 82

"I have an idea." The doctor placed the magazine on the bedside table and continued. "This North Carolina inn looks familiar to you, so I think you should go there. I'll arrange for the trip to take place. You can visit for a week or two and then return here to talk to me about your thoughts, feelings, and memories. We have a small emergency fund we can dip into for the trip. We'll cover the expense, but maybe in the future, you can donate back to us if you have the opportunity." He looked at Joe, and Joe nodded his understanding.

"We've asked a friend of ours to take you to Tasiilaq via helicopter. Then, you'll take another chopper from Tasiilaq to Kulusuk Island. From there, you'll board a plane to Reykjavik and then fly on to the U.S. You need someone to accompany you. I suggest Margret goes as your nurse and as your friend. How do you feel about this plan?"

Joe felt a mixture of emotions all at once. He wanted to leave and find answers, but he was also scared of what he might find. He stood up and began to pace. The doctor recognized his fears.

"You don't have to go, but I really do think it could help." The doctor rose from his chair, stopped Joe's frantic pacing, and assured him. "Joe, you're going to be okay. Margret will be with you. She is a very capable nurse."

Joe looked at him and nodded. "I thought I'd be excited about it, but I'm scared. If you think I'm ready, though, I'll go. Thank you for arranging it and for sending Margret with me. She'll be a big help, I'm sure."

He turned away and looked out the window. *I just don't know about this. I feel so lost. What if...*

The doctor interrupted his thoughts. "I'll take care of everything. You might experience a breakthrough." He shook Joe's hand, picked up the magazine, and left the room. Joe sat down and tried to think about his life before the accident. Nothing new came to mind. *What if I can't remember? What if the trip doesn't work?*

Margret stopped by to check his vitals. "All the pieces are falling into place! I'm so excited!"

Joe looked up at her and nodded. "Yeah, me too, but maybe not as excited as you." She grabbed his pillow and playfully wacked it against his shoulder. He grinned, pulled it away from her, positioned it against the wall, and leaned up against it. She laughed and left the room. He was anxious, but he told himself he could do it. He just needed to take it one day at a time.

By the end of the week the doctor had secured an emergency medical passport, the airline reservations had been made, and the accommodations were booked in Margret's name. She had never traveled so far from home, but she knew it was important for Joe's memory. She promised herself she would stay professional and keep her desires to herself. This trip was for Joe, for his health and for his long-term memory. She would simply be close by and stay attentive to his needs.

Joe woke up early the morning of the trip. He showered, dressed, and packed his few clothes into a bag someone had found for him. He walked downstairs, poured himself a cup of coffee, and sat down in front of the fire. He looked around and was suddenly nostalgic as he realized he was going to miss this place. This frozen world was the only home he knew.

The snowmobile ride to the small landing pad was cold but quick. They boarded a helicopter to take them to the Tasiilaq heliport, and Joe was determined to enjoy the ride as he buckled himself in tightly. As they took flight, his bird's eye view showed more of his temporary home than he had ever seen. He saw brightly colored houses dotting the landscape and then long expanses of ice and snow. He wondered which house was Auntie Imi's and if she was making her famous bread. This small village was a remarkable place, but he knew more awaited him. There had to be more. In Kulusuk, they boarded a plane to Reykjavik, and once there, Margret maneuvered through the large airport with expertise.

"I went to college here. Then once I became a nurse, I went back home. Hard to believe, huh?" She steered Joe into a coffee shop, ordered, and then pulled out homemade sandwiches she had brought with her.

"You never told me you went to college in Iceland. I guess I never thought to ask. It's a lot different from your village. Did you like it?" He was curious, and he turned to her and waited for her response.

"Yeah, it was great. I really enjoyed myself the first couple of years, and then I got serious about nursing. Plus, the classes got harder as I progressed." She sipped her coffee and continued. "When I graduated, I was offered a position here, but my heart longed to go home. I missed my family, and I thought I could make a difference in the village. It was the right decision for me. But this city was quite the experience!" She smiled and pointed to a dog riding on top of a woman's suitcase. They both laughed and continued people-watching.

Joe could not remember when he'd seen so many people. He sipped his coffee, ate his sandwich, and watched them as they passed by.

Soon their flight was called, and they made their way to the gate. "On to New York," Joe whispered. "We're really doing this."

"Are you okay?"

"Yeah. Can't go back now, can we?" Margret looked at him anxiously, but he assured her he was fine. "Let's do this." He handed his ticket to the agent and boarded the plane. His thoughts were chaotic, like snowflakes in a storm. He couldn't straighten them out. He was worried about what he would find, and about what he might not find. After buckling himself in, he closed his eyes and prayed. *Lord, direct my steps, I trust in you. Amen.* He fell asleep and woke up hours later to Margret's voice.

"Hey, Joe. We're almost there. Look out the window." Joe opened his eyes and pushed open the shade. He stared at the landscape but then pulled it back down.

"I don't recognize anything. I'd rather just wait." He felt her hand giving his leg a series of comforting pats and turned to her. "I'm okay. I just want to take it one step at a time."

Their next flight from New York to Asheville arrived on time after a quick layover in Baltimore. They were tired, unkempt, and ready to arrive. Joe looked out the window at the scene before him. He turned to Margret.

"You know, I would have thought getting into a new environment would trigger something in my memory, but nothing has. It's frustrating."

Margret was surprised as well, but she just nodded and reached for his hand. "This is just the beginning. Let's be patient and just see what happens. It will be okay, and I'll be with you." Joe squeezed her hand and didn't let go. He didn't want to. He was relying on her, and her presence calmed his fears.

Celeste flew back home, leaving Luca in Colorado to finish a project. They had decided that The General Store would not fit in at the Colorado resort after all. It was fancier and more elite than the North Carolina Inn. She thought a different kind of store, such as a boutique, would be a better fit. Luca was sad to see her go, but he asked her to look into that idea in more depth and to report back to him with an update.

She arrived home in the afternoon and was bombarded by updates, reports, and problems that had come up while she had been away. A group of two hundred people was arriving one day early for their conference. The rooms weren't ready, the kitchen lost three employees, and several showers were leaking on the second floor. Celeste dropped her suitcase in her office and got to work.

Within a few hours, the showers were fixed, the rooms were cleaned, and three employees were transferred to the kitchen. She called the charter bus line to pick up the conference guests, and they were on their way to the airport to retrieve them. Celeste had a few moments to spare and headed for the barista. A hot mocha appeared a minute after she sat down, and she and Emma both laughed.

"Thank you! I've missed your coffee. It just wasn't the same in Colorado."

"You're very welcome. You looked like you might need it." The barista smiled as she handed Celeste a dark chocolate coffee bean. "I also heard you like these!"

"I sure do! How did you know? Oh, wait, are you friends with the barista at our Colorado resort?"

"Yes, of course. I told her what you liked and to have one ready for you when you arrived. I hope you don't mind."

"Mind? It was wonderful of you. Thank you!" Celeste took a sip and thought about what she'd just heard. Emma was quite good at her job, and Celeste thought she'd make a good leader.

"You have such a heart and head for good service, Emma. Let me know if you're interested in a managerial position. We could hire more help for you here at the coffee bar and you could train and manage them. You would be very good at it."

"I would love to talk to you about that. Thank you! I've actually already asked several of the wait staff to help me with this huge conference coming in, so we don't get too backed up with coffee orders. I hope you don't mind. It won't interfere much with their current positions."

"Well, let's talk tomorrow about making you a manager. Nice job! You're already a great leader."

Celeste was paged, and she ran off to the kitchen to see about a potential issue. Emma grinned and popped a chocolate bean into her mouth to celebrate.

Celeste fixed the problem in the kitchen and then decided to take a few minutes for herself. She turned her phone off, took the tunnel entrance, and headed outside.

Happy to be home, she breathed in the familiar air. She knew just where she wanted to go. As she walked towards the waterfall, she relaxed and breathed deeply. She loved her job, but today had been a bit overwhelming. She pushed her thoughts away and listened to the evening sounds. She heard the wind brushing against the leaves and the whispers of the pines. She loved it here. She pushed back the limbs and walked into her sanctuary. That's exactly what it was to her, a place of safety and refuge. A place where Sergio had taken her, had shared with her, and where he had first kissed her. She sat on the bench and stared at the water, watching it splash into the rocky pool below. She didn't know if anyone else knew about this place, but she liked to pretend that the two of them were its only visitors. It was theirs. She touched her snowflake pendant by habit and thought of the man she loved. *Is he really gone forever? If he is somewhere in the Arctic, why doesn't he call or come home?* She threw a pebble into the water and made a wish. *I wish I could see you soon, my love.* Leaving her refuge, she sighed, turned her phone on, and headed back to work.

Song: *Remain* by Royal Tailor

Chapter 83

As she turned her phone off of airplane mode, Margret heard the ding of a voicemail and held the phone to her ear. From the look on her face, Joe knew something was wrong. She hung up and turned to him.

"What is it?" Joe held his breath as reasons for the call multiplied in his head.

"That was the Inn at Shepherd Falls. They are overbooked because of a big conference, but they made reservations for us at a neighboring resort called Wren House. On a positive note, they are paying for it because of the inconvenience." Margret looked at Joe and reached for his hand. "Are you okay? I know this is important to you."

Joe exhaled slowly. "It's fine. We can stay at Wren House and still visit the original one. Really, it's okay. Right now, I just want a shower and sleep. How nice that they paid for it. That's great management."

Margret rented a car, and Joe watched the countryside pass by as he hoped to recognize something… anything. A few minutes later, he was surprised when he heard the turn signal. He looked at her quizzically as they pulled back off the highway.

Margret noticed the look. "I don't know about you, but I need new clothes." She pulled into a shopping center and parked the car.

"Let's go check it out. I have money, and we can get some clothes better suited for this weather. Ready?"

Joe looked down at his clothes and nodded. They walked into the store looking like a happy couple and then walked out an hour later looking even happier. Margret wore jeans, a t-shirt that said North Carolina across the front, sunglasses and sneakers, and she carried a new purse. She had also found a pink Bible in the book section, and for some reason, one she couldn't yet name, she was eager to read it.

Joe wore a V-neck navy blue t-shirt with jeans and sneakers, and he carried a bag stuffed with toiletries, snacks, and bottles of water. He relaxed in the passenger seat and pulled out his new sunglasses. Turning to Margret, he smiled, and she caught her breath.

"You look great!" She complimented him as she fumbled for her keys.

"Thank you! You look great yourself!" He opened a bag of snack mix and a bottle of water for Margret and then did the same for himself. "This trip is good medicine. I can't remember much, but I'm having fun!" Joe popped a pretzel into his mouth and looked out at the North Carolina scenery as Margret chuckled at his antics.

Thirty minutes later they pulled into Wren House and parked the car. She turned to Joe as he took in the scene. "I know this isn't the inn from the magazine, but it looks nice, and we can visit the other one soon. How are you feeling?"

"I'm fine. I'm actually glad we're here. I feel more at ease since I don't have to depend on my memory at every turn. Let's see what this place has to offer."

They grabbed their bags and headed to the front doors. As Joe approached, he admitted his uncertainties to himself. He knew it wasn't the right place, but the inn from the magazine was nearby. He was on edge. He just didn't want Margret to notice.

Celeste walks along the pine-needled floor and stops to look up at the cathedral ceiling of evergreen trees. Soft feathery snow begins to fall and draws her deeper into the woods. She isn't scared; instead, she feels a sense of purpose and intention. She glimpses a shimmer and walks decisively towards it. It grows as she approaches. It leads her into a small grove of younger trees, not yet bursting to the cathedral's ceiling. She stands in the midst of them, waiting. In a moment of light, Sergio appears in front of her. He reaches out his arms and embraces her. He swings her around, and they laugh and cry and kiss, lost in each other's embrace and filling all the emptiness that has plagued them both for so long.

Celeste's phone rang and woke her up. She answered it, knowing her day had begun. Before she rolled out of bed, she closed her eyes and tried to remember how she had felt in Sergio's strong arms. She reached for her notebook and jotted down as much as she could remember.

Celeste dealt with the demands of the conference guests all day long, handling their questions and requests with grace. Daisy and Bert's pop-up shop had been assembled in the space where the permanent store would soon be, and it was a huge success. They were nearly sold out after one day.

Celeste walked over to talk to them. Daisy and Bert still smiled and chatted with their customers, but Celeste detected their weariness. "You've done so well! How are you both holding up?"

"Oh, my, we're exhausted, but happy. Look how much we've sold! If this is any indication of how we'll do, we need to hire some young help fast!" Daisy looked at her husband and gave his hand a squeeze.

"Yes, I will take care of the hiring soon. For now, though, you need to go home and put your feet up." Celeste picked up the *Closed* sign and placed it on the hook. Daisy dropped the money bag into her purse while Bert secured the retractable belt to the stanchions.

"Yes, it's time. We'll be back tomorrow with more to sell!" She reached for Bert's hand, and they walked to the door. Celeste waved goodbye as she made a mental note to get busy with the hiring.

Suddenly, she turned around and ran after them. "Daisy, Bert," she called. The couple stopped and waited for her to catch up to them. "Would you like for me to drive over to your store tonight and load some things into the truck? I can have my staff unload it and put it all in the shop tonight so it will be ready to sell in the morning." Celeste grinned at the couple. "I'm happy to, really."

Bert looked at Daisy and was about to refuse, but then thought better of it and agreed. "We'll see you in a couple of hours. That will give us some time to get it all together in boxes. Thank you, Celeste. You are incredibly thoughtful." Bert reached out and gave her a quick hug and then helped Daisy into their car. Daisy waved and blew her a kiss as they drove away. Celeste walked back inside, but she was looking forward to getting away soon.

Joe took a hot shower and fell into bed. He sighed, pulled up the covers, and slept deeply.

He stands beneath a canopy of trees so green he can almost hear them growing and stretching to the stars. They seem ancient and wise, as though they hold the answers he desperately seeks. He turns his hand over to catch the falling snow and notices that a large snowflake has landed in his palm. It doesn't melt. Instead, it begins to glimmer and glow. In a moment of light, a beautiful woman stands before him and runs into his arms. He embraces her and feels a joy so strong he begins to weep. As they hold one another, the snowflake glows and rises to join the others in the night sky.

Joe got out of bed and stood at the window. *Who is this woman I keep dreaming of?* He could see the outline of the dark mountain in the night sky and the headlights of a lone truck on the mountain road. He wondered if the woman in his dreams was out there somewhere. *Does she dream of me too?* Wondering what the morning would bring, he sighed and got back in bed.

Celeste jumped into the truck, turned up the music, and rolled down the windows. She was glad she had a reason to visit Shepherd Falls. She knew the trip wouldn't take too long, as Daisy and Bert would have everything boxed and ready for her to pick up. But right now, she desperately needed to get away.

Her fast-paced speed mellowed as she drove. She sang along to the radio, the lyrics winding their way into her thoughts, and thought of the man she loved. She passed Wren House, noticing that some lights were still on, and then continued towards her destination.

She pulled up to The General Store and quickly transferred the boxes to the truck so that Bert and Daisy could get some rest. She waved goodnight to them and drove back to the Inn. A feeling of contentment washed over her, and she felt a new kind of energy. This feeling was something new, a different route her heart had discovered. A tremendous feeling of gratefulness filled her, and she thanked God for the good things that seemed destined to be on their way. "Lord, I'm grateful for my new home. I'm grateful for my friends. I'm grateful for my parents and the time I had with them. I'm grateful for Sergio. But most of all, God, I am grateful for love. Thank you for the love you have showered upon me. I pray I can be a good example of love to you and to others. I don't know where Sergio is, but you do. I pray he is safe; I pray he feels loved, and I pray he comes home soon. Amen." She drove home in silence, feeling God's peace all around her.

Chapter 84

Joe slept better than he had in months. When he woke, he stared out the window and marveled at the scene. Fog blanketed the mountain and held it close. It clung to the earth, not yet ready to let go. The scene seemed familiar to him, but he couldn't place the memory. He turned away from the window but then quickly turned back as something caught his eye. He moved closer to the glass and noticed a glimmer in the trees. *What was that?* He stared until his eyes seemed destined to cross, but he did not see it again. *I need to make a list of things that nudge at my memories: fog, mountains, and something shining in the trees.* He shook his head and headed for the shower.

"I love this foggy weather," Celeste stated as she ordered her coffee. "It's as though we're on an island, away from the rest of the world. It's the kind of weather for a cozy fire, a good book, and a great cup of coffee."

Emma handed the steaming mug to Celeste. "The guests will be in meetings all day, so it's perfect weather for them. Think how sad they'd be if the weather was perfect and they had to stay inside all day. I have a feeling I'll be very busy here making coffee." She wiped down the bar and checked her supplies as Celeste nodded and wandered to the fireplace. She sat down and stared into the fire.

"Hey, Moses." She grinned at the nickname for the fireplace and then whispered, "Sergio, I miss you. I would like for you to just walk in here, order a coffee, and sit down beside me. We can sip and talk and begin our day together. I love you. You are my heart. You are my person." She sighed and stole a quick glance at the door. He was not there, but there was no harm in hoping.

She finished her mocha and headed to the pop-up shop. The employees had done a great job replacing the inventory the night before, but Celeste wanted to double check the placement before Bert and Daisy arrived. All seemed in order, and Celeste wandered back to her office. She was restless. She had not heard from Luca in several days, but she was happy about that. She didn't want to explain to him why she couldn't love him. She just couldn't. Deciding a walk would help, she grabbed her phone and slipped out the back door into the waiting fog.

Joe wandered down to the lobby and headed for the restaurant. Something smelled very good and familiar, and he needed food. He wondered where Margret was and if he should wait for her but decided he would meet her later. As he approached the breakfast buffet, his mouth began to water. He couldn't believe the amount of food before him. Picking up a plate, he filled it with items that looked familiar and delicious, including pancakes, bacon, hash browns, grits, and fried apples. He remembered the meager rations he had eaten in the hospital and shook his head in disbelief at the memory. He thanked God for each item he placed on his plate. He was truly grateful. Finding a table near the window, he sat down eagerly as a young waitress brought him a steaming mug of coffee.

"I may never leave!" he gushed.

The waitress winked at him. "We get that a lot here. I'll check on your coffee in a few minutes. You may want some more."

Joe took a sip and then excitedly dug into his breakfast. He savored each delicious bite, chewing slowly while looking around the room. He watched the people, he looked at the decor, and he stared out the window, but nothing was familiar. He sighed and reached for another slice of bacon.

The forest drew her in with its promise of crisp air and silence. Celeste was intrigued with the denseness of the fog and how at times she could not see more than a few feet before her. She wasn't scared; in fact, she welcomed the fog as a comfort and as a protector. She could be alone, and no one would find her. She slowed her pace, breathed deeply, and closed her eyes. She imagined the tendrils of fog to be Sergio's arms wrapping around her and holding her close. She longed for his touch, for his kiss, and to be held within his arms. She took a deep breath, and for a tiny moment, she thought she felt his presence.

When she opened her eyes, a beam of light caught her attention off to one side. *How was light shining in the foggy woods? That's impossible.* She turned to her right and walked slowly towards it. *What on earth could it be?*

Joe finished his breakfast and charged it to his room. He still had no money and no idea who he was, and the emergency ID listed him as Joe Doe. He knew it was not his name, and now he hoped to recognize something to help him remember. So far, he didn't recognize anything. He was frustrated, and as his stomach was full, he decided to take a walk. He considered telling Margret where he was going but thought better of it. She could still be asleep, and he didn't want to wake her. He headed out the front doors into the crisp, cool air. Hoping for direction to the trails, he spotted a wooden sign in the distance and walked towards it. The sign pointed him to three different trails, and he chose the one that looked like it would take him to the highest point. He felt better walking after the meal, and he began to relax as he climbed higher and higher. He couldn't see very far in front of him, but he grinned as he realized it was a metaphor for his life: walking through the fog, not knowing or seeing where he was going, nearly invisible to others, no trace of where he'd been, and no sight of what was before him. He picked up a walking stick and climbed.

Celeste kept hiking in the direction of the light, but it seemed farther and farther away no matter how far she walked. "I think my eyes are playing tricks on me," she murmured, but she kept going.

Joe stopped and stood still. The fog surrounded him like a thick blanket, and he felt strangely safe and comforted. He closed his eyes and listened to the woods. Everything seemed asleep; there was no chirping of birds, call of frogs, or scurrying of small animals. He opened his eyes and noticed that the fog was beginning to evaporate. He nodded and walked on.

Celeste had no concept of time. How long had she been walking in the fog? She glanced at her phone but had no reception. As she slipped it back into her pocket, she missed a step and stumbled on a rock.

A cry escaped as she fell into the bramble. She lay in the leaves and wondered what she was doing alone in the foggy woods. She sat up and took inventory of her legs, ankles, knees, and hands, but all seemed fine. There was no blood or broken bones. She pulled leaves from her hair and stood up. Suddenly, the object she had been seeking was right before her, and she was a bit disappointed. A flashlight, lying on its side, had been left on top of a boulder, and it was still on. She had been walking towards an old flashlight the whole time. She picked it up and noticed it wasn't old at all. It looked unused and probably had a brand-new battery in it. Someone had been there recently and had left it. *Had they left it on purpose? And if so, why? If someone left it on for a reason, I will not be the one to turn it off.* Celeste placed it back exactly where it had been and turned around. She followed the path the way she had come and headed back home. It had turned out to be an interesting morning. She wondered if the flashlight had a deeper meaning. As she followed the path slowly downhill, she promised herself she would write about this adventure in her journal when she had time.

Joe felt more and more comfortable in the woods as he walked. He wondered if he had known these woods before. They seemed somewhat familiar. He walked on, using his new walking stick as a guide. His stick struck a rock that was, unfortunately, right in the middle of the path, and he veered around it.

"That could be dangerous," he said as he considered it. "Someone could trip if they didn't see it." He glanced up from the path and noticed something shining from a nearby rock. He stared at it for a minute before walking closer. It didn't seem real. It was a flashlight lying on its side with the light on. *I think this must be the light I've been following, but why? Who would leave a flashlight on in the woods? Maybe someone is hurt, and this is a beacon to draw someone in to help.* Words floated into his subconscious and mingled with the fog: *Your word is a lamp for my feet, a light on my path.** He closed his eyes and tried to remember where that was in the Bible. He couldn't recall exactly, but he liked it, and it gave him a sense of peace.

He turned around and called out, "Hello? Are you there? Do you need help? Hello?" He stood still and listened but there was only silence. He called out again but there was no response. A sudden memory came to him, and he saw himself standing on the edge of a cliff yelling something. He closed his eyes and tried to remember. He wanted to know what he was saying. Was it something good or was he trying to get help? He noticed his hands were fisted, and he stretched his fingers out and breathed deeply. He concentrated again and heard himself yelling, "I love you!" He heard it over and over again. He opened his eyes and voiced, "Well, that's cool. Can't wait to remember all of that!" He turned, left the flashlight where it was, and walked away. As he walked, the fog lifted, and he found his way easily, wondering about everything: a flashlight in the forest, who had left it, why they had left it, when did he yell love notes, and where was he when he had proclaimed that love?

Celeste sat down on a log to rest. The fog seemed a bit thinner, as if it were thinking about lifting but wasn't quite ready. She looked down at the ground and noticed the ants were hard at work. She was watching them with interest when all of a sudden, she heard Sergio's voice. She jumped up and turned in its direction. She whispered, "Sergio?" and then shouted, "Sergio!"

She listened and heard his voice again saying, "Hello?"

Celeste couldn't move. Was her mind playing tricks on her? Was it the fog? She broke out in a cold sweat. She didn't know what to do. She listened but heard only the beating of her own heart. She realized she was holding her breath and let it out in a huge gasp. She shuddered and turned to go, moving into a slow jog. The fog lifted as she picked up her pace. She was ready to get out of the woods.

Song: *Somewhere in Between* by Lifehouse

*Psalm 119:105

Chapter 85

Celeste was distracted as she walked to the Inn. She mumbled to herself about getting a grip and how she couldn't possibly have heard Sergio's voice in the fog. Luca watched her from the window and frowned.

"What's going on with her this morning?" He looked at his watch to note the time and headed downstairs. As he neared the lobby, he caught Emma's eye and held up one finger and then the shape of a C with all five. Emma immediately understood the code and began to make a mocha for Celeste. By the time Celeste made it to the lobby, Luca was waiting with steaming coffee. He placed his hand on her elbow and gently ushered her back to the office suite as she vaguely wondered when he had arrived. Celeste latched onto the cup and held it tightly. She thought about mentioning hearing Sergio's voice but thought better of it at the moment. When they arrived at his office, Luca motioned for her to sit. She did so, took a sip of the hot brew, closed her eyes, and exhaled. Luca watched her and waited.

"Celeste, are you okay?" His voice sounded forceful.

Opening her eyes, she answered, "Something happened in the woods this morning. It was the fog…"

Luca interrupted and looked at her intensely. "What happened in the woods? Are you okay?" He paced, his face turning red. Celeste watched him and didn't understand his reaction. She simply turned to look out the window and was surprised that the sun was shining and the sky was blue.

"Celeste!" Luca nearly yelled. "Are you okay?" Celeste turned to look at him and realized he was truly worried. Little beads of sweat shone on his forehead, and his eyebrows were furrowed.

She shivered. "Luca, I'm fine. Let me explain." Luca grabbed a bottle of water from the mini fridge and sat down. "I went for a walk in the woods and followed a light in the distance. It turned out to be a flashlight someone had left there. On the way back, I heard…" She wasn't sure if she should go on. Maybe Luca would think she was losing her mind.

"What did you hear?" He was insistent.

She answered calmly, "I heard Sergio's voice calling out. He was saying, 'Hello.'" Celeste looked up at Luca but couldn't read his face. She took a sip of coffee and waited.

Luca wiped his brow. "Hey, there, it's okay," he began. He moved his chair closer to hers and placed his hand on her knee. "It's not uncommon to hear voices of the ones we love. It sounds like you had an interesting morning in the woods. I understand. You miss him and long to hear his voice, so you imagined hearing it, but what you have to realize now, Celeste, is that he's not coming back. You have to move on with your life and make room for new people and new experiences." He let the words hang in the air as he took advantage of the placement of his hand and patted her leg.

Celeste looked at him intently and purposely removed his hand. "Luca, I'm in love with Sergio. I fell in love with him in a minute, and I knew he was my person. When I read a book, I want to share it with him, when I laugh at something funny, I want to laugh with him, when I travel, I want to be beside him. Our love is steady and strong. It has grabbed hold of my heart and has not let go. With him, I felt seen and heard and loved and special."

"Celeste, I understand, and I'm here for you, but…"

"You don't understand. Please listen to me! If this deep love for him fades, it will simply become a beautiful memory. But it's not fading! When I close my eyes, I can trace the curve of his face, run my hands through his hair, and wrap my arms around him. I picture his quick smile and the way his eyes look at me with fascination and interest and love. Love is a risk, and it's one I'm willing to take. So, if I hear his voice in the woods, that's just fine with me. I know he's coming back. I just know it!" She stood up and looked at him with such intensity that he couldn't look away.

Without hesitation, Luca took the coffee out of her hand, pulled her into his arms, and kissed her passionately, his mouth capturing hers with reckless possession.

From the doorway, a new coffee shop employee started to knock but thought better of it when he saw his boss locked in an embrace. He grinned and walked away, knowing he could come back later to sign the new-hire paperwork.

Celeste reached her hands up to Luca's chest and pushed him away. "Luca, stop it. I love Sergio, and I always will. Don't do that again!" She trembled as she stared up at him.

"Celeste, what do you have to show for this relationship? What are you even fighting for? He's gone, and besides, he's not the perfect man you think he is." Luca's eyes were bright, and a sheen of sweat covered his forehead.

"Are you kidding me?" She stepped away from him. "I have all the words he said to me etched in my heart and in my head, and I remember how he made me feel. We love each other, Luca. It's a love I can never forget." She turned to leave and then spun around again to face him. "What do you mean he's not perfect? No one is perfect, but we do the best we can. Look, I love my job, but I can't work at the Inn if you're here too. If you're staying, I quit!" She stormed out of the office, slamming the door behind her. Luca ran after her.

"Celeste!" He reached for her arm and pulled her into a corner of the hallway, nearly hidden by a large Ficus tree. She was breathing hard, and he couldn't take his eyes off of her lips. He shook his head and switched his gaze to her eyes. They were fiery and fierce. He took a breath. "Celeste. I know that no one is perfect, but did Sergio ever tell you about the incident? No, I'm sure he didn't." When she didn't respond, he continued.

"In college, he was part of a group that altered online grades for money. They were all expelled and jailed. But for some reason, Sergio was able to finish his classes online and graduate. He was the only one. Sounds devious to me, and to everyone else. His reputation was ruined. Did he tell you? It was a huge scandal. He is not the perfect man you think he is." He wiped his sweaty hands on his pants as if the memory was dirty.

Celeste regarded him, dodged his grasp, and was out of sight before he knew what was happening.

Luca watched her leave, trudged to his office, and hurled his water bottle at the wall. He stood in the middle of the plush carpet and watched it splash across the bookshelf. He was angry at himself for kissing her but also for telling her Sergio's secret. He sat down, put his head in his hands, and groaned, "What am I going to do?"

Celeste headed straight for Sergio's room. She wanted a new shirt to hold onto. She didn't just need his shirt, though, she needed him. But right now, holding onto something of his would help ease the pain. Using her master key, she slipped in, made her way to his closet, and opened the door. His scent wafted towards her, filling her senses. She pulled a t-shirt off its hanger, held it to her nose, and breathed it in. With her eyes closed, she imagined him beside her, and she relaxed. The morning's events had taken their toll, and a weariness came over her. She made her way to his bed, slipped under the covers, cuddled his shirt, and fell asleep.

Joe made his way out of the woods and followed the path back the way he had come. He couldn't quite explain his feelings. He needed to think. He also wondered where Margret was. As he approached Wren House, he took the side steps that led up to the deck at the back of the building. It was a wrap-around deck with a spectacular view of the mountains. Guests could sit or lounge in one of the many chairs and stare out at the incredible countryside. He stepped onto the expansive area and saw Margret. She was lounging on a chair, holding a cup of coffee, and soaking in the sun. She looked like she was asleep, but every now and then she would move the cup to her lips for a sip and then move it back down to rest on the arm of the chair. Joe watched her. *She loves the sun*, he thought as he approached her, but he didn't notice the way the sunlight played on her hair or how her foot was tapping at music only she could hear.

As his shadow fell across her face, she opened her eyes and looked up at him. "Hello, Joe. What have you been up to this morning?" Joe pulled a lounge chair beside her and sat down on it, letting his legs stretch out to their full length. He reclined and closed his eyes to the sun.

"Ahhh, this is nice. I see why you're here." He accepted a glass of lemon water from a waiter. Margret giggled and closed her eyes again.

"We're a long way from Greenland," she whispered as she took another sip of the strong brew.

Joe thought about his morning. "Margret, do you think people in love once can find one another again? What I mean is, if love is meant to be, can its force bring them back together, even in the face of obstacles?" She didn't answer, so he looked over at her. She was sitting up and looking off into the distance. "I think I am just looking for answers, and now that I'm here, I'm wondering if there was love in my life."

Margret turned and looked at him and reached out to hold his hand. "I understand. You are searching for answers, for who you are, for your name, for your place in this world, and for love. It's okay. I'm your friend, and I'm here for you. Now, tell me about your morning." She pulled her hand away and settled back into her chair.

Looking off at the mountains, he began, "This morning I followed a light in the woods." He told her how he had felt drawn onto the path and up the trail as if on a quest. He explained how he kept going on and on as if a force was pulling him deeper and deeper into the heart of the mountain. He told her about the flashlight and the fog and the walking stick and the rock in the path. He described how it had all seemed familiar yet unfamiliar at the same time. He sighed, leaned back, and closed his eyes to the sun. Then he sat up and asked, "Do you think that's crazy?"

Margret took a sip of coffee and looked at the mountain. "No, you are not crazy. You are a man who has forgotten, but I believe you are on the path of healing and remembering. It will come back to you little by little. Be patient." She stood up and stretched. "I need to take care of a few things, and then I think I'll go into town. Would you like to join me in an hour?"

He nodded. "Yeah, sure. I'll meet you in the lobby. Thanks, Margret."

She looked pensive as she left to retrieve her new flashlight from the rock high upon the hill.

Song: *Clocks* by Coldplay

Chapter 86

Celeste slid deeper into Sergio's bed. Her responsibilities floated into view one by one, and she knew she had to get back to work. Pushing the covers down dramatically, she huffed. *Why was Luca here anyway, and when did he arrive?*

"Ugh." She moaned and threw her legs over the bed, hoping her body would follow. It did not. She lay across the bed with her legs dangling to the floor. *I must look like a forgotten doll lying here like this.* She wondered what time it was and then raised her head to glance at the clock on the bedside table. She had to scrunch up her eyes to make sure she was reading the display correctly. *Three hours? I've been asleep for three hours?* She quickly jumped up, smoothed the bed, and walked into the bathroom to splash cold water on her face. Five minutes later she slipped out of Sergio's room and onto the service elevator. She knew exactly where she needed to go.

Daisy beamed when she spotted Celeste and reached out to grasp her hands. "I love how the merchandise is arranged. It was so sweet of you to have it all ready for us this morning. What a treat! We are selling out again!" Celeste hugged her friend and allowed Daisy to lead her into the store. Daisy pulled her to the farthest point from the doorway and faced Celeste. Her kind face turned serious, and frown lines appeared out of nowhere. "Now, Celeste, dear, you need to tell me what's wrong. I see a story behind those beautiful green eyes, and it needs to be told."

Celeste held Daisy's strong hands and told her about the experience on the mountain, and then about her incident with Luca.

Tears welled up in her eyes. "Daisy, I just miss and love Sergio so much, but I feel so alone in my feelings, and then Luca wants me to love him instead. It's just too much!" She closed her eyes and let the tears flow. She thought she would feel Daisy hugging her or murmuring soft words, but she didn't. She opened her eyes. Daisy stood in front of her with a knowing look on her face. She handed Celeste a tissue and nodded at her to use it. Daisy's look was not uncomfortable; it was all business, and it was surprising. Once Celeste had wiped her eyes and stood up a little straighter, Daisy led her to a chair and sat down beside her. She cleared her throat and looked as though she had prepared for this moment all her life.

"Celeste, you have embarked on a great adventure. In fact, it's the greatest adventure of your life. Do you know what I'm talking about?"

"I think you're talking about love."

"That's right. We seek love all our lives. We seek it from our parents, our siblings if we have them, our friends, and then from a potential partner. You found love with Sergio, and it is a true, deep, lasting love that has not grown dim with time and distance. You are a part of him, and he is a part of you. Your love is intense and strong. It's a love that has grabbed your heart and held on tight, and when love is that strong, it hurts when it's away." Celeste nodded and Daisy took a breath.

"Luca doesn't quite understand this love you have for his brother. He must now believe that Sergio is not coming back. He is reaching out to you to help you heal as well as to enable his own healing. The problem is, though, it will never work. You'll always love Sergio, and

Luca will always resent it." Daisy patted her hand. "It's going to be okay because Bert and I are here, and we are going to cheer you up." Bert heard his name and walked over to them.

He put his arms around the two women and felt very blessed as he spoke words of wisdom, "Sometimes, all the doors slam shut, but with hope, there's always another door that will open. And when it does, it just so happens to be the perfect door." Bert pulled them in for a double hug and gave them each a wink before he walked away towards his customers. Celeste whispered a thank you into Daisy's ear, and the older woman smiled at her.

"Love is precious, my dear. Hold onto it and never let it go." She paused and then continued. "You have been holding on to so much for so long; I pray you also feel held by those who love you." Daisy squeezed Celeste's hand and then joined her husband.

Celeste watched them and then stood up to leave, but then she stopped. *Doors. Bert had mentioned doors. He said that with hope, another door will open, and it will be the perfect door.* Her mind whirled and she sat back down. *I dreamed of a door once; it was an old door. I could have ignored it, but it was the only option, the perfect door for me, and I walked through it.* She gulped. *I think my relationship with Sergio is the door. I walked through it intentionally. It was a choice I made, the right choice. I will not walk back out and close the door. I'm committed to him. We're in this together. He's my perfect door, and maybe I'm his. Maybe he walked into his own door to meet me… maybe he made his choice. Maybe we're each other's perfect door…*

She suddenly remembered where she was, cleared her throat, and left the store. She knew she had to find Luca, but she wasn't looking forward to the conversation she knew needed to happen.

Luca stood on the deck that overlooked the valley. He had picked up leaves from the floor and watched them drift on the breeze as he dropped them one by one. Most of them found their way to the ground below, but others rode the wind until finding their place to rest. He was angry at himself and knew what he needed to do. He turned to the building to gather up his nerve but saw that she was coming towards him with a look of determination. He tried his best to smile at her.

Celeste walked with strength of mind she didn't feel, but possibly exuded. Although her stomach was turning flips inside, she wanted to look calm but firm.

"Hey, Luca, can we talk?" she said as she reached the railing.

"Of course. I was actually about to come find you. Celeste, I'm so sorry."

"Thank you, Luca, but I need to speak. I'm in love with your brother, and I still believe he'll be found. I am not giving up on him, and I cannot love you the way you want me to. I love you like a friend or a brother, and I always will. I've never loved anyone the way I love Sergio. It's a love in my heart so deep it can't be removed. I am his forever, and I can't change the way I feel."

Luca flicked another leaf off the edge. "I'm just so sorry I tried to replace him. It wasn't fair to him or to you. I think I just miss him so much and want his love to be my love. I'm uh… I'm also sorry for telling you something that only he should have explained." Luca's phone rang, and he reached into his pocket to retrieve it. He glanced at the screen and frowned. "Sorry, I need to take this. Give me a minute."

Celeste nodded and moved away, keeping her eyes on the valley before her. It was lush and beautiful, and she started naming the types of trees she saw. Once, a guest had asked her what the trees were, and when she couldn't answer, she decided to learn their names.

"There's a beech tree, that one's a yellow birch, and I see a mountain maple and lots of dogwood." She started to smile as she named them. It was calming, and she breathed deeply. She loved it here, and she knew one day she'd share it with Sergio again. She glanced over at Luca and saw a strange look on his face. She moved closer to him but wasn't sure what to expect.

Luca ended the call and stared at his phone. Then he looked up at Celeste with tears in his eyes. "Celeste," he whispered.

She brought her hands to her face and shook her head. "What is it?" A mixture of fear, terror, and dread came over her as she looked at him. Her pulse quickened.

Luca grabbed her hands and looked into her eyes. "Celeste, they may have found Sergio. They need me to go see if, well, they need a family member to go see." Luca pulled her into his arms and let go of all the emotions and tears and anger he had been trying to contain.

Celeste stood still but was able to get her arms around Luca to support him. *It couldn't be, it just couldn't be.* She knew that Luca would make the trip, but she would stay here and spend time in their special places. He couldn't be gone. She still felt him alive in her heart.

He pulled himself away. "I'll leave tomorrow." His voice still shook. "Can you stay here and take care of things? I know it's a lot to ask, but I don't know what else to do."

"Yes, I'll stay here. I do not want to go because I know he's alive and well. I just know it!" Celeste led Luca into the building and helped him with his flight reservation. He would travel to Iceland and meet with the doctors at the hospital there. Luca then took off for his room and Celeste sat down at her desk. She closed her eyes and talked to the one who could give her real peace. A verse immediately came to her from Philippians 4:6-7, and she whispered it out loud: "'Do not be anxious about anything, but in every situation, by prayer and petition, with thanksgiving, present your requests to God. And the peace of God, which transcends all understanding, will guard your hearts and your minds in Christ Jesus.' Lord, I present my requests: please let Sergio be alive, please keep him strong, please be present with him as he endures these difficulties. I thank you for also holding me up and for helping Luca during this trip. I love you so much, and I feel your love all around me. Thank you, Lord. Thank you."

Joe and Margret wandered through Shepherd Falls looking at all the sights, stopping at a variety of stores, and resting at a coffee shop.

"This seems so familiar, Margret. I wonder if there's a little park around that corner." He grabbed her hand and led her around the café, hoping he was right. They both stopped and stared at a small, charming park. The ground was paved in red brick, and several fountains bubbled from different corners. There were benches, hanging plants, and lovely paths to follow. Joe let go of her hand. He took his time as he wandered to every fountain, touched the water, and walked down the paths.

He turned towards her. "I know this place. I remember it." He broke out into a smile and then ran back to her, embraced her and spun her around. "I remember!"

Song: *Blow Away* by George Harrison

Chapter 87

The new day dawned with promise. The sun shone brightly, flowers stretched towards the light, and birds chased each other in a frenzied game of tag. Celeste took it as a sign of hope on this difficult day. It was time for Luca to leave for Iceland, and he was being dramatic. She walked him to the truck, and he leaned into her, hoping to gather strength for the journey. He then planted himself in the passenger seat with a thump and a groan.

She walked around the car and opened the door, her thoughts absorbed by the heaviness of Luca's trip. Looking over at him from the driver's seat, she took a deep breath that sounded like a sigh with an attitude. "Luca, you're going to have to be strong for this trip. Can you handle it? Do you need me to go for you?"

Luca snapped out of it and shook his head. "No, I'll be okay. I'm just stunned, I guess. No one ever expects that kind of phone call."

"But it was just a phone call. We don't really know what's up there. You have to be brave," Celeste advised as she drove out of the parking lot. Irritated and sad, he turned his head to the window and thought about his brother as the mountain scenery sped by.

Joe looked at Margret and told her it was time to visit the Inn at

Shepherd Falls. "If I remember this park with its fountains and paths, then maybe I'll remember something there. I think we need to go now." His heart was beating fast. He was excited about the possibilities. Soon, he might know who he was. Soon, he might remember everything!

Emma reviewed her inventory and knew she needed to restock. The coffee bar was low on everything from stir sticks to lids, and there was a lull in business at this time of day. She had trained Ben on a few things, but he couldn't really run the place by himself. But maybe, just maybe, she could leave him in charge for half an hour while she collected her supplies from storage. Ben walked up to the coffee bar carrying a rack of clean mugs. He was smiling from ear to ear.

"I love this job. I can't wait to learn more. Thanks, Emma!"

Emma looked at him in his uniform and noticed how carefully he shelved the mugs. She looked around the quiet lobby, noticed that The General Store was closed for lunch, and decided to trust him with the task.

"Ben, I need to go to the storage room to restock. It usually takes me about thirty minutes. Do you think you can handle running the coffee bar while I'm gone?"

Ben was confident he could handle it. "Go ahead; I'll take care of everything." He continued putting away the mugs and grinned at her. "I've got this." Emma nodded and headed towards the kitchen. She turned around and watched him as he wiped down the bar and straightened the napkins. She breathed a sigh of relief and kept walking.

Margret pulled up to the Inn and noticed Joe was holding his breath. "Are you okay?"

"Yeah, I'm okay." He stared out the window, hoping that his memories would come flooding in. He breathed out a long, slow breath and unfastened his seatbelt. "Let's do this," he said shakily, as he opened the car door. His long legs stretched out, he stood to his full six feet, and faced the building. He didn't know what to expect, but he was ready. Wasn't he?

Margret walked over and stood beside him. She squeezed his hand. "Let's go."

Joe and Margret walked to the front doors. They were wooden double-arched doors, and he regarded them intensely. *Hmm. I think I would have remembered those. They're beautiful.* He kept walking and took a breath as he opened the door. He stepped over the threshold and cautiously took it all in. He looked at the lobby, the stairs, the windows, the little store in the corner, but nothing seemed familiar. There also seemed to be no one around. The registration desk was empty and there were no guests lingering in the lobby. It was very quiet.

Margret squeezed his hand again and whispered, "Let's try the coffee bar. Maybe we can ask some questions." They walked over to the bar and sat down on the polished round stools before it.

"Hi there," began Margret to the young man behind the counter. "We'd like two black coffees, please."

Ben looked up and nodded to the couple. "Right away," he said as he poured the brew. He was glad they hadn't ordered anything fancy. He probably would have messed up their orders.

Joe took a sip and spoke to the young man, "This is a nice inn. Can you tell me about it?"

"Thank you, Sir. Well, the owner and his fiancée run and manage this lovely place. They are just the cutest couple. Celeste is the best and has been so good to me. I'm really glad she's so happy now."

Joe heard the name, stopped in mid-sip, and stared at the young man. "What is the fiancée's name again?" He suddenly felt weak, afraid to hear the answer.

"Her name is Celeste. Do you know her?" Ben asked as he moved napkins from one side of the counter to the other.

"Um, no, I don't think so. It's just a nice name." He stole a glance at Margret while she stared at the barista.

"So, you say they're engaged?" she asked, trying to get more information.

"Oh, sure, they run this place together. They're the best," he answered. "If you're visiting, you may want to walk around the grounds or have a snack on the deck. Our scones are great with coffee." Ben looked pleased with himself and did not notice that Joe had grown increasingly pale.

Margret nodded at Ben and took a sip from her mug. She placed her hand on Joe's arm and whispered, "Maybe it's a different Celeste. This is only one place. The world is filled with women named Celeste. Also, the one you love couldn't be engaged to someone else already." She patted his arm and took another sip, but she had a strange feeling. Something wasn't right.

Joe turned to look at Margret and nodded. "You know, I don't remember Celeste, but I did call you that name by mistake, and there's a woman who occupies my dreams. I see her face, I hear her voice, and I feel like my dreams are trying to help me remember. But hopefully I am not dreaming about a woman who is engaged to someone else." He sighed and looked wistful.

Then he continued, "I think there's a point when you look at the one you love, and you don't see her face or her hair or her body. You see her wholly – body, mind, and soul, and that's who you love. I think it must be a feeling of complete knowing and therefore complete loving. It takes time. It takes joy, trials, disappointments, grief, experiences, and learning. And when it happens, it's as if contentment surrounds you both. You are connected. You are known. You are loved." He took a sip of coffee, turned around on the stool, and stopped short as his gaze fell upon the fireplace. He stood up and walked slowly towards it as a fleeting memory came and went like a wave on the ocean.

Margret stared at Joe and gulped after hearing his monologue on love. She took a deep breath and then asked, "What is it? Do you know this fireplace?" Margret turned from the counter and hopped down to follow him. She was curious, not only about his words on love but also about the fireplace he seemed to recognize. He stood before the stone structure trying to remember.

"I don't know. There was something there for a moment, but I can't seem to recall it. Let's go for a walk." He placed his mug on the table beside the couch and turned to the door. A thought suddenly presented itself, and he looked back to the barista.

"Excuse me, but what is Celeste's favorite coffee drink?"

Ben smiled and said with certainty, "She loves a good mocha."

Joe gasped audibly and headed for the front door. Margret nodded to the barista as she followed quickly outside.

Joe shook his head as if the movement would slide memories back into place, but it was no use. He looked at Margret and noticed she was looking off into the distance.

"Margret, she likes a mocha. Remember when I drank coffee in the hospital and recalled that I had a friend who liked a mocha? Do you remember that day?"

"I do remember that. Let's go for a walk down this way," she suggested. She crooked her arm through his and led him away from the building. "I discovered a little path this morning and found something nice. I think you'll like it."

Joe was pulled along by the motion, but his heart wasn't in it. He thought about how he had found the ad in the magazine. He had been so sure this place would hold all the answers and open the door to his memories. He was tired of having a foggy brain and was suddenly angry. He kicked at a stick on the path and watched as it flew into the brush. Margret stopped and smiled at him.

"Good," she said. "It's healthy to be angry in this situation. It helps me know you're going to keep fighting." She began leading him again. Joe felt like a child being pulled along by his mother, but he grinned and dug his elbow into her side. She laughed out loud and pushed him away.

They made their way down a slight hill to a gazebo. He followed and stepped into it with her. A soft breeze wrapped around him, and he felt a familiar comfort. It was a cozy feeling, but it was hard to describe. Was it this place or was it this mountain? He looked around and stood at the railing taking in the view.

"I think I've been in this place before. I may have been at this exact spot with someone very special to me." He rubbed his hands along the soft wood. It seemed to be a motion he'd made many times before. He began to hum a song he didn't know the name of and looked off into the distance. The sun sparkled on the mountains; the fog was long gone. He sighed.

Margret sat down in a chair and looked at him. "Tell me about Celeste."

Joe looked at her quickly and grimaced. "I don't know anything about Celeste. I just see a woman in my dreams."

"What does she look like in your dreams?"

He stood against the railing for support and let out a breath. "I don't really know. In dreams, there's a cloudy quality to people, and I rarely see her face." He paused for several minutes and then began again. "She's petite but athletic. Her smile captures the sunlight and radiates it back to you. Her eyes are the deepest green. She doesn't know how beautiful she is. She's kind and thoughtful and thinks of others first. She loves music, and she loves me." He sat down in a nearby chair, covered his face with his hands, and cried.

Margret had been watching his face as he described the woman in his dreams. She knew dreams were significant, and she would try to help him find her. *Did he realize he just remembered things about her that he couldn't possibly have learned through dreams?* It was strange to her that his memory had not fully returned, and she wondered why. What trauma was keeping them hidden? She reached over to him and placed her hand on his knee.

"Joe?" she whispered. "Joe, I want you to look at me." The whisper got his attention, and he wiped his tears with the back of his hand. He looked at her and waited. She sat up straight and folded her hands in her lap, looking businesslike.

"You have been through a traumatic experience, but it's time now to talk about it. I believe that once it's out in the open, you will be able to remember your life. You may begin now." She looked at him with determination, but he could also see friendship and warmth in her eyes. She couldn't hide that from him. They'd been through too much for that.

He straightened and turned his chair so that the mountains were before him. It grounded him somehow. He closed his eyes and breathed deeply. He was silent for a long while. Then he spoke quietly.

"The building we were in was getting colder and colder. It was hard to work, and the computers were beginning to malfunction. We could barely use the keyboards or input any data. One of us had to go out back to the electrical panel and generator, so I volunteered. I was hoping to find a solution to our impossible situation, and I thought I could just turn a switch or twist a knob to make it warmer for us all. I was already wearing my heavy coat, boots, hat, and scarf, but I put on extra socks and a pair of gloves." He sighed and opened his eyes. "Why am I able to remember this now?" He didn't look at her, but he could see her in his peripheral vision, and he could feel her eyes upon him.

Margret tried not to move as he spoke. She didn't want to break his train of thought or memories as they came flooding in. She was as surprised as he was, but perhaps this trip really was helping. She wanted to wrap her arms around him and tell him he was doing a good job. Instead, she whispered, "Keep going. What happened next?"

He nodded and continued, "The guys slapped me on the back and cheered me on as I headed to the door. I looked back at them and gave them a thumbs-up. Then I opened the inner door and closed it quickly behind me. I remember standing in the lockdown section. We called it no man's land because it was a frigid place between two sets of doors. I took a breath, pulled my mask over my face, and opened the outer door. It was brutal. The blizzard was worse than I had thought, but I knew if I didn't try, someone else would have to. The first thing I did was clasp my carabiner to the rope to make sure I didn't veer off course, and then I took my first step towards the back of the building. The rope was connected from a bar beside the door to the generator at the back. All I had to do was stay linked to that rope, and I should've been okay. After three or four steps, I seriously had my doubts that I would make it. I couldn't see anything, and my hands were so numb I could barely feel the rope. But it was fastened to me, so that helped my nerves. I think I fell once and hit the ground with my face." He winced and continued. "I kept thinking about the guys inside and how they were depending on me to get the heat started. Without it, we probably wouldn't make it out alive."

Tears ran down his face, but he didn't wipe them away. Margret moved her chair closer to his and reached for his hands. She squeezed them gently and whispered, "Take your time."

Suddenly, he jumped up and pounded the wooden railing with his fists. "I failed them! I failed them!" His body shook as he sobbed. Tears fell onto the wooden floor like raindrops as he continued his attack on the railing. Margret knew he had to get through this on his own. She stood nearby, but she let him cry, remember, and mourn. She would help him once the tears subsided.

Chapter 88

Celeste guided Luca into the airport and then steered him to a corner where two white rocking chairs faced one other.

"Sit down for a moment; I want to talk to you." She reached across their knees and held Luca's hands. He grabbed on tight and searched her eyes, waiting. "Luca, are you familiar with the words from Habakkuk 3:17-18?"

"Uh, no, not off the top of my head." He rolled his eyes. "Seriously?"

She tightened her grip on his hands to get his attention. She was serious. "Yes. It starts off by listing all kinds of things that are going badly. Like, the fig tree doesn't bud, there are no grapes growing on the vines, the crops fail, there's no food, no sheep, and no cattle, but then it says, 'Yet, I will rejoice in The Lord. I will be joyful in God my savior.'" Luca looked at her with confusion.

"Don't you see?" She gripped his hands tightly. "The most important word in those two verses is yet. Yet! Even though bad things were happening, there was hope. Yet means that no matter how bad things get, no matter what is happening, we must trust in God because He is our strength. Luca, we must have faith and believe that God loves us and is here for us. Even if bad things happen, we are not alone." Luca looked off into the distance and nodded. He squeezed Celeste's hands and leaned in to kiss her forehead. Then he stood up and walked through security, turning back slightly to nod goodbye. Even though he was across the room and in the midst of a crowd, she could still recognize the pain in his eyes.

Silently praying for him, Celeste watched him until he was out of sight and then turned to go. *What now?* She needed to think, but she also needed action. She had to do something. Suddenly, an idea came to mind. As she stopped walking to consider it, several people mumbled under their breath as they dodged her to avoid collisions. Unaware of the annoyed travelers, she left the airport and headed straight into town. She was on a mission, and she knew exactly where she needed to go.

Song: *I Knew You Were Waiting for Me* by Aretha Franklin and George Michael

Chapter 89

Bert had given Celeste a key to The General Store, and she used it now to open the back door. She texted Bert to let him know she was there and asked if he needed any items for restocking. Daisy responded and told her to eat some cookies and drink some lemonade. Celeste headed for the cookie tin Daisy kept on the table. She grabbed a Cranberry-White-Chocolate-Oatmeal cookie and headed to the front.

Bert and Daisy had closed the store for the week while they launched the little shop at the Inn. Daisy said it was their vacation. Soon they would return and have Celeste's employees run the day-to-day operations of the new store.

Celeste slowed down as she always did when she walked through the doors. She felt safe, as if nothing in the world could be wrong here. She wandered to the candle section and found what she was looking for. She picked up twelve boxes of votives and placed them on the counter. Then she wandered through the store, calming her mind and breathing deeply. She chuckled at dishtowels with funny sayings, rubbed her fingers along the soft blankets, looked at the jewelry, and even tried on a dress. She liked the way it looked and placed it on the counter with the candles. She then picked up a leather journal and placed all the items into a bag. She turned around to look at the store and noticed the twinkle lights shining along the rafters. She sat down to study them. *Strands of twinkle lights are like stepping stones. They are little bursts of light that illuminate a place or lead the way to something meant to be seen.* She stared at them and quietly sighed.

"I think we are supposed to be like twinkle lights to others," she said aloud. "We shine our light with kindness and thoughtfulness, and we lead others to the source of the light: God." She closed her eyes and prayed that she could always be the person God intended her to be, and to have faith and strength in the coming days. She prayed she could be a light to others, like a twinkle light or a stepping stone to God. As she prayed, she felt a wave of peacefulness envelop her. She sat in the stillness, enjoying the embrace, and whispered a thank-you.

As she left the shop, she took two cookies and a bottle of water for the road and headed for her truck. A little bit of retail therapy and prayer had helped, but now she also had a plan. She wondered about her sense of calm. Why wasn't she frantic and worried? Why wasn't she crying? Didn't she just leave Luca at the airport so that he could fly to Iceland? She shook her head to get that thought out of her mind.

She gazed upon the mountains as she drove. *I feel at peace because I don't believe that Sergio is the man they found. I truly believe he's okay and that he will come back to me. I don't know why I feel this calm. It's as if I just know. Wait, I do know why I feel this way. God's peace is real, and I trust in him no matter what. He is with me, and it will all be okay, no matter what happens.* She reached for a cookie, finished it off in three bites, and turned on the radio.

"Ooh, this is the song I would text him right now!" She started singing along and arrived home ready to spring into action.

Song: *Signed, Sealed, Delivered, I'm Yours* by Stevie Wonder

Chapter 90

NORTH CAROLINA

Totally spent and groaning with desperation, Joe dropped to his knees and rested his head on the wooden railing. Margret sat beside him, waiting. She knew there were no words to say at the moment. Words weren't needed. He would have to get to a point where he was ready to talk, but she knew that would take time. She placed her hand on his back and massaged his shoulders where she knew he carried his stress. She felt the tension release a bit from his muscles, and she continued to rub.

Celeste arrived at the Inn, carried her packages inside, and headed straight to the little shop. "Hi, Daisy! I found some treasures at the store in town and want to pay for them here."

Daisy peeked into the bag. "Oh, I just knew that dress was meant for you. I can't wait to see it on you!" She chatted happily as she pulled the items out of the bag one at a time and rang them up. "Twelve boxes of votives? Gracious. What will you do with these?" Celeste grinned and told Daisy her plan.

"I once heard an old tale about true love. In the story, a woman waited for her love to return from war. It had been years since she'd seen him, but she believed he would return to her one day. She kept hope alive by burning candles and praying. One day she had the idea to light all her candles at once. If she placed them outside on a ledge near her home, maybe the light would lead him to her. Maybe he needed the light to help him find his way home. She waited until nightfall. The evening was perfect; there was no wind or rain in sight. She placed the candles on the ledge and lit them all. Then she sat nearby and waited.

Soon she fell asleep. As she slept, her love saw the light from the road and knew he had made it home. The lights told their own story, and he knew in his heart she had waited for him all this time. She woke up to see her love standing before her. She jumped up, ran into his arms, and, well, and then they lived and loved happily ever after."

"That's a beautiful story, my dear. May I help you place the candles and light them tonight?" Daisy asked.

"Yes, thank you. There are so many, I'd love your help." They planned the evening and then Celeste headed to her office. She studied a spreadsheet, fiddled with some entries, and then closed her laptop. She couldn't concentrate. Plopping down in a chair beside the windows, she gazed out over the mountains and prayed.

Joe's cries softened until Margret could barely hear them. She continued to rub his back softly, as if he were a child in need of soothing. She wasn't sure what would happen next, but she would wait for him to make the next move. It was his story to tell, and she would wait, and watch, and listen.

Celeste fell asleep in her office chair. She dreamed a montage of strange scenes: a light shining in the forest; someone calling to her from the ocean; candles on a ledge flickering softly; a helicopter rising into a snow-filled sky, and other vague images she couldn't quite understand. Her phone woke her up, but she ignored it and tried to recall the images. Then she reached for her journal and quickly jotted them down. She began to sketch some of the images so that she could think more about them later, but she finally gave up the idea. She had things to do and a plan to implement.

Daisy was pulling votives out of the bags when Celeste joined her on the deck. Celeste looked lovely, wearing the new dress and looking determined.

"My dear, you look beautiful," Daisy exclaimed as she reached for Celeste's hand. "I love how the ocean-blue of the dress makes your eyes sparkle. It's perfect. Now, where do we begin?" Celeste turned around and pointed to the deck railing, explaining her ideas to her friend.

"I think it's important for the light to be seen from all vantage points. This deck is our highest one, and the light will be seen from quite a distance." Daisy nodded and chatted happily as she unwrapped the packages.

Joe's knees hurt. He slid into a sitting position against the railing to relieve the pain. He sighed and then looked up at Margret. "Thank you for allowing me to vent like that. I guess it was all bottled up. Did I fail my friends? Are they still there?"

Margret sat down beside him. The wooden floor was hard, and she wasn't sure what to say. She didn't know if the men were still there or in a hospital somewhere. She knew he blamed himself, and she didn't want to give him false hope. He turned and rested his head on her shoulder.

"Thanks for just listening. I know you don't have all the answers. I'm glad I remembered some of that awful day, but remembering has consequences too. I don't know what happened to my friends, and it hurts." He sighed and continued. "I think maybe we should leave soon. This place is familiar, but I'm exhausted, and I need to rest somewhere without the memories." Margret dipped her head. She wasn't quite ready to go home yet, but she knew she needed to do what was best for him.

Joe moved away from her, grabbed onto the railing, and stood up. "I'm pretty hungry. Do you want to get some food?" He looked at Margret with sad eyes. She nodded and turned away, but he didn't follow. "I'll be right there. I need a minute."

Margret headed to the parking lot. "I'll be in the car. Take as long as you need."

Joe leaned into the railing. The scenery was beautiful, but tears spoiled the view. He wiped them with the back of his hand and choked back a sob. *I think I'm forgetting some very important things, and it's so frustrating.* He looked out at the mountains again and then turned towards the Inn. The rays of the setting sun touched the window panes all at once, and they sparkled and shone with crimson light. As he watched, the light faded, and his eyes were drawn to the top deck. Someone had placed candles all along the edge, and they were coming alive with light. He watched as the light progressed from each end until they met in the middle. He heard laughter and saw a figure wearing a blue dress that swished around her legs. He hoped the breeze wouldn't blow out her lights. For a moment he considered walking to them, but then he remembered that Margret was waiting in the car. He made his way to the parking lot and looked up at the lights once more before the corner of the building hid them from view. He sat down in the passenger seat with a feeling of defeat.

"I have dinner planned and then you can get some rest," he heard Margret say. He didn't care. He just didn't care.

Song: ***Something in My Eye*** **by Callum Beattie**

Chapter 91

Celeste reclined in a deck chair next to Daisy and watched the candles flicker in the wind. Daisy chatted about the store for a while but soon rested her head on the back of the chair to gaze at the stars. As the crickets and frogs began a concert on the ground below, Celeste listened while keeping an eye on the dancing lights of the candles. She knew it was a long shot, but maybe, just maybe, the light would draw Sergio to her.

"You know," whispered Celeste, "we all have to be like candles lighting the way. Light chases away darkness: it's a sign of hope, and it creates a feeling of safety and trust."

Daisy reached out and grasped her hand. "That's beautiful, dear, and so true." They held hands and watched the lights. Bert joined them and offered blankets to chase the chill away. Celeste hadn't realized how cold it had become, and she was grateful for the warmth. Soon Daisy and Bert said goodbye, and Celeste hugged them both.

"Thank you for your help. I'm just going to stay here a bit longer."

Daisy nodded. "I'll see you tomorrow, Celeste. Goodnight."

Celeste watched her friends leave and then turned back to the votives. A few of them had gone out, but she didn't relight them. She snuggled into her blanket and sat for hours, watching them go out one by one. She wondered about Sergio's incident in college and what had really happened. She didn't believe for a second that he was involved, but she needed to hear the story from him. She wouldn't cast guilt from gossip or second-hand accounts. She snuggled deeper and closed her eyes.

She was awakened by some distant noise and checked her phone. It was midnight, and she was freezing. Gathering her blanket, she stood up to leave and stretched her sore muscles. All the candles were out now, and he had not come. She was disappointed but not surprised.

"I may keep lighting them to keep hope alive," she whispered into the wind. "Although true hope comes from God. He is my hope, and I trust in Him." She prayed silently, *God, you know my path, and you know what's right for me. Your timing, God. Your timing.* Then she turned around and headed into the warmth of the building. Within minutes she was in bed and sound asleep.

Joe and Margret shared a pizza on the deck of Wren House. They ate in silence as they watched the flickering lights on the deck of The Inn at Shepherd Falls.

Margret took a sip of hot cider. "In the Arctic, candlelight is significant because it lights up the darkness and signifies hope. A single candle can light the path and help someone find his way home." She glanced over at Joe, but he didn't notice. His eyes were focused on the candlelight. Every now and then he'd take a bite of pizza, but she could tell his mind was elsewhere.

He asked, "Do you think those lights over there are significant or just decoration?" He continued watching as he took another bite.

"Oh, I don't know. It's nice to think they're significant, though.

Do you want to go back over there to check it out?" Margret looked at him for his reaction.

He thought about it but decided against it. "Thanks, but I think I just want to go to sleep. It's been a big day. I may even want to leave tomorrow." He looked at Margret and smiled a sad smile. "Thanks for everything."

"You're welcome." She stood up and placed the remaining pizza back in the box. "By the way, I also bought chocolate. Would you like a piece?" She held up a chocolate bar, but he shook his head.

"No, thanks. I'm not really in the mood for G-squared right now." He looked and sounded dejected.

"What did you call the chocolate?" Her head tilted curiously.

"What? I don't remember," Joe muttered. Margret looked at him and shook her head. He was exhausted.

"Are you ready?" He nodded, followed her inside, and wondered how he'd even make it to his room.

He felt a steadying arm on his and a whisper in his ear, "It's going to be okay. Sleep as late as you want to. We can make plans tomorrow." Margret led him to the elevator and then down the hallway to his room. He mumbled something to her that he hoped sounded like goodnight as he closed the door. His emotions were all over the place. He was tired but also angry and irritated. He stood with his back against the door and wasn't sure if he should cry or hit something. He was beyond frustrated and needed a plan. But first, he knew he needed sleep. He climbed into bed, closed his eyes, and succumbed. He dreamed of candles, wind, and a fluttering blue dress.

Song: *Broken* by Lifehouse

Chapter 92

Knut looked intensely at each male passenger arriving from the latest flight, but his eyes did not linger on Luca. Knut was a large man with a big personality. His beard was big and full, and his body tall and stocky. He looked like a man who lived and thrived in the mountains.

Luca passed easily through security in Reykjavik and saw his name scrawled on a paper sign. He regarded the man holding it and noted his size. He imagined even his voice would be big and loud. Luca, on the other hand, was tall and slim, clean shaven, his dark hair neat. They looked like a pair of opposites. Luca managed a slight smile as he approached.

"Hello, I'm your guy," Luca said as he held out his hand in greeting. The man's mouth turned up in a cheerful response, and he shook the offered hand.

"Hello! Welcome to Iceland. Follow me." He grabbed Luca's bag and led him out to a waiting car. Luca slid into the back seat of the warm SUV, and the door closed behind him. His host sat up front and continued talking.

"My name is Knut. We're glad you're here in our beautiful city, but I'm sorry it's under these circumstances. We'll go straight to your hotel and get you settled. Afterwards, I'll take you to the hospital."

Luca watched the scenery pass by and listened to his new friend describe the city, the weather, and the excellent people of Iceland. Luca thought the landscape was beautiful. Then he remembered why he was there, and his head began to throb with the difficulty of his upcoming task.

Joe woke up with determination. He knew he wasn't well yet, but he felt fine, and he was ready for a change. He needed new scenery, and he had a plan. He hoped Margret would agree. He showered, shaved, and packed his bag, and then he went downstairs for breakfast. He was seated at his favorite table when Margret walked in. She hesitated when she saw him and then headed his way.

"Good morning, Joe. You look like you're ready for the day and for whatever it brings." She pulled out a chair and sat down to join him while watching his response.

"Good morning," he said as he picked up a piece of bacon. "I know one thing for sure: I love bacon!" He laughed out loud, and Margret looked on with interest. She ordered coffee and a bowl of fruit.

"What are you up to, Joe? What's going on?"

He wiped his mouth with a white cloth napkin and took a sip of coffee. "I think I need to see something different. This place has been nice, but it might be a good idea to see more of the country. I'd like to see the ocean." He looked directly into her eyes to gauge her response and noticed a flicker of interest.

"Well, it just so happens that I spoke with the doctor last night and suggested that very thing. It's a five-hour drive to the coast. Let's head out after breakfast." She laughed, and they high-fived across the table.

Celeste was at her desk before the sun greeted the mountain with its warm rays and beautiful colors. She was behind on several projects, and she thought if she stayed busy, her mind wouldn't wander, but it was no use. She pushed her laptop away and walked to the window. *I can't sit still today. I just can't. Luca is in Iceland, and I'm here lighting candles in the wind.* She sank into the cozy chair by the window and uttered a sob. She pulled a throw off the shelf nearby and gathered it around her. Somehow the soft material helped soothe her grief. As she stared outside, tears pooled in her eyes, making the trees look like a blurry child's painting.

"Sergio, I miss you so much. I miss you like breath. I want to breathe the air you breathe; I want your arms around me, I want to feel your hand squeezing mine, I want to share my day with you, I want to walk with you, read with you, travel with you, and be yours forever," she whispered into the warm office air. "But, if you don't come home, I will still love you always." Celeste sat for an hour staring out at the mountains as she watched the world wake up. Finally, she stood, stretched, folded the throw, and headed outside for a walk.

As they finished breakfast, Margret told Joe about her plans. "I spoke with the front desk attendant earlier this morning, and she suggested Ocean Isle, North Carolina. It's about five and a half hours away. If we leave soon, we'll be there by early afternoon and can find a place to stay. We don't have to hurry. We can enjoy the trip and see if anything looks familiar to you. Does this plan sound okay?" Joe grinned. It was a good sign. "Okay, let's get packed and checked out. Want to meet me in the lobby in thirty minutes?"

Joe downed the last sip of coffee and stood. "Let's do this! I'm ready!"

They headed to their rooms and then met in the lobby. Joe was there before her and asked the desk attendant for hotel or resort options in Ocean Isle. By the time Margret arrived, he had several brochures and recommendations for hotels. Margret chatted with the clerk while she checked out. He reminded her that their bill was paid for by The Inn at Shepherd Falls.

"Thank you very much," she said. "We loved our time here, and I'm sure we'll return one day. Now, we're off to the sea."

Celeste took the inner loop trail for her morning walk. The trail wound its way around the lower edges of the bluff, close to the property line of Wren House. As she walked, she thought about the two inns, how they were different and how they were similar. She knew hers was much grander and could hold large conventions, but Wren House was relaxed and comfortable, and she considered stopping by for a quick look. The gardens were beautiful in the morning light. She passed the tiny white blooms of the Flowering Dogwood and the lovely pale yellow and bright orange of the Flame Azaleas. She smiled at their beauty and at the perfection of God's creation.

As she continued climbing the hill to Wren House, she wondered if they had good coffee. She rounded the hill and walked to the front doors. Something in her peripheral vision caught her eye, and she casually glanced towards it. It was a laughing couple just getting into their car. It was a split second of color, gestures, movements, and laughter, and she looked away. As she approached the door, a young man opened it and greeted her.

"Good morning. How are you this fine day?"

"Good morning! I've been walking, and I wondered if you have a coffee bar."

"We certainly do. I'll show you right where it is." The young porter led her into a comfortable lobby with overstuffed chairs and several fireplaces. She followed him and took in little details all around. She smelled breakfast somewhere nearby and heard the clink of dishes. The place was smaller than hers, but it was inviting.

"Here we are. We have excellent coffee and hot chocolate. Enjoy!" He tipped his hat to her and headed back to his post at the front door. Celeste thanked him, sat down, and ordered a hot chocolate. As she waited, she thought she should probably speak to the manager and apologize for never having visited before. After all, they should know each other. They were neighbors.

Suddenly she froze. The couple in the parking lot: the way the man moved was so familiar. What was it? It was something subtle, but it was something she knew. Did she know him? And his voice, did she recognize it? But it couldn't be! She jumped off the barstool and ran to the door. The startled porter opened it quickly and looked concerned.

"Are you okay?" he began, but she didn't hear him.

Celeste ran out into the parking lot, but the couple was gone. She turned around and ran back to the young doorman.

"Do you know the couple that just left?" she pleaded.

"Yes, I do. I talked to Margret many times. Do you know her?"

"Tell me what you know about her! Please!" Celeste raised her voice and must have looked intense because the porter backed away from her. His calm demeanor, though, was reassuring.

"Well," he began, "I talked to her about her work. She's a nurse up north somewhere and loves taking care of people. She's never been this far south. She likes to hike and..."

Celeste interrupted his litany, "But what about the man? What's his name?"

"I believe his name is Joe, but I'm not really sure. I didn't speak with him." Celeste stumbled over to a bench and put her head in her hands.

"I'm sorry. It's just that I thought I knew him. He looked so familiar, like a long-lost... I apologize for my behavior." She shook her head and stood up. "I'll go grab that hot chocolate now and meet your manager."

"Of course," said the young man as he opened the door. He was glad the situation was over, and he watched as Celeste made her way back to the coffee bar. The drink was waiting for her, but she looked at it and realized she didn't want it anymore. She took one sip, complimented the barista, paid for it, and asked to see the manager.

"She's away for the day, but she'll be back tomorrow. Would you like to leave a message?" The barista handed her a notepad and a pen. Celeste wrote a quick note, included her name and phone number, and then headed home. Still rattled, she needed the exercise to calm her nerves. She walked at a brisk pace back to her inn thinking about the man she had seen for no more than a few seconds and wondered who he was. Taking the path that wandered towards the back of the property, she found her way to the waterfall. She sat on the bench and stared at the water.

Something was nudging her mind. *If I knew him, why didn't I recognize him?* She sighed deeply and then whispered to the waterfall, "Don't forget me, don't forget me, don't forget me. Sergio, my love, don't forget me."

She turned to leave and walked away from the garden. She didn't even turn back for a quick glance at the water, as was her custom. Her nerves were raw, and she needed to keep busy. She headed for the office, determined to keep her mind on her work, but once there, she looked at pictures of Sergio on her phone, focusing on each handsome feature. She longed to be held in his arms again. She sighed, searched her playlists, and texted him a song.

Song: *From Where you Are* **by Lifehouse**

Chapter 93

Luca walked into the Icelandic Hotel and stopped to stare. It was a modern marvel of glass and steel. Everything was white: the walls, the floors, the tables and chairs. Snowy landscape pictures covered the walls, and steel beams near the ceiling shimmered white. He turned to the front desk and noticed it was gleaming white marble that mirrored all the white around it. Even the enormous fireplace in the center of the lobby was white marble with flecks of glitter scattered through it. Luca noticed that the firelight reflected the glittering specks and gave the illusion of snow on fire. It was mesmerizing. The only color noticeable was in the uniforms of the employees. Everyone was dressed exactly the same: white shoes, white pants, and lime green shirts with a white name tag near the right shoulder. It reminded him of a large white bowl he had seen once in a store. The bowl had been filled with fresh limes. He stood in the grand lobby marveling at the scene. The white and green complimented each other and looked fresh and clean. It was strange, but Luca loved it.

Knut led him to the front desk and assisted him with the check in. Then, pointing in the direction of the elevators, he asked Luca to be back in the lobby in an hour.

Luca's room was all white with lime green throw pillows on the bed and clusters of green ferns in white vases placed throughout the room. The theme of the hotel was definitely white and green, and Luca wondered if it was meant to represent the snow of winter and the hope of spring in green. He shook his head, set his alarm for 30 minutes, and lay down for a quick nap. He was asleep immediately.

As Margret drove away, Joe looked back at Wren House in an effort to commit it to memory. A pretty woman approached the porter at the front door, and his heart picked up its pace. He liked the way she moved, and he noticed how the wind picked up her hair to play with it. She brushed it off her face and walked through the door. He reluctantly turned in his seat and felt empty, as though he were missing something. He looked for her in the side mirror, but she was gone. As he wondered about her, he turned on the radio. For some reason, he needed to hear some music.

Luca slept until his phone alarm woke him thirty minutes later. He stared at the white ceiling and dreaded what he had to do. He wished Celeste were with him. He was braver with her nearby. He picked up his phone and called her, but it went to voicemail. He listened to her voice and felt more at ease. It wasn't the same as talking to her, but it helped. He turned it off and headed for the shower.

Knut was waiting in the lobby and nodded when he saw Luca. He led him outside and to the waiting car. There wasn't much talk on the way to the hospital, and Luca was glad. He didn't want to listen or have to answer any questions. He just stared out the window and thought about his brother.

It didn't take long to reach their destination. Luca thought about asking Knut to drive around town just a little bit longer. But in his heart, he knew he needed to identify the body and arrange for him to be brought home. He got out of the car slowly as Knut directed him into the building. They took the elevator to the basement, where the morgue was located, and stepped out into a gray hallway with too many lights. Luca wondered if they were overcompensating. *Maybe the bright lights are here to make the place feel less desolate.* He followed Knut down several hallways until they reached a room with double metal doors. Luca tried desperately to remember the Bible verses Celeste had spoken to him in the airport while holding his hands. He didn't know if her words or the memory of his hands in hers brought him comfort, but he grabbed onto the memory for its strength. As Knut swiped his badge and the doors swung open, the word *Yet* cemented itself in Luca's brain. Yet. It gave him hope. Luca didn't move, but Knut understood and linked his arm through Luca's so they could enter together. Luca slowed his steps, felt his stomach gurgling, and wondered if he could find a bathroom before he got sick. Knut kept nudging him farther into the room. As they approached, the doctor turned around and acknowledged them.

"Hello," she said to Luca as she reached out to clasp his hand. "Thank you for coming. I'm Doctor Larsen. Since yesterday, we have found and brought in three more men from the accident site. I know this is terribly difficult for you, and I know this is not what you expected, but we will need for you to look at all four men. Let me know when you're ready, and I'll help you." She looked him in the eye until he looked back at her and nodded.

Luca knew he had to look, but until he did, he could pretend that it was all just a mistake. And now there were four men to look at? Was his brother really lying there under a sheet? He knew he would have to tell Celeste everything, and that frightened him too.

How would he tell her? Could she handle it? Luca finally took a deep breath. "I'm ready."

Dr. Larsen led him to the corner of the room where sheets covered four different examination tables. Luca could tell a body was under each sheet, and he broke into a sweat. He paused, and the doctor paused as well.

"Take your time. There's no rush," he heard her say. He took slow, steady breaths and then continued walking. When they reached the tables, Dr. Larsen led him to the first one. "Now, I will pull the sheet down. All you have to do is tell me if this is your brother. If not, we'll move to the next one and so on. Here we go."

Luca watched the sheet being pulled back in slow motion, and then he saw a face he did not recognize. It was bigger and broader than his brother's, and he shook his head. He wiped the sweat off his forehead and took a breath. They moved down the line, and each time, Luca shook his head. He was feeling lightheaded and faint, but he only had one more to go. Dr. Larsen pulled back the final sheet, and Luca immediately turned around and threw up in the corner. Dr. Larsen pulled the sheet back in place, grabbed cold cloths, and sent Knut for a bottle of water. She placed a wet cloth on the back of Luca's neck, and then she handed him another cloth to wipe his mouth.

"I'm so sorry I made a mess." Luca took the offered bottle and swished the cold water around in his mouth. Then he spit into a nearby sink and repeated the process. He turned to face Dr. Larsen and stated, "That is not my brother." Dr. Larsen and Knut looked at each other and then back at Luca.

"Oh! We thought…. Are you quite sure?"

"I'm positive. None of these men is my brother." Luca managed a tiny smile but felt weak. "I'd like to leave now."

Knut nodded to Dr. Larsen and led Luca back into the bright hallway and straight to the car. Luca rode in silence, his mind jumbled with contrasting emotions. He didn't know whether to cry, yell, or laugh. He walked through the lobby of the hotel, not even noticing the lime and white, took the elevator, and slumped down onto the white couch in his room. He rested his head in his hands and thought of Celeste. He wanted to call her, to hear her voice, and then head home as soon as possible. He wondered who the men on the examination tables were, and he hoped their loved ones would be notified soon. He was glad he hadn't seen Sergio, but then again, where was he? He reminded himself that his brother could still be dead, just buried under the snow. He stood up, sat back down, and then punched a lime green throw pillow. It sagged to the floor as Luca began to pace. He needed answers. He wondered if he should visit the village where Sergio had been working before his team made the trip farther north. He called Knut to get more information and to formulate a plan. He couldn't just sit around. He had to do something.

Chapter 94

Celeste's phone rang, displaying the name Wren House on the screen, and she answered it quickly. Pulling a sheet of paper, she was ready to jot down any important information. Instead, she stared at it until the paper became blurry. She wasn't sure she was hearing correctly, and she was certain she would have stopped breathing if breathing weren't an involuntary process. She thanked her neighbor, ended the call, and sat still for a moment. She didn't understand. The manager had received Celeste's note from the barista. She had called to chat but also to tell her about the couple who had stayed at Wren House. She thanked Celeste for paying their bill and was intrigued that they had traveled all the way from Greenland, of all places. She was a nurse, and the man's name was Joe. They had enjoyed their stay and were now headed to the beach. *What?*

Celeste stood up and began pacing. *Greenland? A nurse? A man named Joe? That's way too close to the name Sergio. It's too coincidental. What kind of game is he playing? Does he have a devious side? Why didn't he come see me? Is it my Sergio? Of course, it's not. He loves me, and he would do everything he could to find me. He would rush here and fall into my arms and hold me and tell me everything was going to be okay. But he didn't.*

She didn't know whether to cry, to scream, to throw something, or to just stare out the window. Her phone rang again, and she reached for it eagerly, but it was Luca. She let it go to voicemail and ran upstairs to her room. She needed to run. She needed to pound the trails and let her music take over her thoughts for a while. Ten minutes later she was out the door with her music blasting into her ear buds. She didn't know what else to do.

She chose a trail that headed down the mountain, knowing it would lead her away from the stepping stones. She just couldn't go anywhere near them today. She ran hard and listened for answers in the songs. The music and the lyrics kept her from thinking about what-ifs. They gave a steady beat, words, and lines to consider. She finally slowed down and came to a stop near a clearing. She wandered into it and sat down on a tree stump, calmed her breathing, and turned off her music. The silence of the woods was peaceful, and soon her ears picked up the sound of running water. Setting off to explore, she walked deeper into woods and soon discovered a generous stream on its journey through the valley. As she watched the water, her breath slowed, and her mind cleared.

It reminded her of the little creek in the park in Chicago. She had compared her life to the journey of its water. Each stream had its own course, its own problems, and varied destinations. Her life was different now, and she had learned something since she'd been here. She could be scared of the unknowns up ahead, or she could enjoy the ride. She became lost in her thoughts as she watched the water flow.

Lakes can't compare to the beauty of a stream. A lake is stagnant. It doesn't move. It feels stuck. Oceans lap in and out but they don't get very far into solid land. Streams are journeyers: seeking, reaching, and finding. "I think I'm a lot like you, little stream. I see that there are obstacles in my way, but I'm not going to let them stop me. I will find a way to get over them. I will figure out this situation, no matter what. Love is a journey, and every step is worth it." She placed a leaf in the water and watched it hurry down with the current to its unseen destination. It bounced over rocks, skirted a branch, and rushed out of sight. She nodded, texted a song, and turned to go.

Song: *All In* by Lifehouse

Chapter 95

NORTH CAROLINA AND ICELAND

Bert waited patiently in the parking lot, and as Celeste rounded the bend, he looked up and waved.

"Hello, dear girl!" Celeste headed towards him and was engulfed in a huge hug. She relaxed in his arms and squeezed him back.

"I needed that bear hug!" She pulled away, smiled at him, and continued, "I've had quite a day."

Bert nodded and pointed to a little bench near the edge of the lot. "Let's sit for a while. Tell me what's going on."

Celeste sat beside him and explained the events of the day. She wasn't angry anymore, she was just confused, and she was working on a plan. She told him about the little stream and the wisdom she had gained from it.

Bert patted her hand. "There was a time when Daisy and I separated. Did you know that?" Bert looked off into the mountains and slowly nodded his head. "Longest week of my life."

Celeste was taken aback. "No, I had no idea. How did you get back together? You seem so much in love."

Bert turned to her. "I was sitting by a rock down by the river one day. I was mad at her; I don't remember why. I was trying to figure out what to say and what to do. Nature always helped me with the big questions, you know." Celeste nodded. "Out of the corner of my eye I saw Daisy making her way to a rock on the other side a bit downstream from me. I just sat and watched her. I started naming all the things I loved about her, and pretty soon, I couldn't remember why I was mad. I put some pretty leaves into the water so that she'd see them. I watched her as they floated by. I kept adding leaves to the water to make her happy. It took a while, but at some point, she looked upstream to see where all the leaves were coming from, and she saw me. She smiled at me, with that face and those eyes that I loved, and I knew I had my answer. I waded through the stream and brought a leaf right to her. She took it, and then she took my hands. She told me that moving water, and particularly this little river, had the answers we needed, and if we were ever in need of help or advice, that's where we'd go. We're still riding that water and getting to our destination together, no matter what's in our way."

"That's beautiful, Bert. Thank you. I know every couple has problems, but you two seem so happy."

"It's because we were friends first. If you marry your best friend, you have the perfect person to journey with." His kind eyes regarded her. "Now, let's think about your dilemma. Have you talked with Luca? Wasn't he in Iceland today?"

"Oh, yes, that's right, and he called me. He left a voicemail." Celeste played the message on speaker so they could listen together. She let out a sob of relief when she heard that Sergio wasn't one of the men under a sheet. "I feel sorry for the men and their families, but I'm also relieved. But, Bert, if he was here, why didn't he come see me? I don't understand."

Bert looked thoughtful for a few minutes. "Well, the reservation was made at the Inn, but he had to stay at Wren House because you were overbooked. The reservation wasn't in his name, but a nurse's name. The nurse is from Greenland. He is going by the name Joe.

I think, if this is really him, that Sergio doesn't remember who he is. But, for some reason, he convinced a nurse from Greenland to bring him here."

Celeste jumped up. "Bert, that makes sense. I was told they were headed to Ocean Isle. I have to go!" She reached down and hugged him again and then ran to the Inn to make arrangements to leave. Bert nodded thoughtfully. Then he picked up a pretty green leaf from the ground and tucked it into his front shirt pocket for Daisy.

"No, we're sorry," Luca heard them say. "We cannot legally divulge any more information about OEC or the accident. All we can tell you now is that Liam, the project manager, has been let go. We are continuing the investigation. It's best you go home. We will contact you when we have news." Luca hung up from the call and ran his hand through his hair.

"What do I do now?" His phone rang, and he quickly picked up. "Celeste, I don't know what to do." He began to speak but she had a story of her own to tell. She was speaking very quickly and was out of breath. "Celeste, please slow down. I can't understand what you're saying."

"I'm sorry, Luca. It's just that I'm trying to close the office while we're talking. Then I have to speak to the assistant manager to take over for a few days, and then I have to pack."

"What are you talking about? Celeste, what's going on? Where are you going?" Celeste stopped and realized she hadn't explained very well.

"I apologize. Luca, you need to come home. I think Sergio and his nurse may have been here on the mountain. They were staying at Wren House. I think Sergio has amnesia. I'm going to Ocean Isle to see if it's really him."

Luca froze. When he was able to make sense of her words, he responded. "What did you say?"

"I'm going to Ocean Isle." Celeste hung up as Luca was trying to get a word in. He stared at the phone, incredulous that she had ended the call so abruptly, and then he leapt into action. He opened his flight app to see how quickly he could get to Myrtle Beach. Once he was there, it was only a short drive to Ocean Isle. He didn't know what was going on or who Celeste thought she saw, but he wanted to be there to comfort her when all was revealed. He suddenly couldn't wait to get out of the lime green hotel. He headed downstairs, checked out, and called a car to take him to the airport as quickly as possible.

Joe rolled down his window and watched the scenery as they drove east on I-40. He was looking forward to seeing the ocean, but he felt anxious. He didn't know who he was, and he had no real home. He closed his eyes, and his mind drifted to the beautiful woman in his dreams. Who was this woman he dreamed of? He wasn't sure he should be leaving the mountain, but he wasn't really sure of anything right now. He glanced over at Margret, but she seemed lost in her own thoughts. He closed his eyes again, succumbing to sleep, and praying he would be able to dream.

Song: *Edge of the Ocean* by Stick Figure

Chapter 96

NORTH CAROLINA

Celeste needed to leave. Now. She called her assistant manager into the office to explain that she would be gone for a few days. "I think Luca will be here soon, but you'll be in charge until one of us gets back." She went on to give him the customer data for the next few days and showed him the spreadsheet. They were down a couple of housekeepers, but she thought it would be fine. She told him to keep Emma, the coffee shop manager, in the loop so that she would be prepared. "In fact, I need to remember to see her before I leave," she murmured. She then reminded him about the engagement party that was coming in for the weekend. She felt oddly calm as she explained everything to him.

When she felt as though she had given all the details she could, she locked her office and headed upstairs. She threw a bag together quickly and then headed to Sergio's room. She looked in his closet and pulled one of his shirts off a hanger. She held it to her nose and breathed it in, placed it in her bag, and walked out. Her last stop was to see Emma and grab a coffee for the road. Emma was in the midst of training Ben, but they both stopped what they were doing when Celeste approached.

"Ben, would you like to prepare Celeste's favorite drink?" Emma looked at Celeste to make sure she wanted one, and Celeste nodded.

"Thank you, Ben. I'd love a large mocha. Emma, may I speak with you for a minute?" Emma nodded and walked to the edge of the bar. Celeste explained that she had an emergency and had to leave for a few days. She thanked her for taking good care of the coffee bar every day, but especially now that she was leaving.

"I'll take care of everything," Emma said. "Don't worry. Are you alright?"

"Thank you, Emma. I'm okay; I just need to follow my heart. I miss Sergio every day, and I think I may have a lead on where he could be."

Emma shook her head. "Celeste, what do you mean? I thought you and Luca were engaged. Everyone thought so."

Celeste's body stiffened. "Engaged? No. I have never stopped loving Sergio. I have a feeling he's near, and I have to go. I always thought he'd come back for me, but now I know I have to meet him halfway." Emma swallowed hard, and Ben handed the coffee to Celeste. He had overheard the conversation and knew he had to say something.

"Excuse me, Celeste. There was a couple here recently. They seemed very curious about you. They both seemed to recognize your name, the man, especially. When he heard your name, he got a look in his eyes like he was trying to remember something. Then, he really liked the fireplace. He took a good look at it, and then they left."

Celeste looked intensely at the young man. "Ben, think hard. Did you say anything else to them?" Ben squirmed and tried to recall the dialogue.

"Um, I think I told them you and Luca were engaged. Yeah, I said that you and the owner were engaged. I haven't seen them since."

Emma thanked Ben for his honesty, and then she apologized. "I'm so sorry, Celeste. If I had been here at that precise moment, I could have gotten more information." Celeste stood still, but her mind was whirling.

"It's okay. I have to go now. Thank you for the coffee." She took a sip, nodded, and then walked out the door. She hopped into the truck and set her GPS for Ocean Isle. She could be there in six hours.

Song: *Say You Will* by Fleetwood Mac

Chapter 97

Celeste drove in silence through the mountains. Her right foot was heavy on the accelerator, but she knew she had to be careful on the winding mountain roads. She forced herself to slow down. She tried to stay calm. She thought about Sergio and what he must have been through. *If he doesn't know who he is, then it is very possible he has no idea who I am. But, if that is true, why had he been here?* Suddenly a thought worked its way through the fog. *He didn't come here for me. He came to the Inn because it's where his brother was, where he had lived and worked. It was a second home to him.* She pulled over to the side of the road where a lookout offered safety from passing cars. She stared out the window. *He truly does not remember me.*

Celeste didn't know what to do. The thought of driving to Ocean Isle to see a man who used to love her but now did not remember her seemed like a very bad idea. But then again, turning around and driving home seemed hopeless. *If it really was Sergio and he doesn't remember who he is, maybe I can help him. But, maybe he's happy with the nurse from Greenland. Maybe they are now a couple, and they're looking forward to being at the beach together. Come to think of it, why would they even go to the beach?* Celeste squeezed the bridge of her nose to release some of the tension that was forming. She needed someone to talk to.

"Please, Lord, send me what I need." She closed her eyes and breathed deeply. The answer would come; she knew she just needed to wait.

Celeste heard her phone ringing from the depths of her purse and picked it up just before it went to voicemail. "Daisy?"

"Hello, Celeste. Bert filled me in on the new developments. I wondered if you needed someone to talk to as you're driving. Those mountain roads can be treacherous. Where are you?"

Celeste felt the tension ease out of her tight muscles. "I'm still on the mountain. I'm starting to have doubts about this trip. I don't know if it's him, first of all, but if it is, what if he doesn't remember me or even want to be with me? I'm scared." Celeste put the phone on speaker, placed it on the seat beside her, and grabbed a tissue. "I just don't know what to do. I'm sitting on the side of the road doubting myself."

"It's an easy question, honey. Do you love him?"

"Yes, I love him very much."

"Then you're going. You have no choice. You have to at least go and see."

Celeste nodded and sighed. "I think I know that. It's just that I'm a bit afraid I'll come back alone. If I don't go, I'll always have the hope of what could have been."

"You'll always have that hope. But, if you go, you'll know for sure. Knowing is always better than just wondering. Life doesn't always go as planned, but we can decide what we do next."

"Daisy, I love him so much that I will let him go, if that's what he wants. I won't stand in the way of his happiness. If he wants to go back to Greenland with his nurse or even be with her here, I will know that I have had the love of a lifetime." Celeste began to cry huge wracking sobs. Daisy prayed for her on the other end of the phone. She waited until Celeste cried herself out and then cleared her throat. Celeste jumped at the noise, having forgotten that Daisy was still on the line.

"Oh, I'm sorry, Daisy. I just, um, I just…"

"It's okay. But, Celeste, you need to go and find out all you can. Talk with him, talk with his nurse. You must find out what's going on, not only for your sake, but for his sake, as well. This is important. You can do it. Now, wipe those tears and take a sip of that coffee that I'm sure is right there beside you, and get back on the road. You know," she paused, "our experiences are necessary stepping stones to get us to the place God wants us to be. Think about that and call me if you need me. I'll be praying for you."

The connection ended and Celeste stared at her phone. *Our experiences are necessary stepping stones to get us to the place God wants us to be? Every one of these experiences with Sergio will lead to where God wants me to be … well, I like the sound of that, but how does Daisy know about the stepping stones?* She closed her eyes again and whispered a prayer, "Lord, thank you for sending me exactly what I needed. I know you are with me, and I trust in you. You led the Israelites through the sea, and now I believe you are leading me to the sea. I will go where you lead me. Thank you for Daisy, and thank you for the stepping stones you've laid out before me."

She blew her nose, took a sip of the lukewarm coffee, and shifted the gear back into drive. She felt stronger and more determined as though she now understood her purpose and mission. She turned on the radio and got lost in the music as she drove carefully down the mountain and towards the sea.

Song: *Ain't No Mountain High Enough* **by Marvin Gaye and Tammi Terrell**

Chapter 98

NORTH CAROLINA

Joe woke to the unfamiliar sound of the car on the interstate and panicked. Margret looked at him worriedly, and as he focused on her face, he relaxed. "I must have slept hard. I didn't know where I was."

Margret looked back at the road before her and pointed to a sign. "We're an hour closer to the beach. Are you hungry?"

"Starving! We need snacks. How about stopping at the next exit?"

Margret glanced at the gas indicator and nodded. "Good idea. We can get gas there as well."

As he watched the scenery pass by, he turned his head and looked at her as she drove. He felt comfortable with Margret and was grateful for all she had done for him. She still wore her hair in two braids, like a teenager. Her face was pretty, and she looked happy. He wondered if she had a boyfriend but then awkwardly remembered the kiss in the hotel in Greenland. He had completely forgotten about it, and he wondered if she ever thought about those moments. He thought of her as a friend or even as a sister, but certainly nothing else. The tik-tik of the turn signal broke into his train of thought, turning his focus again to food.

"How about we fill the car's tank first," she said. "Then we can choose a place for our lunch. Do you want to eat in or take it to go?"

"Let's take it to go. I don't want to stop any longer than necessary, if that's okay with you." Joe walked into the market connected to the gas station and bought bags of chips, candy bars, and bottles of water with money Margret had given him. While paying at the register, he heard a song on the radio and listened intently to the words. He suddenly had a strange desire to text the name of the song to someone. He shook off the feeling and headed back to the car. *I don't even own a phone. Strange.* Margret drove down the road to a fast-food restaurant for burgers and fries, and then they hopped back on the interstate and headed east towards the sea.

Song: *Don't Lose Heart* by Stephen Curtis Chapman

Chapter 99

ICELAND AND NORTH CAROLINA

Luca's flight was scheduled to take off at eight p.m. He had walked the length of the airport many times over, had eaten lunch, and had bought a paperback claiming to be the next bestseller. He stuffed the book in his bag, not having the patience to read it, and started to walk again. Turning a corner, he noticed a door he had not seen before. A small sign labeled "Chapel" was displayed discreetly on the wall beside it. Although he had grown up going to church, Luca had not been to one in years. He now walked to the chapel with the realization that it was truly where he needed to be.

The door opened silently, and he stepped into a peaceful room with benches all facing one direction. The room was quiet and inviting, and he made his way to the back corner. From where he sat, he could see the entire room. Breathing deeply, he looked around. A stained-glass window of a beautiful garden glowed in the center of the front wall. Its effect was inspiring. Beside it, an angel looked quietly at him from another stained-glass window, also shining softly. She had a sweet look on her face, as if she watched over everyone who entered this room and loved them. *Loved them?* Along the side of the room, a row of battery-operated candles flickered on a railing. It was a pretty scene, but most of all, it was peaceful. He looked up at the candles and then dropped his head into his hands and began to pray. At first, he wasn't sure what to pray for, but as he began, the words just seemed to come, and he talked to God in a friendly, yet respectful way.

I've been away a long time, God. I'm sorry. I know I need you, and I hope you can hear me. He looked up at the candles and then bowed his head again. *I know you are here, and I believe you do hear me. Celeste says that you know what we need more than we know what we need. So, would you please send me what I need? She also tells me you love me, no matter what I've done or how long I've been away. Thank-you doesn't really seem to be enough. I don't really think I'm worthy of so much love, but I'm grateful. I'd like to start fresh with you, God. I'd like to ask your forgiveness for things I did that I shouldn't have done. I'm sorry. Thank you for everything. I'm really going to try to get to know you better. Truly. Thank you.*

A peacefulness came over him. He eventually sat up and felt lighter, as if a load had been lifted from his shoulders. He looked at his watch, surprised he had been there for two hours. It had seemed like minutes. He smiled, turned on a candle, and left as quietly as he had come in. He bought dinner at the food court and settled in to read his new book. He couldn't wait to get to the beach to help Celeste, but he was now less anxious about everything, and he had renewed energy to keep searching for his brother.

Celeste took care not to speed, even though she was anxious to arrive. Then again, she was also scared to get there. What would she say? Would Sergio remember her? What would she do if he told her he was in love with his nurse and was moving to the Arctic? She shook her head at the possibilities.

She pulled off the interstate for gas and then into a coffee shop drive-through for more caffeine. The car ahead of her paid for her order, and she smiled and waved her thanks. It was exactly what she needed at the moment, and it gave her the boost she needed. She continued east on I-40.

Working towards the sea... isn't that what I dreamed about one night? I wrote a poem about working or walking to the sea, and here I am, working towards the sea. She had brought her journal along with her, and she promised herself she would read the poem again when she arrived. She shivered, took a sip of coffee, and turned on the radio to drown out her thoughts.

As she drove, her mind wandered to the stepping stones and to the mysterious signature on the note. She turned off the music to give all her attention to the topic: *First, he separated the letters of his name. S E R G I O. Why would he do that? Do the spaces between the letters mean something? And why was the I underlined?* She ran the questions through her mind and pictured the scene again and again. Suddenly, she understood. *Oh, wow! The spaced-out letters represent the stones! The letter I is underlined because there's something extra special about it.* She gasped. *I think there's something buried under the I stone!* Cold chills ran over her body. It was too late to turn back, but she knew exactly where she would go when she returned to the mountain.

Joe was antsy. He and Margret were driving to the beach, and he was excited to see the ocean, but there was something bothering him.

"Margret, where were you the morning I was walking in the fog chasing the light? You weren't at breakfast either." He had a strange feeling that she knew something. His mind was itching to put the pieces together. He looked over at her, but she kept her face on the road. "Margret?"

She glanced quickly at him and relented. "What would you like to know?"

"Did you have something to do with the flashlight I found up on the mountain trail?"

"Why would you think I had something to do with the flash-light?" She continued to stare straight ahead, keeping emotion from her face. He turned to her.

"Is there some Arctic belief about lights? Like finding a light in the dark, or in this case, fog? I don't know, Margret, but if you know something, please tell me."

"There's an old tale I grew up hearing. Every child I know grew up hearing it, so it just became a story many took for granted. I took it very seriously. I think there is something very beautiful and mysterious about light in the darkness."

Joe watched her. He was patient as she spoke softly. What was it about light in the darkness he needed to hear so badly? "Please tell me the story."

"My mother, my grandmother, and even my great-grandmother told this story to me and to whoever would listen. I always loved it, and they loved how attentive I was. They told it and retold it, no matter how many times I had heard it before." Margret looked ahead at the pine trees along the side of the road. She took a breath. He waited.

"Once, in the ancient days, there was a woman who waited for her love to return from a hunting expedition. It had been over a year since she'd seen him. Even though the rest of the hunting party had returned months earlier, she believed he would come back to her one day. She kept hope alive by burning candles and praying. One day she decided to light all her candles at once, and she placed them outside on a mountain ledge near her home. She prayed the light on the mountain would lead him to her in case he had lost his way. She waited until nightfall. The evening was perfect; there was no wind or rain in sight. Then she sat nearby and waited. Soon she fell asleep, but as she slept, her love saw the flickering light from the trail. He knew he was finally home. She woke up to see her love standing before her, watching, and waiting. She jumped up, ran into his arms, and they lived happily and in love the rest of their days." Margret turned to look at him, and he noticed she had tears in her eyes.

"Hey, why are you crying?"

"I'm crying because I know I'm not destined to be your true love. Someone else is, but you just don't remember her yet." She pushed her thumb into the corners of her eyes with one hand while keeping the other on the wheel.

Joe turned to the front window and stared at the road. "Um, I don't really know what to say. But I'm wondering if there's something else you need to tell me." He looked back at her, his eyes caring and kind.

Margret laughed and wiped the tears from her face. "Yes, there is. You're quite perceptive. I think you're getting better every day." Joe took a sip from his water bottle as she continued. "I wanted to see firsthand if the story would work for you. I thought that if you followed the light, you might realize you were home. I admit that I placed the flashlight in the woods for you to find. I wasn't sure you would find it. I was actually kind of surprised that you did, but I guess it didn't work. I'm sorry."

Frustration seeped into his voice. "But Margret, we don't even know if this is my home. And it was deep within the woods on a foggy morning. I was following it into the woods alone, not towards someone. The man in the story followed it home to his true love. I was following it away from everyone. It doesn't make sense."

"I know it doesn't make sense now, but my instinct told me where to go and where to place it. I've never been here before, but for some reason I went there. I woke up really early and had this urge to reenact the story for you. I walked into the woods before the fog even appeared, placed it on the rock, and then left. It was only after I was back at the Inn that the fog rolled in. I guess you happened to see it, got curious, and followed the light into the fog. When I went to retrieve it, it was just where I had left it. I picked it up, turned it off, and brought it back. I'm sorry. I guess I'm just being sentimental. I love a good story."

Joe rolled all these thoughts and emotions around in his head, but her actions just didn't make sense. It would only make sense if two people had seen the light and met at the rock. He mentioned this to Margret, and she wondered as well.

"Hmmm… well, that would have been something," she stated wistfully.

"Remember that night we saw all the lights on the deck at the Inn at Shepherd Falls? I wonder if someone else knew your old story and was doing the same thing." He leaned back in his seat and thought about it as Margret considered. Suddenly she clicked on the turn signal and pulled over to the side of the road. Cars whizzed by them, causing the car to shake. Margret turned to face him.

"Joe, what if it was your true love awaiting your return? I know it's a long shot, but maybe it was her, hoping you'd see the light… the light that would guide you home. Should we turn around and go back?" She turned towards the speeding cars as she contemplated getting to the exit.

Joe shook his head. "No, let's go see something new. We'll have to come back this way to get to the airport. Let's go see the ocean, and then we can visit the Inn again if we want to. I don't want to go back now."

Margret searched his face and then nodded in agreement. Pulling back onto the interstate, she resumed her speed. She was glad to be heading east, although she now wondered about the lights and if someone had lit them especially for Joe.

Song: *Love Stands Waiting* **by Matthew West**

Chapter 100

ICELAND AND NORTH CAROLINA

Thinking only of Celeste, Luca boarded the plane. He pictured her teary-eyed and desperate and running into his arms for love and support. Of course, he would hold her and comfort her and make everything all right. He would marry her and take care of her. They would work together at the resorts, traveling between the two. Maybe they should hire a manager for North Carolina and live permanently in Colorado. It would be easier for her there, and they could visit Shepherd Falls when necessary. He pulled out his laptop and began making plans. If only he had a ring with him, he would propose right there on the beach. Was this what God had planned for him? In the airport chapel he had asked God to send him what he needed. He took a deep breath, let it out gently, and continued to plan.

Margret took the Ocean Isle exit and headed for the hotel that had been recommended to them. She looked at Joe with enthusiasm. "I can't wait to see the ocean! But first, we need swimsuits, towels, and flip flops. Let me know when you see a place we can stop."

He opened his window, enjoying the warm, salty breeze, and spotted a store that looked as though it would have what they needed.

Margret pulled in, and they got out of the car. There was a small harbor nearby, and Joe watched the boats swaying in the water. He was curious and walked closer to them. As he neared the water, he stared at the tethered boats and became lost in thought.

"Hey, are you coming in with me?" Joe turned and saw Margret motioning to him. He looked back at the harbor and then jogged over to her. They walked inside together to buy the supplies they needed.

Soon after, Margret pulled into the Windswept parking lot. *This will do*, she thought. Palm trees swayed in the wind, and she imagined them as guardians watching over the expanse. She paused, examining her thoughts. *Why do I need guardians or protectors? Ugh… I know exactly why. I don't want him to leave. Those palms look sturdy and strong, exactly the opposite of how I feel right now.*

Margret gathered herself, glanced up at the guardians looming high above her, and walked into the lobby to register. Joe opened the car door. The parking lot was hot and breezeless, but he knew the ocean beckoned beyond. *It must only be windswept on the ocean side!* Chuckling to himself, he stuffed their car trash into paper food bags and threw them into a nearby bin. Then he collected their suitcases and new beach supplies. It wasn't long before Margret walked out with two sets of keys and brochures for things to do in Ocean Isle.

"Here's your room key. We're at opposite ends of the second floor. The elevator's just inside." He followed her, anticipating his first look at the ocean. Once on the second floor, they parted, and Joe found his room. It was painted light blue and decorated with nets, seashells, and paintings of the ocean. He threw his bags on the bed and headed for the sliding glass doors, opening them quickly.

He stood on the balcony and stared, the sight taking his breath away: white sand as far as he could see, the ocean before him sparkling in the sunlight, white frothy foam along the edges, and a pier in the distance that stretched far out into the water. He was mesmerized as the waves ebbed and flowed in a graceful dance. He sat down on a plastic deck chair and simply took it all in. He heard a light knock at his door and was reluctant to move, but he knew it would be Margret. She was already wearing her new swimsuit and looked surprised that he wasn't ready.

"Joe, let's get down there. I can't wait to put my toes in the water! Oh, no, I forgot my sunscreen. I'll be back in five minutes." He rummaged through his bag, found the suit, and was ready to go when she returned. Margret looked at him in his bathing suit and flip flops and smiled with admiration. He was looking better than ever.

"Let's go!" he exclaimed as they both hurried to the elevator. He beat her to it, pushed the button, and turned around. She reached the elevator, elbowed him in the ribs, and they laughed as they made their way to the lobby.

Joe's skin tanned nicely as he walked along the beach, waded in the water, and relaxed in a beach chair. The sun seemed to soak into his skin and tan him at once. It also brought out the coppery tones in his hair, and as he brushed it out of his face, he wondered if he should get a haircut. Margret, on the other hand, was uncomfortable as her skin baked in the sun, turning pink and warm.

"I think my skin has never felt this much heat before. I may have to go inside for a while. I don't want to burn on my first day." Joe looked at her and nodded. He could see the color of her skin that promised to turn red soon.

"I might stay out here just a little bit longer if you don't mind. Should we meet for dinner later?" Margret nodded and headed back up to the hotel. She bought lotion at the store in the hotel lobby and headed to her room for a shower.

Joe moved his chair to the water and let the waves lap in closer and closer. He looked out at the horizon and wondered again who he was. *Why hasn't my memory returned? Why am I really here?* He thought about the mountain resort and all the emotions he had experienced there, including the tears and the scattered memories. He thought about the recurring dreams he had, especially the one about the woman at the ocean. *What was she doing? Who is she?* He closed his eyes. He heard gulls overhead, the roar of the waves, and the wind in his ears. He could hear nothing else. What else even mattered right now?

Celeste was making good time but realized she had no idea where she was going to stay when she got there. She called her assistant manager and asked him to research nice hotels on the beach. She didn't know where Sergio and his nurse might be staying, but she was sure it would be beachfront property so they could get the full ocean experience. He called back within fifteen minutes with her reservation information. He had booked her into a suite at a hotel on the beach and had even made sure she had an ocean view. Celeste thanked him and hung up, accelerating just a little so she could get there sooner.

Song: *Beautiful Day* by Joshua Radin

Chapter 101

NORTH CAROLINA

Celeste's GPS guided her to the Windswept, but she was so tired, she couldn't enjoy the beauty of the surroundings. It was dark and she was just grateful to have a nice place to stay. She made it to her room quickly, placed her bags on the bed, and headed for the glass doors. The ocean beckoned, and she wanted to hear it and lose herself in its comfort and strength. She had worked her way to the sea. Now what? She sat down on a chaise lounge and then stretched out on it, listening to the waves crash softly onto the beach below. The salty air embraced her as she thought about her day: the tears, the travel, the point of it all, and she closed her eyes.

She turned her attention to the one who held all the answers. *God, what's the reason for all of this? Why introduce me to Sergio, why fall in love, why long for him, if there's no point? What's your purpose in all of this grief, and longing, and fear? What's the point?* The waves continued to creep upon the sand, the wind continued to blow, the stars continued to twinkle, and she knew in her heart there was a purpose to everything. *I know you are love, and so I believe that every opportunity to love someone brings us closer to you. You must weep when we travel far away from your love. You must grieve when we don't come back to you. You shower us with love, and then sometimes we walk away. I feel only a tiny fragment of the pain and sadness you must feel. Thank you, Lord, for loving us. Thank you for the experience of caring for someone and feeling a love so deep that it hurts my heart when it's gone. I think that real love is wanting good things for the other person, even if it means it takes them away from us. I guess the point of it all is to experience love and therefore grow closer to you. Thank you.* She sighed and fell asleep to the rhythm of the waves.

Joe and Margret enjoyed a great meal at a recommended restaurant and stuffed themselves with seafood platters. Joe couldn't remember the last time he'd had so much good food, and Margret looked sick with overeating.

"I think I had too much sun and too much food. I may be sick." Joe put his arm around her and helped her to the car. She drove them back to the hotel and immediately headed for her room. He wasn't quite ready to go in, so he walked around the building and took a sandy trail to the beach. Several stepping stones were placed along the path to keep people from trampling the plants, and he stopped to look at them. A faint memory tried to rise to the surface of his brain, and he saw letters in his mind trying to spell something: S E R … He couldn't figure it out, so he shook his head and continued on.

The beach was deserted at this hour as he walked to the water. There were no gulls, no voices, and no sound of any kind except for the waves before him. He found a forgotten beach chair and relaxed into it. Closing his eyes, he began to pray, letting the words of thanks and gratefulness wash over him. The sound of the waves rushing in and out intertwined with his prayers, becoming one. He knew that God was in control of the sea and of his life. All he had to do was be still. He listened to the waves and felt their strength and their peace. God was embedded in his heart and in his soul. He sighed, continued to listen with his eyes closed, and began to pray.

God, I'm sorry I drifted away from you for a while. There were years when I didn't feel I needed you. But now I need you desperately. Sorry it took a tragic experience to realize how much. You're always there for me. Thank you. Joe felt at peace, and he knew for certain he had never been alone.

Luca landed in Myrtle Beach after changing planes in New York and Chicago. He was exhausted, and he needed food and a shower. He wanted to drive to Ocean Isle, but he knew the better and safer option was to get a good night's sleep and wait until morning. He rented a car and drove to the nearest hotel, checked in, and was asleep before his head hit the pillow. His plans and a shower could wait.

Joe woke up on the beach to the water lapping at his feet. He was still wearing the flip flops from the night before, and the water tickled his toes as it greeted him. He yawned and stretched and unfolded his body from the small beach chair he had slept in. It was early. The beach was still empty. He looked out at the ocean and thought about its constancy. *Every day is the same to you, isn't it? You ebb and you flow no matter what. I think you're a good example of what God is. You're always here, you are constant, steadfast, and deep. You listen and you provide. You are beautiful, and you are home to many. You provide wisdom and peace. Lord, I know you are the God of the universe. You are my God, and I am your child. Thank you for loving me and thank you for guiding me home.* He then turned towards the hotel, where he thought a hot shower and a hearty breakfast sounded just about perfect.

Song: *Trust in You* **by Lauren Daigle**

Chapter 102

NORTH CAROLINA

Margret was restless. Had going to the beach been the right plan? Now that she was here, she had concerns. She was homesick. She missed her people, her hospital, the patients, and her home. She missed the cold, the traditions, and the food. This trip was a good diversion, but it had taught her she really did love where she came from. She knew she could never live anywhere else. She understood how things worked there, how people lived. It was comfortable and familiar. She missed her own mountains, the cold air, the trees, and the snow. She laughed at the realization. Yes, she missed the snow. *I really can't stay here much longer. As nice as this is, it is not my home.*

She pulled her phone off the charger and called the doctor to check in. She did not know why Joe's memory had not returned, but now she believed she needed to get him back. Back to the snow, and to the place where his accident happened. More tests needed to be done there. After speaking with the doctor, he agreed, and she made tentative plans to return. She knew he would not want to leave because, after all, they had just arrived the day before. But she was getting antsy, and her skin was burnt. Was she also scared of losing Joe? She considered this fear, closed her eyes, and spoke to the one her heart needed now.

God, I don't know how to pray, but I believe you are here, and I want to get to know you. Please help me know you better, and please help me do what is right. Opening her eyes, she sighed and looked out the window. The waves continued to journey in and out, the gulls continued to fly, the wind still blew, but she had changed. She had made a connection to God, and she was ready to pursue that relationship. It was a beginning. She pulled on a loose sundress that would be gentle on her skin and set off to find Joe. As predicted, she found him at breakfast sitting before a plate piled high with pancakes and bacon. He was sipping coffee when she approached, and he grinned from behind the mug.

"Good morning!" he said happily, as he pushed strands of hair back behind his ears.

"Good morning. How are you feeling today?" It was hard not to smile at his exuberance.

"Feeling great. I actually slept on the beach last night. What a feeling to wake up to the sunrise over the water. It was incredible. But more importantly, how are you?" He noticed she looked unhappy. He placed his mug on the table, concern filling his eyes.

"Joe, um, I think, and the doctor agrees, that we need to get you back home, back to the hospital to run some more tests and to figure out why your memory has not returned. We probably need to leave tomorrow." She looked at him sadly and turned her coffee mug over for the waitress to fill.

"Tomorrow? We're leaving tomorrow?" he sounded like a little boy whose vacation had been drastically cut short.

"I'm afraid so. We can drive to the Myrtle Beach airport, leave our rental car there, and head north. I'm sorry." He sat, dumbfounded, but then noticed her pink, tender skin and realized she did not want to be at the beach any longer than necessary. She wanted to go home, and she and the doctor probably needed to understand why he still had no long-term memory. He nodded.

"Sure, we can go tomorrow, if that's what you and the doctor think is best. I would like to enjoy the day in the sun, though, if you don't mind."

"Yes, enjoy your day. I'll take care of all the arrangements. Should we meet for dinner here at 7:00?" Margret's voice already had an uplift to it as her mood lightened with anticipation.

Joe nodded and picked up his fork. "See you here at 7." Margret walked away with a mug of steaming coffee and a banana. She was ready to plan the trip home.

Luca woke up and walked sleepily to the window of his hotel room. He opened the curtains and grimaced as he realized where he was. His window looked out over a parking lot with the airport in the distance. He remembered why he had stayed there and was grateful for the good night's sleep, but he was eager to plan his day and find Celeste. He called the assistant manager at the Inn to find out where Celeste was staying. Then he hung up and devised a plan.

Should I go right away and just rush headlong into her, sweep her off her feet, and propose? Should I call her from the lobby and ask to meet her on the beach to talk? Luca shook his head and headed for the shower. He knew he had to respect her feelings and take her lead. Rushing into this would not be smart. He was excited and nervous all at the same time. But he knew he had to talk to her, listen to her feelings, and respect her wishes. Decisions could then be made. He left the room thirty minutes later and headed to Ocean Isle. He couldn't wait to see Celeste.

Chapter 103

NORTH CAROLINA

Celeste woke up on the chaise lounge at 4 a.m. Her neck was cramped from an awkward position, and massaging it offered no relief. She rubbed her arms for warmth and looked out at the ocean. It was dark, but dawn was not too far off. She could see someone on the beach and wondered if it was a fisherman getting an early start. She yawned and walked into her room, closing the sliding door behind her. She found a granola bar in her purse and ate it quickly, followed with water from her bottle. She didn't care if she slept the entire day. She just wanted to get warm, fall asleep, and dream of Sergio. She changed into her pajamas and crawled into bed.

Joe ate his pancakes while considering the day. He decided he would take a long walk and do some good thinking. Maybe if he remembered one thing, all his memories would come flooding back. Maybe then he could stay. *What is keeping them hidden? Why can't I remember? I should at least know my name.* He finished his coffee, charged the meal to his room, and crossed the lobby. A family was registering at the front desk, and as he watched them, he felt a raw ache in his gut. *Where is my family? Doesn't someone need me to come home?* The two boys escaped their mother's hands and ran through the lobby playing tag, nearly knocking over potted plants and end tables. Their joyful squeals tugged at his heart.

"Marco, Sergio, come here right now! You do not run through a hotel lobby knocking things over. Come and apologize. We will not go to the beach until you can show us your good indoor behavior." The two boys froze in mid-tag and walked quickly to their father. They apologized to the manager and held on to their mother's hands again while waiting to get checked in. The manager accepted their apology and thanked them. The family then walked to the elevator together, talking excitedly about what they wanted to do first.

Joe stood still as an electric current raced through him. Something whirred in his mind. *What names had the father called out? Marco and Sergio? Why was that familiar? Sergio. Sergio.* He suddenly felt ill and needed to get upstairs. He hurried to the elevator, stepped inside, and pushed the button. As the doors were closing, he felt as though pieces were fitting together in his brain and falling into place. He felt keys turning into keyholes that opened doors long closed. He arrived at his room and proceeded straight to the balcony. He dropped onto the deck chair and stared out at the view before him. Images swam across his vision, just out of reach. His stomach churned. He stood up unsteadily and ran to the bathroom to throw up. Afterwards, he splashed water into his mouth and all over his face, then he gripped the sides of the sink and stared into the mirror. *What is going on?* He left the bathroom, fell onto the bed, pulled up the covers, and closed his eyes. He wondered if he was sick or if his brain was just working overtime. He didn't wonder for long, as he fell asleep and let his brain do what it needed to do. It needed to rest, and it needed to heal.

Margret spent the day making reservations, consulting with the doctor, and packing her bags. There was a part of her that was sad to leave, but she realized how much she missed home, and with that realization, she was ready to go. When all the plans had been made, she slathered sunblock on her tender skin and made her way to the beach. She assumed Joe was enjoying the water, the sand, and the sun. She hoped he was having fun, but she didn't see him anywhere as she scanned the long expanse. Wondering vaguely where he might be, she began collecting shells and did not think of him again.

Luca checked into the Windswept. He glanced around as he made his way to the elevator, hoping he would run into Celeste, but the lobby was deserted. He found his room, unpacked, and quickly changed clothes. He started to grin as he thought of surprising Celeste, but then he sat down to think things through. *What will I say? Am I going to wing it, or do I have a plan? Maybe I should just see what her mood is and go from there. Yeah, that's probably the best thing to do. I just need to see her.* He grabbed his room key, zipped it into his pocket, and left the room.

Luca shared the elevator with a father and two boys who were eager to build a sandcastle. As he listened to them, he remembered that excitement as a young boy. He felt an ache in his heart for his brother.

"Hey, Serg, do you wanna build a castle with a moat around it? We can fill our buckets with water and float our boats in it." The other boy answered, but all Luca had heard was the name Serg. It was exactly what he had called his own brother. The realization of what he was planning hit him hard. *I'm such a fool. My brother is who-knows-where, and all I'm thinking about is taking the love of his life for my own. Ugh...*

He gritted his teeth and silently berated himself. Then he sighed and shook his head. *I will see Celeste, but I will not make any kind of move, and I will not take over the situation.* He felt dirty and disgusted with himself. The elevator ride with the two boys had affected him, and he exited the elevator with a new strategy. *I will be her friend. If more develops later, then it will have to happen naturally.* He shook his head and headed to the beach.

Joe woke up wondering why he was in bed in the middle of the day. Then he remembered seeing the boys in the lobby and feeling sick. He placed his hand on his stomach, but the queasiness seemed to be over. *Was it my breakfast or was my body reacting to the name I heard?* He got out of bed slowly and sipped water from a bottle. He did not feel queasy or have a headache, but his mind began buzzing again. He sat back down on the bed and thought of the two boys he had seen. *Two boys, brothers, Sergio...* Suddenly a name rocketed to the surface of his thoughts. *Luca. I have a brother named Luca, and my name is Sergio! I thought it was Joe. I had no idea how close I was. Sergio... Sergio... My name is Sergio!*

He jumped up, fist bumped the air, and yelled loudly, "Yes!" Then he began to pace the room as thoughts and memories came crashing in like floodgates opening wide. He had to sit down as they came in fast and furious. He tried to sort through them. It was a lot to take in all at once, but he was smiling. He had to find Margret. Then he froze. The name Celeste raced into his mind, and a warm feeling spread throughout his body. *I love her, and she loves me. I do have family. I have a brother, and I have Celeste.* Then another thought rammed into his brain. He remained still as he remembered. *Didn't the barista say that Celeste was engaged to the owner? To Luca? What?* He needed Margret's calm demeanor and quick thinking. He grabbed his key and a beach towel and ran out of the room.

Margret had long since abandoned her shell collecting. She had taken a walk, eaten lunch at an outdoor snack shack, and had settled into a beach chair under a large umbrella. She didn't want to get any more sun, but she enjoyed the warmth and the constant breeze. She closed her eyes and fell asleep to the rhythm of the sea.

Sergio walked to the beach and spotted Margret right away. She looked very still as she sat under her umbrella, and he wondered what she was thinking about. As he got closer to her, he realized she was asleep. He spread his towel out beside her and sat down on it, waiting for her to wake up. He stared at the ocean while thinking of different ways to tell her his good news and wondered if, instead, he should just blurt it out.

Sensing he was near, she woke up, opened her eyes, and yawned.

"Hi, there, Joe. How has your day been? Looks like I fell asleep." She sat up in her chair and reached for her water. Sergio waited for her to finish her sip, and then he began speaking. Once he started, he couldn't stop.

"I heard a name in the lobby, and something just shifted into place in my brain. I took a nap, and when I woke up, all my memories came flooding back!"

Margret's mind was spinning. *All it took was hearing a name?* She shook her head and focused on what he was saying.

"Margret, I remember everything! My name is Sergio, I work in IT, but I also help my brother Luca run The Inn at Shepherd Falls. I was in Iceland for a job when they sent us to Greenland to work on an abandoned project. I walked outside to restart the generator, and something large, maybe part of the roof, fell on my head. I saw the building begin to cave in from the weight. I must have fallen into the snow." At this point, he closed his eyes and whispered a prayer as he remembered his friends. He continued more slowly. "I also remember Celeste." He looked at her expectantly, noticing her smiling face.

"Well! Our trip here was worth it! We did it, Joe, er… Sergio, we did it! You have regained your memory! You are going to be okay!" She jumped up and hugged him, falling over onto him, and causing him to fall back onto the towel. They erupted into laughter and rolled into another hug. Sergio pulled her up, and they ran to the ocean hand in hand. As they waded into the water, Margret let go and then stopped to catch her breath. The significance of his news was becoming clear, not only in her head but also in her heart.

Margret looked up at him. "I'm proud of you. You've come a long way. You're on your way to full healing." Her heart ached. Was she happy? She knew she should be, but now everything would change.

"Thank you for sticking by me, for helping me, and for being my friend." Sergio reached out and wrapped his arms around her. She moved into the embrace and hugged him back. She was happy for him, wasn't she? There was a part of her that wished he could be with her forever, but she also knew that wasn't practical. He would need to stay here, to be in familiar surroundings, to talk with Luca and Celeste, and to continue to heal, physically and emotionally. She knew she needed to let him go.

"I will never forget you. We will definitely keep in touch," Sergio whispered in her ear. She pulled away from him and looked into his eyes. He returned the gaze. "Thank you, Margret. Thank you."

Margret brushed away a tear. "So, you will not need to come back with me tomorrow. We can contact Luca and have him come get you." She cleared her throat. "I will need to know who your doctor is so that we can send your medical reports."

Sergio shook his head and grinned. "Always the nurse, aren't you?"

She motioned to the hotel. "Yeah. Um, I need to make some calls. Meet me later for dinner?" She turned away from him, her heart a jumble of mixed feelings.

"Of course. See you then." He watched her leave and then turned to the sea. He raised his arms in celebration and shouted, "Thank you, Jesus! Thank you!"

Song: *Celebration* by Kool and The Gang

Chapter 104

NORTH CAROLINA

Luca left his flip flops and t-shirt on a pool chair before heading to the beach. Once on the hot sand, he jogged to the water and cooled his feet in the incoming tide. In an orderly fashion, he turned to the right and walked away from the hotel to avoid running into Celeste too soon. He wanted to think carefully about the words he would say. He knew he would only offer his friendship and a listening ear, but he wanted to ready himself for the conversation. His dark hair whipped around in the wind, and he likened the chaos of it to his life. He was an analytical man, a man who made decisions neatly, but here at the beach he noticed there were no straight lines. There were curves in the shells, in the waves, and in the foam from the tide. There was the crashing of waves, the call of the gulls, the brokenness of the sandcastles left behind. It was all very present and chaotic and loud, and he suddenly felt like running. He wanted to feel the sand on his feet and the air pounding in and out of his lungs. He wanted to be at one with the sea, the sand, and the wind. He took off running, feeling confident and strong and sure. The exhilaration pushed him farther and farther, and then he slowed down into a comfortable jog and then into a walk. He felt at peace, as if the run had forced all the restlessness out of his system.

He walked a bit farther and then sat in the sand facing the ocean. He began to pray.

"God, thank you for the majesty of the ocean, for Celeste, for the brother I miss desperately, and for your presence in my life. I don't know if Sergio is alive or dead, but I pray he is at peace. Please give me strength, and please guide me as I move forward in life. Help me to know that you are always with me. Amen." He stared out at the water, watching the waves crash in and then fade out. He was content.

Sergio made his way through the thick, soft sand to a gazebo set back on the beach between the hotel properties. It was situated perfectly so one could simply sit in peace. He wanted to think, to consider, to remember, and to plan his next steps. There was so much to do, but he wanted to think about it calmly. He sat down on a sturdy chaise, leaned back, and closed his eyes. He needed to remember everything.

Celeste woke up and realized she had almost slept the day away. *Ugh, what a waste.* She quickly changed into a sundress, brushed her teeth, washed her face, and pulled her hair up into a clip. Then she applied a bit of lipstick and headed out the door. She didn't know where to look for Sergio and his nurse, but she wanted to work her way closer to the ocean. She took the elevator down to the lobby and then made her way to the beach-access doors. They opened with a slight swoosh as she approached, and she walked outside. She followed the pathway around the pool and through the gate to the beach, keeping her eyes open for Sergio. She was excited, her heart nearly pounding out of her chest with anticipation. She stopped and took a deep breath.

Lord, be with me. Make me strong and courageous. Help me. I know you are with me every step of the way. Thank you.

She left her sandals on the walkway, and then turned to the water. It was beautiful, and she knew she could watch it for hours. She noticed a gazebo that looked like it had been placed solely for that purpose, and she walked towards it. A movement caught her eye, and she reconsidered, but then her eyes grew wide, and she froze. It looked like Sergio, but his hair was long, almost to his shoulders. *Could it be? Was he alone in the gazebo watching the sea?* An idea came to her. She turned back to the hotel and ran up the walkway, past the pool, and into the lobby. She asked for the restaurant and was directed to it. She spoke with the manager, asked for a pen and paper, and set her plan into motion. Then she waited a few minutes and retraced her steps to the beach. If it wasn't him, she could apologize later.

She watched as a waiter made his way to the gazebo, holding a tray in one hand. He looked over at Celeste, gave her a quick nod, and then focused on walking through the soft sand. Celeste wondered if it was the right thing to do, but it was too late to change her mind. In a few moments, everything would be different.

Sergio sat with his eyes closed but opened them as he heard the waiter approach. The man offered him a cold ginger ale, and he eagerly accepted it and thanked him. Then the waiter pulled an envelope off the tray, handed it to him, and left. Thinking the note must be from Margret, he opened it right away.

Celeste watched from her post and wished she could read his thoughts. Her palms were sweating, and she thought seriously about taking up the habit of fingernail biting.

The note was written in a handwriting he didn't recognize. He placed the glass on the table and read:

I once had a dream about the sea, and I
wrote a poem about it.
You are like the sea: deep,
beautiful, mysterious.
I waded in cautiously, not quite under-
standing the risks of love.
I then turned towards the shore, but
you pulled me back in,
with laughter, warmth, and songs,
and I felt at home.
But then again, I turned to the shore.
I was afraid and unsure of love.
Then with determination, I turned
around to face you.
I moved towards you. I was confident.
I couldn't keep away.
Love encircled me.
Joy consumed my soul.
I am yours. I will always be yours.

Celeste

She made her way closer to him until she stood directly behind
the gazebo where he sat. He read it again, glanced around, and tried
to make sense of it.

"I don't understand," he said aloud. She took a step closer. It was
him. She would know his voice anywhere. She was trembling, but
all she wanted to do was rush into his arms. She knew she needed to
explain everything to him. She had to be gentle, not knowing how
much he remembered.

She took another step and cracked a shell under her foot. He
tensed and slowly turned around. She stopped and looked up at
him, her sundress dancing wildly in the wind.

"Sergio. My Sergio." Tears pooled in her lower lashes. They
weren't tears of sadness but, finally, tears of joy. She recognized the

difference and allowed herself to take a breath. Sergio stood up and walked towards her. She met him halfway. The look on his face was a mixture of curiosity, joy, sadness, and need.

"You're Celeste." He walked towards her. As they neared, they came together with magnetic force, arms encircling, holding, embracing. He pulled away for a moment to look at her and to touch her face. Then he grabbed her again and held her tight. His heart tensed. Could he let himself feel so much joy? There were so many unknowns. She clung to him and felt his heart beating near hers. Her heartbeat matched his, seeming to beat as one. Sergio calmed his breathing and then pulled away again. He grasped her hand as if it were a lifeline, but then dropped it, and nodded to the chairs. They sat down, feeling flustered and suddenly shy. There was so much to say.

Out of the corner of his eye, he saw her note fluttering in the breeze. He picked it up and pocketed it. Taking a deep breath, he thought about what he needed to say. But how could he? His heart was breaking, and he had just found her again. "I don't know what has happened, but I will let you go. I know you are engaged to Luca." *My brother! How can I live with her as my sister-in-law?* He couldn't look at the woman he loved, knowing she belonged to someone else. To his brother! *I can't do it!* He stood up, stepped out of the gazebo, and headed to the sea.

Celeste sat frozen. *What just happened? One minute we were hugging, and the next... Oh no! He thinks I'm engaged to Luca! And he is letting me go.* She hurried after him, calling his name. The wind picked up and the gulls cried. She felt as though her world was crashing around her and roaring in her ears. She had to make this right. She had to make him understand. The fact that he loved her but was willing to let her marry his brother was all wrong. Chivalrous but wrong. *No!*

Catching up to him, she latched onto his hand, causing him to spin around. He looked at their hands and shook his head. "Sergio, look at me, please. I am not engaged to Luca. I'm not engaged to anyone."

"But I heard …" He wasn't sure he could continue. He swallowed and began again. "Have you been engaged to Luca? Do you love him?" He looked at her with searching eyes. God, she was beautiful. *Does she still love me?* He wanted desperately to reach out to her, to touch her face. He wanted his Celeste.

Celeste regarded him tenderly. "No. I have never been engaged to Luca, nor do I love him. I have never stopped loving you. I have written to you, I have thought about you, and I have dreamed about you. I have prayed for you every day. I love you, Sergio. I love you." She stood up straight, allowing the stance to give her courage. She waited for him to speak.

"I heard you were with Luca. It crushed me. I… I had just remembered you, and then…" He paused and watched a Sandpiper searching for food in the wet sand. He recalled an odd fact about the birds as he watched it. They were monogamous, and they defended their nests. Strange what he remembered.

He shook his head and looked at her. "I love you, Celeste. I want to be with you. Are you sure you want to be with me? There's something I never told you. Maybe after you hear it, you'll change your mind."

"I only want to be with you! If you're referring to the grade-altering scandal in college, I trust you enough to hear your side of the story. You can tell me when you're ready." Looking down at their clasped hands, she noticed the tide coming in, the water creeping towards the sand. It reminded her of the stream near the Inn. The movement of water brought change, newness, and hope. They had a long road ahead of them, but they also had a lifetime to get to know one another again. They could do this.

Sergio took a ragged breath. "Did Luca tell you?" He suddenly realized Luca had to have been the one. But why? Was he trying to make himself look better so that Celeste would choose him? "Don't answer that. I want to tell you the truth." He faced her and exhaled.

"One night at a local bar, my friends and I talked about a computer program we were working on, and then the conversation morphed into a discussion about the ease of changing grades online. I told them not to do it, that they would get caught, and that they could be expelled. It wasn't ethical. I was the project manager, and my name was first on the credits. The team just laughed at me and continued to plan. I left the table and went home. Someone at an adjacent table heard the whole plan and wrote down the names of everyone who had been sitting at the table, including me." He took a breath, suddenly glad to be unloading this burden. "They were caught. We all spent a night in jail, and then they were expelled. In the inquiry, they all admitted I had nothing to do with it. The person who exposed their plan also stated that I had left the table before they got out of hand. I was allowed to finish all my classes and graduate. But my name was still linked to the scandal. Some people still believe I was in on it. Obviously, Luca is one of them." He searched her eyes. He wanted to see love, belief, mercy, and grace.

"I believe you." She looked back at him and pulled him close. No other explanation is needed." He held her, his arms reaching around the small of her back. He gulped back a sob and allowed his heart to open back up to hers with love and hope.

He pulled her in closer. Her wind-blown hair tickled his lips as he whispered in her ear, "Have you ever seen a harbor?"

"Yes." Celeste wondered where he was going with this topic and waited for his explanation. She was patient. She was holding onto the love of her life. The man who until just a few minutes ago was missing. He was here now, warm and alive, and holding onto her. That was all that mattered.

Feeling suddenly bold, he pulled back, looked into her eyes, and explained, "I saw a harbor recently, and I was intrigued. There was something so organized about it. All the boats fit perfectly into their slips. They were where they were supposed to be." Celeste nodded and continued to wait. She knew more was coming.

"I think a good relationship must be like a harbor. When two people are a perfect match, they know where they belong. They know where they fit. I haven't known who I was for so long, but all of a sudden, I have memories, I remember who I am, and I remember you. I appreciate that you accept me and love me as I am. It is incredibly securing, like tying in a boat to its slip." He looked down at their clasped hands and then back to her face. "We are moored together, anchored. I know we have to get to know one another again, and I look forward to it, but I already know we're right for each other. We know where we belong. Thank God you waited for me!"

Celeste reached her arms up around his shoulders. "I love you, Sergio. I am yours!" He looked into her eyes and smiled his crooked, handsome smile. Then he bent down and kissed her lips, tender and exploring. Soon, passion overtook them, and they unleashed all the feelings and emotions they had held onto for so long. The kiss was desperate, needing, searching, longing, and full of love. As a wave crashed into their legs, they nearly lost their balance and began to laugh.

"Wow!" Sergio picked her up and twirled her around. She spun in his arms, joy filling her soul.

Sergio placed her down gently on the wet sand and gathered her into his strong arms again. He held her and knew that wherever he was with her, he would always be home.

Luca headed back towards the hotel. He did not know what he would find, but he felt peaceful. He knew he would accept Celeste's decision, whatever it might be. As he drew closer, he noticed a woman standing on the beach staring out at the ocean, her two blonde braids whipping in the wind behind her back. She was lovely, and Luca was intrigued. As he looked at her, he realized she was not gazing at the ocean. Instead, she was watching a couple playing in the water. Luca followed her gaze and watched the happy couple run, splash each other, move in for kisses, and then run again. He could hear their laughter on the wind. He looked back at the woman and then headed to her. He felt drawn to her, but he did not know why. He kept his eyes on her with glances towards the playful couple just beyond. Suddenly, he stopped. He recognized the woman playing in the water. It was Celeste. Then he looked over at the man, almost in slow motion, already knowing the answer. There he was. It was Sergio, his brother, with Celeste. But how? He stared and then broke into a smile, walking, and then running to them.

"Serg! You're here!" He ran fast, sand and water spewing around him, coating the backs of his legs. Sergio heard the call, recognized his brother, and ran to meet him.

"Luca!" Sergio shouted. They hugged and pounded each other on the back, grinning from ear to ear as they celebrated.

Celeste watched them with joy. *There would be peace… happiness and peace.* Celeste glanced over at a woman standing nearby and guessed who she might be. She walked to her and introduced herself. "Are you Sergio's nurse?" Margret nodded and looked at Celeste curiously.

"Yes, my name is Margret." Celeste reached out to Margret, pulling her into a quick embrace.

"I'm Celeste. Thank you for everything, absolutely everything you have done for him. I know he would not be here without you."

Margret smiled and nodded. She was overcome with emotion, but she was grateful for Celeste's attention. Luca and Sergio made their way to the women and introductions were made. Sergio put his arm around Margret and told them how thankful he was for her care, her time, and her belief in him. Margret brushed a few errant tears from her face and tried to smile. She knew her time with Sergio was nearly at an end. But then she heard him speaking.

"One day soon, I would like all three of us to go to Margret's village and to the hospital. I need to see them one more time, and I need you two to see where I've been. If possible, I would like to visit the accident site as well. I know I'll still need to see a doctor here and continue my care, but I'm on my way. I'm going to be fine." He squeezed Margret's shoulder, and she wrapped her arm around his waist. It wasn't the end. She would see him again. They would be friends, and now she would have Luca and Celeste as friends too.

Luca suggested they go inside the hotel for a celebratory dinner. Luca and Margret walked ahead but Sergio stood still. He reached for Celeste's hands and held on tight. She turned to him.

"Looks like a storm may be coming in," Sergio said as he glanced at the sky.

"That's okay. You're here now, and we can handle any storm headed our way." She squeezed his hands and looked into his eyes. "The poem I wrote in my note, I'd like to explain." She looked to the ocean and then back to him. "It was a dream I had about our relationship. At the beginning, I was eager and excited, but then it got so serious so fast, and, although it was thrilling, it scared me a bit. I was reluctant, and so I swam to shore. But then with all the courage and strength and determination I had, I swam back out to you because I just couldn't be without you. I wrote the note because I thought it was a good analogy for our relationship. Does that make sense?"

Sergio reached out and stroked her cheek with the back of his fingers. He wanted to kiss that cheek. "I get it, but somehow, I know that dream. Could I have dreamed it too?" He shook his head. "I know that sounds strange, and I don't know how dreams work, but I'm very glad we both made our way to the sea." He glanced down at her neck and noticed the snowflake necklace. Celeste watched him as a memory flickered across his eyes.

"Is that the necklace I bought for you?" He looked at her incredulously. "I bought it in Iceland at a festival. It reminded me of you. How did you get it?"

"Your coworker Oliver sent it to me. It was in your room, and he thought I should have it. I love it. I have never taken it off." She clasped it and continued, "Thank you. It has been very important to me."

He traced it with his finger and then looked back to her eyes. "I'm so glad you had it and wore it near your heart all this time." He kissed her lightly on the lips and hugged her again, loving the feel of her body against his. He remembered the stepping stones in the woods near the Inn's property and smiled to himself. He had something buried there for Celeste. They would dig up the fifth stone, the *I* stone, and gather the treasure underneath. At the right moment he would ask her to share her life with him, and he would slip the ring onto her finger. He hugged her tight and then reluctantly let go. They clasped hands and turned towards the hotel, but then he stopped.

"I'd like to thank God for this… for all this." He gestured at their surroundings. "Could we pray together?" He looked at her expectantly. She nodded and bowed her head.

"God," he began, "We thank you for bringing us back together in your good timing; for orchestrating the stepping stones that brought me home. Thank you for giving me strength as my body and mind healed and for all the good people who helped me along the way. The dreams, the nudges, and the little reminders that helped the healing process had to come from you, and I'm so grateful. Thank you for keeping Celeste safe, and for giving her hope." He squeezed her hands and she continued.

"Thank you, Lord, for the hope that you embedded within me. Thank you for keeping Sergio safe, and thank you for bringing him home. Please walk with us, Lord, as we continue our journey together. Amen."

"Amen," he agreed. He couldn't believe he was here with her, talking and praying together. There was so much to say and to share. He wanted to know everything. He wanted to spend every moment with her.

The wind had released some of her hair from the clip, and Celeste brushed it away from her face as she spoke. "Stepping stones have become important to me since that day you showed me the waterfall garden. And look where they've led us!" She thought about mentioning the stones she'd discovered in the woods, but decided that conversation could wait for another day.

"Yeah… if we look back at our lives, we can see how God has placed stepping stones to lead us where he wants us to be. We just have to decide which direction to go and which stones to follow." He sighed and looked to the sea.

She suddenly wondered what else he remembered. "Sergio, do you remember texting song titles to each other?"

"Huh…" he looked back to her. "I kept thinking that music was really important to me, but I didn't remember the song titles until just now. There were times I'd hum a tune I didn't even know, or I'd hear a song and have the urge to text it to someone. Wow! I remember it now! That's fun!" He laughed at the wonder of it all. "I know exactly which song title I would text you right now."

Before she could ask which one, he gently cupped her cheeks and looked deeply into her eyes. She felt cherished, she felt loved, and she felt whole, as if part of her heart, her soul, had been missing but was now complete. He lowered his lips to hers and kissed her. Time stood still. The wind whipped around them, and the waves crashed in the distance. Celeste was with the man she was meant to be with, and all would be well. She sighed, and he ended the kiss. A flirty smile graced his lips, and he began to hum a tune. She recognized the song and joined in.

As they walked across the sand, she asked, "When we get up to the door of the hotel, can we walk through it together, side by side?"

He dodged a clump of seaweed and turned his head to her. "Yes." He paused and thought about doors. "You know, I think we are going to come across all kinds of doors in our lives, and I'd love to walk through them side by side with you."

Celeste leaned in and surprised him with another kiss. Sergio rested his hands at the small of her back and pulled her in tight. They heard Luca calling to them from the open doorway, his voice fading in the wind.

"He can wait. What I need to do is more important right now."

Sergio grazed her lips and then continued following the slope of her neck, pressing kisses at every turn. He whispered, "I love you, Celeste. I can't imagine spending the rest of my life without you." At his words, all the fear and worry she had held onto since his disappearance evaporated into the salty air. She clung to him, needing to feel the closeness of the man she loved. She knew without a doubt they would follow the stepping stones placed before them, and they would enjoy each moment of their journey together. They turned and walked through the open door together hand in hand.

***Song: Everlasting Love* by Carl Carlton**

Love is worth the wait.

Enjoy the journey.

Author Bio

ANDREA HERLONG was drawn to Jesus as a child while living in Italy. Her daily studies with a nun in a convent helped her learn and grow in her faith. That experience was the beginning of a beautiful journey with Jesus. She is an Anglican Priest, a Spiritual Director, an Ignatian Guide, a retreat leader, and an educator. She finds joy in writing inspirational fiction to spread God's message of hope, love, forgiveness, and peace. She has three children and lives in Nashville, TN